THE BACKSLIDER

THE BACKSLIDER

By
LEVI S. PETERSON

Levi S. Peterson

Signature Books
Salt Lake City
1990

To
Althea, my wife

COVER DISIGN: BRIAN BEAN

COVER ILLUSTRATION: MARK W. ROBISON, OIL ON CANVAS, 1990

©1990 Signature Books, Inc.
All rights reserved.
Signature Books is a registered trademark of Signature Books, Inc.
Printed in the United States of America.

First published in 1986.

93 92 91 90   4 3 2 1

LIBRARY OF CONGRESS CATALOGING-IN-PUBLICATION DATA

Peterson, Levi S., 1933-
    The backslider / Levi S. Peerson.—2nd ed.
      p.   cm.
    ISBN 1-56085-015-9
    I. Title.
PS3566.E7694B3   1990
813'.54–dc20   90-37395
                                               CIP

Contents

1.

Marshalled in
the Ranks of Sin

At three-thirty on a May morning Frank Windham got out of his bunk and said his prayer. He reminded God of their bargain, which was that if God would give him Rhoda, he would live up to every jot and tittle of the commandments. Actually it was Frank's bargain, God having never confirmed it. That was the way with God. He never offered Frank any signs, he never gave him any encouragement. He left him penned up with his own perversity like a man caught in a corral with a hostile bull.

In the bunkhouse closet, tucked into his shirt pocket, was Rhoda's letter, tattered from reading and rereading, telling him she was engaged to Milo Terrance Jacobson, who was about to graduate from the university with a bachelor of science degree in accounting and an ROTC commission in the United State Navy. When the letter had come, right then was the time Frank should have driven to Salt Lake City and straightened things out. Instead he wrote one letter after another, which Rhoda never answered.

Frank went to the corrals and loaded the three mustangs into the stocktruck. By the time he had clanged the steel gate shut on them, Wesley had come from the ranchhouse. In the dark he was nothing more than a silhouette with a big stomach leaning against a fence post.

"One of those mares is in estrus," Wesley said.

"I know. She's in heat."

"The estrus period is a curious phenomenon among the placental mammals," Wesley went on.

1

"Well, at least I hope she doesn't get any more notions," Frank said. "She's already got that gelding boogered. She wants him to be a stallion and he doesn't think that way."

"Are you all set now?" Wesley said. "Have you got in mind all the errands you're going to run?"

It was a complicated itinerary. In Howell Valley, at the other end of the state, he would deliver the three mustangs and take on a load of nine milkgoats. The next day, coming back, he would stop at the Trailways bus station in Salt Lake and pick up Marianne, Wesley's and Clara's older daughter. He would also buy three fancy tablecloths for Clara to donate to the Lutheran church in Richfield, and he had to go to a building supply and get five cans of creosote for Wesley. Of course before he left Salt Lake, he would run his own little errand and have a talk with Rhoda.

"I have not come to peace over those goats," Wesley said.

"I imagine you can palm them off on somebody else."

"It was never my ambition to see this ranch become headquarters to a herd of milkgoats," Wesley continued mournfully. "But Clara thinks Jeanette is allergic to cowmilk. And it's also her idea to make goatmilk cheese. Have you ever tasted goatmilk cheese, Frank? My gad, it is the collected, condensed, rarified essence of goatstink. It tastes just like they smell."

The two men went into the ranchhouse where Clara had Frank's breakfast ready—eggs, sausages, pancakes, and milk. Besides that, she had packed a double lunch so he wouldn't have to stop on the road. Clara had the shape of a tripod: fat thighs, big buttocks, narrow shoulders, a little head. She had tartarred teeth, ruddy cheeks, and cheerful eyes, and this morning she wore a blue kerchief over her uncombed hair. She was the sweetest, most motherly person on earth, and Frank wouldn't have traded her for six of Wesley.

"It will be so fine to have Marianne with us," she said. "I never thought I could survive nine months without laying eyes on her."

"Yes, ma'am," Frank agreed, though he had never seen Marianne. When Wesley had moved Clara from Colorado to the ranch in southern Utah, they had brought along Jeanette, their younger daughter. Marianne had chosen to go to Illinois to spend the school year with her aunt. According to the photograph on the living room mantel, Marianne wasn't destined to win any beauty contests.

"I'm excited about my goats, Frank," Clara went on. "I'm so glad we're getting them at last."

"Yes, ma'am," Frank said again, watching Wesley roll his eyes and suck in his lips.

As he put the truck into gear and rolled out of the yard, Frank felt depressed. In the autumn he and Wesley had spent some nice days running down the three wild horses in the Escalante desert. Frank had worked with the mustangs off and on all winter and in April Wesley had bought out Frank's share for $30, not mentioning the trade he had arranged with Mr. Morris, whom he had met at a Hereford convention in Reno.

Frank wondered whether Wesley's profits would exceed the intentions of the Fathers of the United States Constitution. Supposing that milk goats were bringing $25 apiece, Wesley would be realizing close to $100 from Frank's share of the horses. He deserved a certain nice gain, of course, because, as he often pointed out, he was positioned in the market. That was why he could buy up old hay farms around Escalante, fix them up with wells and pumps, and get rich selling alfalfa in Salt Lake, Las Vegas, and Flagstaff.

On one of those bright days in the fall when Frank and Wesley had roped the mustangs, they took a break in the shade of an old gnarled juniper. While they finished off the apples and cheese sandwiches Clara had sent along, Wesley propped himself on an elbow and gave Frank a lecture on economics.

"Don't become a mere millhand. Don't get bogged down earning a simple wage while you make another man rich. There are two avenues upward, one of which is education." Wesley flung an arm for emphasis. He was a tall, big boned, hard eating man with a chubby, sincere face and a middle which bulged like a sack of wheat. From his appearance a person might not have guessed that he had a Ph.D. in agronomy from Colorado State.

"The other avenue is the great American marketplace," he went on. "You don't have to go to college to get rich. You just have to be smart. And be positioned in the market. Knowing who wants what, that's everything." This was the avenue Wesley had in mind for Frank. "Or, of course, like myself, a person can do both."

Unfortunately, Frank wasn't positioned in a market. He was twenty years old and worked from dawn till dark six days a week feeding cows, plowing fields, loading bales, heaving sacks, and driving Wesley's trucks. He had his compensations. He had fancy boots and pearlbuttoned shirts and a shiny blue Chevrolet pickup with overload springs and a four speed transmission. He received free bunk and board for himself and stable and hay for his roping horse. Also Clara did his laundry and cut his hair and cheered him up. Nonetheless, he could see he was one of those fellows who got bogged down making another man rich.

As he drove through Panguitch about a half hour after sunrise, Frank had to decide whether to stop and say hello to his mother and brother. His hauls for Wesley brought him through Panguitch a dozen times a month, but usually he put off making up his mind until he had got to the opposite edge of town and then it seemed a waste of gasoline to turn around and go back. When he did manage to stop, Margaret pumped him about his church attendance and let him know how grieved she was by his absence. "I don't know why you couldn't get a job here at the mill," she was likely to say. "It seems like to me if a young man isn't married and isn't on a mission then there isn't any sense in him not living at home."

A mile or two north of Panguitch, Frank was thinking that a fellow who wouldn't stop to visit his mother and brother ought to have his head pounded with a rock. Soon, however, he began to feel better. A long haul in a truck pacified him. Having left one place, not having arrived in another, he could put off his worries. The roar of the engine, the rumble of the tires, the rush of the air gave him a nice feeling in the stomach.

For a while he pondered about Wesley, who confided a good many personal matters to Frank. For example, he told him how hard life was for a man who had to get up two or three times at night to urinate and also how hard it was for a man who truly believed in science. When Wesley talked about science, his face took on a cloudy, poetical appearance and his voice a half peeved, half marveling tone.

"I can't speak of these things around Clara," he said one day as he and Frank lay side by side welding a strut beneath a horse trailer. "When people let you know they have no tolerance for your private view of things, what do you do? Do you change that view? Do you obliterate it, wipe it out? Not at all. You simply take it underground. That's where I'm at, Frank—underground. I hide in my secret self."

By way of emphasis he waved the welding electrode around, setting off showers of sparks as the rod struck the undercarriage in promiscuous places.

"Does Clara know that I am a free thinker?" he went on in astonishment. "Does she know that I stand side by side with Galileo, Darwin, and Einstein? Not on your life! It would frighten her to know that! My gad, Frank, knowledge of my fundamental character would break her. She has no courage for such a recognition. What Christian has? Therefore I hide and dissemble, I protect her innocence."

Frank was thinking that a welding job that should have taken three minutes was taking twenty. Also he was wondering whether in the afterlife Wesley would make it to the Terrestrial Kingdom or whether God would lock him up in the Telestial. Even though Wesley knew how to make money raising hay, a thing nobody else in Garfield County could do, he had his oddities, he didn't quite add up, which might cause God to give him the benefit of the doubt and let him into the higher kingdom. Clara would be in the Terrestrial Kingdom, which belonged to the goodhearted people of the earth who had been deceived by the craftiness of men, and it was nice to think Wesley might make it there too. As for Frank himself, he would be lucky to inherit even the Telestial Kingdom. A fellow who belonged to the true church and who believed in God but wished he didn't was in big trouble.

At Circleville Frank stopped the truck and inspected the mustangs, which were snubbed by halter ropes to the stakes of the truck. The estrus mare showed the whites of her eyes and pranced in place as if she thought she was headed off to find a stallion. He went into a grocery store and bought a strawberry soda pop, which he drank while finding out from the proprietor whether the opening of trout season had been successful in this vicinity. Frank had a square jaw, a big mouthful of white teeth, a button nose, and a shock of brown hair which bounced above his shingled temples like loose hay on a wagon. He wore Levi's, engineer boots run down at the heels, a white tee shirt, and an unbuttoned, tails-out shirt of faded red flannel. In the cab were his Sunday shoes and a nicely pressed sports shirt which he intended to put on before going to see Rhoda.

Back on the road he was tempted to pass time with a daydream about Rhoda. For a year and a half, ever since meeting her at a dance at Escalante high school, he had made up heroic stories about the two of them. He would rescue her from a fire or from a runaway horse or from a New York racketeer who happened to be passing through Garfield County, and Rhoda would hug him and kiss him and tell him he was the one she had been waiting for all her life. Then his fantasy would jump to their wedding night. It was a good fantasy but it had its limits. For example, he had to omit the wedding night when he was making up a daydream during Sacrament Meeting because God would naturally keep a close lookout for lewd thoughts in his own house. And now, as he steered his truck north along Highway 89, Frank couldn't make any part of the daydream take fire. It didn't seem respectful to think about romancing with Rhoda when she might become another man's wife.

Before she left for the university, Frank and Rhoda took a drive up New Canyon where cold, clear water rushed and steep, fractured slopes bristled with pine and aspen. From a high viewpoint they gazed over the simmering Escalante desert, then meandered along the creek until it looped into a deep, clear pool. They took off their shoes and stockings and waded, she leaning on his arm, her light brown hair glistening in the sun, her voice full of squeals and laughter. Later they sat on a log and watched trout hovering in a riffle above the pool.

"This sure will be empty country without you," he said.

"I'll come back," she murmured. "I'll be home at Christmas and maybe Easter."

"I wish you wouldn't go," he said.

"I couldn't pass it up," she protested. "At least one year. I wouldn't ever know what it's like if I didn't go."

"You'd better go then," he said. "But I won't love nobody in my whole life but you."

"Oh, Frank," she wailed, nonplussed and grieving. She put her arms around him and hugged him tight. She closed her eyes and took a deep breath, expelling it in a whisper. "We'll get married next year, Frank, I promise we will. When I come home next June, when I've had my year, I won't leave any more."

They sat on the log for a long time while she told him all the things she had always hoped her husband would be. He listened closely, wanting not to disappoint her in the tiniest particle. That night he was feverish from love and couldn't sleep at all. While Nathan snored across the room, he knelt at the side of his bunk and made his bargain that if God really would let him have Rhoda he wouldn't hold back on anything a righteous man was supposed to do.

He began to attend meetings at the Escalante North Ward, and he began to pay tithing. He stopped drinking coffee and tried to avoid going around with Jack Simmons and Red Rollins, who were evil company and had tempted him to drink great quantities of beer. He quit poaching trout and deer and gave up roping other people's calves. He tried to stop swearing and he cut down his masturbation to two or three times a week. Each time he masturbated, he felt very contrite and vowed he wouldn't do it again. Occasionally he imposed a punishment on himself like going without his lunch or leaving his waterbag at the ranch so that he had to pass an entire day without a drink of water.

He would have gone to hell for Rhoda so it didn't matter that all this righteousness made his life more or less hellish. That's what righteousness was all about.

About a mile south of Payson the truck sputtered, coughed, lurched, and died. It was two-thirty in the afternoon. Frank got out and kicked the bumper and said, "God damn it all to hell." He got the toolbox from under the seat and removed the fuel pump. Just as he had suspected, its diaphragm had split. He locked the cab, peered at the horses in the back, and headed up the highway afoot, putting out his thumb every time a car came by. By four o'clock he had got a ride to Provo and had found an autoparts store, which didn't have the pump he needed. He got on a payphone and called around Provo without finding the right pump. He got out on the highway and caught a ride to Salt Lake with a fellow who let him off at an autoparts store in Murray. At five minutes to closing time he had finally located his pump.

Outside Frank stood on the curb with his parcel under an arm. Far up State Street he could see the dome of the state capitol. The street was smothered in dust and exhaust, cars moving along its traffic lanes like ants that someone had managed to get into single files. Frank felt like punching himself in the mouth or maybe in the belly or kidneys. If he had had sense enough to change into his good shoes and shirt before leaving the truck, he could have paid Rhoda a visit right now. As things were he'd be lucky to make it back to Salt Lake with the truck by midnight.

He decided to phone her.

"She's not here," a roommate said. "Her and Milo went up to Kaysville at noon. They'll be back sometime tonight. Can I take a message?"

"Tell her Frank Windham called and wants to talk to her about something important. Tell her I'll come by your apartment tomorrow afternoon at five. I've got to look after a truckload of livestock and I don't have any other time I can come by, so I hope she'll be home."

He had just thought up a new itinerary and it seemed sensible while he was near a telephone to call Wesley collect and let him know about it.

For the first minute or two Frank couldn't get Wesley straightened out on what was happening. "Well, just drive on," Wesley kept saying. "If you've got as far as Salt Lake, you can make it to Howell Valley by midnight or a little after."

"But I don't have the truck and horses. They're still down the other side of Payson. All I've got is the new pump. I don't know what time it'll be when I get back down the road and install it."

He could hear Wesley mumbling something to Clara. "What about Marianne?" Wesley said. "Where's she?"

"She isn't in yet. She isn't supposed to be in. That's tomorrow afternoon at two o'clock."

There was more conferring. "Well, my gadfrey, what are you going to do?" Wesley asked.

Frank gave him the new itinerary, saying he would thumb back as far as Spanish Fork, where he had a cousin Emily. He would ask her husband to drive him on down to the truck. Then for the night he'd put up the horses in their corral and throw down his bedroll in their house. In the morning he would drive on slow and easy, taking care of his errands in Salt Lake. He would meet Marianne at two and take her with him to Howell Valley, where they would spend the night. He didn't anticipate any problems in finding a bed for her in Mr. Morris's ranchhouse. However, if necessary, she could have Frank's bedroll and he would sleep in the truckseat. Then, digging in, he and Marianne would drive hard and get to the ranch with the goats just one day later than planned.

There was more conferring. Wesley was very irritated and Frank could hear what he was saying. "I don't like this talk about her sleeping in his bedroll. That's damned near obscene."

Clara mumbled something and Wesley went on, louder than ever. "Hell, no, I don't mean to not have faith in her, but you've got to admit she doesn't have a lick of sense about boys."

Clara mumbled again and Wesley shouted, "I'm not putting ideas in his head. They're already there. I know what's in the mind of a young fellow like that."

Wesley came back on the phone. "Look here, Frank, I didn't mean to bring this matter up until later, but maybe this is a good time for you and me to have something out between us. You just go ahead, like you say, and pick her up at the bus station and take her with you up to Morris's ranch and take good care of her and get her down here safe and sound in both body and spirit. You and she are going to be around each other a lot of the time this summer and maybe next winter too if she decides she's going to stay on and take her senior year in Escalante. Now what I'm telling you is without any rancor whatsoever. Just a bit of friendly, fatherly advice. By God, Frank, you keep your distance from that girl. I'm not having her get bogged down in Garfield County. Not by a damned sight. What I'm saying is, you treat her like a sister. Like a sister. You understand that?"

"Yes, sir."

"All right."

"I didn't have in mind treating her any other way."

"Okay then."

"I try to do things the way they're supposed to be done," Frank said.

"Well, I know you do," Wesley replied in a mollified voice. "By and large, yes, that's a fact, you do try to do things the way they're supposed to be done."

"So you can count on it. I'll look after her. I won't let anything happen to her. She'll be my number one lookout."

"All right, all right," Wesley said, becoming angry again. "I'm paying for this call. Get on with your business."

"Yes, sir," Frank said as he hung up.

The next morning, having slept in Emily's basement, Frank helped her husband, Robert, milk his cows and then loaded the horses. It wasn't easy. The heated-up mare was interested in backing up to the gelding, which took her gestures as a threat and tore out a hitching post.

"Slow down there, you wild puckerassed bastard!" Frank shouted as he chased the careening animal round and round the corral. When he and the gelding had calmed down, he looked sheepishly at Robert, who was startled and perhaps a little scandalized. Robert was a fat, middle-aged man who probably hadn't ever acquired a taste for bad words.

"Horses get kind of skittish in the early morning," Frank explained. "I'll get your crowbar and shovel and plant that post again after breakfast."

After Frank had led the mare up the loading ramp and had snubbed her tightly to a bedstake, the gelding decided he could go up too. Frank couldn't help admiring the mare. It was her bad luck to offer her business end to a gelding, but what she lacked in judgment she more than made up in enthusiasm.

Emily called Frank and Robert in to breakfast. She was a stubby, strawhaired woman of forty-five. There were two teenaged sons, one fat, the other skinny, both with acne. There was a spoiled daughter of nine and there was Emily's mother, Marilla, an old woman with silver hair who was a half-sister to Frank's mother. Breakfast consisted of home-ground wheat cereal, milk, and mashed figs for a sweetener. The family was strong on footreading. Just before sitting to the table, Robert offered to give Frank an exhaustive physical examination by scrutinizing his bare foot, but Frank said he had been feeling well lately and kept on his boots.

After Robert and the children had gone off to work and school, Marilla, the old silver haired lady, kept Frank pinned to the table for almost an hour. She had eaten like a silage chopper, happily smacking her lips and licking her fingers and strewing cereal and figs around her plate and up and down her bib. She had a crush on Frank and called him good looking and wondered why he wasn't married. She liked to preach and wouldn't tolerate interruptions. When she asked a question it wasn't because she wanted an answer but because she meant to move to a new subject. "Did you ever hear about Jimmy Jamison getting his privates shot off in the deer hunt?" she might say, or "I don't suppose you're old enough to remember what a hand my mother was with tatting," and of course Frank had better sense than to do anything except grunt and look interested.

Finally he got up and said he had to plant the torn-out post in the corral. Marilla followed him out and kept talking about all the injustices her poor mother had suffered in polygamy. After he had replaced the post, he shook Emily's hand and thanked her for a place to stay. He tied up his bedroll and started the truck. As he rolled up the window and let out the clutch, he could see Marilla still talking on the front porch.

Frank arrived in Salt Lake a little before noon and picked up the cans of creosote from a building supply. Then he parked in a run-down neighborhood a couple of blocks southwest of Temple Square. He wasn't sure the city fathers should have let a neighborhood so close to the temple go to seed although it was convenient for a man who needed a place to park a truckload of horses. Besides that, these houses and lots weren't much different from most of the houses and lots in Escalante and Panguitch—patches of lawn the size of a bed-quilt with untrimmed edges and shaggy, dark green spots where dogs had defecated, window panes replaced here and there by warped plywood, paint gone dusty with oxidization, front porches that had become storage places, holding old Victrola phonographs and cardboard boxes full of *National Geographic* magazines.

Frank changed into his Sunday shoes and pressed shirt and walked to the Trailways bus station. After seeing he had a half hour before the Omaha bus arrived, he crossed the street and wandered onto Temple Square. For a minute or two he looked at the statue of the handcart pioneers and at the seagull monument. Drifting on, he gazed at the tall, grey granite temple which had six big spires and more little ones than he felt like counting. Opposite the temple was the tabernacle, a long, squat building with small buttresses of hewed stone and a silvery dome for a roof. Frank was thinking about Brigham Young and John Taylor and Wilford Woodruff and all the other great men who had made tracks back and forth across this square like cows in a feedlot.

He entered the tabernacle at the rear and found people listening to a tour guide. He sat down among them and gazed at the wooden pews and posts and at the narrow balcony circling three-quarters around beneath the great concave ceiling. The guide, having explained that the joists and rafters had been joined by wooden pegs and rawhide thongs, was now ready to demonstrate the exceptional acoustics of this marvelous pioneer building. When she arrived at the front, she dropped a pin on an oak railing and, sure enough, everybody could hear the pin when it hit—krip.

Outside, a skinny little man who wore a navy blue suit and a narrow twisted tie and who had eczema patches on his cheeks said to Frank, "That's the first time I ever heard a pin drop in the tabernacle."

"Same goes for me," Frank replied.

"You a Mormon?"

"Yes, sir."

"Likewise. I imagine most of them folks ain't. Wouldn't you think that was likely?"

"Could be."

"They are Gentiles that has come more or less thinking this building is a curiosity, haven't they? Then they heard that pin drop. I would imagine they would be pretty impressed, wouldn't you?"

"Likely," Frank said.

"A little pin! Another witness as to the truthfulness of the *Book of Mormon*," the little man said. "God moves in mysterious ways."

"Nobody can quarrel with that," Frank replied as he ambled off toward the bus station.

He sat down to wait for the Omaha bus. The high-ceilinged lobby smelled of diesel fuel, saliva-soaked tobacco, and urinal disinfectant. Opposite him, sitting on a grimy oak bench with parcels around her feet was a pregnant woman who huddled a small child under either arm. A lanky giant of a man leaned against a wall, his shins gleaming between his pant cuffs and the tops of his cracked brogans. Three Navajos, one of them wearing his hair in the old-style bob bound with cotton string, came from the rest room.

A fuzzy-voiced loudspeaker announced the Omaha bus. Frank pushed through swinging doors into the cavernous loading area where passengers streamed along a dock. A big girl was getting off the bus. She wore sandals, yellow shorts, and a rainbow striped blouse and she clutched an overnight case and a large paper sack. She would measure five ten or eleven, an inch or two shorter than Frank. She had sturdy arms, bulging calves, man-sized thighs.

Stopping in front of Frank she eyed him for a moment, said, "Hello, horseface," and handed him the overnight case. She stepped back to get a good view of him. "So you're Frank Windham. Every letter I've had all winter says you're pure death on calf tying. But you don't look like much of a roper to me. You look like you'd do good at shovel work. Look at the size of those hands!"

Frank's big hands weren't something he liked to have mentioned, but he restrained himself and said, "You're making a mistake, ma'am. I'm not this Frank whatever his name is. My name is Beardsley. Wendell T. Beardsley."

"Woops," she said, taking back the case.

"That's all right," he said, wandering on down the dock craning his neck and peering from side to side.

A little later he returned to the lobby and found Marianne teetering an up-ended trunk toward a bench. "Excuse me, miss," he said, "if your friend doesn't show up, I could give you a hand. I can put you in touch with the police of this here city, who have a department for lost kids. That way, your mom and dad will know where to look you up."

"Wendell T. Beardsley!" she muttered. "Well, my name is Zora Mae Crashcumber and I'm on the road selling fertilizer, which you might know as bullshit. You bet you can give me a hand. There's another trunk and a suitcase right over there."

"Good Lord," Frank said, "where are we going to put all that?"

"You have a truck, don't you?"

"Sure. It's filled with horses and manure."

"These bags will wash off. Where's the truck?"

"Wait a minute," Frank said. "Let's leave this luggage checked here for an hour or so and go do a little shopping for your mother. I'm supposed to run down three tablecloths with flowers on them for the church your folks go to."

They stopped first for a late lunch at Walgren's drugstore. They sat at the counter where they could see the walls and spires of the temple across the street. Marianne ordered a cheeseburger and coffee and Frank had three hot dogs, cherry pie a la mode, and milk. Marianne began to talk in a hearty, uninterrupted way about her stay in Illinois. She lamented leaving her kind, loving aunt and uncle, who lent her their car and listened to her problems. She scorned the riding club at the high school, whose members used English saddles, and boasted about locating a riding stable with western saddles and some nice trails, where she took rides on Saturday afternoons except when the temperatures were close to zero. Her only friends at the high school were on the staff of the student newspaper, for which she was junior class reporter. Her only date was for the Adelia M. Jackson formal, which was ladies' choice. Now, thank God, all that was behind her. She was very excited about living on the ranch at Escalante because after ten months in Illinois she knew she wasn't a city girl.

Listening gravely, Frank decided she wasn't downright ugly, although she certainly wasn't anyone he would have taken up with by choice. She was big and brawny and had a long, bumpy nose, a thin upper lip, and an unbecoming declivity in her chin. However, she also had bouncy auburn hair whose curls she had revived with a comb, nice brown eyes, and white, even teeth. She sat to his right and her blouse gaped so that every time he forgot and took another look he could see her large breast, covered by a bra, of course. He tried hard to imagine what a big brother would do in a case like this since he had decided to take Wesley seriously and treat her exactly like a sister.

As she drank the last of her coffee, she glanced at the temple across the street. "What do the Mormons really do in that temple?" she asked.

"I don't know. I've never been in it."

"How old do you have to be?"

"I'm old enough. I haven't got around to going yet."

"I hear they have sex orgies in there."

"Gosh no!" Frank said scornfully. "People dress up in robes. Then they sit and listen to sermons, I imagine. It's probably like Sacrament Meeting, only worse."

"Worse?"

"I mean longer. More sermons."

"Don't you like to go to church?"

"I go," he said grimly. "I take in Priesthood Meeting and Sunday School and Sacrament Meeting and MIA. Every week more or less."

"What's MIA?"

"Mutual Improvement Association. It's like Sunday School except it's on a week night."

"Do you do a lot of improving there?"

"We mostly have more sermons. Lessons actually, but they're just like sermons. MIA was more fun when I was Boy Scout age. Of course, I learned a lot of bad things in the Boy Scouts."

"Like what?"

"It wouldn't be decent to say."

"Tell me!" she insisted.

"I learned guys could have sex with mares, for example."

She seemed shocked.

"I never did it myself," he went on hastily.

"Thank goodness. How did they do it?"

"On a box. I've seen it done on a step ladder too."

"I guess I wouldn't care to know any more about it," she said. "Do you believe in Joseph Smith?"

"Sure enough. Why shouldn't I?"

"It seems like one Bible is enough. Why do you need a whole pack of prophets running around the country?"

"You can't have too much of a good thing," he said. He was thinking she was getting pretty pushy, considering she was a Gentile and more or less a guest in the state of Utah.

"Do you want to know what I believe?" she asked hoarsely. "I just believe in Jesus. Just in Jesus." She gazed expectantly into his face.

He fetched around in his mind for what just believing in Jesus might mean. "So," he finally said, "maybe you don't believe in God. Just in Jesus."

She slapped herself on the forehead and laughed out loud. "You dummy! You can't believe in Jesus without believing in God. He's part of God."

"Which part?"

"Don't you know anything?" she asked, looking at him as if some of his bolts were missing. "What I mean is that I'm saved if I believe in Jesus. He's all I need, just Jesus. I don't need creeds and churches and big, thick books. God loves me so he gave me Jesus."

He couldn't see anything stupid about thinking she might believe in Jesus and not believe in God. Half of her might be Clara, but the other half was Wesley. He could see that in her face. That long, bumpy nose was Clara's, as clear as day, and so was her upper lip, which came to a tiny point in the center. Her ear lobes, which drooped a little, were Wesley's, as was the declivity in her chin. Why couldn't her religious opinions be mixed up in the same way, Clara believing fervently in Lutheranism and Wesley believing in—well, whatever it was he chose to call it on the particular day he might be secretly expounding to Frank—the Providential Principle, the Fatherly First Cause, or maybe the Great Maternal Bosom of Nature?

At five o'clock Frank and Marianne parked the truck in a neighborhood near the University of Utah, where the yards had lush, clipped lawns and banks of irises, tulips, and daffodils. Some of the houses were old fashioned mansions with signs bearing Greek initials. Frank told Marianne to keep an eye on the horses, then strolled along the street to the house where Rhoda lived.

A roommate in a baggy tee shirt let him into the basement apartment. Rhoda would be home any minute, she and Milo having gone to town for a formal photograph. Milo would receive his naval commission this evening and the next day he would graduate from the university. Looking around, Frank decided it wasn't much of an apartment. Old wallpaper had been painted green, and in spots the dark flowered carpet was worn to its cords. The air smelled of mildew.

Hearing a car door slam, he peered through a tiny window. Milo and Rhoda stood on the grass next to a new Buick, he in a Navy uniform of black and gold, she in a light pink suit. They conferred soberly, holding hands, each nodding when the other spoke. After they had kissed and parted and returned for another kiss, he got into the car and drove away.

As she came down the basement stairs, Frank lost all his courage. He was an intruder, a trespasser, a man caught with a hand in his neighbor's purse. His mind galloped frantically in search of a new reason for his visit.

Rhoda hugged him tight, pressing her cheek against his, saying, "I'm so glad to see you, Frank. I've thought about you every day."

He stared dumbly over her shoulder, wondering what pattern the wallpaper had had before someone painted it green.

"Shall we sit down?" she asked. "Please, tell me everything. I'm so lonesome for home. How are things in Escalante?"

Sitting, he blurted, "Just fine, just dandy, one hundred percent okay. I saw your dad and mom out in their yard the other day. I stopped and said howdy. Their peas are about a foot high. They're likely eating radishes and green onions by now, maybe some leaf lettuce. The weather has been good lately. We had a big fire down at the sawmill in March. Burned up a whole bunch of dry lumber. Brother Phelps doesn't teach our Sunday School class anymore. Sister Hollister has got pulled in to do that. The class had a party in April. They got together at the Hollisters and made ice cream."

He had already run out of words. The Sunday School party he mentioned had led him to shame. All winter, waiting for Rhoda, Frank had spent most of his evenings reading at the ranch. He had a notion he shouldn't go to the party but he did and when he got there, sure enough, he found Jack Simmons and Red Rollins, who were from out of town and didn't have any business being there. They lured him away early to taste some rootbeer Jack's father had made. Jack swore it wasn't fermented but of course it was and Frank couldn't quit drinking it. He parked his pickup high on the road to Hell's Backbone and they sat on the tailgate and drank rootbeer and told stories which, as the evening went on, got funnier and funnier. One rancher had got a cow into a flour barrel and couldn't get her out. A fellow on Canaan Peak had aimed at a four-point buck and shot his own horse. A California elk hunter had come through the Fish Lake checking station with a shod mule, shot, gutted, and tagged for an elk. A homesteader down in the Escalante desert had got the shakes on a moonlit night from seeing a small, furry apparition with a round, white, skulllike head, which turned out to be a badger which had eaten into a cantaloupe until its head had got trapped inside. Frank lay back in the bed of the pickup and pounded his thighs with his fists and laughed in loud, whooping guffaws.

He could see clearly that God wouldn't give Rhoda to a man with such trifling ways.

"I just wanted to say goodby," he said, rising. "I'm on a long haul with some horses. I've got to make Howell Valley, up by the Idaho border, before I get to sleep."

"Oh, don't go yet, Frank," she pleaded, also rising and taking his hand. Her brown hair was soft and wavy and her cheeks were smooth and her smile was very kind.

"I got your letters," she said. He nodded and wiped his eyes with a thumb. Like an auger bit, the fact he couldn't ever have her was boring in.

"I couldn't answer your letters," she went on. "I was going to look you up when I got home and talk to you face to face so I could explain. So you would really know."

"I know now," he said.

"I really will remember you, Frank."

He cried harder.

"I just have to have Milo. I couldn't do anything else. If you knew him, you'd know what I mean."

"I know what you mean. I saw him out the window."

"Will you forgive me?"

"Sure, you bet, I'll forgive you."

"Will you please not feel bad?"

"Sure, yeah, you bet, I won't feel bad."

"Well, then, would you please not cry?" she said. "Maybe we could talk about something cheerful."

Just then he heard a strange staccato rapping, exactly like the sound in newsreels of police horses on city pavements. His eyes, drifting past the open door, glimpsed rippling muscles, shining hide, flying mane. The staccato rapping doubled. A second form flashed by.

"My good hell," he said, "there go my horses."

He ran out onto the street and saw the rumps of two fleeing mustangs. From the opposite direction came a shout, "Stop those sonsabitches!" It was Marianne coming full steam, her head bobbing, her large bare legs working furiously, her hand brandishing a coiled lasso.

"Hold up," he shouted as she dashed by.

"Come on," she called over a shoulder. "Get your butt in gear."

"You can't outrun horses," he cried, pulling up alongside her.

"Well, we can see which street they turn down, can't we?"

"I was hoping you'd keep an eye on them."

"Well, I didn't. I took a walk."

"Where's that other mare?" he puffed.

"She got rustled. By a bunch of frat rats on a toot, drunker than catfish. They put down the ramp and took off with her."

"My God," Frank bellowed, "those horses are going through a red light!"

Tires squealed, a motor roared, a car spun around in the intersection and stopped headed in the opposite direction. The horses veered at a right angle and headed for the university.

Five minutes later Frank and Marianne plodded onto the lower quad of the campus, a large, grassy inverted U rimmed by solemn, venerable buildings. They stopped in front of the administration building, which had broad granite steps and a rank of giant columns. Fresh, green droppings had splattered on the sidewalk.

"That's a good sign," Frank muttered. "They've slowed down to a walk."

They went on. Between the library and the home economics building they passed a student on a bicycle. He hadn't seen any horses. Going by the law building they saw a bearded professor carrying a large paper sack. He hadn't seen any horses either. They didn't meet anyone as they went by the gymnasium and stadium.

"Geez, will you look at that!" Marianne said as they rounded a corner of the bookstore. On the lawn of the union building were the two mustangs, one eating from a bucket, the other stamping idly next to a young man who had looped a waterhose around its neck.

"All right, now we're getting somewhere!" Frank said. "Let me take that rope and I'll go up easy on that mare eating out of the bucket and get a loop on her."

"Howdy do," he said, nodding at the fellow as he sidled up to the mare.

"Just fine, thanks," said the young man, who looked like a janitor. "I take it these are your horses."

"That's so. Much obliged for your help." Having secured the mare, Frank took the other end of the lasso and turned to the gelding. "These animals are suckers for grain. I'm glad you had a little handy."

"That isn't grain in that bucket. It's floor detergent."

"Lordy!" Frank said, pulling the bucket away from the mare.

"I don't imagine it will hurt them any. It'll likely just clean them out. I saw a calf once, three days old; its mother had died when it was born. It had been sucking up tractor oil drainings out of a cut-off barrel bottom. Never killed it. Just gave it the black scours."

"I'll be danged," Frank exclaimed. "What come of the calf later?"

"It got big. It's still ranging up home in Idaho."

"I figured you were a ranch boy," Marianne said. "You look lonesome for horses."

"I hate horses. Cows too. I'm going into pharmacology."

"Good gosh," Frank said, "what's pharmacology?"

"I'm going to be a pharmacist. Going to run a drugstore."

"I sure as hell wouldn't run a drugstore," Marianne said.

"Now that isn't polite," Frank said. "If he's got a notion to sell pills, let him do it." He tugged at the horses and as they fell in behind him he said, "Thanks kindly for rescuing these critters. Good luck in that pharmacology stuff."

It was growing dark as Frank and Marianne arrived at the truck and loaded the horses. Frank rummaged beneath the truck seat and found a ball peen hammer. "Now," he said, "if anybody messes with those horses while I'm out looking for that mare, you wade into them with this hammer. Threaten them good. Put on like you mean to pound in a head or two."

"This is crummy," she protested. "There's nothing to do but sit in the dark."

"That doesn't matter. You keep an eye on those horses. No more wandering around. And don't get excited if I don't get back for a while."

Frank set off along the dusky street, coiling the lasso and muttering to himself. He rang a couple of doorbells but no one answered. Around a corner and up a hill he came to a mansion, larger than any house nearby, whose windows blazed and from whose open doors came loud music and laughter. It seemed stupid to ring the bell, but he did anyway. A pretty blonde, wearing a low-necked, full-skirted dress, paused in the hallway.

"Well, come in," she giggled. "Where did you get that costume?"

"I'm looking for my mare," Frank said. "Have you seen a horse around here?"

She squinted her eyes a half dozen times, repeating, "A horse, a horse? Well, come on in. We'll ask if somebody has got it."

She led him into a parlor where a dozen or so young men and women sat around with mugs and punch glasses and refreshment plates. She cleared her throat and spoke loud. "Has anybody seen this man's horse?"

"I was told some fraternity guys took a horse out of my truck," Frank said. "I'd like it back."

A fellow wearing a short sleeved lavender shirt and a purple necktie said, "Do you see any horses here? Try the stockyards. They keep a lot of animals down there."

"Much obliged," Frank said. "I'll just go on up the street."

"Oh, don't go," said the blonde, frowning with concentration. "It's very important to find your horse. Very important. Let's go ask somebody else."

She took his hand and led him down a hall. He glanced up a stairway and saw a couple in a shadowy corner. It looked as if the man had his hand under the lady's skirt. The blonde tugged Frank onward and led him into a high ceilinged room. A giant table stood covered by punch bowls, a keg of beer, cut vegetables, salted nuts, tiny sandwiches, and little iced cakes.

Gesturing, she said, "Please have some refreshments. You can't hunt for your horse without nourishment." She tottered and swayed and finally leaned against him. "I feel so bad for your horse. I never had a horse, but I know how you must feel."

She put her arms around him and snuggled her cheek against his chest with her body slightly askew so that when he bent his head he was staring into her cleavage. "My name is Inez," she said. "What is yours?"

He had never before in his entire life been hit in the nose by the fact that a man could tell when a woman was ready to fornicate. He was thinking about the estrous mare, about how she had backed up to the gelding, whinnying and snorting and wiggling with excitement, and about how this beautiful, busty Inez had just backed up to him, so to speak, except of course Frank was no gelding. He was wondering why nobody had ever told him a university was like this.

"You haven't told me your name," she said.

"It's Frank."

"Frank! I love a name like Frank."

"My middle initial is J. For Jamison."

"J is beautiful too. What are you majoring in?"

"I don't know exactly. Well, I guess I do. I'm majoring in animal husbandry."

"I didn't know people could marry animals."

"You don't marry them. You take care of them. Like I'm out looking for my horse right now."

He was wondering what God would do if he should shimmy off into a dark corner with Inez and get his hand under her skirt. It seemed reasonable that some sins, committed in out of the way places, might not come to the attention of the Almighty, at least not until Judgment Day, when all the books would be opened and every secret, shameful thing would stand revealed. Long before that dreadful day Frank planned to repent. Adding a few more sins to the truckload he already had didn't seem to matter much. What was the difference between drinking fifty bottles of beer or a hundred, or between breaking his fast on one Fast Sunday in a year or on all twelve of them, or between taking the Lord's name in vain five hundred times or a thousand? Sinning was like keeping hogs in a house. Whether a man kept one or a dozen, the house was still a hogpen.

Another couple were at the refreshments table but Inez paid them no attention. She had both arms tight around Frank and she dipped and swayed with the music floating in from another room.

"Do you think you could fall in love with a girl who flunked English 3?" she asked hopefully.

"You bet," Frank said. "English 3 doesn't mean anything to me."

"Well, I'm the one who flunked it."

"That's okay. When it comes to important things, I'll bet you're sharp as a tack. You are a mighty pretty woman."

"Do you think so? Do you think I'm all right?"

"You come ashouting you're all right. They don't make girls any nicer than you."

Inez tossed her hair and kissed him, saying in a voice that was almost reverent, "You're so good looking."

His mind was going round and round with terrible thumps like a blown-out tire on a highway. The worst sin of all was denying the Holy Ghost, which Frank hoped he hadn't ever done. In fact, he wanted to have as little as possible to do with the Holy Ghost so he wouldn't be tempted. The next most serious sin was murder, which wasn't a problem because Frank didn't lust on killing anybody. The third worst sin was fornication, and that was a problem. Frank needed to know how riled up God might get over a little fornication. He needed a temperature gauge with a little patch of red showing when God had reached his boiling point.

Through the open French doors came a shrill whinny. It was one of the horses in the truck. Then he heard a faint, muffled nicker.

"I'll be damned," he said, detaching himself from Inez and starting for the doors. "That's the mare I'm looking for!"

"Oh, Frank," she wailed, "please don't go away."

He paused to ponder in the doorway, scratching the back of his head with the coiled lasso. He heard the hoarse, hollow grunts of a frightened horse. "Lordy, I better not wait," he apologized. "Maybe I'll make it back."

He groped his way across a dark patio and lawn, knocking over a big urn, stepping into a tub of what seemed to be ashes, and barking his shins on a stack of split firewood. He waded through a hedge, tearing his shirt and scratching his face. He crawled on his hands and knees across a terrace, freshly spaded and planted with tiny flowers. He pulled himself over a brick wall and fell with a clatter onto a lawn chair.

He heard the stamping of a tethered horse and a low, desperate voice. "What was that?"

"Nothing, for hell's sake! It's that dog that was here a while ago."

"Why don't those guys hurry up?" the scared voice said. "What's holding them?"

"Take it easy, calm down!" said the brave voice. "Give them time. They'll get here."

Frank spoke up vigorously. "All right, you guys, I want my mare."

"Who's that?" the brave voice demanded.

"It's me," Frank said.

"I told you, I told you!" the timid voice whimpered. "It's the Phi Kays. Now we're in for it."

"For crap's sake, stay here and help me," the other voice said.

Frank had started forward. His foot skidded and he fell into a small pit half full of empty cans, paper plates, and chicken bones. He pulled himself out on the other side and went forward. He heard other voices and saw the waving beam of a flashlight.

"On 'em, guys, give 'em hell!" someone urged with a half-whispered shout.

Ducking his head and flailing the coiled rope wildly, Frank lunged into a body. He fell, rolled, got onto his feet, lashed out with the coil, threw his fist. In the meantime he got a fist in the nose and another on the cheek and a wild glancing kick on the thigh. He heard grunts, yelps, and profanities. Suddenly he found himself flat on the grass, his arms pinned by strong hands, his eyes blinded by the flashlight.

In the background someone was saying, "Watch out for who you're hitting, you puckhead! I'm on your side."

"Jeeesus Christ! It's just one guy."

"He ain't no Phi Kay."

"That's for sure," Frank said. "You stole my mare. You took her right out of my truck."

"Oh, Lord, I told you. We're in trouble now." It was the timid voice again.

"That's right," Frank growled. "You are in one hell of a lot of trouble. The minimum for horse theft is eighteen months. Plus a fine."

A murmur went around the circle of standing silhouettes. The hands holding him relaxed and he sat up. He could see only shoes and pant legs in the beam of the flashlight.

"Besides that," he went on, "you criminals have committed assault and battery on me when I was trying to recover my property."

"Take your horse," a voice said. "He's right over there tied to that porch railing."

"It isn't a he," Frank said. "She's a mare and I'm afraid you have ruined her spirit. She won't be worth anything after this."

Frank was wondering about the going price of milk goats. He was wondering how much cash Mr. Morris would expect in place of the third mustang. It had come to Frank that he was positioned in a market. One road up, Wesley said, was the great American market place. A man didn't need college. He just needed to be smart, which meant he needed to have somebody down with a knee on his neck the way Frank suddenly had these fellows.

"I've got to deliver that mare to a rancher in the morning and he expects prime horseflesh," Frank said gloomily. "He paid two hundred dollars and she won't be worth fifty now. I'll have to give him back his money."

A belligerent voice said, "Anybody that paid more than five dollars for that crowbait got cheated."

"That's telling him, Shorty," an admiring voice added.

"I've got a witness," Frank said. "She saw you steal this horse and turn two others loose."

"We haven't stolen your horse. There she is. Take her!"

"Two hundred isn't much if you all chip in," Frank said, counting bodies with an extended finger. "Fifteen dollars apiece will do it."

"Take your horse and haul your ass out of here!"

Frank got to his feet, rubbing his swollen nose. "No, sir. I'm heading off to the police. I'm going to file a complaint. I'm going to start with old Shorty there."

Somebody had pushed forward from the rear. "Don't get in a hurry," he said, squatting near the flashlight and motioning Frank to join him. He wore Bermuda shorts and thongs with straw soles and velvet toestraps. After tamping tobacco into a pipe that had a bowl like an old-time ear trumpet, he lit up and Frank saw that he had a heavy black beard and a flat-topped hat.

"This is a very interesting case," said this solemn fellow. "On the one hand, we have done you a wrong. Your property rights, vested in this animal, have been trespassed upon. On the other hand, the brothers of Psi Epsilon have a unique aspiration. Unique indeed!" Now he blew out short, rapid puffs like a two-cycle engine. "In keeping with a long standing custom, this generation of Psi Epsilon aspires to kill a horse in the abode of our traditional enemies, the Phi Kays, who at this moment are in a drunken revel in Lamb's Canyon."

The pipe glowed orange and balloons of silver smoke rose in the dark. The speaker's hands were large, his beefy legs were hairy. Frank was wondering where he had got his talent for tangling up a little idea in a huff of big words.

"It's a shame to abandon this project," the fellow went on. "It's a shame we are stymied here, wasting precious time."

"I'll show you how to get the mare upstairs," Frank offered.

"We have done you an injustice. But now you want to do us an injustice. The problem is your price. I propose fifty dollars."

"I could come down to a hundred eighty."

"Seventy-five."

"One hundred sixty."

"No more of this unseemly haggling. One hundred twenty-five. If that isn't enough, take your animal and go to the law. We will simply have to resign ourselves to your machinations."

"Okay. One hundred twenty-five."

"Done," the fellow said in a cheered-up voice. "Boys, empty your wallets. History awaits our deed. And we're counting on you," he said to Frank, "to help us get this expensive animal up the stairs."

With the money in his pocket Frank showed them how. They tied a hind leg to her belly so that she couldn't kick. They made a nose halter from their rope and a rump sling from sheets torn from Phi Kay beds. Pushing and pulling, they moved the struggling, frightened animal down a hall, up a stairway, and into a back bedroom.

"That's that," Frank said as he untied the leg and retrieved his rope. "Thank you very much. I've learned a good deal about this university tonight."

"Who's going to kill it?" someone asked.

No one answered.

"You can do it with a knife," Frank said, drawing a finger across the mare's throat. "Make sure your knife is sharp. Go for it hard and fast."

"Unsavory!" said the pipesmoker. "Do you have other ideas?"

"I've got a ball peen hammer in my truck. Blood and brains would likely get thrown around the room some. But if you clapped her hard enough she wouldn't know what hit her. She'd drop in her tracks."

"Go get your hammer."

"Well, no, I don't relish that kind of thing."

"We'll pay you ten dollars if you'll do it," the pipesmoker said.

Frank was sorry he had mentioned it. He and the mare had been through a lot of things together. He had chased her through the Escalante breaks and had bucked her out and fed her grain and scratched her behind the ears. Furthermore, she had taught him a thing or two about female nature. As for the brothers of Psi Epsilon, they were wastrels, drunkards, fornicators, and horse thieves.

"We'll give you twenty-five dollars," the pipesmoker offered.

"No deal," Frank said. He took his coiled rope, went out the door, and strolled around the block to the truck.

He climbed in and closed the door. "Lord, I'm cold," Marianne said. "What's more, I'm mad. Where in hell have you been?"

"I told you not to get excited. It took a while to track that mare down."

"So where is she? I don't see any mare."

"I sold her."

"At some livestock auction, I imagine."

"Those sons of bitches broke her leg and she's got to be killed, so I took seventy-five dollars for her which I figure will just about pay for three goats."

"Well, I wish we could get out of here. I'm not only cold, I'm spooked. A man with a big dog came by four times. And a couple of guys parked a car across the street and sat there with the motor running for a quarter of an hour."

"Okay, we're going," he said as he started the engine.

They stopped for supper in Ogden and for a cup of coffee in Tremonton. As they drove northward Marianne slouched against the truck door and slept. Near three o'clock they left the highway and drove along the graveled roads of Howell Valley, searching in vain for an early rising rancher who could direct them to Morris's ranch. At last, when a road they were following ended in a juniper patch, Frank killed the engine, pulled his bedroll from the top of the cab, and got each of them a couple of blankets.

"We're just going to have to wait till daylight," he said. "Maybe you can get some more sleep."

"Sure," Marianne said. "What's one more night of sitting up?"

"I hope you won't tell your folks. I promised your dad I'd get you a decent bed."

"Okay, I won't tell them," she said.

He slumped against his side of the cab, feeling snug and warm in his blankets. Marianne wasn't sleepy.

"Do you want to know what I daydream about sometimes?" she asked.

"Sure, tell me about it."

"I daydream about a cowboy Jesus."

"A cowboy Jesus?"

"I daydream that I am a little girl and I'm lost in the trees somewhere and I feel like I did once in Denver when I got lost in a department store. I'm lost and there isn't anybody to help me. I feel terrible. Then I daydream I see this guy coming through the trees on a horse. He's a cowboy. He is riding a double rigged saddle and he's got a lariat, though that part isn't important. He's got on chaps and spurs and a blue denim jacket and a ten gallon hat. But when he gets up close I see he really is Jesus. He has a beard and he looks like there isn't anybody in the whole world he can't love. He says, I found you; you were lost, but I found you."

She was quiet so long that Frank thought she might be going to sleep. Finally she said, "Do you ever daydream about Jesus?"

"No, I never do."

"Why not?"

"Well, good gosh, I don't know why not."

"Don't you ever think about him?"

"Sure, I think about him."

"Well, what do you think?"

"I think he's down on hellraisers and backsliders."

She laughed.

"That's no joke," he protested. "When he's had enough of all their cussing and drinking and lying and cheating and whoring around, he'll clean them up. He'll burn the goddamned world like a stubble."

"Do you really believe that?"

"Of course I believe it," he said scornfully. "And you would too if you had any sense."

When dawn came Frank shoved aside his blankets and started the engine. Driving along another road, they found a dairy farmer who pointed out Morris's ranch across the valley next to the mountains. As they approached they drove through a square mile of dryland wheat, which stood a foot high, rippled into great green waves by the morning wind. Evidently Mr. Morris was prospering with wheat, having a freshly painted ranchhouse, a half dozen wheat silos of bright corrugated steel, several tractors, a truck, and a new red combine. However, he had apparently neglected his livestock operation, which consisted of a rickety corral full of bleating droop-eared goats and an ancient swaybacked horse.

Three mongrels circled the truck, wagging their tails and barking halfheartedly. Two men came from the house and greeted Frank and Marianne. The older was Mr. Morris, who was bald and portly and wore hornrimmed glasses. The younger was Dave, the hired hand, a huge strapping fellow who wore scuffed cowboy boots and a carved leather belt with a shiny chrome buckle the size of a salad plate.

"Got your horses here," Frank said.

"Don't see but two," Mr. Morris observed, kicking a dog in the ribs.

"We had a little accident last night," Frank said. He told his story and added, "Each horse was to go for three goats, wasn't it? I was hoping we could work out a cash price in place of that mare."

They followed Marianne to the corral. The goats were spotted black and white and yellow and tan and looked as if they hadn't been eating much except the bark off fence posts. Five of them were nannies, three were kids, one was a billy.

"Those are awful run down, starved out, raunchy looking critters," Marianne said.

"Of course them horses aren't so much either," Mr. Morris said.

"How about fifty dollars in place of that missing mare?" Frank said.

Mr. Morris didn't reply.

"I could go sixty."

"All right, sixty."

"You cheating son of a gun," Marianne said to Frank. "You got seventy-five for that mare."

"Well, then, boy," Mr. Morris said, "it doesn't seem right for me to let those goats go any cheaper than seventy-five dollars."

Frank kicked a post, said goddammit to himself, and pulled out his wallet. He backed up the truck to a loading chute and they put the two mustangs into the corral and all went in to breakfast. Mrs. Morris, fat and cheerful, put on a tasty meal of ham and eggs and fried potatoes.

"I was wondering if you could give us a place to sleep for a while," Frank said while they ate. "I hate to turn around and head off for Escalante without catching up on my rest. Maybe you've got a bed in the house here for Marianne. Me, I've got my bedroll and I can throw down under the truck or in your barn."

After breakfast Mrs. Morris led Marianne down a hall to a bedroom. Dave took Frank around back to the bunkhouse, which was a room partitioned from an old saddle and harness shed. There were two iron cots, a little potbellied stove, a table, and a chair. Dust an inch thick lay in the window sill and the floor was littered with orange peelings, empty snuff cans, and clods of dried mud.

Dave explained his housekeeping habits. "My theory is after a while things get evened out and you haul as much out on your feet as you haul in so there ain't no use getting panicked and sweeping it out ahead of time."

He was leaning in the doorway watching Frank spread his bedroll on the empty cot. "You ever screwed a woman?" he asked.

"No, sir, can't say that I have."

"Well," Dave said proudly, "last week I was over at Jackpot, Nevada, with a buddy from Snowville, Lester Chimley. If he ain't somebody! He says, David, you damned virgin, what you saving yourself for? So we looked around for the whorehouse, which wasn't hard to find. Jackpot ain't nothing but three gas stations, a casino, and this here cathouse, which looks like a house some family would live in. It's got five women. There was this real pretty one. Couldn't have been any older than that gal you're traveling with. I went and done it to her. Then I came back an hour later and paid my money and done it again."

"I've never seen a whorehouse," Frank said.

"Just go to Nevada. Look here what I got." Dave got up and dug into a duffel bag and threw down onto the table a box of condoms and a pack of playing cards. "Them rubbers you gotta have or else you'll catch something."

Frank spread the playing cards. On the back of each was a color photograph of a nude brunette lounging on an elbow.

"My gosh, I'd like to have that deck of cards," Frank said. "What'll you sell them for?"

"They ain't for sale."

"How much did you pay for them?"

"Fifteen bucks."

Soon Dave took off for work and Frank got undressed and lay down on the bunk. He was all heated up and wondering about masturbating so that he could get to sleep, but when he wasn't expecting it he dozed off and didn't wake up until sometime in the afternoon.

He lay on the bunk for a while thinking about the last couple of days. He was through being in love. He was going to make sure it never happened again. He had tried it out on Rhoda, had lined himself up true and chaste like a real husband and had repented, as much as he could, and had waited for her and had cut himself off from a lot of fun and pleasure. All his life he had believed in love. Just as sure as the sun would come up tomorrow morning some wonderful woman was going to come along and raise him up and make a better man out of him and make him happy forever, and now he could see what a lot of baloney that idea was because Rhoda had taken an ax and knocked it in the head and killed it stone dead.

He became more and more angry as he thought about Inez, the pretty blonde at the party in the fraternity house. He wondered whether he could have been out of his mind when he took off hunting for the mare and left Inez standing there warmed up and ready to make love. It was crazy to repent too soon. He would get around to it when he was forty or fifty and all the logs on his fire had burned up and there wasn't anything better to do. He was through going to church. He wouldn't pay another penny of tithing. He would look up Jack Simmons and Red Rollins just as soon as he could and would tell them their old buddy had come back from the dead and was ready to go out dancing and drinking and helling around.

He heard a shout from outside. He got up and peered out the window. A couple of goats were in the truck, which was still parked at the loading chute. Then Marianne came from behind the truck. She had on boots, jeans, a denim shirt, and buckskin gloves, and she was looping out a lariat. She opened the corral gate and went inside and started swinging the rope around her shoulders.

Frank got Dave's duffel bag and dug around until he found the condoms and the deck of playing cards with the dirty picture on the backs. He poked around again until he found a writing tablet and a fountain pen. He sat at the table and wrote a note. "Dear Dave, Sorry to steal your cards. You likely will get back to Nevada before I do and can get some new ones. I also took your rubbers. Am leaving $25 on table, which I hope will give you a little profit on the deal. Sincerely yours, Frank Windham."

He tied up the condoms and cards in his bedroll, carried it out to the truck, and went to work helping Marianne load the goats.

2.

Witness at
Canaan Peak

During the Pioneer Day celebration, Frank and Marianne competed in the Escalante rodeo. With Jeanette along for company, they trailered their horses into town and parked behind the holding pens. Marianne saddled her gelding, Chowder, and got set to ride in the ladies' barrel race. She wore scuffed boots and a dusty flat crowned Stetson. When she bent forward over the pommel and shouted into Chowder's back-laid ears, he launched into a frantic run. With dust spurting behind his hooves, he careened around the three barrels and tore away to the finish line, giving her first place in the event on both days.

The first day Frank made third in the calf roping. The second day he had a disaster. When it was his turn, he got behind the starting rope, a pigging string in his teeth and a looped-out lasso in his hand. His gelding, Booger, broke past the starting rope just right and in two seconds was locked on the heels of the calf. Frank whirled his loop and let it fly and it went out wide and beautiful and twisted down over the calf. But he waited one second too long to jerk the line. The loop stayed big and the calf dived through and churned away up the arena, free and safe. "That's a heartbreaker!" the announcer groaned over the loudspeaker. "No time for that cowboy from Panguitch."

Frank sat on a rail and watched the other ropers, fuming because he had been practicing all summer. Pretty soon Jack Simmons climbed onto the rail and said, "Whyn't you ride one of them bareback broncs? They haven't got all the places filled."

"You bet," Frank said.

A half hour later he lowered himself into a bucking chute where a large grizzled white bronc stood, head down and flanks trembling. Frank had on big roweled spurs and buckskin gloves and borrowed chaps.

Jack leaned over the top rail and said, "Hang onto the surcingle with one hand and keep the other hand out there waving so you won't be tempted to grab on with it. Remember you gotta keep raking shoulder to flank with your spurs till the horn blows or you don't make no showing."

"All right," Frank said, "let him rip."

Around the bronco's belly and penis was a cinch which Jack pulled tight to make him fight harder. At the same time Red opened the gate and the big grizzled white came out of the chute, bucking fiercely.

"Here's that young man from Panguitch again, Frank Windham," the announcer said over the loudspeaker. "Works out south on the Wesley Earle ranch. First time he's ever contested in the bareback event, but look at him go, folks!"

The bronco made a series of wide bounds, keeping his front legs stiff as he came down so that the shock would drive up into his rider. Then he put down his head and kicked up his butt and heels, twisting to one side and the other. Frank hung on tight with his right hand, his knuckles cracking between the bronc's bony back and the tough leather surcingle. His left arm waved and bounced in the air and his heels kicked forward and raked the spurs back over the bronc's shoulders and belly.

Then the timing horn blared out and he knew he had made his ride. The pick-up man spurred his horse and came pounding up alongside, and Frank leaned out, clutched him around the waist, and slid off the bronc. As the pick-up horse slowed down, Frank hit the ground running. Car horns honked and people in the grandstand applauded. As he trotted across the arena he raised his arm and waved. The loudspeaker started playing "The Yellow Rose of Texas" loud and pretty. My gosh, he felt proud.

After the rodeo, as Frank loaded the geldings, Marianne gave Jeanette permission to stay overnight with a friend in Escalante. Marianne was in charge because Wesley and Clara had gone to Salt Lake for business and a little relaxation. A member of the governor's Water Board, Wesley had been invited to ride in the big Salt Lake Pioneer Day parade. On the following Wednesday they would return to the ranch with a professor, and on Thursday they would ride out with him to inspect a few fossils near Canaan Peak.

Frank and Marianne climbed into the pickup and drove slowly out of the rodeo grounds. Marianne pulled off her boots and put a foot on the dash board, doubling her leg till her knee almost touched her chin. "You know," she said, "you can't rope for nothing. I could have told you that calf was going to go through your loop before you ever threw it."

"I haven't noticed you catching any of those goats you been practicing on lately."

"Goats are harder to rope than calves. They're smarter."

"Anybody that'd rope goats would suck raw eggs," Frank said.

Wesley said Marianne was unusually intelligent and had to go east to college. Then she had to go to graduate school and get a Ph.D., following which she had to become a college professor instead of wasting her Ph.D. in practical pursuits the way Wesley had wasted his. He worked overtime at the dinner table correcting the bad Garfield County grammar she was picking up. He also worked on Frank because she was learning most of it from him. Frank paid attention and tried to be correct and grammatical around Wesley and Clara, but Marianne went right on saying "ain't" and "it don't" and "we was" just to get under Wesley's skin.

That was part of her tough side. Another part was that she picked on Frank and teased him and put him down as if he couldn't do anything right. She did that especially around Wesley and Clara, which had helped Wesley get over thinking she and Frank would start making love behind the haystacks. He didn't seem worried about the Sundays they spent roping in the big corral or taking rides over the sandhills.

"Actually, you went out that gate real nice, Frank. I thought you had that calf, I really did."

He was surprised at how abruptly her voice had become warm and friendly. She had a soft side, but he wasn't very good at predicting when it would show up.

She stripped off a sock and began rubbing between her toes, saying, "That was some bronc ride. I was real proud of you." She pulled her foot from the dashboard and sat up straight. "Would you take me to the dance tonight?"

"Take you to the dance?" he said, rolling his eyes in disbelief.

"Sure, that's what I said, take me to the dance."

"Good lord, no. Don't you have no sense at all? You know your dad wouldn't stand for that."

"Well, if I went to the dance, would you dance with me some? That wouldn't hurt anything, would it?"

"Nope, can't do it," he said. "Last night I would've. But I'm not going to the dance tonight."

"Where you going?"

"Me and Jack and Red are going to prowl a little."

"Like where to?"

"Like none of your business."

As they pulled into the ranch, she said, "I heard this afternoon you took that Mory Hutter home to Boulder last night."

"I sure did."

"Well, that's damn cozy, I'd say."

"Can't a guy take a poor drunk little critter home without everybody thinking bad of it? She asked me and I took her home and gave her to her mother, safe and sound."

"Oh," Marianne said, sounding apologetic and relieved. Then she became wistful. "I sure would like to go to that dance."

"Well, go. Lots of people will show up stag."

"I hate to go to a dance alone."

"Phone up Jeanette at the Jarmans' and tell her she's got to go with you."

"Like hell I will," she said. "I'm not going."

While he unloaded the horses she stood around depressed and mopy. As he started toward the bunkhouse, she said hopefully, "Do you want to come on over and have some supper after you've got cleaned up?"

"You bet," he said.

When he came into the ranchhouse, his pearly shirt buttons gleamed and his wet brown hair showed tiny combing furrows. She had set on baloney sandwiches and tomato soup warmed up from a can, which he ate with relish, all the while feeling like a skunk because she seemed so grateful to have him eat with her.

A lot of the time she behaved as if she really did want to be a housewife. She washed dishes and clothes, ran the vacuum, and made goatmilk cheese. On Sundays when the family went to the Lutheran services in Richfield, she dressed up in flouncy dresses and high heels and she put on lipstick, rouge, and eye shadow. Her closet was divided between jeans and western shirts on one side and pretty dresses and lacy blouses on the other, as Frank knew because Clara had taken him into her room to boast about it. She had a vanity with a big mirror, and her bedspread was blocked with quilted tulips. On one wall was a poster showing a sweet, starry-eyed blonde in a baggy sweater who looked up toward Jesus in the clouds. At the bottom the poster said, "Heart and Hand for God, Country, and Family." However, on another wall was a poster of Gary Cooper, the good sheriff in "High Noon," and hanging from buffalo horns near a corner were a cartridge belt and holster holding a .22 calibre frontier revolver.

After supper she followed him out to the white picket fence that enclosed the ranchhouse and its little patch of lawn. The sun had dropped over Fifty Mile Mountain and blue shade covered the ranch.

"I hope you have a good time," she said.

As they stood on either side of the fence, their hands resting on picketpoints, he struggled with a mean idea, which was that if he worked at it a little, if he went slow and easy, if he had the guts to tell her a few lies, she would let him do whatever he wanted.

"See you later," he said, swinging away abruptly. He got in his pickup and started the engine. The pickup lurched forward, spun gravel, and rattled over the cattleguard. In a moment it was racing along at seventy miles an hour, leaving a trail of billowing dust in the evening air. Frank felt virtuous. Though he meant to show God a thing or two, he wasn't going to use Marianne to make his point. He was going to go on treating her like a sister. He was on his way to a bar in Fredonia, Arizona, which was over a hundred miles from Escalante. Jack claimed there was a woman at the tavern who took on young men for a ten dollar fee. She wasn't really a whore because she wouldn't do it with everybody. She simply wanted to help inexperienced fellows go forward with their careers. Her name was Sally and she lived in a trailer behind the bar.

Frank picked up Jack in Henrieville and Red in Cannonville, and they drove on over the mountain to Highway 89 and headed south.

Knowing this was the first time for Frank and Red, Jack unloaded a truckload of advice while they were driving.

"First thing to remember is don't start nothing till you got your rubber on."

"I already know about that," Frank said.

"Also," Jack went on, "if she grabs your whang, don't get jumpy. You'll never figure out how to hit the hole by yourself. Let her put it in for you."

"What's so hard about it?" Frank said. "Seems like a bull can find the hole without anybody grabbing his whang."

"You don't know nothing about it," Jack insisted. "Pay attention and don't think you're so damned smart." Jack was as tall as Frank and perhaps a little heavier. He had a large, bent nose and coarse, sandy hair. He worked at a feedmill in Tropic, but that was just a sideline to his real business, which was hellraising.

About a mile out of Fredonia they parked at the Purple Sage tavern and went in. It was dim and smoky and crowded with cowboys and millhands and summer workers from the Kiabab Forest. Frank and his friends took a table in a corner. Across the room a blond woman hammered at a piano.

"That's Sally," Jack said. "We're in business."

Right away she got up and came over to their table. "Hi, fellows, nice evening, isn't it?"

"Sure is," Jack said. "Remember me? I'm Jack Simmons from Henrieville. I have drug some buddies along tonight."

"I see you did. If you fellows aren't a sight for sore eyes! You want a little beer? We'll serve you some of that without no I.D. Behave yourself and we'll treat you good."

"You bet, bring us some beers," Jack said.

"Not me," Red said. "I ain't feeling so good. Bring me a Seven-up."

"A Seven-up!" Jack said. "Whyn't you just drink pee?"

"Beer for me," Frank said.

When she had brought the drinks Jack said, "Sally, me and my buddies here are looking for some time out back in that trailerhouse with you."

"My God," she gasped. She laughed and sat down and pulled her Mexican peasant blouse a little higher on her shoulder. She wasn't exactly a blossom. At the roots her hair was grey instead of yellow and crowsfeet tracked at the corners of her eyes. Her cherry red lipstick needed blotting and her cheeks looked like soda biscuits dusted with flour.

"Holy Moses, all three of you?"

"One at a time," Jack said.

"If you ain't three big rams!" she said, pinching Frank's arm. "Where did you get such big ideas? Who told you I'm into that kind of thing?"

"Well, I just heard about it when I was down here last month," Jack said, starting to sound ashamed.

"Okay, boys," she said, standing up. "I got to play piano and wait on table till eleven. You wait till then and we'll go out back to my trailer. When I go out the back door, you go out the front and circle around. It's eight bucks apiece. And you're going to have to do your business in a hurry. There isn't no time for frills."

When she was back hammering at the piano, Jack laughed and said, "Eight bucks! Ain't that nice? I thought it was going to be ten."

"That lady looks like she's got coccidiosis," Red said.

"That's a poultry disease," Jack said.

Red had pushed his chair back and had slouched down with one leg thrown over the other. "I don't care if it is a poultry disease. She looks like she's got it. You fellows better count me out. I ain't feeling so good. Besides, I've about made up my mind to go on a mission next summer."

It wasn't surprising to hear Red talk that way. He was only a part time heller to start with. He went to church frequently though he didn't like to let on that he did. He was tall and thin, almost skinny, with red hair, of course, and red freckles on his nose and cheeks. He went everywhere with Jack to be his guardian angel and pick up the pieces and get him home safe after one of his wild sprees.

"I gotta side in with Red on this much," Frank said ruefully; "that Sally ain't no teenager."

Jack was getting mad. "God Almighty, all summer you fellows been pissing and moaning about not getting any loving and now we drive all the way down here and she's only charging you eight dollars and you're too delicate to take advantage of it! You ain't men. You're steers."

Frank said, "I'm not backing out on you." But a fellow couldn't help being nervous when it was the first time.

At eleven, after Sally had disappeared through the back door, the three friends got out of their chairs and went out front. Jack went on around back and Frank and Red leaned against Frank's pickup, washed in the blue light of a blinking neon sign. The door of the tavern opened and two Forest Service men came out, one of them remaining on the porch, the other, a tall, chunky man, sauntering toward Frank and Red.

"I saw what you boys are up to," he said. "I saw Sally get up and go out back and then you boys came on out here and now one of you is gone out to her trailer. It wasn't so long ago she was going to marry me and I was going to quit the Service and take her back to Kansas. Now she don't want any of that. She isn't for anything decent. She wouldn't want to cook a guy's meals and wash his dishes and be home every night when he came in from work. That isn't her way."

The man leaned toward Frank. "I know you. I was at the district office in Panguitch for a while. You played football for Panguitch High School."

"That's right. Frank Windham is the name."

Frank put out his hand but the man refused it. "Yeah," he said, "the Windhams. If we didn't have all the trouble in the world with old Lonnie Windham overloading his summer allotment! Is he your dad?"

"My uncle."

"If we allowed him twenty cows on the Forest, that son of a bitch had to try to sneak in forty."

"He isn't any son of a bitch," Frank said.

"He's a son of a bitch all right. And you're one too. And this redheaded pimple is another."

Frank lunged at the man and hit him in the nose and knocked him against a parked car. Then he hit him in the stomach and knocked him to the ground, and when he sat up he kicked him in the jaw.

The other man thrust his head into the tavern and shouted and then came running. "Why did you have to pile into him?" he said to Frank. "I wasn't going to let him fight you."

A crowd came from the tavern. The Forest Service man knelt by his friend, pulled out a handkerchief, and tried to stop the blood which dribbled from his nostrils over his lips and chin. "God,

Jimmy, he broke your jaw!" He pushed aside an onlooker who blocked the light coming from the neon sign and, sure enough, the fellow's lower jaw was oddly askew.

Jack had come around the corner. "What's going on?" he asked.

"He called Uncle Lonnie a son of a bitch," Frank said. "So I knocked him down and kicked him one."

The tavern owner tugged at Frank's arm and pulled him away from the circle, saying in a deep, angry whisper, "Every time, every time, it don't never fail! You young fellows come in here under age and we try to treat you decent and you got to end up half killing somebody and then where does that put me, I want to know! Now I got to call the deputy sheriff and he ain't but in Fredonia and will likely make it here in three, four minutes, so you ain't got much time to get across the Utah line. Get going! I'll stall five more minutes, then I got to call."

As Frank and his friends headed north in the pickup, Red moaned about what would happen next. "That deputy will radio up to Kanab or Carmel Junction and they'll stop us. So now what are we going to do?"

"They can't stop us in Utah, can they?" Frank said.

"Sure they can. They trade favors like that all the time."

"So we go home by Skutumpah ranch road," Frank said.

"That's a poor track," Red said. "It don't get traveled much. It's likely washed out in a hundred places."

Nonetheless Frank took it. Most of the way it was nothing but two dim tracks, and it went on endlessly through juniper and pinion forests, across broad sage brush flats, up and down hills, over patches of slickrock, through arroyos and ravines, and along the base of black, invisible mountains. Every few minutes kangaroo rats scampered across the tracks in front of them. Once a bunch of deer dashed by. Sometimes jackrabbits ran directly before the headlights for a hundred yards or more, as if they enjoyed racing in a tunnel of light. A half dozen times they got onto dead-end roads leading to water tanks or salt licks. Another half dozen times they had to stop at a washed-out ford in the bottom of a draw and cut brush with an ax and throw in dirt with a shovel, making themselves a new road.

Once when they were working in a wash bottom Jack said, "If this ain't crappy! We been building road all night."

"And old Frank never got any loving either," Red said. He leaned on the shovel and laughed. "You poor broke-down old magpie. You never do have good luck, do you?"

After Jack and Red had got into the pickup, Frank stood outside a minute. Sweated up from digging and chopping, he had rolled up his sleeves and unbuttoned his shirt and the night air tasted sweet on his bare arms and belly. Except for the blood in his ears, he couldn't hear a thing, not a thing at all. Around him he couldn't see anything, no trees, no rocks, no hills, just the dead dark, but overhead he could see the big upside down pan of a sky filled with glowing dust and bright burning stars. He had the feeling there were places not even God could track a fellow. Gosh, he felt good.

By the time Frank returned to the ranch, it was nine in the morning and the sun was already high and hot. Marianne was heading toward the corrals with a couple of pails for milking Clara's goats. She wore faded jeans, a battered straw hat, and a halter instead of a shirt. Frank climbed from his pickup and said he would help her milk.

"Do you want me to fix you some breakfast?" she said.

"No, thanks. I just ate at Red's house."

"You must have had a swell party."

"Not so as you'd notice it. I'm plumb tuckered."

"You've been driving the back roads. Look how dusty your pickup is."

"That's right. Me and Jack and Red went up behind Fifty Mile Mountain and had us a wienie roast."

"I'll bet you did," she said. "How come you've been out on the back roads?"

"It wouldn't edify you any to know."

"I'll bet you've been poaching deer or something."

"Maybe we have," he said. It wasn't such an unlikely idea, considering that when times got hard the Simmonses and Rollinses more or less lived on venison. Also, as usual Frank had his thirty-thirty behind the seat of his pickup.

Marianne drove a goat onto the milking platform, sat on a stool, and went to work. Frank squatted on his heels by a nanny and set his pail in the dirt beneath her. He couldn't milk fast because the hand he had used to knock down the Forest Service man was swollen and sore. Marianne finished first and she leaned against the fence watching, her pail dangling.

"How did you hurt your hand?"

"A giraffe bit it."

"You've been in a fight," she said. "You've been on a real toot."

A roan steer which Wesley was fattening for the ranch table, standing not five feet from Frank, let go with a big lazy drizzle of urine. It made Frank nervous and he looked over his shoulder four or five times to make sure he wasn't being splattered.

"You never saw a steer pee before, I guess."

"Oh, hell," he said, disgusted.

"I hope it drenches you. You've been out all night and you haven't been up to any good either."

That made him mad. For one thing, it wasn't any of her business where he had been all night, and for another, it wasn't decent of a woman to talk about steers peeing. Furthermore, he wished she wouldn't run around without a shirt. Her bare belly, shoulders, and back were brown as juniper bark, and her halter gaped at the top, showing where brown skin faded into white.

"Dad and Mom phoned from Salt Lake this morning," she said. "They're for sure going to bring Professor Critchley down. So we really are going to ride up to Canaan Peak Thursday."

"Swell," he said.

Wesley had been promising for a long time to bring Professor Critchley from the university to examine some fossils in a little canyon near Canaan Peak. Wesley meant to make a party of it. Along with the professor he intended to take Clara, Marianne, Jeanette, and a biology teacher from the junior college in Cedar City who was a family friend. Frank was going along to wrangle the horses, which suited him just fine. In fact, he would have paid money to go.

"Too bad you're in trouble," Marianne said.

"Me?"

"Yep, you."

He tried to look calm and steady. He was wondering how many months in jail a guy could get for kicking a man in the jaw.

"Dad found out about that mare you said had to be killed last spring up in Salt Lake," she said. "It never had any broken leg. You sold it to those frat boys and they dragged it up into somebody's bedroom and it dumped horse biscuits all over the carpet. Then it got hauled off to the city pound and now a guy out in Cotton-wood or somewhere like that has got it. There was a letter to the editor about it in the *Tribune* the other day and Dad saw it. He said on the phone he's going over tomorrow or the next day and see for himself if that mare is still alive."

Bursting into laughter, Frank shoved the nanny away and sat back in the dirt. "That's so danged funny," he whooped.

"What's so funny about it? Dad's madder than a wet hen."

"Okay, let him be mad. I'll cool him off."

Frank walked to the bunkhouse and went to bed. He went to sleep quickly and didn't wake up until three in the afternoon. The July sun had heated the bunkhouse and, though he had thrown back the sheet and wore nothing except briefs, he felt sweaty and smothered. He had dreamed his penis was a water hose which was punctured in several places and let out water where it wasn't wanted. He pulled down his briefs and took a look at himself, then was ashamed for checking up on something he was already sure about.

He got to thinking that God had showed what he thought of people's sex organs when he put them into such cozy company with their bladders and guts. He had created people with sex organs so they could get married and use them once in a while to multiply and replenish the earth. But even before he started, God knew people wouldn't stop at multiplying and replenishing the earth. They'd jack off and pet and fornicate just for the hell of it. They'd lust and lasciviate and tickle themselves any old time for fun and pleasure.

He dressed, washed his face, and combed his hair and went up to the ranchhouse to see if he could get some lunch. The house was cool because bushy elm trees shaded the roof and all the doors were open and little fans whirred in a couple of windows. Marianne and Jeanette were sunk in easy chairs, reading. Marianne jumped up and went out to the kitchen where she made him cheese sandwiches and poured him a glass of cold apple cider.

When Frank had taken a chair at the table, Jeanette stood behind him, scrutinizing his hair and stirring it with a finger, saying, "You need a shampoo." She wore a yellow sundress and had big wood-chuck teeth, honey-gold braids, and a chest as flat as a board.

"Better get your finger out of my hair before something bites it," Frank said.

"Let's go hunt for rattlesnakes."

"All right, let's do it."

"I've got some bad news," Marianne said. "Harvey's mother called a little while ago. Him and Jerry and LaMar are hung up in Grand Junction, Colorado, with a broken down car. They don't think they'll make it back to work before Wednesday, maybe Thursday." Harvey, Jerry, and LaMar were high school boys who had summer jobs with Wesley hauling bales from the fields and stacking them in the yards.

"My gosh," Frank said, "how did those boys get in Grand Junction?"

"They went to Denver over the holiday. Coming back, their transmission went out."

"Who let them all three go at once?"

"I guess they've got a right to go on a trip together if they want to," Marianne said. "There's no big problem, is there? Everything will hold for a day or two."

"No, it won't," Frank said. "They were behind schedule before the holiday. Nathan'll be champing at the bit wanting to get water going on the big field east of the corrals. The hay on the lower Jamison field is baled and ready for hauling too. And I'm supposed to cut a field at Hogan Wash in the morning and go right on to the upper Jamison field as soon as I can get to it."

During the growing season Wesley spent long hours in his office making flow charts and schedules, according to which a fresh field came up ready for cutting every three days. But of course what actually happened was that every thirty days all of the fields blossomed at once. Two weeks out of four, all summer, everybody on the ranch went crazy trying to cut, bale, clear, and irrigate all at the same time.

Frank could see his ride to Canaan Peak going down the drain. There was no room in the schedule for Harvey, Jerry, and LaMar to have a breakdown in Colorado.

"Look," Frank said, crumpling his paper napkin, "there's four or five hours till dark. I'm going to hook up the loader and go haul some bales off that field east of the corrals."

"What about hunting rattlesnakes?" Jeanette complained.

"I'm sorry about that. We'll do it next Sunday."

"What's the big rush?" Marianne asked.

"What's going to happen is your dad will get back and blow up and say, No, sir, Frank, you ain't going to ride up to Canaan Peak to see those fossils. You and Nathan can get your hind ends out there and help Harvey and Jerry and LaMar clean off the fields. But if I get a head start on it, maybe he'll let me go."

As Frank hitched a tractor to a wagon, Marianne came from the house dressed for work—jeans, shirt open over her halter, battered hat, and heavy gloves. "I'm going to help you," she said, "though it isn't my idea of fun."

"You don't have to do that," he protested.

"I'm in a mood for suffering. Now give me a pair of them," she ordered, pointing at his canvas haying chaps.

In the field Marianne steered the tractor and Frank trotted from side to side throwing bales onto a hydraulic lift, which shoved them into position on the wagon bed. In the stackyard, Frank tumbled bales onto a roaring, clanking elevator, and Marianne placed them as they arrived at the top of the growing stack. It was mean work. The sun burned in the sky and the ground radiated heat. Leaves and dust got into their eyes, clogged their nostrils, and set their sweaty skin to itching.

They quit working long after dark. Before dawn Frank was cutting hay in the upper Jamison field. In the afternoon he asked Marianne to help haul hay. Again working till after dark, they finished clearing the field east of the corrals. Before dawn Frank was cutting hay in a field at Hogan Wash. Mid-morning his swather broke down and he had to return to the ranch for the other swather. He told Marianne to call her father and tell him to pick up a part before he left Salt Lake. Otherwise it would have to be sent on the Trailways bus and someone would have to drive over to Panguitch to get it.

In the afternoon he and Marianne went out to the Jamison place and began to clear the lower field. Frank wasn't trotting from side to side now, and often Marianne had to stop the tractor while he caught up. When they were unloading, he bent wearily for each bale and tumbled it onto the clanking chain of the elevator. Marianne wasn't so lively either. Catching the bales as they came off the elevator, she pivoted unsteadily and dropped them into place. Between bales she rubbed her back and wiped the sweat from her eyes with a crumpled bandanna.

While they were having a drink of water, she said, "You think you're Sampson, but you aren't. You're not doing so good, you know. Let's go into town and get a milk shake."

"Criminy no!" he said. "Let's keep working. Maybe the boys will get in tonight."

They quit at dark and went back to the ranch. On the back porch they sloshed the dust from their faces and went in to the supper of macaroni and cheese and canned peaches that Jeanette had fixed. They chewed slowly, staring indifferently around the room. Marianne's hair, doused at the wash basin, had kinked into tiny wet curls.

Nathan, the old man who bunked with Frank, came into the ranchhouse to find out when he could start irrigating the lower Jamison piece. Frank said, "It isn't but two thirds done. Let me call town and see if the boys have made it back."

Harvey's mother gave him bad news. Harvey had got his car out of the shop in Grand Junction at noon, and he and Jerry and LaMar had headed for home. About twenty miles the other side of Green River, a seal had loosened on the new transmission and they had required a tow into town. Mrs. Coppins didn't know whether the transmission had been fixed before closing time. It looked as if they would be held over one more day in Green River.

Frank looked at Marianne as he came back to the table. She said, "You gotta slow down. You're going to kill yourself and maybe me too. You don't have to carry this whole ranch by yourself."

The phone rang in the office and Jeanette answered. It was Clara wanting to talk to Marianne. At first Marianne murmured pleasantly into the phone. Shortly, however, she became strident and everyone could hear what she said to Clara.

"If Dad wants to make things so nice for that professor, let him get the dinner himself."

"Well, that's just the way I feel. That's the way I talk when I feel this way."

"No, nothing's the matter. Just tell me what you want done."

"Gosh, yes, I'll remember. Roast beef, mashed potatoes, wine for us heathens and grape juice for Nathan. China, goblets, butter knives, and salad forks."

"Yes, correcto, you bet, I'll order a cake from Mrs. Henderson."

"And sack lunches for the ride! Well, good hell, Mom!"

"I know I'm sounding like Dad. That's how I feel."

"No, go on, dump it on me. What else?"

"Okay, a soup in the refrigerator for when we get back off the ride."

"No, I ain't mad. Yes, I know you love me."

Marianne banged the phone down and returned to the table, pulling her chair up close. "Mom and Dad will be here around six tomorrow afternoon. We're going to have a big dinner. Dad wants to make the professor think we run a southern plantation around here."

"That'll be a sideshow," Nathan said.

She reached for the dented pot in which Jeanette had served the macaroni and cheese. She dug into it with a serving spoon and came up with a big wad. She gave her wrist a flip and splattered her plate and the cloth around it. "Well, hot shot," she said to Frank, "you'll have to get somebody beside me to help you tomorrow."

"Maybe Nathan will help me," Frank said.

"My job is irrigating, not hauling bales," the old man said.

"Seems like you ought to help haul if you've run out of irrigating."

"There's other fields I can irrigate."

"Wesley'd tell you to help me if he was here."

"Maybe he would, maybe he wouldn't."

"I'll drive the tractor," Jeannette said.

"He doesn't need anybody's help," Marianne said. "Old do-it-all can handle it all by himself."

Frank got to the Jamison place by three the next morning. Having serviced the tractor and baler, he turned on the tractor lights and lined up on a windrow. The tractor putted calmly down the field. Behind it, the baler clattered and clanked, its rotating tines eating up the windrow and funneling the hay into a packing chamber. A big fly wheel went round and round, cranking a ram that pounded the hay into tight, rectangular bales.

At six-thirty Frank saw dust on the road and soon Marianne pulled up in Wesley's pickup. She walked out into the field carrying a basket covered by a gingham towel.

"I brought you breakfast," she said, "so you won't have to lose time coming in to the house."

"Gosh," he said, "you sure didn't need to do that. Not with all you've got to do today."

"It's okay. I'll take care of everything. I kind of went to pieces last night. I feel a whole lot better this morning."

He shut off the tractor and climbed down. She spread the towel and set out fried egg sandwiches and a big can of tomato juice and a thermos of coffee. "I'll eat with you," she said, sitting down crosslegged. "We'll have an early morning picnic."

He leaned back against the tractor tire, chewing and looking around and feeling good. The arm on the baler ram was cocked like a cast-iron elbow. A bale was two-thirds out the chute, a big rectangular egg ready to drop. Everything was pretty—the early slanting sun, the blue sky, the dew on the alfalfa stems, red-wing blackbirds warbling in the weeds along the ditch.

Marianne had covered her uncombed hair with a red kerchief and she hadn't put on makeup. Her nose looked longer and bumpier than usual. The little point in the middle of her upper lip, which looked like Clara's, was acceptable, but the cleft in her chin, which looked like Wesley's, was ugly. She wasn't saying much while they ate, but he could tell she was peaceful, she was soft. Taking her all around, she was just a heck of a decent person, and it was too bad she wasn't prettier.

That evening Frank came to dinner scrubbed, shined, and combed. Marianne had gone all out, and for a girl who specialized in goat roping and barrel racing she had done very well. The table was set for a captain's dinner—crystal goblets ready for wine; plates with a band of gold around the rim; pure white napkins folded into triangles; two tall blue candles; a bouquet of snapdragons and larkspurs and a wild yucca stem. The mashed potatoes were lumpy and the gravy was scorched, but the roast beef was moist, the green peas tender, and the hot yeasty rolls delicious.

Wesley and Clara had arrived around five o'clock with Dr. Critchley from the University of Utah and Mr. Woorbeck from the College of Southern Utah. Mr. Woorbeck had a way of making people laugh, and Frank could see he'd be the kind of teacher students would like. He combed his wavy hair straight back and he wore a pearlbuttoned western shirt and a turquoise bolo tie. Dr. Critchley was a big baldheaded man with a round face, droopy jowls, and thick glasses that magnified his eyeballs.

As the meal began everybody was a little stiff and cautious. Jeanette reported that Mrs. Coppins had called, saying Harvey, Jerry, and LaMar had finally got home and would show up for work the next day. Mr. Woorbeck talked about the big airliner collision over the Grand Canyon. Clara thought it was disloyal of Harold Stassen to try to push Vice President Nixon off the Republican ticket. Professor Critchley said it was irrelevant because President Eisenhower hadn't yet made up his mind to run again.

Soon the professor was doing most of the talking and everyone else was asking humble, polite questions. Especially Wesley. Frank could see Wesley was as respectful and cowed as if he was eating supper with the queen of England. Dr. Critchley was just back from a field trip to Sumatra with a colleague, a big gun at the University of California at Berkeley, and they had uncovered some fossils of a new species of marine turtle.

Gesturing with his fork, on which he had skewered a morsel of roast beef, the professor said, "We were certainly lucky in choosing our location. You may know that dating fossils is a more difficult task than finding them. Many splendid fossils are sitting around in desk drawers useless and forgotten because they can't be dated. But thanks to ancient volcanic activity and some clear sedimentary strata, we could date our pieces rather precisely. We have placed them in the late Triassic era—two hundred five million years ago."

Wesley said, "Imagine that!" and Clara said, "Good gracious!"

After dessert, the professor pushed back his chair and dug a cigarette out of his shirt pocket and lit up. Nathan, who had dressed up for the gala evening in his grey double breasted suit, scowled and snuffled and coughed. He had told Frank a hundred times how bestial and ungodly smokers were. "One thing is for sure," he said in a loud voice, "there isn't no turtle nor nothing else two hundred and five million years old."

He snapped his false teeth and glared around the table. The professor peered through his thick lenses, his emotions in apparent suspension, as if he hadn't yet determined in which phylum or genus to categorize the old man.

Nathan went on. "The world isn't but seven thousand years old. Hardly that, even. God made it in six days. All those dinosaurs and funny looking fish and flying lizards you see in the magazines, half of them are made up. They're nothing but the inventions of deceitful men, the same kind who write novels and make movies. The other half of them creatures likely roamed around all right. God made them in Adam's time. Then they got drowned in the Flood.

That's where those bones came from you're riding out to take a look at. They got buried under the Flood, them and lots of others too."

The professor became frantic. He rubbed the hand holding the cigarette over his head four or five times, leaving little moist tracks where the wet filter dragged along his pate. "My God, Adam and Eve, Adam and Eve! The Flood! The Tower of Babel! Is this the twentieth century or isn't it?"

"Adam and Eve are also mentioned in the Book of Mormon," Nathan said. "They were real. There can't be no mistake about that."

Wesley was looking as if he and Nathan had been sneaking by a mean, red-eyed dog that was sleeping and just when they had got safely past Nathan had turned around and kicked it. "The Bible is poetry," Wesley said. "Folklore. Old stories passed on by word of mouth. Wonderful old narratives like *The Iliad* and *The Odyssey*. Literature, not scientific truth."

"Gracious!" Clara said, rubbing her cheeks with her palms. "What's a person to believe?"

Jeanette said, "I believe in the Holy Ghost and in the holy Christian church and the communion of the saints and the forgiveness of sins and the resurrection of the body and the life everlasting." She was sitting between Frank and Nathan in a chair that was too low for her.

"What does all that barf mean?" Marianne said.

"That's what the catechism says."

"Well, yes, you sweet thing," Clara said, "we do believe in the Holy Ghost and the holy Christian church."

Frank was inclined to think the Adam and Eve story was correct. It stood to reason that creating people was easier than evolving them. God didn't have to do more than scoop up a handful of dust, spit in it, stir it around, and mold out a little figurine and then breathe on it and, lo and behold, there was Adam. He could have done the same with Eve, but he apparently got bored with doing things the easy way and knocked Adam out with a dose of chloroform and took one of his ribs.

"The way I look at it," Mr. Woorbeck said, "evolution is God's way of creating. You don't have to take Adam and Eve literally to be a Christian."

"Yes, that's it exactly!" Clara said. "Evolution is God's way of creating."

Nathan pushed back his chair and got up, saying, "No Adam and Eve, no Fall. No Fall, no Christ. No Christ, no salvation." Then he flung down his napkin and walked out.

Clara jumped up too. "Here I sit like a wart on a toad! Coffee anybody? Marianne has perked a nice pot for us."

"Yes, ma'am, I'll have a cup," Frank said.

The professor was wagging a finger at Mr. Woorbeck. "God is extraneous in the evolutionary scheme. We don't need him to fill out the hypothesis. There is a rule of logic called Occam's Razor by which the simplest explanation for any set of phenomena is the preferable one."

"Oh, can't we have God, Dr. Critchley?" Clara said from the kitchen door. "Not even if we agree to get along without Adam and Eve?" She wore a silky black and gold dress. Her grey hair frizzled in a little circle around her head and her cheeks were ruddier than usual.

"I'm with Mr. Woorbeck," Marianne said. "Why can't evolution be God's way of creating?"

Frank was also swinging around to Mr. Woorbeck's view. The more he thought about it the more he could see evolution fit in just fine with God's tendency to do things the hard way. It would be just like God to do something as crude, inefficient, and roundabout as evolving people. There he was, up on the royal star Kolob millions and billions of years ago, planning how things were going to be in the twentieth century, seeing the future plain and clear and saying to himself, Considering how you're going to behave once I do get you evolved up to being people, you don't deserve anything better than apes and monkeys for ancestors.

The professor was becoming aggressive. "I find the Bible a downright nuisance. We'd be lightyears ahead in education if we could abolish it. And these other holy books of the local culture—incredible! Here in Utah we live in a medieval mentality!"

"Dear me!" Clara said as she poured the professor a cup of coffee. "The Bible is certainly a comfort to me. I do sometimes think these good Mormon folks are benighted and superstitious, the way they substitute their Book of Mormon and Doctrine and Covenants and Pearl of Great Price for the Bible, but then I think maybe they get some godly comfort out of their books too, and I say to myself, Who am I to judge?"

"The Mormons believe in the Bible," Frank said. "They believe in all of them. You can't have too much of a good thing."

A little later as Frank crossed the yard heading for the bunkhouse, Wesley stopped him and said, "That Nathan! For crying out loud, he's got as much tact as a rattlesnake. Prof. Critchley is a world authority on fossil turtles and that old bat has to shove the Book of Mormon at him."

"Yes, sir," Frank said, "Nathan goes up in smoke pretty easy."

"I gathered from Marianne and Jeanette that you have more or less kept things caught up in the absence of the boys."

"Yes, sir," Frank said. He felt proud of himself.

"That's commendable. There is no question you are a hard worker."

"I just wanted to make sure I could go on the ride tomorrow."

"That makes my next task very difficult, Frank. You are not coming on that ride. I am angry with you. I am disappointed. I am deceived and disillusioned. I have trusted you. I have turned the management of my ranch over to you many a time. I have made you privy to my financial affairs. I have relied on you day and night. And now what do I find out?"

The corral floodlights lit up Wesley's face. He had hooked a thumb in his belt and waved his other hand like an orchestra conductor.

"Right there in my Salt Lake *Tribune*, delivered to my own box in the Escalante post office, right there in a letter to the editor I found out that some fraternity boys had left a mare in somebody's bedroom and that mare was still alive and in the city pound. And when I got up to Salt Lake I went out to see for myself. Yesterday, Frank, I spent the afternoon tracking her from the pound to Cottonwood to Draper to West Jordan. She didn't have a broken leg! I have seen her with my own eyes! Without my consent you sold her."

"Well, sir," Frank said, "those boys just seemed to need a horse so bad I let them have her. I figured it wouldn't hurt as long as you got your goats. I brought back all nine of them."

"Now what I want to know is how much you got for her. Don't you lie to me. You tell me straight how much you got for her."

"A hundred twenty-five dollars."

"And you gave Mr. Morris seventy-five."

"Yes, sir."

"You sneaking, conniving, low-down rascal! You pocketed fifty dollars that belonged to me and never said anything about it."

"No, sir, the goats belonged to you and I delivered them just like you wanted."

"None of that, none of that! If you are going to defend yourself you're through! Finished! Fired! I'll pursue you, I'll harry you, I'll see you won't find employment in this county ever again!"

Frank shoved his fists into his pockets and looked at the dark ground.

"So do you admit it was my fifty dollars? Do you? Say it out loud!"

"Yes, sir, it was your fifty dollars."

"All right, now we are getting somewhere. I am going to dock your check twenty-five dollars for the next two paydays. No interest, just the strict amount you embezzled from me. And you aren't coming along tomorrow on the ride. You get out early and cut that field at Hogan Wash. Then you and Nathan hitch up a tractor and loader and help Jerry and Harvey and LaMar haul hay."

Frank was remembering how first he had punched the Forest Service man in the nose and stomach and then he had kicked him in the jaw.

"We will see if you're willing to make up for your deceit," Wesley said. "We'll see if you'll accept a little discipline. Are you going to do as I've said? I want to hear you say."

Frank couldn't see breaking Wesley's jaw when he didn't have money ahead for the next payment on his pickup. "All right," he said, "I'll help get the hay in."

"Good. On top of everything else the radio says there are thunderstorms on their way up through Texas and New Mexico, and I want this whole cutting down, baled, and hauled before they hit."

Then he said, "One more thing. I want to take your horse for Tom Woorbeck. I don't trust that patchy gelding I borrowed from Cyril Hobson."

Frank turned and walked off in the dark. "What do you say?" Wesley called after him. "I need that horse."

"Sure, take him," Frank said, going on to the privy where he sat for a long time and cried and ended up kicking the door off its hinges, which he knew he would have to repair before Wesley got back and saw it.

Frank was out cutting hay by four o'clock so that he wouldn't have to watch the party load up and leave without him. About eight o'clock Harvey, Jerry, and LaMar came up the road with a tractor and loader, ready to haul hay from one of the other fields. Harvey walked out and had a chat with Frank.

"Well, we're back. Bet you're surprised." Harvey was a fifty gallon barrel with legs and arms and a head. He wore size fifteen shoes, and his hair was supposed to be crew cut but lay flat on one side and bristled like lawn grass on the other. He had a crush on Marianne.

"You had a good time in Denver, I reckon."

"Real good. We saw a hot movie. Took in a girlie show. Haw! Also we watched some summer baseball. Didn't do nothing in Grand Junction and Green River but read comic books. We sure do want to thank you for doing our job for us."

"I didn't do you any favor. You aren't getting paid for it. Neither am I. The only one who is ahead is Wesley."

"We thought you was going on the big ride."

"Wesley had other ideas. He says it's going to storm."

At ten Frank finished cutting and drove back to the ranchhouse, which was empty and quiet. He made himself some breakfast and put together a lunch for later. He found Nathan irrigating in the field east of the corrals.

Nathan said, "I notice you ain't off on that ride you were so excited about."

"No, sir, I ain't."

"I didn't think Wesley would give you another day off right after Pioneer Day."

While they were driving out the road to the Jamison place, Frank saw a magpie on a fence post. He stopped the pickup and took his thirty-thirty from behind the seat. He rested the rifle on the open door, aimed, and fired. There was a shower of blood and feathers.

"You always got to be shooting things," Nathan said.

"Yep," Frank said as he put the pickup into gear and drove on.

"Too bad to shoot magpies."

"Why? They're common as horseshit at a rodeo."

Frank parked his pickup at the stackyard and lubricated the tractor and loader with a grease gun. Nathan stood at the gate, arms akimbo, gazing over the fields. Probably he was feeling that all this

pretty alfalfa was his. He had come back to Escalante during the
Depression, bought the old Jamison place, and tried to make a go
of farming. However, he had gone bankrupt and lost the place a
long time before Wesley came along and bought it.

Nathan was too old to pitch bales. He climbed into the tractor
seat, saying with a groan, "I'm quitting this fall. Going to move
to Provo and be with my little wife."

"I hope you do," Frank said but he knew he wouldn't.

On Sundays, after returning from church in Escalante, Nathan
wrote long letters to Dora, which Frank read when Nathan went
out to the privy. The letters were full of lies about how much Wesley
leaned on him for advice and counsel and about how close he was
to raising the capital for buying back the Jamison place. The letters
were also full of Frank's crimes. "He's wild and notional," Nathan
would write. "Figures he's got to be breaking the commandments
every half hour or he isn't having any fun. He sits at the breakfast
table and blows on his coffee in my direction like I might be tempted
by the smell. Profanest young man I ever met. If it wasn't for him
things would be okay here."

Nathan could get as mushy as a rotten cantaloupe. He would
write to Dora, "I have woke up nights, thought I heard your steps
out the door. Didn't my heart beat though thinking about my little
darling. Isn't it cruel the miles that keep us apart? If I could hold
you close to my bosom. Here's a kiss for my sweetie top of page
left side." Provo wasn't more than two hundred eighty miles from
the ranch, but Nathan and Dora hadn't seen each other in five or
six years.

When they came out of the field with the first load, Frank sat
on the front of the load where he could shout at Nathan if he turned
too sharply crossing the ditch. Nathan had spilled more than one
load by running the hind wheel of the wagon off the narrow bridge.
There was no advantage in mentioning it beforehand because that
put the idea in his mind and made him more likely to do it.

Nathan pulled the wagon to a bare spot where Frank could start
a new stack. For a while he wouldn't need the elevator, which was
too bad. When the noisy engine was running, Nathan couldn't talk.
Frank began tumbling bales off the load. Nathan stretched and spit
and got himself a drink of water.

He had three topics. One was his gift of healing through the Spirit and another was dryfarming and the third was the pioneers. Frank couldn't always tell which one he was on because he talked slow and meandered like a flatland riverbed. He paused frequently to talk about people's ancestors or about their kids who had gone off to college and lost their testimonies or about the list of people who had owned a particular piece of land or about the fact that if a plowshare was shaped in a certain way it poisoned the soil. If Frank tried to steer him back to his topic so he'd get through and shut up sooner, he would glare at him with disgust and say, "What's your hurry? If I'm going to tell this story I just as well tell all of it."

"Now you take dam building," Nathan said, standing on the tractor like a preacher in a pulpit.

"You'd imagine it would be easy to build a dam in the Escalante river, wouldn't you? Well, then, how come the Escalante pioneers had three dams wash out before they finally got one to stick? Which by the way you probably didn't have any idea of, did you? That dam west of town is the fourth one the pioneers built and it has been there since 1887."

He paused to let all that sink in.

"That dam will be there when the Savior returns and I'll tell you why. One day about noon, when the men from town were standing around at the old dam site, this stranger came riding up on a crop-eared jack mule. The men thought he was one of them mining engineers from down on the Colorado. He sat a minute looking things over and then he says, It won't ever do, but I'll tell you what will do. And he took them up river about a quarter mile to where the stream cuts through rock and he told them to blast out two keys on either side of the river and to make a little, low dam of solid concrete and rock anchored into them two keyholes, the whole idea being that the big floods would just run over the dam and never tear it out because it was so low and solid, but it was high enough to divert water into the town ditches which is all they needed anyhow."

Nathan stopped a minute to hawk up and spit out a big piece of phlegm.

"It only took about a minute to make them catch on. Then the stranger got on his mule and rode over the hill. Somebody looked around and says, Boys, it'll work and we owe that guy something if it ain't no more than a good dinner. They ran up the hill to holler him back, but they couldn't see him anywhere. And you know what? Right there in the dust, just over the hill, the tracks of that crop-eared jack mule disappeared all of a sudden. Into thin air! Then they all knew it was one of the Three Nephites God had sent to help them build their dam. And that's why that dam will hold till the Millennium."

When Frank had finished unloading, the new stack was two layers high. He took a drink from the bag and let water slosh from the corners of his mouth and run down over his chest. He corked the bag and hung it under the tractor seat.

He said, "I always heard it wasn't a crop-eared jack mule. It was a white jenny." That was a lie. He had never before heard a story like Nathan's.

"Who said it was a white jenny? It wasn't no white jenny. I never heard any such thing. It was a crop-eared jack."

Frank shrugged. "You hear that story over at Panguitch all the time. It was a white jenny."

Nathan started the tractor and headed off for the field, shaking his head and muttering. Frank lay on the empty loader with his hat over his face. He could have laughed if he hadn't been hurting so much from the treatment Wesley had given him.

At two they had lunch under an old juniper on a little hill above the stackyard. Nearby sat a big flop-eared jackrabbit which frequented the stackyard. Frank would have shot it long before if Nathan hadn't told him not to. A fly buzzed around its head and it flipped its upright ear. The fly went on buzzing. The rabbit lifted its hanging ear, hopped a yard or two, then dangled the ear again.

"Ain't he cute?" Nathan said. "It tickles me how he flops that ear."

"Five jackrabbits eat as much hay as a goodsized calf."

Nathan chuckled. "He don't hurt anything. Wesley's got hay to spare. I can't get over how he lets that ear flop."

Propped against the juniper trunk, Nathan took out his false teeth and put them into his bib pocket. He tore off a morsel of bread and ham and gummed it rapidly.

"I imagine those teeth of yours are good for something," Frank said. "Maybe you could throw them at rats."

"You're pretty smart. Someday you're going to look in a mirror and see what I see. That'll take you down a peg or two."

Frank leaned on his elbow and looked out over the fields. In pioneer times his grandfather Jamison had homesteaded this farm. On a little rise was a rock chimney, half ruined, the remains of the shack in which Frank's grandmother had once lived. In those days the farm hadn't been more than twenty acres watered by a spring. Later, Nathan had cleared off more acres. Later still, Wesley had sunk a deep well, rigged it with a diesel and a pump, and cleared land till he had a hundred acres. The fields were enclosed by fences and ditches grown up with weeds and longstemmed grass. Over everything the hot air shimmered.

"What I want to know," Frank said, "is how come when Grandpa damn near killed himself and Grandma too clearing off this place, how come God let it fall into the hands of a Lutheran."

The trouble with Nathan was nine tenths of the time he didn't know Frank was baiting him. "That don't mean nothing," he said. "Back in Nephite times this country was paradise. Green grass, trees, vines, bushes, flowers all over the place. But the Nephites waxed wicked and God got a bellyful of them and let the Lamanites destroy them and he turned this country into a desert. He sent your grandpa here to redeem a little bit of it. He sent me in to redeem a piece. So I'll tell you about Wesley Earle since you bring him up. He thinks well of himself, don't he? He's got a Ph.D. and he stashes money in the bank and he buys up old hay farms from people who've had a run of bad luck. But someday God will bankrupt him, and then the land he's cleared off and fixed up, it'll be ready for Mormon buyers. This country is for the Saints, not for the Gentiles."

According to Nathan, God hovered over this wild country with a notebook in his hand keeping tally on everything. Frank hoped that wasn't true. He hoped there was somewhere a fellow could get away from the Big Son of a Bitch in the Sky. He lay down flat in the shade and put his hat over his face.

"Right here is where your grandma went crazy," Nathan said. "She lost four babies. They're all buried down in the Escalante cemetery. I've seen their stones a time or two. They ain't all in the same part of the graveyard. A couple of them died out here."

"We might get ourselves a little nap before we go back to work," Frank said.

"Your grandma more or less made her own living. She ran this farm with some help from your grandpa's older boys by his first wife.

That wasn't so unusual in those days. A lot of the polygamous wives supported themselves."

"I know all that. I just as soon not hear it again."

"When she lost her last baby—she had your mother and your uncle, which was the only ones to grow up—but when she lost that last baby she sent your mother and your uncle into town to live with your grandpa's other wife and she went loco. She went around the junipers in a tore-up dress hunting for isinglass. I don't know what she wanted isinglass for. She did that for a couple of years. Then one day all of a sudden her wits came back to her and she went into Escalante and took her kids and moved over to Orderville and got your grandpa to build her a rock house there which is where your mother did most of her growing up. Ain't that true?"

Frank got up and put on his hat. "You old maggot," he said. "My grandmother never went crazy, and if you ever say she did again I'll knock your false teeth down your throat."

They went back to work, and as they came in from the field with the next load Nathan turned the tractor sharply and ran the rear wheel of the wagon into the ditch. The load tilted, lost a few bales, then slid, pinning the wagon obliquely to the ground.

"You did that on purpose," Frank said.

"I never either."

"It isn't you who is going to have to reload it, is it? All morning I knew this was going to happen. You just can't be happy till you run a load off that bridge, can you?"

Nathan got back on the tractor and started the engine. He let the drive wheels spin in the dirt for a while. Then, letting the clutch in and out, he rocked the tractor back and forth. Frank went up to the tractor and brusquely turned off the ignition. He climbed on the load and tossed off bales. Later he shoved Nathan from the tractor seat and pulled the empty loader from the ditch.

Nathan stooped, picked up a bale, and shuffled toward the wagon. Taking the bale from him, Frank said, "You aren't up to throwing bales. Go sit down."

"I never done it on purpose."

"You sure as hell did."

A load later, when he had finished stacking, Frank got the water bag and had a drink. The big rabbit sat flicking its upright ear, not fifteen feet away. He picked up a rock and threw it. The rabbit didn't move.

"Okay for you," he said. He walked to his pickup and pulled the thirty-thirty from behind the seat.

"Don't you shoot that rabbit," Nathan said. Frank pushed by.

The rabbit hopped a few yards. Frank put the rifle to his shoulder and fired. There was an awful roar and rabbit skin with head and feet attached looped into the air and came sailing down to the ground. Frank went back to the pickup and put up the rifle. He heard the tractor engine start and then he heard the clanking of the loader. Nathan drove out the far end of the stackyard, circled, and got onto the road leading to the ranch. Dust roiled up behind the tractor and loader and they became smaller and smaller. At last they went over a hill and were gone.

Frank sat in the open door of the pickup and let his legs dangle. He felt lower than a gopher hole. He was in big trouble and there wasn't any way through it. Wesley had rubbed his face in manure, and now it was too late to get mad and quit. Wesley would come home and see Nathan was gone and the hay was still in the field and he wouldn't give Frank a chance to quit, he'd fire him. He had just as well drive in to the bunkhouse and gather up his clothes.

For a minute he thought about setting fire to some of the stacks for a going away present. But that wouldn't do any good. Wesley had insurance and beside that he would know who had done it and he'd clap Frank in jail. He sat there a long time wondering how he was going to make his pickup payments while he settled into a new job. He could see the rabbit skin halfway up the little hill. For some reason it gave him an idea. My God, it was a good idea, so good that for a minute he couldn't believe in it. Then he lay back across the pickup seat and laughed. He felt fine. He saw just exactly what he was going to do.

He would come back with the tractor and loader and go on hauling hay. He'd stay out hauling till Wesley got home from the ride and came looking for him. He'd tell him he was sorry he had offended Nathan but he had gone on trying to get the hay in anyway. He'd apologize for not telling him the truth about the mare. He'd tell him he was glad he was docking his pay and he would do just whatever he could to make up for cheating him. In the days following, he would go on working just as hard as he could and being as nice and respectful as ever. In the meantime, he'd secretly get ready to quit. He'd get another job lined up and he'd move his horse over to the Rollinses' place in Cannonville. Right in the middle of the next hay cutting he'd quit. One morning he'd get up from breakfast and tell Wesley to go to hell, and he'd get in his pickup and drive away.

But that wasn't the best part of the idea. The best part was he'd screw Marianne two or three times before he left.

It wouldn't be hard to do. Before he moved his horse, they'd go on a Sunday ride. Out in the junipers somewhere they'd dismount and have a good talk. He'd warm up to her and try to kiss her and then act helpless and flustered like he didn't quite know what it all meant and couldn't help himself. He'd tell her he had been in love with her for a long time. Pretty soon he'd take off her halter and get a hand into her britches, and when she'd ask him if he'd marry her he'd say, You bet I will; I want you for my wife; we've got to keep it a secret for a while; but, sure enough, next year when your school is out, we'll get married.

Frank drove back to the ranch. Nathan had left the tractor and loader at the corrals and had taken off in his old car. Frank pulled the loader back out to the Jamison place and went to work hauling hay. Long after dark he saw lights along the road. When he got to the stackyard with a load, he could see the shine of parking lights and the grill of Clara's Chrysler.

"I thought you'd be out here," Clara said. Even in the dark he could see she was still dressed in boots and jeans.

"Yes, ma'am. But I have treated Nathan dirty and have drove him off."

"Well, then, that's another worry, because he isn't at the ranch. I was hoping he'd be out here."

"He's okay. He's got lots of friends in town. He'll show up in the morning and I'll make up with him. I sure am sorry I hurt his feelings."

"And you've been working here all alone till this late hour."

"Yes, ma'am. Though I didn't get too much done."

"Nobody else in the whole world would do this, Frank. You just stop now and come on back to the ranch. Likely you haven't had any supper."

"I just want to show Wesley how sorry I am. I'm a no good coyote for selling that mare and keeping fifty dollars."

"You saint," she said. "I never saw such a boy in all my life. You come get in this car with me and we'll go get you some supper and then you go to bed. We're all very tired from the ride but, gracious, we can't be anywhere near as tired as you must be."

While they were driving to the ranch, she told him about the ride. The weather had been just right—sunny but not too hot. The horses had behaved well. And, my goodness, the fossils! They were really there, four of them, sticking out in half relief from a limestone ledge. Dr. Critchley thought they were very probably dinosaur bones. He had seen several traits that caused him to think of Allosaurus, a genus of large meat eating dinosaurs.

"So that was very exciting," Clara said. "However, in one way it was a miserable day. When Marianne found out you weren't coming, she bowed up and said she wasn't coming either. She certainly did lose her composure. She reminded her father of all the extra work you put in this week. I hadn't realized how much you had done, and I must say I sided with Marianne. Wesley has done you a gross injustice, Frank. But he commanded her to get into the truck this morning. He is a firm man when he puts himself to it."

It was four miles from the Jamison place to the ranch. Clara drove very carefully, never getting over thirty miles an hour and slowing down to twenty when she came to dips.

"She more or less pouted all morning," Clara said. "She dallied along behind till I thought she'd get lost. Finally Wesley rode back to have it out with her. I could see he was boiling. I half expected he'd try to give her a licking, big as she is. The rest of us waited for them twenty or thirty minutes. I could see them afoot, holding their horses by the reins in a little wash. But I will say, Frank, Wesley is not a petty man. Do you know what? He apologized to her for doing you a wrong. And he promised to apologize to your face, which I know he will do. And I also apologize to you, Frank. You are a wonderful, hardworking young man. Please forgive him. And please forgive me too."

"Gosh," Frank said, "you don't need to apologize. Neither does Wesley. I'm the one who was in the wrong."

While Frank was eating supper, Wesley walked through the dining room with Dr. Critchley, but he didn't say a word to Frank. When

Frank got up at four, Nathan's bunk hadn't been slept in. Frank drove to Hogan Wash and began to bale. At seven, wanting to do a favor for Nathan, he got his rubber knee boots from the pickup and started the diesel on the pump above the fields.

Water gurgled deep down in the well, then erupted in a cold, clear stream. Frank walked down the ditch ahead of the water, his boots thumping loosely on his feet. He almost stepped on a slithering rattlesnake, which coiled and began to buzz. He chopped off its head with his shovel and threw it out of the ditch. He opened certain headgates and closed others and watched until the water was spreading through a field.

When he returned to the ranch, Frank saw Nathan's sedan parked in its usual place at the bunkhouse. Moreover, he could hear the diesel east of the corrals, which meant Nathan was at work. Clara gave Frank a cheery good morning and put him down to scrambled eggs, hot biscuits, and raspberry jam. Wesley had already left for Cedar City to take Mr. Woorbeck home and to put Dr. Critchley on the airplane for Salt Lake. Marianne brought a hollyhock sprig from the garden and placed it in a vase on the table. Jeanette stopped stirring cheese curds and stood with an elbow propped on Frank's shoulder. He could see he was somebody special this morning.

When Wesley returned from Cedar City, he walked directly from his pickup to the toolshed where Frank was repairing a baler. He cocked a polished brown boot on a crate and picked at a snag on his tan twill pants. He clucked and sighed and glanced guiltily at Frank two or three times before he said, "I understand you had a falling out with Nathan."

"Yes, sir. I'm sorry about it and I'll make up with him as soon as I can."

"I don't blame you for quarreling with that old marsupial, Frank. He's too old to be working on a ranch. He's too cranky. Nine times out of ten, he's a hindrance, not a help. But I keep him on as an act of charity. I am not without Christian feelings, you know. Any civilized person should have them, though some people have an excess. Like Clara, for example. At any rate, I am supporting Nathan more or less in a state of retirement. I am his pension!"

"Yes, sir, you're real kind to him."

Wesley seemed to relax a little. "Now you really will patch up with him, won't you, Frank?"

"Yes, sir, first good chance I get. I feel bad I hauled off and shot his rabbit."

Wesley kicked in the oily dirt with the toe of his boot. "My daughter says I have to apologize to you, Frank. She says I owe you a day off."

"You don't owe me a day off. You don't have to apologize either. I'm the one who was in the wrong. That mare was your property and I played fast and loose with her. I won't ever do it again."

"No, Frank, I've done you a great injustice. I have been under terrible tension these past few days. I have been distraught and emotional. College professors do that to me. I can't think about anything but whether I'm going to pass muster. Your little joke on those frat fellows seemed like an enormity, a felony. I felt betrayed and hoodwinked. But I was in the wrong and I beg your pardon. And of course I won't dock your paychecks."

"Thank you, sir."

"My gad, all the extra work you've done this week!" Wesley struggled to keep his composure.

"It's all right. It's just my job."

"It being mid-season and all, Frank, if you'll forgive me, I won't give you that day off. I know we are almost through with this cutting but the radio still says we have a storm coming. I would appreciate you helping out till all the hay is in."

"You bet, sir, I'll sure help out."

Wesley had kicked up an old sagebrush root. Now he was slowly working his way around it, banging the stub first with one toe, then with the other. "Marianne says she's going to take you up to Canaan Peak and show you those fossils. She says if I don't give you a day off she's going to take you up on Sunday."

"I'm not anxious to see them fossils. They don't mean anything to me."

"That's what I told her. I said, You're presuming on Frank's interest in a dry academic subject."

"I'll figure up something else I've got to be doing on Sunday."

"That's the idea."

But it wasn't really the idea because Wesley kept on kicking a circle around the root. "To be truthful with you, Frank, I am in the doghouse with Marianne right now. So unless it is actually disagreeable to you, I would take it as a kindness if you'd let her

take you up there on Sunday. She fancies it's a way to make resti-
tution to you."

"Yes, sir, I'll sure go if you want me to."

"I'd be grateful if you'd start early and get back before dark. I
won't get anxious until dark."

"You bet. You can count on me. We'll get back safe and sound
with plenty of time to spare before night."

Wesley looked much happier. He shook Frank's hand and said,
"What a travesty! I strain at a gnat and swallow a camel. I get all
heated up over you selling a mare I had already traded off anyhow,
and I overlook the unending loyal service you give me. A son couldn't
be any better than you are, Frank."

After supper Frank stayed at the corrals currying his horse until
he saw Nathan return to the bunkhouse from the privy. Frank gave
him ten minutes more so that he would be ready for bed and couldn't
walk out while Frank was trying to pacify him. Sure enough, when
Frank went in, Nathan had his shirt off and his pants unbuttoned.
His irrigation boots stood by the bunk smelling worse than a rotten
carp. The bunkhouse was still hot. Through the open windows came
the chirping of crickets and, from the pond back of the corrals, the
grumping of a frog or two.

"I've been a good deal remorseful over shooting that jackrabbit
yesterday," Frank said. "Also over that magpie I shot in the morning."

Nathan was winding his clock. His thin grey hair was damp
with sweat.

"I'm sure a bummer," Frank went on. "It seems like I've got to
be shooting things all the time that don't need to be shot."

Nathan pulled off his pants, stuffed them under his bunk, and
stretched out without covering himself. He said, "I never spilled
that hay on purpose. I didn't mean to let that wheel run off the
bridge and put you to all that extra work."

"I know you never. I said you did just to get your goat. Just to
be mean."

"You're the only family I've got," Nathan said weepily. "For two
years you and me have bunked in this bunkhouse."

"That's right. For two years."

"I've been feeling terrible. I've been asking myself how I was ever
going to partake of the Sacrament next Sunday, me feeling so bitter
and vengeful. I have had ungodly thoughts. I've been thinking what

a scourge you are and how you have to be taking God's name in vain all the time and how you take pleasure in scorning the commandments. I've been forgetting all the nice things you do for me, how you keep work off my shoulders. This morning I notice you got the water going for me out at the wash. And lots of times you've brought me a candy bar or a doughnut when you stopped by the store in Escalante. I didn't mean to run that wheel off that bridge, I truly didn't. And I repent of the bad thoughts I've had against you. What's a jackrabbit between two sons of God?"

On Saturday evening Frank hitched the two-horse trailer to his pickup and loaded saddles and blankets into the hutch. Marianne came from the goat pen carrying pails and singing "My Bucket's Got a Hole in It." Setting down the pails, she went into the tackroom for ponchos. She bent into the trailer hutch and tied the ponchos onto the saddles. The sun was down, dusk was on, and the air was starting to cool. Over Boulder Mountain an immense black cloud had gathered and lightning flashed every three or four seconds, lighting up the cloud like a movie marquee, but the storm was too far away for anyone to hear thunder.

"I hope that storm doesn't spread," Marianne said.

"It won't," Frank asserted. "It was flashing like that last night and nothing came of it. The sky was clear as a bell this morning."

"Breakfast at four-thirty."

"Okay. I'll be up and the horses will be loaded."

She went across the driveway singing "The Tennessee Waltz." His eyes followed her round, flexing buttocks. For a couple of days he had been as hot and lusty as a bridegroom; he hadn't had anything but sex on his mind. Along with the usual things like wire cutters and matches, he had put condoms in his saddlebags, which were still in the bunkhouse.

When he got up at a quarter to four the sky was on fire with stars. There wasn't a cloud anywhere. He sat in the privy moping, remembering a dream about Clara. In the dream she had brought him a piece of raisin pie and a mug of coffee while he was out at the Jamison place adjusting the diesel. Her hair was covered with a kerchief and her cheeks were rough and chappy, but she spoke to him with great kindness.

Frank sat in the privy with his elbows on his knees and his chin in his hands, wondering why God had put up for so long with a deceitful, malicious shitheel like Frank J. Windham. For two days he had been acting repentant and good natured, exceeding himself in being moral and Christian for no other purpose than catching Wesley off guard—quitting him when it would hurt most and soiling his daughter for good measure.

What about Clara, who washed Frank's clothes and cooked his meals and cheered him up when he was down? What kind of a skunk would dirty her daughter? What about Marianne? What had she done to deserve him telling her lies and fixing her so that another man wouldn't want to marry her? And for crying out loud, what about Wesley himself? These last two days he had been contrite and humble and friendly, showing Frank the most consideration a boss could. Nathan too. That old badger had been as sweet and decent as if the Millennium had arrived and human nature had at last been sanctified.

Frank wasn't going to quit Wesley and he wasn't going to make love to Marianne. All that was totally out of the picture. When he went into the bunkhouse, he took the condoms out of his saddlebags and locked them in the little red box under his bunk.

It was daylight before they got off. They drove into Escalante and took the road up Alvey Wash, which ran between high ridges covered with juniper and pinion. The road crossed the wash every half mile or so and sometimes ran in the wash itself. A two-horse trailer was a big load for Frank's pickup, which growled and whined and creaked through the sand and over the rocks. After an hour and a half they turned up a side road into Little Valley Wash. The road was steeper and rockier and ran through gorges so narrow a person on either running board could have touched the cliffs.

"I hope this road holds up," Frank said. "This would be a heck of a place to try to turn around."

"Isn't this great country!" Marianne said. "This is how come I left Illinois."

When the dark gorges opened a little, they saw sunlight on the billowing tops of cottonwood trees. Sage brush, some of it as high as a horse, covered the flats. They passed clusters of prickly pear with yellow flowers and tall yucca stems with waxy white blossoms.

"Have you ever had a visitation?" Marianne asked.

"What kind of visitation?"

"Of the Holy Ghost."

"Never have. Lots of my relatives have had visitations, though."

"Last winter," she said, "when I was in Illinois, I thought I'd go crazy. The temperature was below zero, had been for days. So I prayed and Jesus sent the Holy Ghost and it witnessed to me."

"I always thought the Holy Ghost was a he," Frank said.

"It couldn't be a he," she said. "It is part of God. Like a fender is part of a car."

"I always thought God was a he."

"Sure, but you don't call a man's leg *he*, do you?"

"The way I see it God is the president and Jesus is his first counselor and the Holy Ghost is his second counselor."

"That's dumb."

"No, it ain't."

About seven-thirty they parked on a little hill and unloaded the horses. They saddled up and headed crosscountry, Marianne showing the way. She was wearing a neat chambray shirt, he a tattered flannel, unbuttoned with tails out. They passed over into Horse Spring Canyon, followed its dry, rocky bed for a mile, then rode over a pass between two giant knolls into Canaan Creek. Tall pines stood among the junipers and pinions on the roundabout ridges. To the west loomed the sloping blue ridge called Canaan Peak. The sun burned hot above puffy, drifting clouds, on which Frank kept an eye, hoping they wouldn't stack up and make a storm.

Marianne reined in Chowder and pointed. Standing at the edge of an aspen thicket was a steer, a black and white yearling.

"Let's rope him," she said, unstrapping her lasso.

"He's pretty big."

"Let's try it. Let's see if we can team rope him. You get his head and I'll go for his heels."

"What if you couldn't get your lasso on his hind legs? Then I'd be in a mess, wouldn't I?"

"Why couldn't I? Especially if you already had his head?"

"Yeah, and in the meantime he'd jerk the horn off my saddle. He's too big. Besides, these flatcountry horses don't know anything about chasing steers through the rocks. They'd stumble and kill us."

They rode on by, leaving the steer staring after them with wide, spooked eyes.

A tiny stream of water had appeared in Canaan Creek. It was clear and cold and they dismounted and had a drink. They sat for a while on a grassy bank, holding bridle reins and watching their horses graze and stamp and swish their tails.

"There's where we're headed," Marianne said, pointing to a side canyon about a half mile ahead.

Frank was thinking this was a place God wouldn't keep an eye on; it was too wild, too far away. All morning he had been repressing a shivery idea. It was like having a snake in a bucket; once in a while he'd lift the lid just a fraction of an inch to see if the snake was still there. He had been hoping something big would happen to him when he got to the fossils; he had been hoping he'd see there wasn't any God. Maybe, come Judgment Day, he'd be in big trouble. But out here in the silence of Canaan Creek, he felt bold. He wanted to whoop and holler and flail his arms and dance a jig. Maybe when he saw those fossils he would have a visitation, a testimony and witness; maybe he'd know for sure there wasn't any God.

They mounted, rode on, and entered the little canyon, whose limestone walls were fissured and bouldery and tangled with wild grape vines. The horses picked their way carefully over rocks and fallen trunks.

They came to a lateral ravine. "This is it," Marianne said. "End of the trail for these horses."

They dismounted, loosened cinches, and tied bridle reins to aspens. Frank took Marianne's saddlebags, which held their lunch, and they climbed into the ravine. Among jumbled boulders nestled tiny pools of clear water and patches of bright green cress.

"That's them," Marianne said. Having climbed onto a flat-topped boulder, she squatted and pointed toward a vertical limestone face.

There were four fossils, white-grey shapes standing out slightly from the blue-grey of the surrounding rock. Three of them, set obliquely, might have been almost any part of a big animal. The fourth one, in line with the limestone wall, was clearly a giant leg with joint knobs at either end.

"Praise God," Marianne said.

Frank let his fingers run over the fossils. "They sure do look real."

"They make me want to pray," she said.

He couldn't stop fingering the fossils. He was relieved to see they were ordinary, everyday rock. He had half expected they would be hot and toxic and corrosive. He didn't have any idea how old they were. Four thousand years? Two hundred million? How was a person to know?

"Did you ever pray with somebody?" Marianne asked.

He was disgusted. "Hell, yes. Every day when I lived at home."

"No, I mean like out here. Just two people like you and me."

He could see what she was driving at. "No, ma'am, not me, not here. I ain't in a praying mood."

The sky had begun to fill with dark grey clouds and a cool wind was funneling down the ravine. A big bird suddenly swept over them, its outstretched wings tilting this way and that as it rode the wind downward.

"An eagle," Frank said.

He felt a prickle on the back of his neck. His arms had goosebumps and they were sweating cold. He felt as if somebody had got a fist around his liver and had squeezed it dry. Even out here a fellow had to keep his thoughts penned up. Even out here a man couldn't wish God was dead. He wanted to squall, shout, and run. But he kept control of himself and didn't move a muscle.

Marianne unpacked the lunch and offered him a couple of sandwiches and an apple. They sat on the edge of a boulder and watched a chipmunk in a stunted spruce tree. Frank took off his hat to keep the wind from blowing it away. There wasn't anywhere a man could go to get away from God. A herd of dinosaurs stampeding down Canaan Creek couldn't change that fact. Maybe it was proper to believe in evolution six days a week and in Adam and Eve on Sunday. Maybe God had done it both ways—created the earth billions of years ago and then created it again six thousand years ago. It was just like him to do impossible and contradictory things. He was God and could do anything he wanted.

By the time they had finished eating, the sun was gone. They climbed down over the rocks to their horses and tightened their cinches and mounted. They rode down Canaan Creek and went over the pass into Horse Spring Canyon. A fierce wind spilled black clouds over the ridges and whirled mist in the canyon bottom. Westward, over the flank of Canaan Peak, lightning flashed and thunder rumbled. They put on their ponchos. Raindrops pattered, picked up speed, then turned into a downpour.

"Let's get over under that cliff until it lets up a little," Marianne said.

"No," Frank said, whipping up Booger, "let's get on down into the bottom and get across the wash before it floods."

They hunched in their saddles, clutching their ponchos at the neck. The horses laid back their ears, tossed their heads, and slipped and slid down the steep slope. When they came to the wash it was running with muddy water. They rode downstream, found an easy slope, and rode into the wash. The water splashed around their stirrups.

"It didn't look that deep from the other side," Frank said as the horses struggled up the bank. "You can't trust these washes."

By the time they reached the pickup and trailer, the wind had calmed, the thunder had died, and the rain had settled into a steady drizzle. Despite their ponchos they were wet through.

"Look at that wash," Frank said as he tied his horse to the trailer. The narrow defile carried a torrent of rumbling, frothing water. "Look at it rain! It isn't going to quit. Anybody can see that. Every wash in the country will be running full."

"At least we've got a dry place to sit."

"I told your dad we'd be back before dark. I promised him."

He walked to the wash and squatted close to the rushing, roaring water. She followed and squatted nearby. "You know what?" he said. "Alvey Wash ain't going to dry out for two or three days, and until it does this pickup and trailer are going to sit right here. We're going to be here all night, and when we go out tomorrow it will have to be horseback."

"So what? That won't hurt anything."

They walked back to the pickup. Slapping his thigh with his wrung-out gloves, he said gloomily, "Your dad is going to get a shotgun and shoot me. He figures you're a lamb and I'm a coyote."

"No, he doesn't. He thinks you're one of the twelve apostles."

Frank unsaddled Chowder for her. He had planned to do Wesley a wrong, then repented and planned not to. Now he'd have to stay out all night with Marianne, and Wesley would think he'd done him a wrong when he hadn't. It seemed as if virtue never was rewarded.

"This is kind of fun," Marianne said. "There's even some lunch left over."

She put a hackamore on Chowder and led him to the trailer. He hesitated and she jerked and he scrambled in. Frank rode Booger into a clump of junipers, put a loop around a big dead limb, and dragged it to the truck.

"This is so we can have a fire and dry out when it quits raining later on," he told her. "Sitting in our wet clothes in that pickup all night ain't going to be any picnic." When he had built up a pile of dead juniper, he loaded Booger into the trailer and climbed into the pickup.

The rain splattered steadily on the cab. They still wore their ponchos for warmth. Frank started the engine and ran the heater for a while. When he turned it off they became cold again, so he fetched the saddle blankets from the trailer. "They're horsy and wet but they'll help a little," he said.

"A little clean horse dirt won't hurt us any," Marianne said, adjusting a saddle blanket over her lap. "You know something, maybe we ought to sit close to one another. Two bodies make a lot more heat than one."

"I guess that's right," Frank said.

"It's a good idea, isn't it?"

"Sure, you bet, it's a dandy idea." He had already decided he wouldn't think of her as a big steamy girl with thighs, belly, and breasts. He would think of her as a sack of wheat that he had snuggled up to because it had a little warmth.

She pulled off her poncho and after she had glanced at him expectantly he pulled off his. She slid close to him and he adjusted the ponchos and blankets over them like bed quilting. She was just a sister, he was saying to himself. Her thigh against his, her arm suddenly embracing his shoulders, they didn't mean a thing.

He could see this wasn't a good idea. It was about as smart as wandering around on a dark night in the vicinity of a cliff. Already he had reached for her hand and their fingers were intertwined. She was telling him about Harvey, who had asked her for a date to a movie.

"I acted real touched. I said, I can't, Harvey; my dad won't let me date much. Then he pulled out an imitation pearl ring and said it was for me. He had it wrapped in a nice little package. I said, Oh, Harvey, that's so sweet, but my dad won't let me take gifts from boys."

They both had a good laugh about that. Outside the rain pounded and everything was dim and grey. Inside the windows were steamy. Marianne's hair was frizzly and tangled and her eyes were shadowy.

"You have such a big hand," she said, feeling each finger in turn.

"It just grew that way. I didn't ask it to."

"I like your big hands. They wouldn't let a person drop."

He kissed her and she responded, moving her lips over his, then pulling away to look at him with eyes half wistful, half proud.

He couldn't help himself. He said, "I've been in love with you for a long time. Ever since the day I first saw you."

"Oh, golly."

"I love you. I just do."

"Nobody ever said that to me before," she whispered. She kissed him and hugged him tight and whimpered.

They went on hugging and kissing and he let his hands roam around. He felt her breasts outside her shirt, and when he unbuttoned a couple of buttons she didn't stop him and he put his hand inside her bra.

"Your dad is down on me because he wants you to go back east to college, and your mom is down on me because I'm a Mormon. But I keep thinking about us getting married. I keep wondering if it'd work out."

"Oh, golly," she said. "Oh, golly."

"When your school is out next June maybe we could get married. We wouldn't want to get in a rush telling your folks. Next winter sometime maybe."

"Oh, gee," she said, "I prayed I wouldn't love you, but I do." Her face was pressed against his neck, her eyes were closed, her breath came in little pants.

He tried to get his hand into her jeans, which were very tight.

"Please," she said. "Not that. Not yet."

He held off for a while, hugging and kissing her and stroking her arms and shoulders and belly. Then he tried again, saying, "I wish I could. I love you so much."

She murmured again and unbuttoned her jeans and shifted so he could get his hand into her panties. Her face looked peaceful and kind as if she was saying, Go ahead, don't be ashamed, it's all right.

"I'm just burning up, I love you so much," he said.

He waited a while and then said, "I want to go all the way. I want to so bad it hurts."

"Oh, Frank," she said, "please, let's don't. Not yet."

He shook his head and looked flustered and let down. "I wish I could. It's killing me not to."

"We can't do it here," she said. "There isn't any room."

"We can figure out how," he said.

When they had finished and were pulling on their jeans and boots, she said, "So what if I do get pregnant? We'll just have to get married a little earlier, that's all."

"Sure," he said, "that's all."

That word pregnant frightened him. He was ready to promise God that if he would keep her from getting that way, he would repent and live decently. He wished he had somebody to explain to, somebody like Red who would listen without saying a word. He would tell him he hadn't done this dirty thing to Marianne out of malice and meanness. Honest to Pete, he had got over his grudge against Wesley. And he never had had a grudge against Marianne. He had made love to her just because he was a goddamned lustful coyote who didn't have any self control.

Marianne found a sandwich and a candy bar in her saddlebags and Frank divided them with his pocketknife. After eating, they cuddled again and tried to sleep. Night had come and rain beat on the cab, sometimes hard, sometimes easy.

An hour or so later Marianne said, "I've got to pee." When she returned she said, "Do you get scared in the dark?"

"Not much."

"How come?"

"Because there isn't anything around here to be scared of."

"Bears and mountain lions," she said.

"No bears around here," he said. "Very few mountain lions. They're afraid of people."

About midnight the sky cleared and the bright stars glimmered. Deciding to make a fire, Frank took a hose from behind the seat and siphoned gasoline from the tank. He broke off juniper limbs, stacked them in a pyramid, and doused them. He threw on a match and bright yellow flames danced up. He added branches one by one until he had a large, crackling fire. He and Marianne stood close, first facing the fire, then turning their backs to it, and steam rose from their legs and shoulders.

"This feels good," she said. "A fire cheers me up."

"You bet. It cheers anybody up."

He put down the ponchos and saddle blankets and they sat close to each other. He could hear rocks rattling and rumbling in the flooding wash. He thought about how much water was going downstream, and he knew the people in Escalante had been driving out all evening to where the road first crossed Alvey Wash, saying things like, "Ain't that a doozy?" and "Good hell, if that ain't a flood!" He hoped Wesley and Clara weren't too worried.

Marianne laughed. "Isn't it funny how we've both been in love with each other all along and we didn't dare tell?"

"It's pretty danged funny, all right."

After a while she said, "Did I ever tell you about the cowboy Jesus?"

"You did once. Up in Howell Valley, which was another time we were camping out."

"Well, I've been thinking about him tonight. When we were in the pickup and it was still raining, I daydreamed about the cowboy Jesus. I could see this rider coming over the ridge. He was too far away for me to see who he was at first, but when he got up close I could see it really was Jesus. He said, You were lost but I have found you."

"That's quite a daydream," he said.

She snuggled in his arms. "Jesus will take care of me. It's so dumb of me to be afraid when I have to get out in the dark."

She went to sleep and Frank held her so that she would be comfortable and wouldn't wake up. His legs began to hurt and then his shoulders, but he held her for a long, long time because he knew he owed her more than he was willing to pay back. It made him bitter to realize that Jesus didn't give a hoot for a sweet girl like Marianne. She was counting on Jesus to keep her safe from bears and mountain lions. She didn't know it wasn't bears and mountain lions she needed to worry about. She needed to worry about coyotes like Frank J. Windham.

3.

Goodby
to Jeremy

Frank found out being secretly engaged wasn't an easy life. On a Sunday morning after he had gone to a dance in Koosharem with Jack and Red, Marianne had a little crying spell in the roping corral. "It just hurt me all night to think about you off on a toot. Doesn't being faithful mean something to people who are going to get married? Don't you want me to be faithful?"

"Sure I do."

"Well, I want you to be faithful too. I just don't know if I can stand it, you going off on toots."

"Okay, okay," he said, "I won't do it again."

After that, she contrived a means for them to get together on Saturday nights. Frank came to supper slicked up and curried and announced he was off for another frolic with Jack and Red. He drove through Escalante and waited at the reservoir west of town. After a while Marianne showed up in Clara's car. She climbed into his pickup and they drove into the junipers.

When Saturday nights were approaching and he was steamed up, he thought it wasn't such a bad life. But on Sunday mornings, he felt maggoty as a manure pile. He woke up without an inch of appetite for Marianne, and while he lay on his bunk pondering a way out of the mess he was in, his deceits, profanities, gluttonies, and scoffings tramped through his mind, clamoring accusations. He knew it wouldn't be long until God would let a hay stack topple on him or let his horse stumble and roll on him, puncturing his lung with the saddle horn.

Things were somewhat better in the fall. The last cutting of hay was in and Frank began taking overnight trips delivering hay, most of them to the big feedlots in Mesquite, Nevada. School had started in Escalante, and five days a week Marianne and Jeanette had to catch the school bus at seven-thirty and didn't get home till five-fifteen. Also, Frank began spending Sundays helping the Rollinses work cattle at Cannonville, which was one of the brightest ideas he had had in a long time.

Red's dad, Jake Rollins, was an eighty percent Mormon. He paid tithing and didn't cuss, drink, or smoke but he couldn't make it to church more than one Sunday out of eight or ten. Beside running two hundred head of cattle, he was janitor at Bryce Valley High School. He wore brogans instead of boots and a striped railroad cap instead of a Stetson.

"What you want to do," he said to Frank one Sunday, "is get going on your own herd. There isn't any way for a fellow like you to start but small. You got to pick up five cows here and five cows there. In the meantime, of course, you got to be working at something else. Your whole life you got to work at something else. You can't make a living on cattle alone."

"I'm going to do it," Frank said. "Wesley Earle says give him five years and he'll be making his living on cattle alone. He's going to build a big feedlot and feed all that hay to his own cows."

"Maybe so," Jake said. "But most of us don't have daddies who leave us a big wheat farm in Colorado to use for a starter."

Frank and Jake and Red were taking a break on the tailgate of Jake's old International pickup. They had been fencing a half acre holding corral. On the ground were hammers, wire stretchers, rolls of barbed wire, and left-over juniper posts.

Jake said, "The whole problem for a guy like you is range. It was all took up a long time ago, and those that have it would rather sell their wife. If you don't have any, you've got to grab a little here, a little there. You've got to be a grunter and a fighter. You've got to horn in."

"That's what I'm going to do," Frank said.

"I hope you do," Jake said respectfully. His own son wasn't interested in cows.

Jake told Frank if he'd go on helping out on Sundays he could pasture a few critters on the Rollinses' winter range. One of the animals would have to be a bull, and Frank would have to find other range in the summer because the Rollinses didn't have much of a summer allotment on the National Forest.

One evening Frank took Wesley, Nathan, and Marianne to see a little piece of land on the upper Paria that he was interested in buying. Though somebody had let the water rights lapse, it was just right for the headquarters of a ranch. He could see his house on it and some corrals and a barn and a little patch of alfalfa. Later he could pick up other acres around it.

They tramped around the acreage and found an iron wheel from a mower and a rusty shovel blade. Then they crawled through a barbed wire fence and climbed a little knoll to look over the country. Below them was the Paria, no more than a glistening trickle. Northeast were the white gullied faces of Table Cliff. Southwest was Bryce National Park, high pine-covered ridges whose flanks had been lathed, rasped, and whittled by wind and rain into curious shapes—miles and miles of corrugated cliffs, coved turrets, and fluted spires in mingled, melted hues of ocher, cream, coral, and rust.

"Anyhow you've got some scenery," Wesley said.

Nathan wasn't so kind. "I gotta tell you, you're daydreaming. No place you'd ever have money enough to buy will let a man make a living. You buy this piddly little piece, you just well tamp your money down a badger hole."

Marianne said, "He's got to start somewhere. I think he ought to buy it."

The next morning she had a talk with Frank at the picket gate in front of the ranchhouse. She had two hundred fifty dollars in a savings account, which she wanted him to use to help pay for the land.

"No, I couldn't take it," he said.

"Why not? It's our ranch, isn't it?"

He wanted to say, "Hell, no, it isn't!" but instead he said, "Sure, but you hang on to that money. We'll need it later on." It almost ruined things, knowing she was interested. However, when he had an appetite up for something, he had to have it, so he bought the little place on installments.

In late September, Frank asked Wesley for time off. On Thursday and Friday he and his brother Jeremy would help their cousin Raymond on his roundup at Antimony. On Saturday and Sunday he would go home to Panguitch to help say goodby to Jeremy, who was leaving for BYU on the Sunday night bus. Frank asked Marianne whether he could borrow her gelding for Jeremy on the roundup, and she said yes. On Wednesday evening she came to the corrals and helped him load the horses.

"I envy you going," she said. "That roundup will be a lot of fun."

"A lot of work too."

"It's the kind of work I like. This school stuff is getting me down."

Their breath was steamy and they both wore coats. A quarter moon hung over Fifty Mile Mountain, and just under it the evening star twinkled. A "V" of wild ducks clamored through the high darkening air.

"I'll sure miss you Saturday night," she said. "It's got to be where Saturday night is the only time we have together."

"I'll miss you too. You're awful important to me."

"Gosh, Frank, you're so sweet." She hugged him and reached up and gave him a kiss.

When Frank got to Antimony, Raymond told him to come in for supper before he unloaded his horses. Everybody was still at the table having a talk—Salsifer; Jeremy; Raymond's wife Helen; his boys Jeff, Harold, and Simms; his girls Rebecca and Sandra. Frank dug into the roast beef and scalloped potatoes Helen had saved for him.

Salsifer joshed Frank about thinking a roundup was nothing but a lark. He was Frank's uncle on his mother's side. "I guess you brung a horse for Jeremy," the old man said.

"You bet. Marianne's gelding. Name of Chowder. Good cutting horse. He's considerable nervous, though. I'm half tempted to let Jeremy ride Booger, who is a little calmer."

Jeremy was tall and narrow shouldered and had a crew cut and a five o'clock shadow. His eyes bulged a little, giving him the appearance of not quite understanding what was going on. Some things Jeremy was perfect at—reading books about birds, bugs, and skunk cabbages and putting up with Margaret and sitting through sermons. He was clumsy around horses and cattle.

"I wish I could go on a roundup," said Rebecca, who was seventeen and had dimpled cheeks and a receding chin.

Raymond said, "We don't need everybody in the family out of school."

"Girls don't go on roundups anyhow," Simms pointed out.

"Girls can't pass the Sacrament," Harold added.

"That's nothing to vaunt about," Raymond said. "They sure made a mistake ordaining that Harold a deacon. He's too dadgummed wicked. He don't mind his parents or his teachers or anybody else. Same goes for you, Simms. When it comes time and the bishop says, All who feel they can sustain Brother Simms Jamison for the office of deacon, I ain't raising my hand, you can count on that."

That kind of talk went off Harold and Simms like water off slickrock. Harold was twelve and Simms was nine. They both had freckles and crooked teeth and wild, glinty eyes that said they didn't give a damn for what civilized people did.

"Grandpa, tell us about a horse called Monty," Simms said.

"No time for that," Raymond growled. "You boys are getting up early. You go on to bed now."

Salsifer had already begun to talk. "Years ago when I wasn't no older than Frank here, when I was cowboying over in San Juan County, I had a horse called Monty like that horse in *The Virginian*, which is the finest cowboy book ever wrote. Brother, was he a runner. For chasing mustangs he was the best horse I ever saw, bar none. He had a chest on him, he could run for hours. One day in Chisel Creek I thought a bunch of broomies was getting away for sure and I kept Monty going and going. Well, we brought them into the trap at last, we had them. Was I ever proud of that pony. But Danny Stowall says, Sals, that horse of yours won't see the sun come up; you've run him to death. Danny was right. That horse called Monty died in the night. He never saw the sun come up."

For a minute Salisfer had tears in his eyes. He was about seventy but looked older. He had got sick and lost weight and his jowls and dewlap drooped. His head was bald except for a little rim of bristle.

"Boys, be good to your horses," he said. "There isn't no nobler animal on earth than a horse. Julius Caesar rode a horse. So did Napoleon Bonaparte. It grieves me remembering the horses I've had. It truly grieves me."

Raymond was stacking dirty plates. He scraped beef fat and little piles of cold potatoes onto a platter, mumbling, "I hate a messy table."

Helen had been leaning in the kitchen doorway. "Land sakes, here I am just plopped on a post," she cried, rushing to the table and picking up knives and forks. She was a skinny, bowlegged woman with grey hair and buckteeth which left her lips wet and unappetizing when she talked.

Raymond shoved a stack of dishes into Rebecca's hands. "Get a move on and help your mother clear this table."

Raymond was also skinny and he had a sharp nose and a droopy mustache. He wore a blue denim shirt and boots run over at the heels. He wiped his greasy hands on his pant legs and went into the living room. Returning with an envelope, he said, "Helen, I see we got dunned again by the light company. Why don't you pay the bills when they come the first time?"

"Well, I never saw it, I just never saw it," she said. "I don't think it ever did come the first time."

"You got to shape up if I'm going to let you sign checks." Then Raymond spoke to Jeff, who was sixteen. "Go out and give Frank a hand unloading his horses, will you?"

"I'll help Frank," Harold said.

"Me too," Simms said.

"No, you won't," Raymond growled. "Now you two skunks listen to me. Tomorrow Frank and Jeff are in charge. You do what they say. You mind business and work hard and don't run off playing Arabs and Foreign Legion on them horses. Frank, you've got my permission to kick the stuffing out of these kids if they don't mind."

Salsifer and Jeremy went across the street to Salsifer's house, where Frank and Jeremy would sleep. After Frank and Jeff had unloaded the horses, Raymond gave them instructions about the roundup. He couldn't go along because he operated a grader for the county road commission. He figured there would be exactly two hundred forty-nine head, not counting calves—eight bulls, a hundred ninety-two cows, and fifty steers less one killed by lightning.

Raymond said, "These boys of mine want to camp out tomorrow night at the holding corral. They're playing cowboy, and they figure that's the way you do it. Jeff's got to be pretty good on Dutch oven cooking. You and Jeremy might want to camp out with them."

"Sure thing," Frank said. "If Jeremy wants to, I'm for it. I haven't slept out for a while."

"Nine of the cows belong to your ma, and three yearling steers. We can tell them by the ear marks," Raymond added.

That made twelve head for Margaret. There should have been fifteen.

Tertullian Jamison had bequeathed a hundred cow allotment on the National Forest to Salsifer and Margaret, the two living children of his second wife, Jerusha. The allotment had been registered in Salsifer's name, but they were to share it equally. Margaret had never summered more than a few head on it, which Salsifer had pastured on his private winter range without charge.

"I've been thinking of buying Mother's cattle," Frank said.

"Buying them?"

"Yes, sir. Take them over on shares. Start a little herd of my own."

The three of them, Frank, Raymond, Jeff, were standing in the barnyard next to Frank's pickup. A cat, a dark blur in the night, rubbed and purred around their legs.

"Are you serious?" Raymond said.

"You bet. Real serious." For days Frank had been plotting, fancying, and calculating how to get Margaret's cows for his own and how to crowd in on Salsifer's summer range on the National Forest.

"I'd winter them down on the Rollinses' range," he went on.

"That'd be something," Raymond said. "To tell you the truth I wouldn't mind getting out from under your mother's cows. They're nothing but a bone of contention between Dad and me."

Frank felt tingly. It was time to tell Raymond about the touchy part of his plan. He wanted Margaret's full share of summer range on the Forest. He would also keep looking for more winter range on the Paria until he had his little herd built up to fifty head. Slouching against the pickup fender, Raymond was a silhouette in the dark. Frank decided to wait. He didn't have the guts to make a man mad when he couldn't see his face.

He pulled his bedroll from the back of the pickup. "I'll mosey on over to Uncle Salsifer's house. See you in the morning."

Frank and Jeremy didn't get much sleep because Salsifer was up every hour or so going to the toilet. Frank could hear him breaking wind and spattering liquid. Once after he had got back to bed, Frank went in to talk to him. "Are you okay? Do you want me to go get Raymond or Helen?"

"I ain't okay but there don't seem to be anything to do about it. I've got the chronic scoots. Helen hauled me over to Richfield and the doctor gave me some pills. They don't help much."

A lamp burned on a tiny table, which also held a small picture of Salsifer's wife, folded spectacles, and false teeth in a glass of water.

Salsifer was propped up by two big pillows and he wore blue pajamas. Frank had pulled on his jeans. He was bare footed and bare chested.

"Don't ever get old, Frank. Have some courage and die first." Salsifer put on his glasses and picked up the picture. His wife was young, had blond page-boy hair, and wore a black dress with a white lace collar. "I never said goodnight to Ora Jean," he said.

He patted the bed, motioning for Frank to sit. When he did the bed dipped and creaked. "We had some good times," Salsifer said. "When I turned the cattle over to Raymond, her and me bought ourselves a camper and a fishing boat. We spent a lot of summer days up at Otter Creek and Koosharem. We caught some fine trout. Her as much as me. She wasn't no mean fisherman."

He kissed the picture and replaced it on the table. "She knows I love her. Up there where she is now, she knows."

Jeremy stood in the doorway, staring solemnly. He wore a white union suit, arms to the wrist, legs to the ankle, buttons from crotch to neck. Frank would put on underwear like that in December.

Salsifer said, "Jeremy here says he's heading off to BYU next week. What you going to take, Jeremy? What you going to be? A doctor maybe. Maybe a businessman."

"I'm going to be a teacher. I'm going to major in biology and come back to Panguitch and teach high school."

"What about you, Frank? You heading off to college too one of these days?"

"No, sir. I'm going to be a cattleman."

"Going to be a cattleman? Well, listen to that! That means you got a taste for poverty and starvation. Why don't you do something where you can make some money?"

"You did all right as a cattleman."

"Not too good, Frank. As far as money goes, not too good."

Frank shifted around and cocked up a leg so he could look Salsifer in the eyes. It was a good time to bring up his little project. "Ain't it right back around 1920 Grandpa gave you and Mom grazing rights for a hundred cows on the National Forest? He gave it to you and said to share it."

"Well, yes, sir, that's correct. He gave it to both of us and said to share it."

"I want to take over Mom's share of that allotment. I'd like to run fifty head on that summer range."

"You?"

"Yes, sir. I want to buy Mom out on shares. Then I want to build up a little herd. At least fifty head."

"Your mama never has run fifty head on that allotment. And I've tried to make it up to her by grazing a few of her cows on my winter range."

"But she's got rights to fifty head. Ain't that so?"

The old man closed his eyes, whose puffy lids were the color of liver. "The cattle ain't in my hands anymore, Frank. I turned everything over to Raymond. He's boss. Whatever you work out, you've got to work out with him."

"The Forest allotment is still in your name, isn't it?"

"Go into trucking, Frank. That's what a young fellow ought to do today. Go down to the bank in Panguitch and borrow enough money to buy yourself a big truck and start hauling livestock on contract. Haul sheep. That's where the money is."

"No, sir, I'm not going to make my living hauling sheep."

Frank got up and the bed rocked. Salsifer held out his hand and Frank took it. "No hard feelings, nephew. But you've got to deal with Raymond."

Salsifer gripped his hand tightly. "Did I ever tell you about the time I swum the Colorado on a bull? Me and Gustavus Liljenquist was trailing fifteen head of purebred bulls into San Juan. It was part of a big project to improve the cattle line over there. There wasn't any way to cross the Colorado but swim. Big, fat Hereford bulls don't amble into the river and start swimming just because you want them to. We pushed and hollered and popped them on the butt with a whip all morning. No luck. Finally we hired us this guy with a rowboat and led those bulls across one at a time. Me and the fellow was in the boat, him rowing, me tugging a swimming bull along by a halter rope. On one crossing a bull got frantic and decided he wanted in the boat. He swum up and tried to hoof his way in. That little boat dipped and rocked like it was in a cyclone. Me, I couldn't swim. But the bull could so I jumped on his back. And that's the way we made it across, that fellow rowing fast as he could and the bull swimming hard so he could catch up and climb in the boat and me riding on his back."

Frank laughed hard. Jeremy smiled a little. The old man smiled too, showing his gums. "Them were the days, boys. Down in San Juan I didn't need nothing but a good horse and I was happy. Golly, the horses I've had. It grieves me to remember them."

After Frank and Jeremy had breakfast with Raymond's boys, they drove into Antimony Canyon, Frank and Jeremy in one vehicle, Jeff, Harold, and Simms in another. By dawn they had crossed the cattle-guard at the boundary of the National Forest. A half mile farther they unloaded the horses next to a large pole corral. Jeff was peevish about the silly noise Harold and Simms were making. He was thin faced and white haired, almost like an albino, and he slumped in his saddle as if to show how relaxed and nonchalant a really good rider had to be.

Frank helped Simms throw his saddle on his horse. "I can do the rest," Simms said, pushing Frank aside. When he had cinched up, he jumped for the horn and kicked frantically until his foot found a stirrup.

"Lucky that little piss-ant ain't riding a bronco," Jeff said.

For a minute or two Chowder gave Jeremy trouble, backing, whirling, and crowhopping. Then he fell into line and they all rode up the bottom of the main canyon. Every half mile or so, where the trail forded the creek, the horses had to splash through the clear, gurgling water. The air was frosty and the horses blew out puffs of vapor. The aspens in the bottom had turned yellow; the maples on the steep slopes had burst into scarlet and orange.

An hour later they came to the head of the canyon, a giant half bowl rifted by outcroppings and covered by oak brush and firs. Frank gave the assignments. He and Jeremy and Jeff would ride out of the main canyon, split up, and haze the cattle off the ridges and down through the side canyons. Harold and Simms would stay in the bottom, collecting the cattle as they came out.

"Peeroonee!" Simms said. "I don't want to stay down here. I want to look for cows."

"Shut up, fathead," Harold said.

Frank said, "You kids ride back and forth in the bottom and keep them moving down. Don't let them go up the gulches and ravines."

"Keep your mind on business," Jeff said. "Dad says we can kick your butts if we have to to make sure things get done right."

About mid-morning Frank and Jeremy came out on a bluff overlooking the bottom, where they dismounted. Opposite, they could see Jeff moving a bunch down a side canyon. In the bottom cattle moved in a straggling file down the trail. Their bellows rose like clear distant bugles.

"Where's those kids?" Frank said.

Jeremy nodded to the right. Harold burst out of a thicket of aspens, riding at a full run, whooping and waving a willow high over his head. Hot on his heels came Simms, beating his horse with the tips of his reins. Harold splashed through a beaver pond, pounded up a ledge, then suddenly reined in, leaped off, and jumped behind a log. He shoved the willow across the log and began to shoot.

"They're playing Arabs and Foreign Legion," Frank said, mounting. "Looks like it's time to kick a couple of hind ends. Whichever one of us gets there first gets to do it." They rode off opposite sides of the bluff, looking for cattle as they went down.

Several hours later Frank ate a sandwich by a seep. His unsaddled horse, stained with sweatsalt, cropped yellow grass. The sun was bright, the sky was blue, and white clouds drifted over the rim of a looming ridge. Fir trees mounted the ridge in dense ranks. A squirrel scolded and a few hardy flies buzzed. Having eaten, Frank lay in the sun with his hat over his eyes. A pretty day, a wild canyon, a good horse, a bunch of cows, who'd want anything else?

Then he heard a clatter, sat up, saw a lean, big-hipped roan cow breaking across a clearing in the firs above him. A second later she was gone.

"Too bad for you, old gal," he muttered. "Now I know where you are."

He saddled up and spurred Booger up the slope into the firs. The groves were dark and cool and littered with fallen trunks and tangled with brush. The gelding slipped and scrambled, his ribs heaving, his breath whistling out in windy gusts. Frank heard a snapping twig, jerked his head around, saw a flash of roan. The cow had doubled back. She was a tough, smart critter. She had legs and lungs for the mountains and a map of the trees. It was no contest; Frank and Booger weren't even in the race.

As he rode down the ravine, Frank wondered what got into some cows to make them offish and lonely. All morning the cattle had been easy to handle. They didn't spook and dodge and try to run away into the brush. They moved off the ridges and out of the gullies as if they knew winter was coming and it was time to clear out of the mountains. But not that gaunt old roan up there in the firs. She thought she was an elk or a deer.

In the late afternoon Frank and Jeremy trailed a final bunch down the bottom. Their tired horses stumbled often and walked with drooping heads, particularly Chowder. Jeremy had fought the gelding all day long, refusing to let him pick his own path through the brush. Jeremy was tenacious, no question of that. He didn't look like a cowboy. He wore pants from an old wool suit, a brand new red leather deer hunting cap, and brogans instead of boots.

Going by a beaver pond they saw a small buck and Jeremy said, "I saw a big one this morning."

"Me too. I saw four or five big ones, plus more does and forkhorns than you could shake a stick at. There's a damn lot of deer in here."

"I'm going hunting this year," Jeremy said. "I want a big one."

"You want a big one?" Frank said, astonished. This was the first he had ever heard of Jeremy being interested in hunting. "I thought you were going to BYU."

"I am. I'm coming back for deer season. I've got a gun. I traded Dad's chisels for it."

"Dad's chisels for a gun! My gosh. Well, I imagine Mom will be really tickled pink if you go deer hunting. She always told me I ought to quit fooling around with guns. She always said I ought to be like you, interested in decent, uplifting things like bird eggs and sunflowers."

"That doesn't matter," Jeremy said. "I'm going this year."

"Okay, fine, slick, great! I'll tell Uncle Lonnie and Uncle Jarvis you're coming. We'll count on you, we sure will."

By dusk Frank and Jeremy and Raymond's boys were making camp. Dust drifted over the big pole corral, which was full of milling, bellowing cattle. Tethered to a hitching pole, the horses had finished their ration of grain and were starting to chew on broken bales of hay. Frank built a fire from scrub oak, and when it had turned to coals, Jeff put on the Dutch ovens. Jeff cut up chicken and mixed dough for biscuits and had Frank slice potatoes and onions for sheepherder potatoes and sent Simms to the creek to fill a pot for making cocoa. Then they built up the fire again and sat in the dancing light, eating big platefuls and drinking all the cocoa they could hold.

"I hate school and I ain't going back," Harold said.

"I'm going to work on a ranch like Frank," Simms said.

Jeff shook his head scornfully. "You're probably going to end up clerking in a store. Neither one of you is worth anything when it comes to ranch work."

"I'm going to teach school," Jeremy said. "I'm going to major in biology so I can teach it. I'm going to specially study birds. I'm going to make ornithology my hobby."

"That sounds like some kind of disease," Jeff said.

Frank and Jeremy threw their bedrolls down in the back of Frank's pickup. Sometime in the middle of the night Frank got up and urinated from the tailgate. It was frosty and he was glad to crawl under the blankets and tarp. The Milky Way cut a glowing, glimmering swath across the sky, and from somewhere up the canyon drifted the soft hoot of an owl.

"I can't sleep," Jeremy said.

"Get up and pee. It ain't all that cold."

"I don't need to pee. I'm thinking about going to BYU. I'm scared."

"There isn't anything to be scared of," Frank said. "Lots of other people have gone off to BYU and it never killed them."

"What do you think? Is it wrong for a young man to leave his widowed mother and go away to school? Especially when he plans to come back and teach school locally and look after her?"

"Why, hell, no, it isn't wrong. Who ever said it was?"

"I'm plenty worried about Mother," Jeremy said. "It's like I had a hammer banging inside my head. What's going to happen to her while I'm gone?"

"Nothing's going to happen to her. Lots of mothers get left behind when their kids go to college. It doesn't kill them."

"She'll go to church and won't have any family to sit by her. She'll come home at night from clerking in the store and there won't be anybody there. She'll sit in the living room all evening and nobody will say a word. She'll wake up in the morning and she won't hear anything but the clock ticking in the other room."

"Geez, are you that torn up about it?"

"So I was wondering about you," Jeremy said. "Couldn't you move home and stay with her? It wouldn't have to be forever. When I finish at BYU you could move out again. Though you wouldn't have to if you wanted to stay."

"You're not serious, are you? I can't go back home. I've got a job. I'm going to be a cattleman."

"Couldn't you be a cattleman in Panguitch?"

Frank raised up on an elbow. "No, I couldn't, so just get that idea out of your head. How come you're taking off for BYU in the first place? If you think it'll rip Mom up all that bad, why are you going?"

Jeremy said, "I wouldn't go if I hadn't been admonished."

"Who admonished you?"

"The Holy Ghost."

"Sure thing. He just walked up and admonished you."

"Don't make light of it."

"The Holy Ghost?"

"For a fact."

"I'll be damned," Frank said. "Really and truly. The Holy Ghost!" They were quiet. After a while Frank said, "Did you see him?"

"No, I felt him. You don't have to see him."

"And you think he told you to go to BYU?"

"I don't think. I know."

"Well, then, I guess you'd better go."

Frank heard the slightest, softest flutter. Overhead he could see the floating, vanishing silhouette of an owl.

"I don't masturbate anymore," Jeremy said. "I got a testimony and quit."

"Flat out?"

"Flat out."

"That's fine, that's great. Cuffing your carrot is a filthy habit. People say it'll make hair grow on the palm of your hand though I can't see any has grown on mine."

"The thing that worries me is if kissing a girl cuts off the Spirit. Do you think it would? I kissed Geneva Eilertsen some this summer."

Frank wouldn't have kissed a girl like Geneva for anything less than a paid off mortgage. She had knobby knees, a curved spine, and a canted head that made her seem to peer at people on the sly.

"I imagine it depends on how you kiss her whether it cuts off the Spirit or not," he said. "Did you kiss her like you'd kiss Aunt Jessica or did you get yourself all heated up?"

Jeremy seemed to be calculating. "I don't believe I kissed her lustfully. I'm going to marry her."

"Does she know about that?"

"No. She's going to Dixie College."

"Too bad," Frank said. "You just as well cut her initials off your tree. I waited for a gal from Escalante for a year just so she could go to the university and find herself another man."

"Mom likes Geneva. When we've graduated from college and get married she can move in with us. Or we'll move in with her."

"You're real certain about that, I guess," Frank said.

"I've had an assurance."

The owl was hooting again, now from far away down the canyon. Shortly Jeremy sighed, mumbled, and went to sleep. However, Frank stayed awake worrying. Maybe he had asked Jeremy too many questions about the Holy Ghost. He hoped the Holy Ghost hadn't noticed. He especially didn't want the Holy Ghost to tell him to go home and stay with Margaret.

By morning a dozen cows had showed up outside the corral. It was clear and frosty and Frank and the others ate their bacon and eggs around the fire, stamping their feet and blowing out steamy breath. As they saddled up, Raymond and Helen arrived from town. Raymond tallied the cattle while the boys drove them a few at a time from the corral.

"Still five critters missing," Raymond said with disgust.

"They'll drift down in a day or two, won't they?" Frank said. "Except for that old roan which thinks she's a bobcat."

"She'll come out when the snow flies. And when she does we'll beef her. She's had her last chance."

It was Raymond's idea that Helen would drive Frank's pickup and trailer to town while Frank and Jeremy helped trail the cattle in. He also hoped they would stick around to help brand the calves in the afternoon.

Frank stood by the pickup window while Helen started the engine. She said, "I was up last night with Dad. Maybe it'd be a blessing if he could slip away quick." She sponged her tongue across her buck teeth and combed fingers through her stringy hair. "Dad says you want to put fifty cows on the summer range. Raymond would jaw at me for a week if he knew I had said anything. It won't happen, Frank. Raymond won't give in. All I can see is two cousins hating each other. I hope and pray you'll change your mind."

He said he'd think about it and watched the dust his outfit made as she drove it away. The boys had started the herd down the canyon road. Frank stayed behind to see whether Raymond wanted to talk. However, Raymond bustled around like a churchhouse janitor. Whistling the "Battle Hymn of the Republic," he shoveled dirt on the fire and threw bedrolls and Dutch ovens into the trunk of his sedan. Finally Frank got on his horse and rode after the herd.

When they had driven the herd onto the graveled road going along the East Sevier, Simms rode in the back and Harold rode in the front with red flags to slow down cars. Frank, Jeremy, and Jeff loafed along on the heels of the herd, which was hemmed in by fences on either side of the road. The sun was bright and blackbirds sang in the willows along the river. Cows bellowed, horses coughed, saddles creaked. Frank was thinking this must have been how things were in the old days. It was too bad he couldn't have lived before cars and fences and indoor toilets and white shirts and ties had come along to spoil the wild free frontier.

Around one o'clock they drove the cattle into a big pasture behind Salsifer's house. They ate lunch and then cut out the cows with calves and put them in a corral. Raymond built a large juniper fire and heated two branding irons and a group of little running irons. On a clean plank he set out a castrating knife, a sharpening stone, and a galvanized pail.

"That bucket is for calf nuts," Raymond said. "Dad wants them. He'll freeze them. He thinks two or three a day of them is sure fire health. They might be for all I know."

They began working. Frank roped each calf from his horse and pulled it along easy to the fire. Jeremy, Harold, and Simms threw it and held it down. Jeff branded it and Raymond earmarked and dehorned it and, if it was a male, castrated it. Soon they had their sweat up and were doing things in rhythm, turning a calf loose every four or five minutes. Cows lowed anxiously and tagged along after their struggling, bawling calves. Acrid smoke rose from seared hair and hide. Bloody triangles sliced from ears littered the ground. Horn stubs sizzled and steamed as Jeff cauterized them with a white hot running iron. Raymond took off the tip of a scrotum with a deft slash, sliced open the membrane surrounding the testicles, squeezed them out, cut off their cords, and threw them into the pail.

In the late afternoon Helen brought cold soda pop from her house across the street. Dismounting and letting the reins dangle, Frank limbered his legs and finished his pop in four or five big swigs. Harold shook up his bottle and squirted the fizz on Simms.

Raymond threw a stick at Harold and shouted, "Do that one more time and I'll larrup the hide off you."

Salsifer came from his back door and limped to the corral, wearing a new Mackinaw coat and a Stetson. Helen opened the corral gate so he could come in. He stooped for a stick to use as a cane. He said, "I've been listening to the calves bawl. I wish I could help you." He leaned over the pail. "There's my Rocky Mountain oysters." They shimmered in a bloody soup.

"I wanted to throw some on the coals," Simms said.

"You don't get none so just shut up," Raymond said.

"Let's throw some on," Salsifer said. "I ain't going to be a hog."

He was raking at the coals with his stick. Frank helped spread the coals and spilled out half the testicles, which steamed and simmered and hissed and then, as they cooked through, split like sausages. Frank speared them with his pocket knife and handed them around. Jeremy and Helen wouldn't take any. The others brushed off ashes and blew on the testicles and bounced them from one hand to the other because they were hot.

"I sure like calf nuts," Simms said. "They're better than wienies."

"You don't have to talk about it in front of your ma," Raymond said.

Salsifer wiped his lips with a handkerchief and said, "Those oysters have got a virtue. Nothing better in the whole world for your kidneys."

Looking pained, Jeremy slowly backed away. Suddenly he began to retch. He ran for the fence, bent over, and vomited.

"Holy Moses, what's the matter?" Frank asked, following.

"It sickens me, us castrating those calves. And then you eat the testicles like you were a cannibal." He put his hands on a rail and leaned again, letting bile dribble from his mouth.

"Well, come on, honey," Helen said, patting him gently on the back. "Come into the house and let me fix you some juniper tea and then you rest a bit. I'll bet you're coming down with something."

She took him by the arm and led him out the gate and across the road to her house.

Frank returned to the fire shaking his head. "Those calf nuts puked him."

"Some men are that way," Raymond said.

"He claims he's going deer hunting this year. He says he won't settle for nothing less than a four point. But how in hell can he stand to gut a deer if calf nuts puke him?"

Harold said, "By durn, I can't wait till I can go deer hunting. It's the stupidest law they ever made says a kid can't hunt till he's sixteen."

"When I was a boy, Cousin Jimmy Jamison got his privates shot off deer hunting," Salsifer said. "Nobody knew where the shot came from. There wasn't anybody around to help him and he bled to death."

"That's just as good," Frank said. "Who'd want to live without his privates?"

"Do you think he'll have them in the Celestial Kingdom?" Jeff asked.

"Sure he will," Raymond said. "How are you going to be gods and goddesses and create worlds without end and have spirit children forever and ever if you don't have your privates?"

"The righteous will have their equipment in the hereafter," Salsifer said. "But the sinful won't have any need for theirs. God will fix them just like you're fixing these here bull calves."

Frank had got a puny, shriveled up feeling in his pants. Nobody had ever told him about God castrating the wicked. It would be just like him to do it.

Raymond built up the fire and Salsifer went back to his house. Frank got on his horse and lassoed another calf. The work went slower now. Jeremy was gone and the others were tired and down in their spirits.

After a while Raymond said, "Get that one right there, Frank! You let it by three or four times."

"I know," Frank said. "That's one of Mont's."

"They've got to be branded like all the others."

"I was going to bring that up," Frank said. "I'm planning to buy Mom's cows. I'm going to go to the courthouse and register my own brand. FW is what it's going to be. So there isn't any need to put your brand on them. I'll take care of them in a week or two."

Raymond stood for a while with his hands on his hips looking back and forth between Frank and the ground. It was clear he didn't know what to say.

"I guess your dad has told you my ideas about some summer range on the forest," Frank said.

"Your ma never has had no fifty cows on the forest."

"That don't matter. What counts is Grandpa gave her and your dad a hundred cow allotment and told them to share it."

"It's in Dad's name," Raymond said. "There isn't any way you can horn in on it. The rangers won't listen one minute to you."

"I mean to have your dad sign it over to us."

"Who's *us*? Grandpa never promised you no fifty cows on the forest."

"He never promised them to you neither."

"I just as well tell you something since you are going to find it out when you get over to Panguitch to visit your ma. I telephoned her this morning and bought her out. I offered her five percent over market and she took it. Them are my critters and let's get them branded."

"Well, shit," Frank said, pulling off his gloves and slapping the pommel. His horse swung in a half circle, ready to go for another calf. Frank remembered what Helen had said in his pickup that morning. She was exactly right. He couldn't take any range away from Raymond, and if he tried Raymond would go the rest of his life badmouthing him and praying for calamities to fall on him.

He didn't know why he had to pick a quarrel. "You had just a phone talk with Mom, I guess. She never signed anything."

"She promised me," Raymond said frantically. "She said, Okay, it's a deal."

"She never signed anything," Frank said. "The law doesn't pay any attention unless something has been signed. I'm going over there tonight and talk her out of it."

"Damn you, get off that horse."

"You bet," Frank said. He swung off the saddle and let the reins dangle. He tugged his gloves on tight, saying, "All right, you little fart, I'm ready."

Raymond was backing away. He looked frightened and shocked, as if he had made a bad mistake.

"You ain't going to hit my dad," Jeff said.

"I'll throw you both over that fence," Frank said.

Simms picked up a stick.

"Put that down, you little skunk," Raymond said. "There isn't going to be any fight here. I ain't fighting you, Frank."

"Okay, we're not going to have a fight," Frank said. He got on his horse and coiled his rope and tied it to the pommel. At the gate he looked back at Raymond and his three boys standing around the fire.

"Go ahead," Raymond called. "Sweettalk her all you want to. Even if she lets you have those cows and calves, you ain't getting one animal onto my Forest range."

Frank loaded Booger and Chowder into the trailer and went into Raymond's house. Jeremy was in the living room sitting in an overstuffed chair. "How are you feeling?" Frank asked.

"Better. I just ate some toast and milk. I was just tired, I think."

"I'm going to pull the horses back to the ranch, so you get in Mom's car and drive home to Panguitch and I'll be along in three or four hours. Tell Mom not to keep supper for me. I'll scout out something to eat at the ranch or I'll get a hamburger in Escalante."

"You sure won't," Helen said. "We aren't about to let you leave here without supper after all the hard work you've done for us."

"I can't stick around for supper. I just had it out with Raymond."

Helen sagged a little, then sat down at the writing table, mumbling without looking Frank in the eye, "I wish you hadn't, I do wish you hadn't! There never was a family like the Jamisons to spit on each other."

"Yes, ma'am," Frank said. He wasn't worth a pile of horse manure. He never had been.

The ranchhouse was dark when Frank pulled in. He unloaded the horses and backed the trailer into its place and unhitched. He grained the horses and while they munched he curried them. Then a door slammed at the house and someone crossed the driveway. It was Marianne.

Pausing at the corral gate, she said, "I didn't think you were coming back until Monday morning."

"I'm not staying. Soon as I take care of these horses I'm on my way to Panguitch."

"Well, I guess I'll go back to bed then."

"Where is everybody?"

"Mom and Dad and Jeanette have gone to Cedar City. Nathan went to Hatch."

The floodlight on the barn lit her up. She wore a jacket and under that a long flannel nightgown. He continued to curry the horses, trying to remember his plans for getting untangled from her. Another idea swaggered around inside him, tall as Goliath, strong as Sampson. When he went out the gate, she was ready. They hugged and kissed and he unzipped her jacket so he could feel her through the flannel. She didn't mind at all.

"Let's go in the house," she said.

"Good gosh, no. Let's go in the barn and get it over with before somebody shows up."

"Nobody will show up. Nathan won't be back until Sunday night. Mom and Dad decided to take a motel in Cedar City and stick around for the meeting in the morning. Mom is being put on the board of the Color Country Concert and Symphony Guild."

She gave him a long kiss and said, "Let's go in. We can shower together like married people."

"Shower together? That's a dandy idea."

Frank parked his pickup at the bunkhouse and got clean clothes. They had a wild time in the shower. Then they got on her bed and made love. Afterward, the bed being narrow, they lay belly to belly with their arms around each other. He went to sleep, and when he woke up Marianne had clapped her hand over his mouth, and he could hear Wesley and Clara and Jeanette in the living room.

"Don't say a word," she whispered. "Don't move an inch."

She got out of bed, pulled on her nightgown, and jammed his clothes into her closet. She was in the doorway when her mother came down the hall.

"Hello, dearest," Clara said.

"Looks like you changed your mind and came home."

"It didn't seem like it was worth getting a room. The new board doesn't really take over till next month."

Clara gave her a kiss. "Goodnight, sweetheart."

"Goodnight, Mom."

Marianne closed the door and sat on the edge of the bed. "Don't get nervous," she said. "They'll get in bed pretty soon and go to sleep and we can sneak you out."

She got under the covers with him and they lay belly to belly again. She let her hands wander all over him, but he couldn't concentrate on anything except Wesley being in the next room. Shortly he wanted to pull on his pants and slip out but she said it was too soon. Just when she finally agreed it was safe, the telephone rang.

"Oh, my aching back," Frank moaned.

Marianne went to her door and stood in it again. Wesley stumbled down the hall and picked up the phone.

"Yes," he said, "this is the Earle ranch. No, he isn't here. He went over to Panguitch to visit his folks. His brother is going off to BYU and they're having something of a family reunion. Oh, is that right? You're Mrs. Windham! Well, no, ma'am, he isn't here. I hope something hasn't happened to him."

Pretty soon he said, "Hang on a minute," and he came down the hall. "Did Frank come in here this evening and unload the horses?" he said to Marianne. Frank could see his shadow on the opposite wall of her room.

"Not that I know of. If he came it was after I went to sleep."

"I wonder if he's had an accident. Clara," he suddenly shouted, "what shall we do? Frank is in trouble somewhere."

Clara had come down the hall and now Frank could see two shadows on the wall. "Did you check the bunkhouse?"

"Well, of course I didn't check the bunkhouse. He wouldn't be there."

"Maybe he just drove in and unloaded and decided to go to bed."

"We'd better contact the Highway Patrol. I'll get dressed and get out and see if there's anything I can do."

"Go check the bunkhouse," Clara said.

Wesley went off grumbling and slammed the kitchen door. Marianne sat on the edge of the bed. She pulled the covers up over Frank's head and he felt as if he was in a coffin. When Wesley came back he'd know he was somewhere on the ranch and it sure wasn't in his bunk. He wondered whether Wesley would take the time to get his shotgun or whether maybe he would just go berserk and try to tear him apart with his bare hands. He wondered if getting killed would hurt a great deal. Maybe it would all happen so fast he wouldn't know anything about it, except of course he would wake up in the afterlife in one hell of a mess. He couldn't blame Wesley for killing him, but he certainly hoped for one more chance so that he and Marianne could get a little self control and quit fornicating. In fact, he had in mind going back to church and cleaning up his language and paying his tithing. He even had in mind apologizing to Raymond and letting him have Margaret's cows and not horning in on his forest allotment.

Then he started to think about that bucket of calf testicles and he began to worry about Wesley shooting off his privates. He decided it would be better to pull on his pants so that Wesley wouldn't get any notions, but every time he tried to get out of bed, Marianne pushed him down and held his arms.

The front door slammed and Wesley's steps thumped across the floor. Then his voice came from the office where the phone was. "You still there, Mrs. Windham? Good news. Frank is down in the bunkhouse sound asleep. Yes, ma'am, that's exactly where he is. I didn't bother waking him. I'm sure he was just too pooped out and figured a good night's rest was what he needed most. We'll tell him you called and I'm sure he'll get on the road early and you'll see him well before noon. Yes, ma'am. No, ma'am, it was no trouble at all. We are as glad as you are he is safe and sound. He's a fine young man. I just want you to know how much we respect and appreciate you, having raised up a hard working, honorable, trustworthy fellow like him. There aren't many like him in the world. Yes, ma'am. Good night now."

Wesley came down the hall saying, "Back to bed everybody. All's well that ends well."

"That's funny he wouldn't wake up when you went in," Clara's voice said. "Did you turn on the lights?"

"Actually I didn't go inside. I just got far enough to see his truck. It's right where he always keeps it."

"Well, now, that worries me. I wish you'd laid eyes on him."

"Worries you! My gad, woman, the horses are in the corral, the trailer is parked where it's supposed to be. Of course he's in the bunkhouse. Where else would he be?"

Wesley mumbled and coughed and went to the bathroom. After a while things became quiet, and Marianne let Frank put on his clothes and leave. He got into his bunk but was so full of fret and worry that he woke up early and drove away from the ranch before any lights had come on in the house.

When Frank rounded the curve on Highway 89 where he could see Panguitch, the little town looked as if the Millennium had come. Chimney smoke rose in thin, straight lines among the roofs and treetops. In a field close to town a crew harvested corn with a silage chopper. Farther away were hay fields silver with frost and dotted by grazing cattle and sheep. Amber sunlight washed the valley. Cottonwoods splotched the wandering line of the Sevier with yellow. The rimming hills and mountains seemed strangely close, their contours sharp and distinct.

Margaret's house was a rust brick bungalow. Two giant poplars, thick with yellowing leaves, stood on the shaggy front lawn. Bright chrysanthemums bordered the house. A few hens scratched and pecked in the back yard. The barn and sheds sagged, their planks weathered and sprung. Weeds grew in the corral and pens. In a little garden were green cabbages, frozen tomatoes, and dry corn stalks.

As he parked in the back yard, Frank saw Margaret at the woodpile, kneeling and loading her arms. She dropped her load and stood. "You're here," she said and turned her cheek for a kiss. He had to stoop to give it to her. Grey curls circled her head; oddly her eyebrows were black. Her jaw was long, her nose round, her cheeks hollow. She wore a blue cotton dress and lowheeled shoes without stockings. She smelled like fresh baked bread.

Frank picked up an armload of wood and they strolled to the house, skirting a hen that refused to give them room. Margaret stopped by his pickup and ran a finger over its hood, leaving a shiny blue track in the dust. "A fancy vehicle," she said. "You're doing real well for yourself."

In the kitchen Frank dumped his armload of wood into a battered box. A teakettle steamed on the range. The smell of baking bread, rich as honey, filled the warm room. On the counter sat a couple of brown, crusty loaves and a pan of rising dough.

"Likely you're hungry," she said. She fried two eggs and poured a glass of milk. She cut off hot, thick slices of bread and spread them with butter, which melted into the spongy centers. She put on a bottle of wild grape jelly, saying, "Sugary things aren't much better than poison. It seems like you never could get along without them. Now honey and sorghum are all right; they're natural sugars."

She sat next to him and explained that Jeremy had gone out to buy cartridges so that he and Frank could get in a little target practice. "I'm just astounded," she said. "I can't pretend to be anything else. I don't understand his sudden passion for instruments of destruction."

"He'll be okay," Frank said. "I won't let him hurt himself."

She looked vexed as if Frank had failed to grasp the point. She changed the subject. "I assume you two had a pleasant time on the roundup."

"You bet. Except Jeremy vomited all over the place yesterday afternoon."

"He's delicate," she said. "It doesn't take much to send him off. I wonder sometimes if I shouldn't have had him held back in school a year or two so his body could catch up with his mind."

"Maybe he shouldn't go away to BYU," Frank said. "I think he ought to stick around here for a while."

"That's a point, that certainly is a point. However, he has had a testimony to go. He's turned very spiritual, Frank. He's like my mother. He has a special ear for the whispering of the still, small voice."

She drummed fingers on the table cloth and picked up a morsel of bread, looking at it closely. "What can we do? We'll simply have to trust in God. When he admonishes someone he knows what he's doing."

"I've got something on my mind," Frank said. "I bought a little piece of land in Bryce Valley. I'm going to be a cattleman and I need some help. I want you to sell me your cows so I've got a start."

"I can't do that. I've promised them to Raymond. He called me up yesterday and said we ought to clean things up between us, and he offered me a real good price."

"I want you to back off on that. I want them. You sell them to me on shares and I'll give you some market steers every fall."

"Cattle!" she said with disgust. "If they aren't a bother. Those who traffic in them suffer vexations, that's for sure. It was your father who got me into cattle in the first place. It wasn't anything I wanted."

"That isn't all I'm after," Frank said. "I want you to get Uncle Salsifer to sign over to you that fifty cow allotment Grandpa gave you on the National Forest, and I want you to let me use it, or if Leola and Susan and Jeremy don't squawk about it, maybe you could give it to me for my inheritance. Because that's what I'd like to have most."

"My goodness, you certainly aren't asking for much!"

"Will you do it? Will you talk to Uncle Salsifer?"

"Gracious, what would I say? I should have brought that topic up thirty-five years ago."

She carried Frank's dishes to the sink, then peered into the oven. Straightening, she said, "There's a lot of talk about you."

"What kind of talk?"

"It's real elevating to hear it. It gives me a whole lot to be proud about. There's word around you dance and drink and roister and fight. There's word you don't dare go across the Arizona line because you nearly killed a Forest Service man down in Fredonia. There isn't hardly anything wicked in the whole world that people don't say you're into."

"It ain't nothing but talk. It's because people figure anybody who works for Lutherans has gone to hell."

"I do hope it's just talk. Good heavens, Frank, if I really believed half of what I've heard, I'd go wild, I couldn't stand it. But you must be up to something or the talk wouldn't have got started in the first place."

"I just been doing a little roping and riding on Sunday, that's all. Folks see I'm not in church and they start saying wild things."

At that point, Jeremy came in with a box of cartridges. He shook Frank's hand as if he hadn't seen him for a long time. Disappearing into his bedroom, he returned with his rifle, which he laid beside the cartridges on the table. He sat before them and gazed, his hands planted on his knees. His scalp gleamed white under a bristling crew cut and his eyes bulged in big sockets. He had a long jaw and sunk cheeks like Margaret. He wore a plaid shirt and stiff new jeans hitched high at the waist and double rolled at the cuffs.

Margaret shook hot loaves from a pan. She threw quick, angry glances at the rifle as if sizing up ways of getting rid of it. "I'm going to say one more time I can't favor you taking up hunting. Not you, Jeremy."

Rubbing the gunstock with a finger, Jeremy said serenely, "Isaac loved Esau because he did eat of his venison. Nephi fashioned a bow wherewith he did pursue the beasts of the field."

"Don't scripture me," Margaret said with disgust. "Behold I have given you every herb and every tree; to you it shall be for meat." She sat by the range, looking glum. "You boys aren't bringing any deer meat into this house."

"I'll take mine to the ranch," Frank said. "Jeremy's too if he wants to donate it. Clara knows a lot of things to do with venison."

"I don't doubt Mrs. Earle can fancy up a table with steaks and roasts and meat gravy," Margaret protested. "That's easy. What's hard is putting on a tasty menu with vegetables and grains and beans. I'd like to see what kind of cook she'd turn out to be if she tried to keep to healthy foodstuffs. Just look at the difference between you and Jeremy." She took a hard look at Frank. "I'm sorry to say it. Your color just isn't good. If you eliminated meat and sugar and white flour from your diet, it wouldn't take you a month to get back to normal."

Frank picked up the long, shiny rifle. Muttering, "Jeez," he put it to his shoulder and peered through the telescopic sight. He stroked the blue, tapered barrel and the fine-grained stock, which had been checkered and finished with amber varnish. "I could fall in love with that gun," he said.

"It's a two-seventy," Jeremy said, opening the box of cartridges and spilling them on the table. Frank picked up a cartridge, scrutinizing its gleaming brass case and lead-tipped bullet. He held it to his ear, shook it lightly, and listened to the swish of the powder inside. "It's alive, plumb alive," he said reverently.

"What I feel worst about is he traded away your father's chisels," Margaret said. "I hoped maybe he would want to learn how to use them himself. He has your father's knack for carving stone."

"Naw, he don't," Frank said, shaking his head.

"He talked a little last winter about trying his hand at it. You ought to read the little poems he made up. He has his father's gift for poetry too."

Frank eyed Jeremy skeptically.

"Let me show him your poems," Margaret said to Jeremy.

He shuffled with embarrassment, mumbling, "They're nothing to look at."

"Come on," she said, heading for the living room. She pulled down the writing plate of a large oak secretary, revealing a row of books and a jumbled sheaf of paper. Repeatedly licking her fore-finger, she sorted through the sheaf. "Here," she said to Frank, "read this one out loud."

> From this world sick and wan
> You have forever gone.
> To a place holy and bright
> Fled from loved one's sight.

Margaret looked over his shoulder, and when he had finished she said, "Isn't that a nice poem?"

"Well, now, it is," Frank said. "That's a mighty good poem. I didn't know he had it in him."

"Read this one," she said, pointing.

> Thou wert but a child
> Obedient, pure and mild
> Bitterly have we wept
> While unto God thou hast crept.

"Oh, that's so lovely, so lovely," Margaret said, dabbing at her eyes with her apron hem. "And you read it so nice, Frank. You have a voice for it."

"These are Dad's poetry books," Jeremy said.

Miles Windham had been a school teacher in Fillmore. On the side he made gravestones, specializing in epitaphs. Sometimes he wrote his own poems and other times he borrowed them from books. He was a bachelor of thirty-five when he met Margaret. She was thirty and released from the duty of caring for her mother, who had recently died. They were married and moved to Panguitch. He drove every weekday to Piute High School in Circleville, where he taught salesmanship, commercial law, and typing. Early one morning he died in a head-on collision.

Frank scrutinized the books. There was one called *The Great Poets of England, Wales, and Scotland,* another called *American Bards,* and another called *The Divine Comedy.* That was the one Frank picked up, saying, "There ain't anything funny about this book." He laid it open on the writing plate. There was an etching of a broad pit with numerous terraces and crowds of people frantically tearing their hair and gnashing their teeth.

"That looks like hell," he said.

"That's what it is," Jeremy replied.

"It sure isn't any comedy," Frank added. "But maybe if you were making gravestones you could find something in a book like that."

Later Frank and Jeremy drove to the town dump for target practice. On the way they visited the cemetery, getting out of the pickup and wandering among the graves. Clouds drifted in the blue sky; bland warmth fell from the morning sun. Sparse plants clung to the arid soil—clumps of yellowing grass, yucca bayonets, grey lacy tumbleweeds. Mounds of red gravel marked recent graves. Old graves, some of them dug as early as 1870, were level with the ground.

They paused before their father's grave. Frank squatted and fingered the lettering on the stone, which said, "Miles Abner Windham June 27, 1890, September 9, 1946."

"It's been a while," he murmured.

Uncle Lonnie had dedicated the grave. His words were as strange and hard to catch as vapor shadows on a summer day. Lonnie thanked God for the life of Miles Windham, for the kindness he had shown his neighbors and loved ones, for the support he had given the church. He blessed the ground, making it holy. He blessed the body of his brother so that it would rest quietly for its due time and so that when the trumpet sounded on the morning of the first resurrection it would rise and come forth, quick, hearty, and whole.

"He used to beat the tar out of me about once a week," Frank said. "Sometimes he did it just on principle. If I didn't deserve a licking at the moment, it wouldn't be long till I did. I was wilder than Harold and Simms."

"I don't think he ever gave me a licking," Jeremy said.

"Why, hell, no, he never. What did you ever do wrong? It's too bad he didn't whop me harder." He pushed back his hat and scratched his forehead. "What do you think? Do you think Dad will make the Celestial Kingdom?"

"Of course, he will," Jeremy said.

"I don't know. He was grumpy with the neighbors. He cussed some. He wasn't regular at meetings." Then Frank became more cheerful. "He took me around with him a good deal in the old pickup. We went horseback lots of times. He had me shooting jackrabbits with a twenty-two by the time I was five or six."

Jeremy wanted to show Frank a stone Miles had carved. They wandered for a while, stopping now and then in front of a marker to talk about an old timer they hadn't thought of for years.

"This is it," Jeremy said at last. It was the stone of Emery Donfeldt, who had died in 1943.

"I guess he's the granddaddy of the Donfeldt boys we know," Frank said. Then he read the epitaph.

> From the fell repast
> Hath he risen
> Freed to go home
> Out of prison.

"Pretty fancy," Frank said. He sat down in the dirt and rubbed his jaw. "To be truthful, it sounds like bullshit. What's a fell repast?"

"I've got an idea about it," Jeremy said. "I looked those words up in a dictionary. A fell repast is a terrible meal, a meal that scares you. So maybe a fell repast means the bonds of mortality. Dad must have meant this world is a prison."

"Well, I'll be damned. That's poetry, no question about that. But you know, I think it stinks. It makes you wonder what Dad had on his mind. Sounds like he wasn't feeling good. Sounds like he had the blues."

They drove on to the dump, a two acre depression in the crown of a hill littered with trash—broken glass, jagged cans, crushed cartons, a ruptured sofa, the bloated carcass of a calf. Frank attached a target to a box and paced off fifty yards. He took his thirty-thirty from behind the seat and slipped three cartridges into the magazine. He leaned across the hood, resting the forestock on his folded jacket. He fired his shots, taking only a moment for aiming. Going forward, he saw they had grouped nicely just above the bullseye.

"I'm through," he said when he had come back. It didn't give him pleasure to shoot boxes. He wanted a live target—a rabbit or a coyote, even a sparrow or a mouse.

Jeremy loaded his magazine slowly, heedlessly letting the barrel waver. Frank pushed the barrel aside and stepped behind him. He leaned across the hood and rested the rifle on the coat. He stretched his neck like a turtle emerging from its shell and squinted into the scope. "I can't make it steady down," he said. "I'm going to flinch.

Every time I get set to pull the trigger I can feel myself already jumping."

"That doesn't matter any. Go ahead and flinch. Shoot a few and you'll get over it."

The rifle roared and his body bucked. "Wow!" he said, rubbing his shoulder.

"A little kick won't kill you. Keep shooting."

He shot twice more and they went forward to the target. One shot had hit high in the left corner; two had missed.

"Not bad," Frank said. "Keep at it."

Frank was feeling hemmed in, locked up. He could see nothing except the dump and the wide blue sky. He ambled up the road until he could see off the hill. Far away the mountains circled the valley. Their peaks and furrowed flanks were black with forests of juniper and pinion and oak. Below, close at hand, water rippled and glinted in a rocky run of the Sevier. In the dump Jeremy still leaned across the hood of the pickup. From time to time his body shuddered, the barrel went up, and a report split the air.

Jeremy would never be a shooter, no matter how much he practiced. He would never look normal, no matter how hard he tried. Yet Frank loved him and wanted now to mourn, remembering the time they had baptized Rupert.

It was a Friday, exactly one week after their father's burial. He and Jeremy headed east along the highway. Rupert tagged along, a surly blue heeler with white eerie irises and a stubby tail that never wagged. All week he had lain in the driveway, waiting for Miles to come home.

They came to the cemetery and went in, pulled irresistibly to Miles's grave. It was a high barrow of fresh red gravel covered by withered flowers.

"I hope the Lord ain't got his eye on me," Frank said. "If you're too good he comes after you like he did Dad. If you're too bad he does the same thing."

They wandered on down the highway and crossed over to the dump, where they scratched around for interesting junk and broke all the bottles they could find. Jeremy began to snivel because Margaret had gone somewhere for the afternoon and he was worried he would never see her again.

"Shut up or I'll knock one out of you," Frank said, and when Jeremy wouldn't quit whining he wrestled him down and ground dirt in his hair. Jeremy struck out for home bawling like a maverick. Frank followed, apologizing and sweettalking. Finally he said, "Let's go down to the river and baptize Rupert."

Jeremy stopped crying and they wandered along the Sevier for a mile or so until they came to a bend where the bank went down gently into a pool.

"Maybe we shouldn't baptize a dog," Jeremy said.

"He won't make the Celestial Kingdom if he isn't baptized."

"It doesn't do any good to baptize a dog," Jeremy insisted. He was still digging gravel out of his hair.

"Let's do it anyway. Let's see if it'll make him easier to get along with."

Frank took off his shirt and sidled slowly toward Rupert, gazing into the sky as if something interesting was going on up there and saying, "We can't let him know what we're up to or he'll tear us to pieces."

All of a sudden Frank threw the shirt over Rupert's head and clenched his arms around his neck. "Get on him!" he shouted. When Jeremy had seized his hindquarters, Frank tied the shirt into a knot. Then step by step they wrestled the scratching, snarling, howling dog into the river.

When they were knee deep, Frank said, "Now hold that son of a bitch tight so I can do this the way it's supposed to be done. If his foot comes out of the water, we've got to do it all over. God will send you to hell if part of you ain't under the water."

He clutched the loose skin of the dog's neck with his left hand and held his right hand high in the air. He prayed, "Rupert Windham, we baptize you in the name of the Father, the Son, and the Holy Ghost, Amen."

"All right," he said, "under he goes."

They pushed the dog into the current and threw themselves onto him. In a wild flurry of flailing feet and cascading water they lost their hold and the dog broke for the bank. They scrambled out and watched while Rupert streaked desperately through the sage brush. The shirt still bound his eyes like a turban. He crashed through bushes and tumbled over rubble, each time somersaulting back into his frantic, headlong flight. He ran through a barbed wire fence and tore the shirt from his muzzle and it flapped from his neck like a wind-whipped banner.

Then, just before he disappeared over a rise, a big black raven flew up, cawing loud, and winged its way into the eastern sky.

"Keeerummm," Frank shouted, "it's the Holy Ghost!"

"It's nothing but a crow," Jeremy said.

For an instant he was dead sober. Then he started to laugh. Frank grabbed him and the two brothers pounded and hooted and shrieked until their bellies ached. That was why Frank loved Jeremy. Sitting there in the dirt on the rim of the dump watching him shoot, Frank wanted to cry, remembering all the good things that had gone into the past, Jeremy included.

After lunch Frank and Jeremy cleaned out a chicken coop for Margaret. She wouldn't eat a chicken but she liked eggs, keeping her own hens because she believed store-bought eggs were full of poisonous chemicals. From the coop floor they raked and shoveled a mixture of dirt, mash, and manure. From under the roost they scooped moist, packed manure so rich with nitrogen that they were forced to wear bandannas over their faces. They trundled the manure in a wheelbarrow and scattered it on the garden.

They took baths and went to the grocery store with Margaret. When they came back, Frank stayed out a while splitting wood. The air was crisp and goldshot clouds floated in the late western sky. Cows lowed and dogs barked and Frank felt as if he wanted to be a kid again. For supper Margaret served a meat loaf made of soy beans instead of meat. To Frank's notion it tasted exactly like hog mash, which he had sampled a time or two. Later they all went to a movie, "Seven Brides for Seven Brothers." When they went by Clay's drive-in for a treat, Margaret and Jeremy relaxed their standards and had soft ice cream cones and Frank ordered a big Coca-Cola.

"That's pure poison," Margaret said.

"I know," Frank said. "That's why I got it." He hadn't had coffee for three days and was nearly dead from lack of caffeine.

Frank slept in his basement room. Until he was twelve he had slept with Jeremy in the room next to Margaret's. Becoming independent, he moved downstairs though Margaret didn't want him to and wouldn't help him fix up the room. A naked bulb dangled from the ceiling on a fly-specked cord. The walls had dirty green paper, the dresser was scarred and without drawer pulls, the oval mirror was cracked. The only nice thing in the room was a black and white poster of a rodeo champion caught mid-air between his horse and the steer he was about to bulldog.

In the middle of the night Frank woke to a knock on his door. It was Margaret, who said, "I can't sleep. I thought maybe you were awake too."

"Well, I sure am now," he said hoarsely.

She entered and sat on the edge of the bed, saying, "The veil between this world and the other is very thin, Frank."

"Yes, ma'am, I know that."

"I've had curious happenings. I thought maybe you'd want to know about them."

"Yes, ma'am, I'm always interested in curious happenings."

"A couple of weeks ago I went into the fruit room where it is dark because the lights don't work in there. I couldn't find the bottled cherries I wanted. I pulled a bottle of beets off the shelf, another of corn. I was getting a good deal of spider web on me, which I hate. Then, Frank, all of a sudden I had a terrible oppression. I couldn't get my breath and I thought my heart was going to stop beating. I began to cry, I was ready to die because I could see into hell. God showed me damnation. I grabbed a bottle, it turned out to be apple sauce, and I got out of there. I went outdoors to make sure the sun was still shining. Now why would God do that? Why did he give me a vision of hell?"

"I sure don't know."

"Was it something I did? Or was it something one of my boys did?"

That meant Frank, of course. Although he could see what was coming, he couldn't get excited. Lying there with a wall on one side and his mother on the other, he felt like a piece of bark floating in the Sevier, bobbing downstream, turning one way and then another, going wherever the water wanted to take him.

She was crying. "Please tell me, Frank. I've got to know. How much of it is true? Have you been breaking the Word of Wisdom? Do you smoke and drink?"

"I don't smoke. I drink a little beer now and then. And coffee."

"Did you nearly kill that Forest Service man in Fredonia like everybody says?"

"I had a fight with him. I knocked him down and broke his jaw. His nose was bloody and he looked pretty rough but he wasn't anywhere near dead."

"Have you been running with wild women, Frank? Have you taken up with taverns and bars? Are you a fornicator?"

"Gosh, no, Mom. I haven't been in more than a couple of bars and that was just to look around. Me and Jack and Red go to the dances up and down the county and get in a few fights with the boys and try to dance with the gals but, good gosh, no, I ain't no fornicator. That's something I don't do."

"Oh, I'm relieved to hear it!" she said. She groped for his hand, took it, gave it quick, anxious pats.

"I feel I should warn you," she said. "I want to put you on guard against the frailty of the flesh. Likely men are more afflicted with it than women."

"Yes, ma'am, you've already put me on my guard plenty of times."

She sighed and shifted her weight. "You were not disobedient when you were a very small boy, Frank. Then Jeremy came and I gave you over to Miles. I will not pretend you were the best possible child after that."

"I was a mean kid. No doubt about it."

She continued to fondle his hand. "Now you are grown so big. Where did you get those shoulders? And these giant hands?"

She pressed his palm to her cheek, which was wet. "I don't know if I can stand Jeremy going away. Life is nothing but leave taking, nothing but goodbye."

She was going to talk about Elizabeth. The tremble in her voice told him that and he didn't like it. Margaret and Miles had three girls in succession, Leola, Susan, and Elizabeth. Elizabeth died at three. Afterward they had Frank and Jeremy. Each time Frank heard about Elizabeth, he wanted to take an ax to himself, perhaps cutting off a hand or splitting open a foot.

"When I got pregnant with you I stopped grieving for Elizabeth," she said. "And then Jeremy came along. What a comfort."

He knew she wasn't telling the truth. She was still grieving for Elizabeth.

"She wasn't quite three. It was the middle of the summer, and I fed her a little clabber, which might have been spoiled. In the evening she was running off and vomiting and crying with the cramps.

She had summer complaint, and I fed her rice water and egg white but nothing made any difference. The diarrhea got worse and the next day I got scared because she was dehydrating. There were doctors in Provo, but it never entered our mind to put her in a car and try to drive up there. Why didn't we? Did God send us a stupor of thought?

"The day she died she was screaming. I couldn't stand it. She looked at me as if she didn't understand why I wasn't doing something to ease her off. What could I do? Three times Lonnie came over, and he and Miles administered to her. Every time she seemed to get a little better. Rallied a bit, wanted some rice water. But the cramps came back and she cried and screamed and got weaker and weaker. The last time they blessed her, I said to Miles, Tell the Lord to take her. But Miles got mad and said, That's the last thing I'd ever do. I couldn't take any more of it. I went out into the garden and I dedicated her. I told God if he would release her from suffering, I would accept it, I wouldn't grieve too much. When I went back in the house, she had quieted down, and twenty minutes later she rattled and died. I took it peacefully for a week. Angels ministered to me because I held up, I didn't cry. But afterward it hit me. I didn't think I'd ever get off the floor."

Margaret sniffled and cried and Frank sniffled and cried too. Lord, he suffered when he heard that story.

The next morning Frank accompanied Jeremy to Priesthood Meeting, dressed in the suit and tie he had brought from the ranch. The North Ward men shook his hand and asked how things were going in Escalante. Most of them were surprised to see him and would have given twenty dollars to know whether all those wild things they had been hearing about him were true. They saw backsliders on the street every day, but they didn't often get a chance to look at one in a churchhouse. Frank felt like a caged coyote at Big Rock Candy Mountain where summer tourists stopped and gawked.

When it was time for Sunday School, Margaret arrived with company—Leola, Lawrence, and their three children and Susan, Cloyd, and their four children, who had driven to Panguitch to say goodby to Jeremy. They made a big stir in the church, and people clustered around them, hugging and patting and bending over to examine the cute little kids.

Frank sat between Leola and Jeremy in the middle of a pew. Hanging lights burned overhead and floor wax scented the air. The pews descended like steps toward the front; dark wood panels decorated the walls. The congregation sang an opening hymn after which old Brother Wentworth offered a prayer and a couple of girls gave the two and a half minute talks. Then it was time for the Sacrament. The congregation sang, "For us the blood of Christ was shed, For us on Calvary's cross he bled, And thus dispelled the awful gloom That else were this creation's doom." The chorister, a thin, peaked lady, dragged her arm through the air as if it weighed thirty pounds. The organist bent over the keyboard, her legs pumping firmly upon the pedals. Two young men from the Priests quorum rose, uncovered trays of bread and water, and broke the bread into bits. After one of them had blessed the bread, boys from the Deacons quorum passed the trays among the congregation.

Frank was in trouble. Night before last he had been in the shower with Marianne, naked as a plucked chicken. People who partook of the Sacrament unworthily were eating damnation. But when the tray came down the pew, handed from one person to another, Frank didn't have the guts to wave it on. He took a bit of bread and ate it.

When it was time to separate for classes, Leola squeezed his hand and whispered in his ear, "Good for you, Frank!"

Leola had lost her waist with her first baby, and she had never possessed a neck to speak of, which meant her body went up wide and then squared off at the top like a large two-legged milk stool with a head perched on it. She had high red cheeks and a hawk nose, also red, and her mouth always looked as if she had just finished laughing at something stupid.

She squeezed his hand again, whispering, "There's a lot worse people in this hall than you."

For a minute that cheered him up, but when he began wondering who they might be nobody came to mind. Besides that, somebody else going crosslots to hell didn't make it any more comforting for him to go there too.

After Sunday School Margaret, Leola, and Susan rushed around the kitchen putting on a big dinner. Lawrence put leaves in the dining room table and Frank put two card tables end to end for the children. On the adults' table the ladies laid a lacy white cloth and set out china and fancy cut glasses. They put on rolls, creamed peas, and buttered mashed potatoes. For the main dish Margaret had prepared a barley loaf by boiling barley with four or five herbs, cooling it, stirring in cottage cheese, baking it, and then garnishing it with parsley and tomato slices. It looked like a baked ham and she was proud of it.

"My, that certainly does look appetizing!" Susan said. "I approve of a vegetable diet."

Unfortunately Leola had brought along a small roasted turkey, which she put beside the barley loaf. "I'm sorry but you're just going to have to grumble," she said to Margaret. "I don't care who else wants to eat your meat substitutes, but I'm not going to."

"That's just all right," Margaret said. "I didn't expect any different. I wouldn't impose my diet on you for anything in the world. I will say, however, that your little girls don't have the best color I've ever seen. Meat is not a natural human food. Adam and Eve didn't eat meat in the Garden of Eden."

"Chapter and verse?" Leola demanded.

"I'm not going to trade contentions with you," Margaret said. "But if you are interested I do have some literature on the subject."

Margaret asked Cloyd to say a blessing, following which they served the children. "I hope you aren't going to object if I give these girls a little taste of this barley loaf," Margaret said.

"Go ahead, it ain't poison," Leola replied.

After dinner Jeremy took Susan's boys outside, and the girls all crowded around Margaret in the living room, who showed them a memory quilt she was making from pieces of cloth that had belonged to family members a long time ago. While Lawrence and Cloyd settled into a discussion of national affairs, Leola and Susan washed dishes. Frank folded the card tables and carried them to the basement. From the head of the stairs he could hear Leola and Susan chatting.

"Aren't those bikini swimsuits a horror?" Susan said.

"I can't say I've ever seen one."

"They're nothing but two little strips of cloth. The bottom part shows all the belly a woman's got and the bra isn't hardly enough to cover up her nipples. You talk about conspiracies of Satan! The bikini is certainly one of them."

"My word! I wonder how I'd look in one of those."

"Modesty is a wonderful principle," Susan said. "Apostle Kimball has been stressing it in all his sermons lately, and I certainly go along with him. It seems like those New York fashion people just can't leave necklines alone. Some of those dresses you see in the Salt Lake and Provo department stores, why, if a daughter of mine came home with one of those, I'd make her take it back. Or maybe I would make her sew on a bit of lace or put a cute little collar on it."

"I haven't bought a dress in six years," Leola said.

"And aren't you just lovely too?" Susan said. "Good decent designs hold up forever and ever, don't they? That red dress you're wearing is beautiful, and that's the nicest little cameo brooch you've got pinned to yourself. The important thing about modesty is that Latter-day Saints have got to be creative in practicing it. We had a Relief Society lesson on all the things you can do to make yourself modest."

"Like what?"

"Well, you take Cloyd and me," Susan said. "This wasn't mentioned in the lesson, but we have always been real careful to be modest with one another so we can be examples to our children. That's what I mean by being creative. So they will grow up modest too. Do you know, I have never seen Cloyd when he wasn't wearing some clothes. At least his underwear."

Frank could hear the clatter of silverware and the swish of running water and Susan's voice going on proudly. "I have never seen Cloyd's arm bare above his underwear sleeve."

"You never have?" Leola said. "Well, a bare arm isn't the dangerous part of a man."

There was a long silence.

"I don't suppose you ever felt his bare arm," Leola said. "And you never felt nothing else he's got either. You got those four babies off a pear tree."

"Leola Windham!" Susan said in a scandalized voice. "You certainly have a way of taking something sacred and beautiful and making it seem vulgar and bestial."

"To tell you the truth," Leola said, "I see Lawrence in the buff every day, and he's nothing to look at. I just as soon he kept his clothes on. He's got skinny legs and starved ribs, and he sure don't stir me up to get out on the town and commit adultery."

Frank could see eavesdropping was another of his flaws. It was pretty damned funny to listen to Leola, but he could sympathize with Susan too. Making babies was like burning weeds on a windy day. Any old time the fire might break loose and burn up the barn and corrals as well.

Later everyone went back to the church for a two hour Sacrament Meeting. The larger children pounded and punched each other and the little ones squalled and had to be taken out to the foyer. Frank didn't blame them for being contentious. He sat up straight for a time, crossed his legs, leaned forward with his elbows on his knees, then started over again, all the while yearning for sleep. Church-going was worse than being staked down on an antheap.

After meeting everybody crowded into Margaret's living room. Miles's brother Lonnie and his wife Jessica came over to help say goodby to Jeremy. The men took off their ties and the ladies kicked off their shoes and the kids ran in and out, shouting and squeal-ing. For supper the ladies put on bread and milk and leftovers from dinner, and people helped themselves. About dark, the visitors prepared to go home. The men shook hands with Jeremy and the ladies hugged and kissed him.

Frank went out to the lawn to watch them get into their cars. He leaned against the trunk of a giant poplar. The evening was sweet with autumn odors. From high dim branches leaves spiraled down through the glow of car lights, joining a moist, golden litter on the lawn. Susan was scolding her children. One, who had preempted a front seat, had to get in the back. Another already in the back had to get in the front. Susan slammed a door, saw Frank, and started across the lawn, her high heels teetering.

She took his hand, saying, "I don't suppose you have considered moving home, have you?"

"What do I want to move home for?"

"What I mean is, would you consider moving home for Mother's sake? It would be so nice if you would."

"Why don't you move home and stay with her?" Frank said.

"It isn't fair to say that. You know I can't move home."

"Well, I can't either. I've got a career to tend to. I'm getting into cattle."

Cloyd honked. "Coming, dear," she called. Thin as a willow, she had auburn hair already touched with grey; sad, sweet eyes;

lips innocent of color. She put an arm around him. "I don't hardly know you anymore. I pray you won't be wayward."

He became stiff. "Don't be mad at me," she said. She squeezed him hard and for a second leaned her head against his shoulder.

When they were gone Margaret and Jeremy had a little quarrel over his suitcases. She made him unpack so she could inspect his shirts.

"I thought so," she said. He had wadded them up and stuffed them in.

"They'll get wrinkled no matter what you do," he said. "I'll borrow an iron and press them when I get there."

"You can do that too," Margaret said as she set up the ironing board. "In the meantime we'll make sure you start with properly pressed, nicely folded shirts. Then there won't be so many wrinkles for you to get out."

Frank sat in the living room twiddling his thumbs. The house seemed empty and sad. He was wishing he could drive back to the ranch right now.

They went to bed early and got up at two-thirty. They put Jeremy's bags in Frank's pickup and drove to Milner's Cafe on Main Street to wait for the bus. The cafe was closed and the street empty. Frank turned on his radio and picked up a station in Clint, Texas, which alternated between one minute of country music and five minutes of advertisements for imitation leather coats and reject baby chicks. After a while the Trailways bus pulled in with blazing red and amber lights. The driver put Jeremy's bags into the luggage bay, and Margaret and Jeremy and Frank hugged each other all at the same time. The bus drove away in a cloud of diesel fumes, leaving Frank and Margaret standing under the bright, twinkling stars.

They drove home and Frank parked in the backyard. He turned off the lights and shut off the key. The silhouette of the old sagging barn filled half the windshield. A shooting star flashed across the other half. A dog barked down the street.

"Well, he's gone," she said.

"That's a fact."

"He won't ever be home again."

"Sure he will. Plenty of times."

"It won't ever be the same."

"Sure it will."

"I've never lived in that house alone. I can't stand it. I think I'm going to go crazy."

"No, you ain't."

"Nothing stays firm ever. All sweet, dear things have slid away like water through my fingers. My poor dead Miles. My poor little Elizabeth. My poor dear mother. She lost four babies. I never left her, Frank. I stayed with her till God called her home."

"Lots of people get along by themselves."

"Come home and stay with me, Frank."

"Gosh, I've got my job over on the ranch."

"Maybe you could drive back and forth. Or get a job at the mill. I could go see Cyrus Dansby for you. He might put you on."

She gagged on a cough and was suddenly sobbing. "I just can't stand this lonely house."

"Well, heck," he said, "maybe I could come home."

She cried harder.

"All right, I'll do it, I'll come home. I'll tell Wesley to plan on a new man. Now please stop crying."

"Oh, Frank, it would be such a trial to you, such an imposition, but it would be so nice for me, it would mean so much."

They went in and he went down the stairs to bed. He lay there for a while smoldering like damp hay. He for damn sure wasn't moving home, and he'd just have to find the guts by breakfast to look Margaret in the eye and tell her so. He wanted to shut a door on his hand to teach himself to face up to a crying woman.

A couple of hours later he got up and prepared to leave for the ranch. Margaret fixed cracked wheat cereal for breakfast, and while they ate she said, "I've been thinking about the cattle. I'm going to phone Raymond today and tell him he can't have them. They're yours. You don't have to pay me anything either. I want you to have them. And I'll see what I can do with Salsifer about putting fifty cows on the forest next summer."

Margaret's cheeks were pasty, her eyelids pouchy, her hair wispy and half unraveled. She didn't need more pokes and punches than she had already had. Besides, a paltry, underhanded idea had got hold of Frank, which was that if he played it smart he could have the cows and range without coming home to live with Margaret. He would drop in once a week and tell her he hadn't quite got untangled at the ranch but would do so shortly. He would dally and stall till maybe she would discover she could get along alone and would quit asking him to come.

"You had better go over and get those animals off Raymond's hands," she said.

"I'll do it next Saturday," he agreed.

They went to the door and she turned her cheek to him. After he had bent down and kissed her, she caught him around the neck and gave him a tight hug. He felt as noble and delightsome as a privy pit. If God didn't kill him off with a car wreck on his way to the ranch, he'd think of some nice things to do for her.

4.

God
Strikes

Frank borrowed Wesley's stocktruck and picked up his cattle from Raymond, releasing them in the Rollinses' corn fields. He registered his FW brand at the county courthouse in Panguitch and had a branding iron made. He and Red branded the calves, Frank roping them and then, while Red held them down, performing the technicalities, which came easy to him—handling the iron, earmarking, dehorning, castrating. It wasn't work, it was fun.

One evening the Earles drove to Cannonville with Frank to see his cattle. The fields were down a lane lined by ripgut fences made from untrimmed, crisscrossed juniper trunks. Frank's critters were mixed in with the Rollinses', but he knew them. They were a handsome cross between Hereford and Black Angus—squat, square, and meaty.

"Pretty fine cows," Wesley observed.

"Lord, I just love them!" Marianne exclaimed.

Frank said, "I've also got to buy a bull. That's part of my bargain with Mr. Rollins."

They drove to Tropic and everybody got a milkshake, after which Wesley drove home slowly because a big moon had lit up the chalky faces of Table Cliff. Wesley was trying to figure out how a poor young fellow like Frank could afford a decent bull.

"There's this rancher up in Heber I meet at the last Hereford convention," he said. "He wanted to sell me a registered bull cheap. The reason was, he's old. Also lame. However, Thornblad swore he has four or five years left in him, especially if he were down here in this country with its mild winters."

121

"The winters aren't all that mild down here," Frank said.

"Now don't get negative till we see what I can work out," Wesley said. "I'll call him tonight. You can't tell in a case like this what I might come up with."

The next morning at breakfast Wesley announced that Mr. Thornblad had agreed to a hundred dollars for the bull.

"No, sir," Frank said. "I'm dumb but I ain't stupid. A lame bull is the same as no bull at all."

Wesley was hot for the sale. "You go ahead and pick up that bull. Look him over, test him out. If you don't like him, I'll take him. Heck, you can sell him to a by-products plant and get nearly a hundred dollars out of him."

Frank left for Heber on the Wednesday morning before deer season, pulling the Rollinses' single-horse trailer behind his pickup. As he returned with the bull on Thursday, he would pick up Jeremy in Provo and bring him back for the hunt. On the way out, he stopped in Panguitch at Minnerly's Mercantile and visited Margaret. He sat on the check-out counter while she put a new roll of paper into the cash register. She couldn't understand why he hadn't quit the ranch and moved home as he had promised. He'd do it shortly, he told her, and diverted her by talking about how nice it would be when Jeremy got home on Thursday night.

"Little good it'll do me," she grumbled. "Him and you both will be off hunting deer."

"Not till Friday night," Frank said. "Also he will likely want to come in Saturday evening so he can go to church Sunday."

"Well, I should hope so," she said.

Arriving in Provo mid-afternoon, Frank drove onto the campus and found the dormitory where Jeremy had a room. Jeremy wasn't there, and the fellow across the hall said he hadn't seen him or his roommate all day. Borrowing paper and a thumbtack, Frank left a note on the door saying he'd be back by nine the next morning. Then he drove up Provo Canyon toward Heber.

Mr. Thornblad's farm, about a mile west of Heber, was prosperous, having a big brick house, a high gabled barn painted rust red, and corrals with strong plank fences. The bull turned out to be one of the biggest Herefords Frank had ever seen. Feeding at a stanchion, he canted his neck and watched Frank with peaceful, sleepy eyes. He didn't have horns and his white spots had turned yellow and his red spots were grizzled. But what testicles! They dangled in their sack of bare red skin like two giant Idaho potatoes. All at once Frank was in love with that bull. He was a bulldozer, a tank, a freight train. He was worth a hundred dollars just for how he looked.

As Frank had expected, the Thornblads invited him to stay the night. In the morning he loaded the bull and drove down the canyon to Provo. Arriving on campus, he parked across the street from Jeremy's dormitory. Sitting for a moment, he watched girls stroll toward their next class. Brother, what a pasture this was! He got out and peered between the trailer slats at the bull, which had decided to lie down in the straw. The bull, his jaws slowly working over a cud, returned Frank's stare. He didn't seem worried about a thing in the world. It was just as well he was lying down, a campus not being a proper place to display all that big male equipment. People said the Hindus believed God would change people into animals in the next life because they had behaved like animals in this one. Frank wouldn't have minded being a range bull. He would have moseyed among the knolls and buttes and junipers, free and unhindered, grazing, belching up cuds, and accommodating ladies by the dozen.

No one answered when Frank knocked on Jeremy's door. At least the note had been taken off the door and a fellow down the hall had seen the roommate. This fellow also advised Frank to check at the cafeteria in the Joseph Smith building because Jeremy had a job washing dishes there. Frank crossed campus afoot. In the basement of a yellow brick building he found a cafeteria full of clatter, steam, and grill odors. When he asked about Jeremy, a girl behind the serving counter called a sharp nosed woman from the back.

"I'm looking for my brother, Jeremy Windham," Frank explained. "I was told he works here."

Squinting, the cook removed her glasses and rubbed the lenses with the hem of her long white apron. "Well, we're looking for him too," she said, resetting the spectacles. "He seemed like a nice boy. I thought he'd work out all right washing dishes for us. For a couple of weeks he showed up like he was supposed to. You have to be regular on this job. Meals have to go out three times a day and in between too, rain or shine."

"Sure," Frank said, "you have to be regular on any job. But my brother is regular. He isn't anything if he isn't regular. You can count on that."

"Could be," the lady said. "But he doesn't work here anymore. He's fired. He hasn't showed up this week. Not one single day. And he missed two days last week. A fellow who acts like that doesn't want a job very bad, does he?"

"He hasn't showed up all week!"

"All week. So when you find him, tell him not to come back."

For a while Frank sat numbly watching crowds of students crisscross the foyer of the Joseph Smith building. When things had got quiet, he wandered down a hall gazing through open doors into classrooms. On an impulse he followed a late student into a classroom and took a seat. The tweedy, wispy haired professor sat on the edge of a table, his gangly legs crossed, the top one giving a special little spurt each time he made an important point. He had a faraway, moon-eyed look, as if there was nothing in the universe he'd rather do than talk to quiet, respectful, paper-scratching students.

It was a religion class and the professor was discussing research he and a colleague were conducting on the grammar of the true Adamic language. He figured that before God had confounded the tongues at the tower of Babel, everybody had spoken the language God had given Adam, which it made sense to believe was God's own language.

"Now it's true," the professor said, "that our holy books are mostly translations into English from some other man-made language like Hebrew, Greek, and Reformed Egyptian. But remember that these books are revelations. No matter how you change a revelation in order to dress it up for the weak understanding of God's people, some of God's original intent has to remain. Otherwise it wouldn't be a revelation. All we have to do is carefully work out the predication and subordination patterns in all four books and compare and contrast them. By golly, when we can see what they have in common, we'll be getting close to the way God thinks and talks!"

He was nearly ecstatic and Frank could see why. Knowing what God thought about "I ain't" and "I done" and "I seen" and how he crossed his t's and dotted his i's would be next best to being in the presence of the burning bush, that was for sure.

At noon Frank returned to the dormitory and found Jeremy's roommate, Bill Taylor, who said Jeremy was at a clinic on the west side of town. He couldn't remember the address but could show Frank the way.

"A clinic? Is he sick?"

"Right, sick is what he seems to be. He ran this here doctor down a couple of weeks ago. A girl over in the cafeteria told him about her. She's a lady practitioner. She cures you with herbs."

"Lordy! With herbs!"

"He's been staying down there. In fact, I haven't seen him since I took him down there Monday. She likes to saturate people. She gives them a bed and doses them night and day."

"What's the matter with him?"

Bill shrugged. "He's just sick, that's all. He was having a lot of pain in his stomach."

"Why didn't he go to a real doctor?"

"Good question. I said the same thing. You can go to the university health center free."

"You know," Frank said, "I just about don't believe you. This sounds fishy."

Bill got testy. "Well, it isn't me that's fishy. I'll show you the way down there and you can see for yourself. I don't know him very well, him and me being roomies only four weeks now, but just to tell you what it seems like to me, it seems like he's crazy. A little bit crazy maybe."

On the west side of Provo they parked by a green clapboard house with a porch sign, "Dr. E. R. Pickett, Herbalist." A tall, heavy woman opened the door. Her face was apple red and her black hair, loosely braided and wound into a bun, was streaked with grey.

"Mr. Windham is here," she said to Frank, "but he is not to be disturbed. He's mid-treatment. You can't come in and out of these treatments like you were running down to the grocery store."

"I'm his brother," Frank said. "I want to talk to him."

"I hope you aren't going to get him all excited. I might say he isn't the easiest one to work with I ever saw. He has a tumor in the bowels though I haven't got a fix on it yet. These herbs will do the trick if you give them time. But if you're going to go rushing him off, he just as well not have come out here in the first place."

"Lady," Frank said, "if you don't fetch him out, I'm going in after him."

"All right, all right," she said, smoothing her hair as she left the room.

Beef soup was in the steamy air and also cat manure. Frank looked around. Slouching on a sofa in a dark corner was a thin, pinchfaced man, whose trouser cuffs were four inches above his ravelly stocking tops.

"Look there," the man said, pointing. "You can see that cat's tail. She's in the organ again."

Across the room was an electric organ. The piebald tail of a cat stretched from the pedal aperture, twitching slowly back and forth.

"That cat just don't like some people," the man said. "When you came in she took a dive for that organ."

Voices came down the hall, a door slammed, and Jeremy came into the room. His shirttail was out and a black stubble covered his chin. He blinked and squinted and finally brought his eyes around to Frank.

"There you are," he said.

"You bet," Frank replied. "I've got my pickup outside and a trailer loaded with a dandy Hereford bull. Also old Bill Taylor, your roommate, is out there. Gather up your gear, if you've got any, and let's get out of this place."

The tall fellow said, "That cat has come out of the organ now. She's gone behind it." Suddenly a mottled cat streaked across the room and disappeared down the hall. "She sure don't like somebody in this room," he said, staring at Frank.

Jeremy leaned against Frank. He seemed tottery and in pain. "Dr. Pickett," he said, addressing the woman, "this is my brother, Frank J. Windham, the bronc rider and calf roper. There isn't anything he can't do off the back of a horse."

"Knock off the chitchat, Jeremy, and let's get out of here."

"Did anyone at Panguitch ever mention to you that man is descended from the ape?" Jeremy said. "The Scriptures do not confirm evolution, Frank. I am happy to say there are professors at BYU who hold the line. My Book of Mormon teacher is one of them."

Frank gripped his arm and pulled him toward the door. "Get your hands off me," Jeremy said, detaching himself.

Dr. Pickett came forward anxiously. "Look at the pouches under his eyes. That's a dead giveaway for a tumor. Especially in a young, thin fellow like him."

Jeremy had gone to the window. "I see your pickup and, yes, there's a trailer too, loaded with a recumbent bull. And there's old Billy Taylor. Why didn't you bring him in? He's a good boy from Twin Falls, Idaho. We take Freshman English from Old Lady Smootzenchamper, or whatever her name is. She eats ten penny nails for lunch."

He turned and elevated an arm. "When I have fears that I may cease to be before my pen has gleaned my teeming brain, before high-piled books, in charact'ry, hold like rich garners the full-ripened grain. . . . I would recite the rest if I could remember it. Something for my gravestone."

"We've got a long haul," Frank said. "Let's get on the road."

"To see Mother."

"Yeah, you bet, to see Mom. Let's go."

"When did you see her last?"

"Yesterday morning. She figures on us tonight."

"Tonight?"

"For heck's sake, Jeremy, don't you remember? I've come to take you home for the deer hunt."

"It is already deer season?"

"Saturday."

"What is today?"

"Thursday."

"Good grief," Jeremy said.

"What are you doing over here? When was the last time you went to class? Why didn't you bother to tell them at the cafeteria that you had got sick? They fired you, did you know that? You haven't been to work all week."

"I came here last night," he said. "It was last night."

"Bill out there says he brought you over Monday night."

"And you need another three or four days at least," Dr. Pickett said. "Why don't you just have a little talk with your brother and then come back in and finish your course. You've been coming along beautiful. It would be a shame to break into your schedule now."

"I haven't been to work all week," Jeremy muttered. "I'm ashamed of myself. All week!"

"Let's go," Frank said. This time when he tugged, Jeremy came.

From the door Dr. Pickett called, "Remember, he's got a tumor. Bring him back. It needs to be treated."

"I'll cut it out with a haymower," Frank shouted over his shoulder.

"What about my fee? He owes me thirty-five dollars."

"You can collect it in cow manure at Earle's ranch in Escalante. Bring your own truck."

They got into the pickup and pulled away. "This is my brother Frank," Jeremy said to Bill.

"I already met him," Bill said.

"We're going home. We're going to see Mother."

"And do a little deer hunting," Frank said.

"That's right. I've got me a new gun."

"We'll get us both a big buck. We'll have a great time."

"I feel better," Jeremy said. "I've had this funny pain in my stomach. But it's gone now."

"Thatta boy!" Frank said happily. "Things will be okay now." Then he began to laugh. "Good hell, did you ever see anything like that lady quack? She's crazier than a locoed mule."

Having let Bill off at the dorm, they headed south for Panguitch. Jeremy talked about his classes and about the peculiar personalities he'd met. He believed he could catch up with his class work easily enough. He said that as soon as he returned to Provo he would apologize to the cafeteria manager and let her know he didn't blame her for firing him.

"So maybe you won't mention anything to Mother," he said. "There's no use worrying her. I'm going to be okay."

"Not a word," Frank agreed.

Margaret had a big supper ready. She was dressed for Sunday and her face was warm and smily. After visiting for a while, Frank said it was time for him to head toward the ranch. Before he left town, he filled his tank at the Conoco station. As he replaced the cap, he heard squeaking brakes and looked up to see a school bus pulling off the pavement. The door folded open and Marianne got off. "Thanks a bunch," she shouted over her shoulder to the driver.

"Wow, am I glad to see you!" she exclaimed. "No use me riding that dumb bus back to Escalante and then having to wait for somebody to come pick me up. I've been to the football game in Circleville. We steamrollered 'em."

She climbed onto the slatted sides of trailer and said, "For goodness sakes, look at our bull! Isn't he big?"

Frank climbed up beside her. The bull, still lying, watched them with restful eyes. "I want to pay for him," she went on. "Let's take the hundred out of my savings."

"You hang onto that money. We'll need it later," Frank protested. What he wanted to say was, Dammit, this cattle operation is mine. Quit trying to horn in.

Driving down Center they saw lights blazing in the Social Hall. "It's the deer hunters' ball," Frank explained.

"Gosh, what do you do at a deer hunters' ball?"

"You dance. What else would you do?"

"Just like Indians, huh? You've got to dance before you go hunting."

"It ain't like Indians. Just neighbors having a good time."

"Sounds like neighbors whipping up a toot."

"Well, some of them will make a toot out of it before the night is over. And they'll go right on making a toot through the whole opening weekend. Those are the kind that shouldn't be carrying guns. By the time Saturday morning gets here they can't tell the difference between a deer and a motorcycle."

"Let's go dance," Marianne said. "Just to be stupid."

"We gotta get home."

"Just two or three dances."

He pulled the pickup and trailer over and backed up until they were opposite the Social Hall. As they crossed the street, Marianne took his hand. They didn't look so bad, he in his dress boots and jeans and ten gallon Stetson and she in her swirly skirt and bobby socks.

"How about half price for us, Gene?" he said to the ticket taker. "Me and this young lady from Escalante are just going to dance two rounds to show these Pangtown hicks how it's done."

"A dollar and a quarter, take it or leave it," Gene said. While Frank was paying, Gene said to Marianne, "Watch out for Frank Windham, miss. He's half goat and the rest of him is skunk."

"I know that already," she said.

The hall was decorated with orange and brown crepe paper, and a man and a woman wearing red hats and vests sold cider and doughnuts in a booth. The band was composed of a piano, a trumpet, and a set of drums, and it alternated between fast and slow numbers. There was a nice little crowd; in the center of the hall couples bobbed and shuffled, and along one side singles clustered in two groups, one of men, one of women.

Some of the dancers paid attention to Frank and Marianne.

"Is there somebody under that hat? Why, look there, it's Frank Windham."

"Hey, gal, you don't have much pride. That fellow you're dancing with just escaped from the city jail."

"Frank can't dance but he can sure haul manure."

Frank pulled his hat low over his eyes and laughed off the banter. Marianne's eyes sparkled. "I love to dance. Don't you?"

He grunted. It wasn't bad at all. When the slow tunes were playing, she pushed back his hat and put her body against his. They danced and danced and when Frank finally remembered to check his watch, it was ten o'clock.

"Scrud," Frank said, "we're in trouble. Your folks will wonder what the hell we've been up to."

They got in the truck and he drove back to the Conoco station and used the payphone. "Hello, Clara," he said, "this here is Frank. I'm at my house in Panguitch and I've got Marianne. She jumped off the school bus and hitched a ride with me. We've been here with Mom and Jeremy having some supper and we got to talking and didn't keep an eye on the clock."

"That's a big relief," Clara said. "The bus driver told Wesley she'd got a ride with you, and we were starting to get worried you had had a wreck or something."

"No, ma'am, we're safe and sound. But I've got to stop in Cannonville and unload this bull. So we'll be a little while yet."

"That's all right. Just as long as we know you're both okay."

Hearing Frank mention supper made Marianne hungry so he bought her a hamburger at Clay's drive-in. An hour later they got into Cannonville. Frank drove into the field where his cattle grazed and backed up to a loading chute.

He took off the tailgate and shouted at the bull, "Get your big haunches off that floor, mister."

The bull shifted a little and sighed.

"Get up," Frank shouted.

The bull didn't move until Frank got inside with him and pulled up his tail and gave it a twist. He groaned and slowly heaved up his hindquarters, groaned again and pulled his front quarters under him. "Looky there," Frank said cheerfully, "he's still got some life in him."

Frank climbed onto the slats and waited. The bull stretched and slowly backed down the loading chute into the dark field, favoring a hind leg.

"He sure is lame," Frank said. "But I'm glad I bought him anyhow."

"You bet, he's a doggone beauty," Marianne agreed.

When they had got back in the cab, they both seemed to have the same idea. They moved close and began to hug and kiss. Pretty soon he tugged up her sweater and got her to loosen her bra. He knew he shouldn't let himself get worked up because he didn't have any condoms. Then she whispered, "We can't go all the way because I'm having a period."

That cooled him off. Shortly he remembered Jack had said a woman couldn't get pregnant while she was having a period, and he got his hand up under her skirt.

"Don't. I really am having a period."

"I don't care," he said. "I want to do it awful bad."

"Please don't."

But he kept trying and pretty soon she said, "Okay, if you're sure that's what you want," and she pulled up her skirt and took off her panties and napkin belt.

When he was through, he got out and leaned against the fender. The moon was high and bright in the cold October sky. A few feet away a cow grazed, big and black. Marianne came around and leaned against him. Knowing she wanted to be held, he hugged her. "I love you," she said, touching his face with her fingers. He had a rock in his belly, a big lump of melancholy. He couldn't think of anything he wanted to do or anywhere he wanted to go.

Friday afternoon Frank loaded Booger and Chowder into Wesley's trailer and pulled them to Panguitch. He picked up Jeremy and they drove west along Five Mile Creek, crossed a divide, and turned up a rutted track. A little before dark they found the Windham camp in a grassy swale west of Five Mile Ridge.

The camp was as busy as an anthill. Trucks, cars, and horse trailers were parked helter-skelter among the aspens. Horses stood at makeshift hitching poles. A walled tent, big enough to sleep fifteen or twenty, and a half dozen small tents were pitched among the trees. A bonfire roared in the center of camp; a smaller cooking fire flickered near a table made of planks and sawhorses. Frank's uncles Lonnie and Jarvis were there and his first cousins Sinclair, Cliff, and Bruno, and his third cousins Lester, Dan, Junius, Hans, and Stanley, and three of Sinclair's friends from Circleville, and at least fifteen children, mostly boys, who ran and shoved and shouted.

As Frank and Jeremy got out of the pickup, Jarvis yelled, "There they are. Come on, boys. Supper's ready." Like his brother Lonnie, Jarvis was a short, overweight man with spectacles. Unlike Lonnie he hadn't overcome his coffee habit. Right now he was superintending a pot that steamed on the coals. "Got some camp Postum here," he said. "The usual rules and regulations are suspended, boys. Crowd around and have a cup. God don't pay no mind during deer season."

"That's pretty weak doctrine," Lonnie said.

Sinclair and one his Circleville friends had bottles of beer. "Danged poor example for them kids," Lonnie grumbled but nobody else seemed to mind.

There was a big Dutch oven full of stew—beef, potatoes, carrots, and onions—and a couple of others with hot biscuits. On the table were pots of jam, slabs of butter, bottles of milk, and five or six pies.

When the men went by to be served, it was like the sifting of Judgment Day, the sheep going on God's right and the goats on his left. The for sure good Mormons passed up the coffee without batting an eye, and the dyed in the wool Jack Mormons held out their cups without any fuss. Two or three were in agony. Bruno shuffled his feet and bit his lip and shifted his plate from one hand to the other. He was second counselor in the Junction bishopric. "Well, golly," he finally said, "once a year isn't going to hurt anything," and he held out his cup.

"Me too," said his son.

"Like hell," Bruno said. "If you don't like that milk, go get yourself some water."

Frank took his plate and coffee cup and squatted on his heels where Bruno, Stanley, and Junius were telling deer hunt stories.

Most of the kids sat around them, chewing their food in big eyed silence.

"You remember that year Cliff and me hunted in the head of Ramshorn Canyon," Stanley was saying, "and it was raining and all fogged up? I never saw more than two or three opening days like that in all my life. We were in a fog that drifted just like you see in those war movies. It was a funny feeling seeing the firs and aspens one minute and then seeing nothing but fog the next. All of a sudden I heard Cliff gagging, like he had a piece of meat he couldn't swallow. He was trying to call my attention to three bucks. Where the fog had cleared away, I saw the three biggest deer I have ever seen in all my days. Any one of them would make one of your big four pointers look like a fawn. But before Cliff and me could even think about getting our rifles up, the fog closed in again and they were gone. Gone! Oh, juzzabell, that hurt!"

Frank could remember a time when that kind of talk made him wild and desperate because he didn't think he'd ever be old enough to carry a gun. He drifted to the other side of the fire where Sinclair and his Circleville friends were talking about an abandoned house on Highway 89 north of Panguitch. Jeremy sat with crossed legs, listening intently.

"It ain't a lie," one of the friends was saying. "You can ask twenty different people, and they will tell you the same thing. That old house has got a spirit in it. It doesn't seem like an evil spirit because nobody has ever mentioned it threatening anybody. But if you go out there on a dark night and just sit in the house a while, pretty soon it comes out and you can see it standing over where the old cook stove used to be. A kid was scalded to death right by that stove, and people think it's her spirit. My Aunt Lorraine remembers about the scalding when she was a little girl."

"That's true," Jeremy said. "I know a guy who has seen her."

Frank got tired of all the palaver and sat with his back to a tree, gazing at the fire while he went to work on a second plate of stew and another cup of coffee. He felt peaceful, like a man who had everything he could ever want. A hand squeezed his shoulder, and he looked around and saw Lonnie squatting a little behind him. His bulbous nose was dimpled with pores, and his thick lenses reflected the dancing flames.

Lonnie said, "I didn't know if I'd ever see the day Jeremy would take up hunting. I'm glad he has come along. When I see you and Jeremy, good looking young men if there ever was any, it seems like I'm seeing Miles all over again. This time of year he gets on my mind, Frank. Him and me hunted together nearly forty years, from the time we were kids. Tonight I feel like I never have got used to him being gone. I keep feeling like in a minute he'll come in out of the dark, like he's out there just a little way, maybe checking up on the horses."

"I remember hunting with him," Frank said. "I don't think I was more than five or six the first time."

"That's right, you were five or six. But he never did bring Jeremy along, which of course gives you extra responsibility. You kind of got to be his dad, haven't you? Taking him out and showing him how to do it."

"That's about it," Frank said. "Yeah, that really is just about it."

At four-thirty the camp woke up. Somebody built a fire and Jarvis fried bacon and eggs while people stuffed sandwiches and apples into pockets, counted out cartridges, and saddled horses. After breakfast they left camp in little groups, their chatter and oaths sharp and ringing in the frosty darkness. Frank and Jeremy mounted their horses and followed Sinclair and his friends along the dim trail in the creek bottom.

"Where you guys going?" Sinclair called back.

Frank yelled, "The bluffs this side of Five Mile. We're going for the big ones."

"Good luck, fellas."

A few minutes later Frank and Jeremy turned off. Branches snapped, saddles creaked, horse hooves thudded on the frozen trail. Frank's breath came steamy and hard. He was scared, out of control, happy. God, he loved a deer hunt! Soon he would tie his horse, would stand in the early grey light, would suffer in the long silence. Then he would hear the first distant shot. He would hear others, a doubling of shots, a twice doubling, a great growing cannonade booming, crashing, thundering everywhere in the mountains.

When they paused to rest the horses, Frank said, "They say the Celestial Kingdom is a globe of fire. Ain't that right?"

"Yes," Jeremy said. "The Celestial Kingdom will be this earth, glorified. It will be a sea of glass."

"That will be the highest heaven, won't it?" Frank said.

"Yes. Only the righteous will be there. They will be lit up with glory."

"Well, I don't want to be lit up with glory," Frank said. "I don't want a sea of glass. Us here on this mountain, that's all the heaven I want."

When daylight broke, they were stationed on a saddle between one canyon and another. During the first hour, while the cannonading went on, deer fled in frantic bunches back and forth across the saddle—altogether twenty-five or thirty does and half a dozen little bucks. Later, when the shooting had died away, they rode onto the top of Five Mile Ridge and ate a sandwich.

Jeremy said, "No big ones."

"Too smart," Frank said. "They don't panic and take off running with the does like the little bucks do. You could have had three or four forkhorns. You sure you want to hold off for a big one?"

"Do you think we can get one?"

"Maybe. We can sure try."

"That's what I want. A big one."

They rode south along the rim of Five Mile until they came to the bluffs, a series of high, broken cliffs at the base of which were ravines and little canyons filled with firs and brush.

"That's where we've got to hunt," Frank said.

It was rough country. They would have to tether the horses and go down through the bluffs on foot. To reach a buck they had killed, they would have to backtrack with the horses and come up from the bottom of the canyon the buck was in. That could easily take half a day.

"We'll have to be patient," Frank said. "We'll have to sit and watch and wait. There's no way to sneak up on them because they can hear us coming. But we can outwait them, sit there quiet for an hour, move a little bit now and then, watch the openings, be ready to take a fast shot."

"Okay, I can do that," Jeremy said.

"Don't shoot a little one, for heck's sake. We can get one of them in a place ten times as easy to pack out of."

Jeremy nodded. Then he said, "When you're cleaning a buck, what do you do with the penis and testicles?"

"Good gosh, just whack them off and throw them away. No need to be dainty about it."

"I mean, how do you do it?"

"You ream out the pelvis with your knife and finger; then cut the pecker away from the belly—it's a slithery little snake about fifteen inches long—and stuff it back up through the pelvis and pull it on out with all the guts and bladder."

"That turns my stomach."

"If you get a buck, I'll gut him for you," Frank said.

"I'll do it. I've got to learn how."

They went together down into a canyon. Frank crossed into another canyon and hunted alone for three or four hours. In a dense grove of firs he jumped a big one, saw the flashing white of his butt and the arch of his antlers, but before he could raise his rifle, the buck was gone. Mid-afternoon he climbed through the trees toward the crest separating him from Jeremy. He stood on an outcropping, studied the canyon, and at last spotted his brother at the edge of an aspen grove. He went on, swallowed by brush. He heard a crash and thudding hooves and saw a flash of grey and white. He plodded on, pushing aside branches, stumbling over roots. He heard a shot, then another and another.

Jeremy's frantic voice came from far away, "I got him, I got him!"

"Whoopee!" Frank shouted. "Atta boy, atta boy!"

It took him fifteen minutes to reach Jeremy, who stood, knife in hand, over the gaping belly and outhanging guts of a little buck.

"A forkhorn!" Frank said. "Well, crum, who cares? That's okay. He'll make good eating. Nobody needs to apologize for a nice little forkhorn."

Jeremy stared at his bloody hands. He shifted his gaze and stared at something across the canyon. He hadn't looked at Frank. His knife still in hand, he turned and ran uphill toward the trees.

"For hell's sake, Jeremy," Frank shouted, "come back. Let's clean this fellow and go get the horses. We ain't got all day."

Jeremy disappeared into a patch of heavy brush. Frank put down his rifle and followed him. As he reached the brush, he heard a scream.

"What's the matter?" he shouted. "Hold on, Jeremy, I'm coming, I'm coming!"

He plunged into the thicket. The branches wove a thick net and he fell. He ran and fell again and again.

He came out of the brush and saw Jeremy without his knife. His belt was loose and his pants unbuttoned and he held them up with a hand. Blood seeped at his crotch.

He began to run and Frank shouted, "Jeremy, wait!" He went up the steep slope after him, lunging and scrambling, his lungs burning, his breath rasping. Suddenly Jeremy collapsed and Frank went to his knees beside him. Jeremy raised an arm and threw his fist, but Frank knocked it down. He rolled him over and pulled down his pants. Where his penis and testicles had been was a patch of red meat from which a thin spray of blood arched into the air.

"Jesus Christ!" Frank cried. He pulled out his handkerchief, wadded it, and clapped it down hard on his crotch.

Jeremy screamed.

"What else can I do?" Frank said. "I've got to shut off that blood." With wild ideas careening through his mind, he leaned away and vomited.

Each time Frank removed his hand from the sticky, wadded handkerchief, Jeremy started to bleed again. "We're in a whole lot of trouble," Frank said. "How are we going to get you out of here?" It was a half mile, straight up and brushy, to the rim where the horses were tied.

Jeremy said, "The rufous-sided towhee is a bird often found in Utah juniper and pinion habitat."

"What's that?"

"She was clad," Jeremy went on, "in a white robe, bright as fire. With glory around her head."

"Dammit, Jeremy, this ain't no time for bullshit!" Frank said, hollow and hoarse. "What did you do it for? That's what I want to know. What did you go cut yourself off for?" Then he leaned away because he had to vomit again, though he couldn't get up more than a little bile.

"It hurts, it hurts," Jeremy moaned.

"I know it does, you poor son of a bitch."

"Herbs will cure you," Jeremy said. "The word is not pronounced with an aspirated *h* as people say it in Panguitch, but *erbs* as it is said in Provo. Did anybody in Panguitch ever tell you about evolution? In Adam's fall we are sinners all. Because of one abominable man, and also Eve, the frogs and mosquitoes must die."

Frank listened with mouth agape. "You're out of your head, plumb crazy out of your head. We've got to get out of here. We've got to get you to a doctor. But, jeez, how are we going to do it?"

He cut off his shirttail with his hunting knife, folding it to make a bigger compress. "I'm going to pick you up and carry you," he said. "It's going to hurt, but there isn't anything else to do."

When Frank tried, Jeremy screamed and kicked. Then he went limp and moaned as Frank pulled him up face to face, lifted him off his feet, and staggered upward, his hand gripping beneath his crotch. Getting him to the rim was something Frank wouldn't want to remember because he had to put him down every twenty or thirty yards to pant and puff, and when he heaved him up again, he screamed and moaned. "I'm so damned sorry, brother," Frank said over and over. "If I knew any other way to do it, I sure would."

It was evening when they got to the horses. They would have to ride on one horse so that Frank could make sure Jeremy didn't start to bleed again. He untied Chowder and wrapped his reins around the saddle horn. He would follow without fuss. Frank untied Booger, swung up, and seated himself behind the cantle, then hauled up Jeremy, scrabbling and screaming, into the saddle seat. My gosh, he was thankful for a steady, well trained horse. He put his arms around Jeremy, holding the reins with one hand and with the other making sure the compress stayed tight on his crotch. He clucked. Booger started off and Chowder fell in behind.

A long time before they arrived at camp somebody fired three signal shots. "We're coming, we're coming," Frank muttered.

By then he was feeling better. At first, as dark came on, he had been frightened. He couldn't see the trail and his gelding had been over it only once and was a flat country horse beside. There was nothing to do but give Booger his head. He knew where he was going. He walked easy, picked up his feet, didn't stumble much. Chowder stayed close behind. For the first time Frank began to believe that he might get Jeremy out alive.

The jolting, shifting ride kept Jeremy shouting and moaning. In between times he talked nonsense.

"I have cleaved," he said. "Therefore shall a man leave his father and mother and shall cleave unto his wife. So I have, yes, I have cleaved."

"You ain't cleaved unto nothing. That's just crap you're saying."

"Shut the headgate! Quick there, close it! A shovelful of mud, please, with a little grass for binding. The principle by which adobes are made. Pharaoh said no more straw for your bricks and the Children of Israel threw down their tools and walked off the job. They quit, they took off, they went through the sea. And they looked upon the serpent of brass."

"Sure they did. The sea opened up like dry land."

Jeremy became very sad. "The little children do suffer, don't they? Suffer little children and let them come unto me. Poor Mother. Eternities without end, suffer little children."

"Mom's okay," Frank said. "She's getting along, don't worry about her."

"If you drive too close to the incinerator at the mill, it will explode your gas tank. The heat of hell. Except Mormons do not believe in hell. There are three kingdoms of different glories. The greater is for the Saints. The lesser is for the wicked. In between is for the honest of heart who have been deceived by the craftiness of men. And outer darkness for the Sons of Perdition."

"Dang it, Jeremy," Frank said, "that kind of talk doesn't cheer me up any. Why don't you just shut up?"

It was one a.m. when they approached camp. Eight or nine men were around a roaring fire. "They're here!" someone shouted.

"He's hurt bad," Frank said. "Start up a car and let's haul him to a doctor."

Hands reached up to take Jeremy. "Back off a minute," Frank shouted. "You've got to keep hold of his crotch. He keeps breaking loose and bleeding. I can feel it when it happens. You've got to pinch him tight."

"Good heavens!" Lonnie said. "What happened?"

"He cut himself off. He did it with his own knife. He shot a little buck, he was gutting it. Then he just went crazy. He ran off into the trees and I heard him holler and when he came out, he had done it. Sheared himself off clean. Pecker and balls, the whole works."

"They're gone? All gone?"

"Clean gone. He's nothing but a woman now."

Arms reached up again and Frank let Jeremy slip into them. The men carried him to the fire and pulled down his pants.

"Bless us, Lord, bless us," Lonnie mumbled over and over.

A boy came from a tent. "Why don't you administer to him? Maybe Heavenly Father will make them grow back."

"Nothing will grow them back. Nothing but the Resurrection," Bruno said.

"Let's administer to him anyway," Lonnie said. "Just to keep him alive till we get him to a doctor. Bruno, you help me. Stanley, do you want to take him in your car? Hans, will you go with him?"

After they had given him a blessing, they put him in the back seat of Stanley's car. Frank started to get in. "Hold up," Lonnie said. "Let Hans get in with him. They can take care of him now. You better stay here. Your guns are still out there, aren't they? And you better take some of us up to look over the scene just in case the law wants a report. It'll be better if two or three of us know where it happened."

After the car drove away with Jeremy, men and children stood around the fire for a long time, talking in low voices. Jarvis called Frank's attention to the bucks hanging on poles at the edge of camp— six of them, including a couple of big ones. Early in the evening Lester and Junius and their children had driven home for Sunday. Lonnie would have also gone if he hadn't been worried about Frank and Jeremy. Now others were changing their minds about staying. Cliff said he intended to gather his gear and leave immediately, having lost his stomach for deer hunting. Dan said he would leave when morning came. He thought the whole camp ought to show its respect for Jeremy by clearing out and going home.

"Not me," Sinclair snorted. "Quitting early ain't going to help Jeremy none. It's the doctors will do that."

"Maybe you should," Lonnie said. "Maybe it's a warning you ought to heed."

Jarvis said, "This reminds me of that Jamison fellow who got his privates shot off years ago."

"Except he never did it to himself," Lonnie pointed out.

Bruno, squatting by the fire, had been shaking his head. "Why would a guy do something like that to himself? It doesn't make sense. No way at all."

"He's gone crazy," Jarvis said, glancing at Frank. "Sorry to say this, Frank, your mother being a Jamison, but there's a good deal of crazy among the Jamisons."

"You better not get to bragging," Lonnie said. "There's plenty of it in the Windham line too."

"What makes somebody go crazy?" Sinclair's boy asked.

"Jacking off!" Jarvis said. "Young fellows get so hot to do what married folks do, they marry themselves to their hand. That's what makes people go crazy."

"Jeremy didn't jack off," Frank said. "I know that for a fact."

"It's notions," Sinclair said. "Notions make people go crazy. They get funny ideas and they get carried away with them and go off the deep end."

"Jeremy didn't have notions," Frank said. "He was smarter than any of us. He was better than any of us. He didn't break any of the commandments. Not a single one of them."

"That's right," Lonnie agreed. "He was good as they make 'em. And let's pray he'll come out of this and be okay again."

"He ain't coming out of it," Frank said. "There isn't anything for him to come out to. Who'd want to spend his whole damned life with his privates cut off?"

He was crying and Lonnie squatted by him, patting him on the back. "Why don't you go get some sleep now, Frank? You've had a rough time."

Frank got into his bedroll in the back of his pickup. Jeremy's empty bedroll there by his side haunted him and he slept fitfully. He had a dream about a Kotex as big as a canoe. In fact, it was floating down a river, dirty and leaking blood into the clear water. He jerked awake, thinking about making love to Marianne two nights before. He couldn't think of anything worse than a man making love to a woman who was having a period. Nobody but a goddamned animal would do something like that.

From overhead came a faint swish, a motion of air like the flutter of a hunting owl. He opened his eyes and gazed around, seeing nothing except a high, late moon and the lacy silhouettes of aspen branches. He had no patience with the darkness, no tolerance for his bed. He wanted sunlight, motion, voices. He heard the swish again and was suddenly stricken. Inside him a connecting rod had sheared loose from a whirling cam.

He peered inside a rifle barrel. He saw shiny spiraling groves and a cartridge locked into the firing chamber. He saw the bead at the end of the barrel, and behind that, the notch of the rear sight, and behind that, oh God, an eye taking sight on Frank J. Windham! God had been tracking him in his sights night and day; he hadn't missed a thing. Furthermore, he wasn't deterred by blood and agony. He didn't mind driving a good boy like Jeremy crazy in order to put fear into a coyote like Frank. He didn't mind watching bad men hammer his own son to death on a cross just so when the time came he could skewer them on the pickets of hell.

After breakfast a bunch rode out of camp, headed for the bluffs where Jeremy had gone crazy. Though Lonnie protested, Sinclair and his friends brought along their rifles. As they rode the men swapped stories and the boys chattered and laughed as if it was just another beautiful October day. Frank neither spoke nor listened. His mouth was dry and little muscles in his wrists twitched.

When they came to the rim of the canyon where Jeremy had hunted, they milled around for ten minutes trying to find a way to take the horses down. "You can't do it," Frank said. "By foot is the only way."

While Lonnie and Sinclair's friends remained at the top, Frank, Sinclair, and two boys started down through the cliffs, slipping and sliding and hanging on to bushes to keep their balance. "I'll be dog-goned," Sinclair said. "You packed him straight up this slope like he was a sack of wheat."

They found the guns first and a minute later, thirty yards down the slope, the little buck. Something had dragged it and had eaten fat from the guts that hung out of the slit Jeremy had made.

"Let's take it, Dad," Sinclair's son said.

"Hell no, we ain't going to take it. Likely it's spoiled. That hill is too damned steep to drag it up anyhow. On top of all that it wouldn't be proper to take it, considering what happened here."

Frank gazed upslope toward the brush patch where Jeremy had cut himself off. "We better go up there and find his knife."

"What for?"

"I've been thinking. If they're still there, I mean if his pecker and balls ain't been eaten by something, I just can't walk away and not bury them."

Sinclair had taken off his red hunting cap and was wiping his bald head with a rag. His mouth puckered as if he had tasted something bad. "Count me out. I wouldn't do that for a thousand dollars."

Frank struggled up the slope and groped through the brush. Though he hoped for failure, he had success, shortly finding the knife and, not five yards away, his brother's testicles and penis, shriveled and black with dried blood. He dug a hole with the knife and shoved them in. He paused before pushing dirt in over them because a prayer had to be said, the grave had to be dedicated.

"God," he said aloud, "I wouldn't do this if there was somebody else to do it. Bless this ground and sanctify it as the resting place of these portions of my brother. Bless them that they may come forth on the morning of the first resurrection to make him whole again. In Jesus' name, Amen." Then he filled in the excavation and piled rocks on top.

Back at camp Frank loaded his horses in the trailer and then, when Lonnie was ready to follow, pulled out for Panguitch. At Lonnie's house Jessica gave them news of Jeremy. Stanley and Hans had stopped in Panguitch long enough to let Margaret know, then had driven on to Richfield. The doctor there had Jeremy transported by ambulance to the Utah Valley hospital in Provo. Leola came from Orderville and drove Margaret to Provo.

Frank used Lonnie's phone to call the Provo hospital, where someone put Leola on. "Is that you, Frank?" she asked anxiously. "Are you okay?"

"There's nothing the matter with me. How's Jeremy?"

She said he was in surgery at the moment. He wasn't going to die, but of course he couldn't be restored to his original condition. "How on earth did it happen?" Leola said. "I just don't see how a man could accidentally shoot his privates off with a rifle. Considering how long the barrel is and all."

"It wasn't with a gun," Frank said. "It was with a knife. And it wasn't any accident. He did it on purpose. He went crazy."

"Oh, no, oh, no," she was moaning. "How am I going to tell Mamma? She's got it all wrong. She's so sure it was with the gun. She's been telling it that way to everybody."

After eating supper with Lonnie and Jessica, Frank headed for the ranch. He stopped first at his mother's empty house, where he rummaged in the secretary. He had never felt so lonesome. He found the Book of Mormon Margaret had given him for his twelfth birthday, and he also took his father's old Bible, which had a cracked binding and tattered pages and an inscription in faded brown ink: "A long and righteous life to Miles, from Father and Mother, Christmas 1898."

At breakfast the next morning he discovered that the word about Jeremy had ricocheted around Garfield County and everyone at the ranch already knew. He filled in the details without hiding anything. Nathan sat shaking his head. Wesley shook Frank's hand and called it a tragedy. Putting an arm around him, Clara said she hoped God would comfort him and his mother. Marianne put her cheek against his and cried, saying, "Why did this have to happen, Frank, why did it?" Wesley and Clara smiled and nodded sympathetically, as if they were happy to see how much like a sister and brother Marianne and Frank had become.

Frank disappointed Clara by turning down his usual cup of coffee, explaining, "I've decided it's time to live my religion. A guy shouldn't try to get out of it forever."

"Well, that's certainly so," she conceded. "Since that's what your religion teaches, you had better pay attention."

Nathan was taking it all in, having stopped chewing so that he wouldn't miss a thing. It would cheer him up a good deal to see Frank brought low. For a moment Frank was tempted to renege on his repentance and send himself to hell just to spite the old man.

After breakfast, having the task of cutting posts for fencing a new field, Frank loaded a chain saw and other tools and drove Wesley's bobtailed truck some forty miles by way of Alvey Wash onto the backside of Fifty Mile Mountain. There the ridges were thick with junipers which, unlike the gnarled trees on lower slopes, grew straight and tall.

First he dug a hole in a hillside, loosening the hard, gravelly soil with a crowbar. Then he dropped in two boxes of condoms and his dirty playing cards. It was like burying somebody he knew. The nude girl on the back of the cards lay propped on an elbow, her smile warm and engaging. Frank had had many a good time with her in the privy or behind a hay stack. But that was over. He would never masturbate again in his entire life.

All week Frank toppled trees and cut them into posts. Having filed fresh, sharp edges onto the teeth of the chain saw, he cranked the engine and the saw roared and bucked and vibrated like a wild animal that meant to get away. The whirring chain gnawed its way through a trunk, spitting a steady spray of tiny chips onto his legs and feet. He wandered from tree to tree, trimming smaller branches with an ax, and when evening came he maneuvered the truck over the rough hillsides, following the helter-skelter trail of scattered posts. He stacked the posts lengthwise on the truck bed, and when they came cab-high, he cinched them with heavy chains. Then he drove the groaning, lurching truck down the rutted road leading to Escalante and the ranch.

He carried the Scriptures in the glove compartment, and every day at lunchtime he read from the Book of Mormon, sitting in the bright sun with his back to a truck wheel for protection against the cold north wind. He could see he had a bad spirit because he didn't like Nephi, who was the humblest man on earth. Nephi certainly didn't mind telling his brothers Laman and Lemuel what low class skunks they were. He had considerable trouble keeping those fellows under control, though once in a while God gave him a hand by sending an angel to shake them up. That didn't seem to change them any. They went on helling around and scoffing at Father Lehi and thinking up dirty tricks to play on Nephi.

Frank was lower than a snake. He didn't know whether he wanted to go on living. It gave him the sweats thinking how God harvested people when and where he pleased. People thought they could earn some credit by being good, by keeping the commandments. They thought they could buy a little more joy and a little more time to live. When it suited him, God dumped them, good or bad, into his mill and ground them into chaff. He hadn't sent an angel to warn Frank, as he had to Laman and Lemuel. He had wasted Jeremy.

Another problem bulldozing around in his mind night and day was how to come clean with Marianne. He knew his next step was to go home to take care of Margaret and Jeremy, which meant he should give Wesley two weeks' notice. Clara would cry and Wesley would try to talk him out of it, and Marianne would get excited and get him in a private place and ask him what in the hell was going on. He wasn't worried about having sex with her again because simply looking at her turned his stomach. It wasn't God's idea that he should marry a Gentile girl, that was for sure, but it also wasn't God's idea that he should sneak away from all the lies he had told her. He would have to tell her straight and clear.

On Friday night Margaret phoned Frank and asked him to drive her sedan to Spanish Fork. If she had it, she could look for a cheap room in Provo. Leola had gone home on Thursday and things were not pleasant at Emily's, Aunt Marilla behaving in her usual deceitful, malicious manner. She harped constantly on the evils Margaret's mother had done to her poor mother. What a travesty! Anybody with any sense of fairness at all knew that it was the other way around, that Cynthia trampled on Jerusha at every turn. Cynthia had worked night and day to undermine Jerusha in Tertullian's affection, without success, thank God, and now, without any slacking off, her daughter Marilla was carrying on her vendetta of slander and badmouthing.

The doctors had moved Jeremy to the psychiatric ward, which was a terrible insult. He wasn't crazy, he was sick. Anybody would be sick who had had an accident like his. What he needed now was healthy food and the kind of care a mother could give. That peevish little psychiatrist, Dr. Berendsen, was trying to talk her into going back to Panguitch without Jeremy, but that ploy wouldn't work.

On Saturday afternoon Frank left his pickup at Margaret's house and drove her sedan north toward Spanish Fork. Clouds blanketed the sky and a cross wind made the car wander from side to side. He passed dozens of cars and trucks full of deer hunters. Many of them had deer hooves hanging out the trunk or a little buck or a doe draped over the hood or a big set of antlers propped on the tailgate where everybody would be sure to see.

By the time Frank reached Emily's, it was dusk and the wind drove a slushy rain. Margaret was in the tiny, cluttered living room watching television with Emily's daughter. Taking her car keys from Frank, she murmured and let her eyes wander back to the grey and black screen. Somewhere in the house a washing machine thumped and sloshed, filling the rooms with a damp, loamy smell. Frank went out back where Robert was feeding his milkcow. The skirt of his denim coat flared over his round belly and he waddled like a duck, his goulashes pulling from the miry corral with a noisy suction. He stopped at the gate and shook Frank's hand. He had the sweet uric stink of cows.

His voice was low and confidential. "I've been thinking about your brother. An evil spirit has got hold of him, that's clear as day. What them psychiatrists and doctors tell you why people go crazy isn't anything but lies. They pretend if you don't have sex with every woman that comes along you will get warped and go crazy. They'll be telling you Jeremy is out of his mind because he didn't fornicate and carry on with the girls."

"Well, he didn't, that's for sure," Frank said.

At supper Marilla sat across the table from Margaret and Frank. She had pulled her thin white hair into a little bun on top of her head. Her dentures clattered and she picked up her food with her fingers, though she kept a fork in one hand to show she was civilized. She kept a wary eye on Emily, as if her fear of her daughter's scolding was all that kept her from saying catty things to Margaret.

After they were through eating, Robert said, "If I were you, I'd get Jeremy a special blessing."

"He's been administered to four or five times," Margaret said.

"Well, I'd get him a special one just in case it was an evil spirit that took possession of him."

"He's just sick," Margaret said. "He's had an accident. He's on the mend. He'll be fine soon as I can get him home. They are feeding him way too much meat, and it wouldn't hurt him any to cut down on the sugar. You should see the desserts they feed them in the hospital. I'll give him wholewheat bread and lots of vegetables and soybeans instead of meat." Margaret's eyelids were puffy and discolored, her hair frowzy.

"There was a widow's family over in Santaquin last winter kept hearing noises at night," Robert said. "One morning they got up and every one of them said they felt something go by in the hallway exactly at two-thirty. They had all looked at their clocks and watches. So brethren from the Priesthood came in and blessed the house and commanded in the name of Jesus Christ there wouldn't be any more visitations."

Emily said, "Dad's Aunt Hattie saw an evil spirit in the snow once. When everybody had gone to bed and all the lights were out, she peered from the back window and there in the back yard was this thing, which looked like a man only it was bigger. Her hair went straight up in the air and she couldn't sleep and she kept looking out and it wouldn't go away. Finally about four o'clock when she looked it was gone. But you know what? The next morning there weren't any tracks in the snow."

"Jeremy's just sick," Margaret said.

Margaret had been sleeping on a sofa in the basement. Emily gave Frank a pad on the floor in the same room. Late in the night he woke up because someone upstairs had flushed the toilet and water rumbled in the soil stack.

Margaret said, sounding wide awake, "Frank, are you asleep?"

"No, ma'am."

"Do you think Jeremy is possessed of an evil spirit?"

"I don't know anything about evil spirits. I never saw one."

"If I can get him home, he will be all right," she said.

"I expect that's true."

"This has been a terrible week, Frank. Nothing seems natural. I feel like I am running a high fever. I have weird dreams about things I never saw before. They say it wasn't an accident, Frank. They say he didn't do it with a gun. He did it to himself with a knife. Did you know that?"

"Yes, ma'am. I was there."

"Yes, that's right, you were there."

After a while she said, "The question is why did he do it."

"He went crazy."

Her sheets rustled and the sofa springs creaked. She went on, "People say Mother went crazy, but she didn't. I know the truth about her. Like people say, it's true she wandered in the sandhills under Fifty Mile Mountain. She sent me and Salsifer in to Escalante to go to school. She stayed on the ranch and looked after the stock and did a little farming. And she searched the sandhills. She wasn't crazy. It was her time of atonement. She was seeking her true punishment. She wanted to know why her babies died."

"Why did they die?"

"Her sins."

"Did she steal something?"

"Mother? Good heavens, no!"

"Did she commit adultery?"

"Frank! Not my mother!"

"What were her sins?"

"Maybe pride. Maybe too much confidence. Maybe thinking too much of this world."

The sofa creaked again and he could tell she was sitting up. "The Savior appeared to her at Reston Spring."

"I know. You told me that."

"Frank," she said in a strange voice, "a frightful comfort comes to me."

"What kind of comfort?"

"If it wasn't an accident, if Jeremy really did do it to himself, I think maybe he did right. Maybe he has sanctified himself."

"That's a tough way to sanctify yourself," Frank said.

The next day Frank and Margaret went to Sunday School with Emily and her family. In the early afternoon they drove to the hospital in Provo and visited Jeremy. He lay on a bed by a window and looked out while Frank and Margaret sat to one side, trying to think of things to say. His skin was pale, his chin was stubbly, his crewcut needed clipping.

When they got up to leave, he took Frank's hand and said, "When copper corrodes it is quite green. When iron rusts, however, it's black."

"Yeah," Frank said, "that sure is the truth."

Mid-afternoon Frank set out to hitchhike to Panguitch. He caught a ride to Nephi with deer hunters and got as far as Levan with a woman and two children headed for a missionary farewell in Fillmore. The driver of an empty coal truck took him to Salina. As he walked around the curve where the highway left Salina, he saw a man and a woman on the doorstep of a stone house. The woman wore heels and hose and the man had on a suit and tie.

The woman was saying, "I told you to get it killed before we went to meeting. Never mind about it now because everybody's hungry. We'll have creamed green beans on toast."

"Well, my good hell, Patricia, we don't have to stop and boil up water to scald with. You just heat up a frying pan. When you're in a hurry, you don't pluck a chicken. You skin it." The man went down the porch steps saying to a girl, "Come on, help me catch one of them hens."

Frank thumbed four cars in a row, then turned back to watch the man, who emerged from a chicken coop dangling a White Leghorn. He paused to scrape manure off his shoe. "Bring me that ax," he said to the girl. "Now watch this." He squatted and put the chicken on a juniper log. He rotated his palm twenty or thirty times over its neck. It stayed in that position. The girl put the ax into his groping hand and with a sudden blow he cut off the chicken's head.

The headless chicken went wild. It threshed its wings, leaped into the air, and thudded to the ground. It circled on its side, scratching and kicking, then leaped and thudded, leaped and thudded. Blood spurted from its bare, bony neck, staining the chips and bark roundabout. Finally it flopped and quivered and was still.

The man looked at Frank across the fence. "Damnedest thing, ain't it, how a chicken won't die?" He picked up the bird and followed his daughter around the corner of the house.

Frank got a ride with a man from Hatch, who took him all the way to Panguitch. He didn't say much, having a cleft palate which made his words sound lost in a deep cave. Frank watched the countryside go by—a muddy stretch of the Sevier, a sage covered plain, a feedlot full of Black Angus cattle. In his mind the demented chicken still jumped, flapped, and thudded. Its neck protruded from its feathery skin like a bony, red, cut-off penis. Maybe a man was better off without a prod. Maybe Margaret was right, maybe Jeremy really had sanctified himself.

He had got up his courage and the next morning after breakfast, standing on the kitchen stoop, he told Wesley he was quitting. Wesley hadn't shaved and his stubble was grey. The bottom three buttons of his shirt were undone, showing a bit of his hairy belly. "You can't do that," Wesley said. He opened the kitchen door and shouted, "Clara, come out here a minute. There's an emergency."

"Gracious," Clara said, wiping her hands on her apron as she came out.

"He's trying to quit. Don't let him."

"I've got to go," Frank said. "I've got to go back to Panguitch and take care of my folks. In about two weeks. Sooner if you can find somebody else."

"Oh, Frank, don't do that," Clara said, starting to cry.

It took him a half hour to talk them down. He was in a mood to face Marianne too, but by evening, when he had got home from cutting posts, he had lost his nerve.

At supper Clara said, "Well, we have come to an end. Life goes along in certain ways and nice things happen to us every day and we don't think about how much they mean to us, and then all at once they stop. Frank won't be with us much longer. He has decided his place is with his mother and brother, which we can certainly understand. But gracious, Frank, we surely have relied on you, and this table will seem empty, just empty as can be."

"Oh, Frank, that's terrible," Jeanette said, mocking a crying face.

"Now that saddens me," Nathan said, "it really saddens me." He had broken a roll in two and was blading a dab of butter.

Marianne said, "When are you quitting?"

"As soon as your dad can find another hand." He couldn't keep his eyes steady. He skimmed broth from his bowl of beans and blew on the hot, steaming spoon.

Marianne dipped her roll into her beans and bit off the soaked tip. She glanced at Wesley, saying, "Who are you going to hire?"

"I've got a couple of leads. I've been on the phone today," Wesley said. Hunched over his bowl, he didn't look happy.

Frank's eyes wanted to wander and circle but her eyes stopped them, asking, What will happen, where do we go from here? His eyes didn't have an answer. Her auburn curls straggled and her lipstick was eaten half off. She wore a tight lavender sweater and a dangling gold chain and locket.

"Like Mom says, it's a new era," she said. "How will we get by without old horseface there?"

"Marianne!" Clara said. "That's irreverent. This is a time of great trial for Frank and we mustn't make jokes."

"Who's making the jokes?" she said, emitting a strange, choked laugh. She rose with a sudden shove against her chair, clattered across the room, and disappeared down the hall.

"What's the matter with her?" Wesley said.

"That certainly was a touchy demonstration," Clara said. "She hasn't bit back at me like that in months. Well, it's a time of strain for us all. You'll have to excuse her, Frank."

Frank returned to the bunkhouse with Nathan, who stoked the stove with juniper and sat at the table to finish a letter. From under his bunk Frank pulled a box full of magazines, canceled checks, receipts, and letters. He had to decide what to burn and what to pack and take away.

Nathan couldn't get into his writing. He bent forward and flourished his pen over the paper two or three times, then looked around and slumped back in his chair. "This is going to be a lonesome place," he said. "I'll miss you."

"I'm going to miss you too."

"Maybe it's getting to be time for me to move up to Provo. Dora keeps telling me to do it. She don't miss saying so in every letter. It's a rotten shame two people who love each other like Dora and me do would get separated this way."

"Maybe it's time," Frank said.

"I got a letter from her today. I told her about your brother in my letter last week. Also about how your mother is up there looking out for him. Dora says for me to tell you to tell your mother to get in touch with her. She says her house is open to your mother."

"That's mighty kind, but we've got relatives up there," Frank said.

A knock came on the bunkhouse door. "Come in," Frank called.

Marianne came in, closed the door, and stood against it. She wore her heavy coat. "Could we have a talk?" she said to Frank.

Nathan looked at her, then at Frank.

"Sure," Frank said. He went to his closet and put on his coat and Stetson and followed her from the bunkhouse.

"Do you want to take me for a ride?"

"Sure," he said.

They got into his pickup and he drove down the driveway and turned south toward the Jamison place. He drove on until he came to the new place Wesley was developing at the edge of the sandhills. He stopped the pickup and for a minute left the headlights beamed onto a stack of posts.

"That's the bunch I brought in this evening," he said. "There's about enough now to start the fence."

A coyote called and Frank rolled down his window a little. The high, shrill wail carried through the night.

"Well," Marianne said, "I guess Nathan knows now there's something between us."

"Likely. He isn't stupid about everything."

"It really hurt me, Frank, you telling Mom and Dad before you told me. It seems like I ought to have known first."

"I guess that's right. You ought to have."

"It scared me for a little while. I went into my room and about went up the wall. Then I decided it was the right thing to do. You really should go home and look after your mom and Jeremy."

The coyote howled again, close, and then, from an opposite direction came another howl, also close.

"They're looking each other up," Frank said. "That's their telephone system."

She went on. "It seems like it's time now to tell people about us. I thought for a little while I couldn't take it, you being gone from the ranch. Seeing you every night at supper and sometimes at breakfast—it's the only thing that keeps me going. So if you're going to move back to Panguitch, isn't it time to tell Mom and Dad we're getting married? Then you can come over open and clear and take me out. We can go on dates. We can be like other people."

"I've got to tell you something. I've got to come clean with you. We're not going to get married. It isn't on the books."

"It isn't on the books?"

"We're just not going to get married. That's all there is to it."

"Frank!"

"I've been deceitful. I've been telling you lies. I don't love you. I never did love you."

"That isn't true," she said hoarsely.

"It is true. I've been lying to you."

"I know you love me! What we've been doing with each other, that's because we're in love."

"I'm a no good son of a bitch," Frank said. "I just wanted to have you. Just because you're a woman and I'm a man. It's the worst thing I ever did in my life. I ain't got no excuse. I've been sweet-talking you just so you'd let me do it."

She spoke a half word, sucked in air, broke into rasping sobs.

"It wouldn't be any different even if I did love you," he said. "I've had a visitation. What I saw wasn't any fun. I don't dare do anything but mind."

5.

The Outcasts

Frank borrowed the Rollinses' trailer and pulled his horse to Cannonville. The Rollinses gave him board and room for a week while he fixed fences and plowed fields, building up credit against running his cattle on their winter range. He also had a chance to watch his bull. When cows came in heat, the old fellow limped patiently behind them, lowing softly, but as far as Frank could tell, he never managed to top them.

Then Frank pulled his horse to Panguitch and settled in at Margaret's house, where he set up a routine of working on the place every morning. He swept and mopped the floors, repaired broken screens, and fixed leaky faucets. Going outdoors, he burned weeds and patched fences and pens, replacing broken rails and driving nails into sprung boards. He split and stacked wood and tidied up the workshop. Afternoons he rode his horse for two or three hours, starting by riding through town to see what was happening. At night he had supper with Lonnie and Jessica, who helped him stay cheerful.

On a Friday night Margaret phoned from Provo in an excited state. Dora Woodbarrow, the wife of the old man Frank had bunked with on the ranch, had got in touch with her—Margaret didn't know how she had found Emily's phone number—and had insisted she move in with her, rent free. Dora maintained a little bookstore in her house.

"So I'm living in the back of a book shop," Margaret said. "My bedroom has a shag carpet and a vanity with the cutest little yellow hooded lamps. You can't imagine what this does to my spirits. I just feel totally at home. She's a wonderful woman, Frank. So cultivated, so kind!"

"That couldn't be Nathan's wife!" Frank said in disbelief.

"It's her, all right, Frank. She is simply beautiful."

Margaret had bad news about Jeremy. Over her protest Dr. Berendsen had transferred him to the state hospital on East Center. The director there, a Dr. Washley, predicted at least a year before Jeremy's release. It was terrible how those doctors could enslave somebody, could just take complete possession of him and say yea and nay about his whole life.

"Of course," she went on, "Jeremy does behave peculiarly, no one can gainsay that. He thinks he's a girl. He calls himself Alice, he won't tolerate anything else. If you call him Jeremy, he gets very sharp with you. Where on earth did he get that Alice from? We never knew anybody named Alice. I don't know that anything about this whole situation has driven my spirits any lower. And he plays with dolls! That is the honest truth, Frank. The first day I noticed it he had salt and pepper shakers, three of them, which he had dressed up with Kleenexes and a handkerchief, and he gave them names, John and Joyce and something else, and he cuddled and cradled them like a little girl playing dolls. Exactly like that!"

"My gosh," Frank lamented, "what are people going to think about us with him caged up in the ninny bin playing with dolls?"

That was all the more reason, Margaret believed, why they should bend every effort to bring him home. There was absolutely nothing wrong with him that good healthy food and a mother's love wouldn't remedy. "So what I really called you about, Frank," she said, "was to see if you wouldn't drive up here and try your luck with Dr. Washley. He looks like the nicest man you ever met, but he won't budge an inch. He says, Mrs. Windham, we really do have the best interest of your son at heart, we really are the ones who can help him the most. But he'll listen to you, Frank. You are a very forceful person. If you say very firmly that we are through shilly-shallying around, that we are absolutely serious about taking him home, he might listen."

Early Sunday morning Frank decided to visit Bishop Bidley. Pulling his knit cap over his ears as protection against the bitter wind, he climbed through fences and trudged through backyards until he arrived in the bishop's backyard. He found the bishop shelling corn in a shed, feeding ears into a cast-iron mill with one hand while cranking with the other, causing yellow kernels to trickle from the spout.

"I'm getting up a little hog feed here," the bishop explained. "If you throw the ears in whole, the hogs lose half the kernels in the muck. If you shell a quart or two and put it in the trough, why, the pigs pretty well get it all." The fur-lined flaps of his Yukon hat dangled over his ears and his spectacles had steamed up from his breath.

"I've got a thing or two I want to get off my chest," Frank said.

The bishop stopped cranking and came to the door. Frank saw he hadn't shaved the grey bristles on his nose for a week or two.

"What I want to talk about is all the things I've been up to lately."

"All right, talk about them."

"I've been swearing and drinking beer and coffee and visiting bars and fighting. I broke a fellow's jaw last summer."

"I knew all that," the bishop said. "I was surprised the law never came after you for beating that Forest Service man. Anything else?"

"I've been fornicating too."

"I'm not surprised. I don't know when you young fellows will ever get enough sense to quit hanging around loose girls. What else do you expect when you know they're all ready and willing?"

Bishop Bidley's past wasn't exactly pious. The word was he had run wild when he was young, tampering with tobacco and liquor and chasing wild girls up and down Highway 89. Hardly ten years ago he had knocked out a fellow's front teeth in a fight over a sheep trade. That didn't make any difference, of course, because nobody was perfect and if a bishop was prayerful and sincere the Spirit would tell him what to do.

"If you think I ought to be excommunicated, go ahead and do it," Frank said. "It don't hardly seem like anything would be tough enough to make up for all the rotten things I've been doing."

"You been jacking off, I imagine," the bishop said.

"Yes, sir."

"Have you quit?"

"Yes, sir."

"Tell me the rest of it. Have you been over to Nevada to the whorehouses?"

"No, sir."

"How many girls have you been carnal with?"

"Just one."

"Was she a good girl or was she a loose one?"

"She was a good girl. I took advantage of her. I told her I loved her and was going to marry her."

"Then you better go do it."

"I don't think God wants me to. She isn't a Mormon, for one thing."

"She isn't? Well, that's different then. Likely she is a loose girl, no matter what you say."

The bishop took off a glove and dug up a handful of kernels from the bucket, letting them dribble through his fingers. "Come on over to the hogpen with me," he said. When they reached the pen he leaned over the fence and spread corn along a V-shaped trough. Three grunting barrows shoved and shouldered each other and scooped up kernels with drooling, champing mouths.

"It's a pleasure to watch hogs eat, they enjoy it so much," the bishop said. He took Frank into the barn and up a ladder to the hay loft, and they threw hay down into a stanchion.

"What I'm going to do," he said, leaning his pitchfork against a wall, "is put you on probation. You've given up your helling around; you're trying to live decent now. That's what counts. I want you to be extra good. You come to your meetings and pay your tithing soon as you get yourself a job. I'm calling you to be a ward teacher right now. And of course you look out for your mother and your brother. Now I want you to check in with me once a month for a while and I'm going to ask you if you're keeping up a good life, and if you say yes, then pretty soon we'll know you've repented for sure and you've paid your bills and your slate is clean."

"Yes, sir," Frank said, "I will sure check in with you every month.'

Monday morning Frank drove to Glendale looking for a polygamist who sometimes hired a truck driver. His name was Farley Chittenden and one of his wives kept a mercantile in Glendale. After Frank had parked at the side of the store, he could hear the sputter and smell the fumes of an acetylene welder. Then he saw the heels and butt of a man who was kneeling under a battered semi-trailer. The fellow was groaning and hissing and breaking out with homemade swear words like "Wheegizz!" and "Goldummit!" and "Oh sweet horse-puck!" Shortly he backed out and pulled off his welding goggles.

He was a short man with narrow, frail hips and mammoth, muscle-bound shoulders. He had a redbrown walrus mustache and a shiny bald dome circled by a rim of wild prophetical hair.

"I'm looking for Farley Chittenden," Frank said.

"Me and him is one and the same," the man said, eyeing Frank calmly as he shut the valves on the welding tanks. "You're looking for a job driving this truck. You may not favor visions, but I saw you this early morning in a dream. Knew you were coming today. What's your name?"

"Frank Windham."

"Know a good many Windhams, Panguitch, Circleville, parts north. Okay bunch on the whole. None as I know of practice plurality, but that don't matter so long as they ain't hostile to those of us who do. Got three wives myself. Right there in that store is one. Another up at my ranch at Alton. Another over at Pioche. Now that's settled and you don't have to wonder about it any more. You've got a clean eye and I trust you. Got a chauffeur's license?"

Frank nodded and pulled out his wallet.

"This is your rig," Farley said, gesturing toward the trailer and the aged Chevrolet truck to which it was hooked. The tires were half bald and the air hoses were tangled. A fender on the truck was crumpled; its green hood had oxidized into a tired grey.

"Runs," Farley said. "Sometimes requires the laying on of hands. Can't pay much. Goes by the job. First one is this. You and me drive up to Alton today. Load her with wheat. Then you drive up to Draper. Know where Draper is? South Salt Lake Valley. Unload the wheat, take on apples and squash. Then you drive back down this way but you don't stop. Keep going till you get to Short Creek. Unload the apples and squash, take on a load of frijole beans. Haul the beans to Pioche, Nevada. Load up with alfalfa hay. Back to Alton with that hay. Four days, maybe five. Thirty bucks total and meals at every destination. Take along a bedroll and they'll give you a place to throw down at night."

"Thirty bucks for a five day haul?"

"Not enough? Don't have no more."

Frank was thinking he would pass through Provo and could pay his visit to Margaret. "All right."

"Good! We're in business," Farley said cheerfully, putting out his hand for a shake. "Now go on into the store and get Bertha to feed you some lunch. I done ate."

After Frank had eaten, the two men set out by a back road for Farley's ranch near Alton. Frank was at the wheel of the rattling, wheezing truck. The rough graveled road went up by switchbacks, then cut across a high plateau. On each summit they looked out on a wild and broken world. Tilted, terraced plains were dark with forests of juniper and pinion. Ridges bristled with tall ponderosa pines. Fanciful erosions abounded—deep canyons, broad sheets of grey slickrock, pillars and arches cut in relief upon yellow cliffs, knolls and buttes jutting like stark islands of creamy red.

After a while Farley said, "Gets on your nerves, being a polygamist. People play games with you. They let you go along for a long time like everything was friendly and all right. Then all of a sudden one morning there's the sheriff parked in your yard. Somebody made a complaint. They haul you off and throw you in jail for a while and then they can't find anybody who'll testify so they let you go home. Meantime your wives and kids have had slim pickings."

"I imagine it could be pretty tough," Frank said.

"A lot of bother!" Farley gnawed at the whiskers over his lip. His wiry hair partly circled his pate like brush around a pond. "People think a polygamist is an old crock with a horse-size pecker just panting to breed every woman in the county. Ain't so. Ain't something you do for fun. So why do it? Every wonder that?"

"Yes, I've wondered."

"It's a commandment, that's why. God told Joseph Smith a hundred fifteen years ago for the Saints to take plural wives. Said it was the highest order a man could enter into. Said you could get closest to godhood that way. Ain't that right?"

Frank nodded.

"But now, says the Brethren up in Salt Lake City, God's gone back on all that. Changed his mind! So be it. What can I do with my puny arm? Ever been to California?"

"Once I drove some hay to Bakersfield for Wesley Earle."

"Now me, I been there all the way. Knocked around southern Cal before the war. Was thirty years old when the war broke out. Saw action in the Pacific. Didn't have no wives. Knew something of sin. Hung around the joints in San Francisco and Honolulu. A foolish Marine pounding on the table with his beer mug, shouting for the strippers to take 'em off faster, that was me."

Farley snorted and put a leg over a knee, then changed his mind and put the other leg over the other knee. "Book of Hosea. Whoredom and new wine take away the heart. Ye have plowed wickedness, ye have reaped iniquity, ye have eaten the fruit of lies."

The truck was pulling hard and slow up a hill and Frank was busy shifting gears.

"New year coming," Farley said. "Time to make resolutions so you can bust them. Time to wonder if this year is the big one. The year when God finally gets puked with all the robbers and murderers and gamblers and embezzlers and badmouthers and sodomists and liars and self-abusers and fornicators and slams the door shut. Says it's over. Had enough! Ain't that so? Don't you wonder if this ain't the year?"

"Might be," Frank said.

"Ever see them pictures in *Life* magazine how they blew up Bikini Atoll? Nothing left of it. Vaporized!"

"I saw some of those."

"I was in construction for six months over at the Nevada test site couple of years ago," Farley went on. "Helped to build some buildings in the blast center just so they could see what would happen."

A jackrabbit raced ahead of them in the roadway, then darted to the side and disappeared in a stand of buckbrush. Powdery dust rose behind the trailer.

"Got up early one morning at Pioche. Knew a blast was coming. Lit the sky red, yellow, white. Bright as day. Hundred and fifty miles away. Had a vision then, understood the End. Saw how it would come, saw how God has departed from among wicked men, has left them to their own devices. The day of the Lord will come as a thief in the night, in the which the heavens shall pass away with a great noise, and the elements shall melt with fervent heat."

They came to Alton, a tiny village of perhaps fifteen houses. They drove through and went on up a narrow canyon, coming finally to a little farm having a dilapidated barn and a white frame house with steep gables. A woman with one child in her arms and two behind her skirts came out and talked to Farley, who introduced her to Frank as Judy Vinharth. Her husband and Farley were partners. After Frank had backed the trailer up to a shed, Farley unfastened a padlock and they peered inside. A purring cat slid between their legs.

"Mouse insurance," Farley said. "Need more of them. Them sacks weigh one hundred pounds more or less. Want five tons on that truck—hundred sacks."

They began with Frank carrying the sacks from the shed and Farley positioning them on the bed. When the trailer was half loaded, Farley jumped down and said he had a little business in the house.

"Think you can finish it off by yourself?"

Frank said sure. An hour later, as it was getting dark, he completed the load and walked slowly around the truck, inspecting the worn tires and the sagging midbeam of the trailer. Mrs. Vinharth invited him to supper, which was creamed corn and sausage gravy on biscuits. For a while at the table it was just Frank, Mrs. Vinharth, and her three children. She explained that her husband worked in Price and came home only on weekends.

Shortly a young woman emerged from a back room. Her hand clutched the collar of her bathrobe, which lacked a top button. Her loose, bronze hair was crinkled from braiding; her face was square, her cheeks plump, her nose pug and freckled. Behind her came Farley, yawning, buttoning his shirt, and nagging his fingers through his flattened hair.

"This here is Gomer," Farley said. "Honey, this man is Frank Windham."

She sat down carefully, murmuring something nice to Frank. She took a plate, split a biscuit, ladled on gravy, and put it before Farley. As she reached for another plate, her robe gaped and Frank saw her plump, pretty cleavage.

"Did you notice how the mice have chewed up them sacks?" Farley asked.

"There were holes in a bunch of them," Frank said. "We couldn't help but spill some grain."

"Ought to get more cats. Though that ain't the real answer. No way to keep vermin out of your wheat except metal bins. Too poor to buy metal bins."

"It looks like you do some swapping between one outfit and another."

"Two outfits. Us here at Alton, them down at Short Creek, them over at Pioche, we're all one big outfit. The Draper bunch is different. A gentlemanly agreement, you might say, to trade amongst one another. What makes one different from another is who you take as your prophet. Us, we got Onis Bollinger down at Short Creek. Them at Draper have got another. Who's right, who's wrong, God knows."

"That isn't so," Mrs. Vinharth said. "Those Draper people are in the wrong. So are all the other little bunches spread around. Time we unite under the true prophet, then we'll prosper, then the Spirit will go forward. Brother Bollinger is the right man."

"Say," Farley said loudly, "you never did meet a woman named Gomer before, did you?"

Gomer blushed and dug into her biscuit and gravy as if eating took all kinds of concentration.

"Must be a Bible name," Frank said.

"Book of Hosea. Wasn't her christened name. She got it from God through the instrumentality of me. Told you I was at Pioche when they were testing atomic bombs. Went weeks with something on my mind. All them pictures you used to see in the war about people burned up by incendiary raids. Skin bubbled up, then turned black and crisp. Burned toast, only they were people. Couldn't get them pictures off my mind. Going crazy with it. One night I had a vision. Prophet Hosea came to me. Said, Farley James Chittenden, I command thee, Arise and go down to Caliente and enter in unto the whorehouse. Whorehouse right in the middle of Caliente. Janet's Place. It's been there for years. Hundreds of souls have gone to the devil in that house. Thousands have spilled their seed in those hellish cribs."

"That's mean talk and I don't want my kids to hear it," Mrs. Vinharth said.

Farley glared her down. "Straight talk for straight facts. Go down into the whorehouse, Hosea said to me. Go forward until you meet one whose face I show you. Command her in the name of the Lord to repent and come forth. Take her unto your bosom and call her Gomer."

He stopped eating, bit a nail, and spat out a paring.

"That's what he did," Gomer said. She had watched Farley closely, her face moving while he talked.

"Hosea said to me, Go in. Did so. Five in the morning. Neon lights were on, house was open. No one at the bar. Went down the hall. She was there, the one I saw in vision. This woman sitting at this table. I commanded her and she believed. Came forth.

Gave up her filthy life. Repented. Changed her name, became Gomer. A Baptist girl gone wrong. No wonder. Baptists ain't no more true Christians than a goldfish is an elephant. Big with child now. I have seen the child in vision. A boy. Jezreel will be his name. Next one will be a girl—Loruhamah. One after her will be a girl too—Loammi. A sign to the world of God's wrath. But a means of salvation for a few. A mercy the Lord has put into my hands. A gift. When I call people to repentance, when I put my mind to it, pick somebody out and pray for the poor son of a bitch, he hears. Repents!"

Farley looked around as if he had just awakened. He took another biscuit and ladled more gravy. His wide shoulders touched Gomer on one side and little Brackley Vinharth in his high chair on the other. "I ain't going to preach to you," he said to Frank. "Me and you, we got a commercial connection. A contract. You load and drive, I pay. Going to say this to you just this once. Please don't forget it. You're on my mind. I'm praying for you. Let me know if I can help you."

Frank drove the truck to Panguitch and spent the night at home. When he went to bed he knelt and prayed for the president of the Church and the twelve apostles and for Margaret and Jeremy. He also asked God to help him not think about Marianne so much, also to help her not feel too bad about what had happened to her. When he got out of bed in the morning, he said the same prayer. After breakfast, having asked Lonnie to look after his horse, he loaded his bedroll and headed north.

It was a grey, windy day, likely to produce snow. The truck had loose steering and wandered on the road. His hands gripping the shimmying wheel, Frank thought about the ranch at Alton. That Farley was rappier than a pen full of turkeys, crazier than a drunk racoon, believing himself visited by old time prophets who told him to fetch sinners out of whorehouses. Gomer worshipped him as if he was God the Father and Jesus Christ rolled into one. She was young, maybe no more than twenty-one or twenty-two. Frank wondered what kind of men she had had sex with, and how many. He wondered how long it took before God would forgive a repented whore.

Circleville, Richfield, Gunnison came and passed. He heeded the roar of the engine and when it flagged or raced he shifted gears, his foot working the clutch, his hand shoving the stick. Past Fayette he caught sight of Mount Nebo, its high sharp peaks mantled by fresh snow. The sky was a cloud-grey arch. For a moment, noon sun broke through and burned on Nebo's snow. Frank could have cried, it was so pretty. Then he wanted to punch himself in the mouth. He had to get over loving vain, worldly things, things that would pass away.

He pulled into Provo and parked across the street from a little house with a neatly lettered sign that said *Woodbarrow Books*. A bell tinkled when he went in. A woman looked up from behind a counter, then suddenly smiled and emerged with both hands extended, saying, "So you are *the* Frank Windham!" Frank couldn't believe his eyes. She wore a white blouse with a ruffled front and her silver hair was delicately curled. She laughed and hugged him. "Nathan wrote about you every week without fail. You can't imagine how respectful he is of your many talents and how grateful for your many kindnesses."

Frank could have crawled into a crack with a cockroach because he couldn't remember doing any kindnesses for Nathan.

"You just missed your mother," she said. "She has a part-time job clerking at Penney's. This is her second day."

She took him into the kitchen, put on an apron, and made him a sandwich. While he ate, she began a cherry pie. "You'll stay the night, won't you?"

"Yes, ma'am, if I may."

"I'm hoping Nathan will come up for Thanksgiving."

"You better not count on him."

"Maybe Christmas."

"Likely not."

"Yes, likely not. Well," she said, resuming her cheerfulness, "it's a great comfort to me to have your mother in the house. She and I go together like bread and butter."

She rolled out dough and stretched it across the bottom of a tin. She poured in the cherries and laid on another crust, then pinched the edge into corrugations and cut tiny chevrons across the top.

"You may not feel encouraged when you see your mother. Jeremy does keep her off balance. She can't get over that name Alice. She broods about it and keeps wondering where he got it."

"We never knew anybody by that name."

"I have to say that Jeremy seems happy in the hospital. I went over the other day with your mother. He had himself a rag doll, which one of the aids brought him. So your mother took over some pieces of cloth that could be tied into sashes and a little skirt and so on. Rather unusual, I would say, but he does seem happy."

"If I had him home I'd kick that out of him in about ten minutes," Frank said. "Who ever heard of a man playing with dolls?"

Frank thanked her for the sandwich and headed for Penney's on West Center. Inside the store he gazed around. Counters, spread in a grid, were stacked with shirts, scarves, stockings, and union suits. A male manikin in a tweed suit stared at him. Margaret was waiting on a woman at the fabric counter. She tumbled a bolt along the counter, measured and cut the cloth, and tied the piece into a small bundle. Her grey hair was short and frizzly; her eyelids were puffy and blue. As the customer left, she saw Frank and broke into a smile.

"Here you are, come to visit," she said, "and I'm all tied up at work."

"I'm staying the night," he said. "Dora's baking a cherry pie. I wouldn't miss that."

"Well, what I hope you'll do now, Frank, is go see Dr. Washley and tell him we've decided to take Jeremy home. Tell him we'll wait till New Year's, since I promised to stick with this job through the holiday season, but not a minute longer. You can indicate that we are very firm about it and don't intend to be put off."

"He isn't going to listen to me any more than he listened to you."

"Oh, yes, he will. You're a man. Now he will try to derail you. He'll tell you they've just barely got Jeremy on some of these new pills, they call them tranquilizers, and he is just certain they are going to do wonders. They are going to wake him up and he'll quit calling himself Alice and he'll be his old self, Dr. Washley says. But I don't believe it, Frank. It's good food and a loving home that will do that for him."

Margaret followed Frank from the store. "I can't say that I relish clerking here. It isn't like Minnerly's in Panguitch." A cold wind fluttered her dress and rattled grit against the store windows; brown leaves tumbled in the gutter. Eastward, the mountains were a looming wall of cliffs, canyons, and ridges, their crest lost in high grey clouds.

"I get a feeling those mountains are moving toward town," she added. "It seems like to me they lean a little farther every day. Do you think they could fall over on us?"

"Gosh, no, they won't fall!"

"I suppose not. But it's too bad this town is so close to them. You'd think they'd have put it out closer to the lake."

Frank walked almost a mile along East Center to the state hospital, which consisted of a hulking four storey building of white stucco and several small new brick buildings. Having made an appointment to see Dr. Washley in one of the little brick buildings, Frank crossed the driveway to the large white building, where he asked to see Jeremy. An aid guided him into the day room where a dozen patients sat, some of them wearing pajamas and bathrobes. A couple of visitors, a man and woman in their sixties, talked with an unkempt man who might have been thirty-five. Soon Jeremy came down the stairs, put his arms around Frank, and for a moment leaned his head against his shoulder. His face was flushed from hydrotherapy; his chin was shaved, his crewcut fresh cropped, his eyes serene. He wore a flowery Hawaiian shirt and carried a small wool bag.

They sat opposite each other at a table. "No one has compassion for birds here," Jeremy said. From his bag he pulled a glossy-backed book titled *Rocky Mountain Birds*. "The female blue jay is of the same hue as the male. It's hard to tell them apart."

"I imagine that's about right," Frank said, glancing at a pretty young woman in a bathrobe who stared out a window. Her hands were trembling. "There's something I've been needing to ask you," he said. "Where's the crowbar? I've been looking all over Mom's place and can't find it. I've been trying to tidy things up a bit down there."

"Hollister Bremer borrowed it last spring," Jeremy said.

"Well, doggone," Frank said, cheered up by the sensible answer. He propped his elbows on the table and started telling Jeremy about quitting Wesley and moving home. Jacksons' milk shed had burned down a couple of weeks ago. A construction worker staying at the Clearwater Motel had nearly died of asphyxiation from a faulty wall heater. That big yellow, stiffhaired dog of the Reynolds had been caught in a coyote trap and the vet in Richfield had amputated the leg and the poor critter was hobbling around the streets on three legs. Albert Johnson had been called on a mission.

"I know Albert is going," Jeremy said. "Mom told me."

Frank leaned forward, saying in a low, conspiratorial voice, "Jeremy, why don't we bust you out of this place and take you home?"

"My name is Alice," he said. His eyes were very calm.

"Dammit, Jeremy, that ain't true!" Frank cried.

"Alice," Jeremy insisted. He turned his chair around and sat with his back to Frank.

"Okay, okay, okay, Alice it is!" Frank said. "You bet you're Alice. I knew that all along. Mom told me. It's a swell name. Now turn around. Okay?"

Jeremy threw a half glance over his shoulder.

"I want to see your dolls."

Jeremy turned around, muttering, "They aren't dolls." He opened the wool bag and pulled out a salt shaker, which was tied with a scrap of red cloth. "This is Millicent."

"She's mighty cute," Frank said.

Suddenly Jeremy's eyes became frantic. "Danny!" he whispered. He plunged his hand into the bag and groped. He came out with a shoehorn. He groped again and came out with a handkerchief.

"There, that's Danny," he said, wrapping the shoehorn in the handkerchief.

"Well, look at that little feller, would you?" Frank said admiringly.

Jeremy pulled a rag doll from the bag. Its makeshift calico skirt had slipped down, exposing a single small ink mark at the crotch.

"That sure enough is a baby girl," Frank said. "Look at its little old tootie."

Jeremy pulled a tangle of cloth scraps from his bag. Frowning with concentration, he spread them out and experimented with them on his rag doll, one as a dress, another a shawl, another a breechclout. Although he at first explained each piece to Frank, he quickly forgot about him and began talking to himself.

"All right, have it your own way. You always do. But I can tell you this, I'm not putting up with much more of it." He poked a finger in the air like a preacher. "She stands right by the stove. It could burn you just as easily. A good many birds are incinerated at the mill. I saw it happen once to a swallow. Take all of Garfield County, there might be a couple of million swallows. In the summertime, that is. A flock like that can eat tons of insects in a single evening. Tons!"

After fifteen or twenty minutes of this Frank stood and said he had to go. Jeremy hugged him and refused to let go. "Now don't you cry or anything like that," Frank said, gently patting his bristly head. "I'll be back. Me and Mom are going to bust you out of here and take you home to Panguitch. It might take a little while, but we'll do it. In the meantime, you behave. Don't do anything wild and mean. Do what they tell you."

Frank waited to see Dr. Washley in an outer office where his secretary clattered on a typewriter. Two men came from the inner office, one of them looking mournful. He wore soiled slacks, and the tip of his belt dangled like a black tongue. The other wore a sports jacket and a bow tie and talked cheerfully about how being recommitted was actually a step forward if considered from the correct angle.

When Frank went in, Washley stood and leaned over his desk with an outstretched hand, saying, "Pardon me for making you wait." He appeared refined and precise—a fine weave jacket with a Rotary pin on the lapel; gold rings on white, tapered fingers; a thin pencil-line mustache; hair neatly parted and glistening with oil. He motioned Frank into a chair, saying, "I have relatives down Piute County way. Do you know Cy Washley in Marysvale?"

Frank didn't, but the first thing he knew, he was talking and Washley was listening. What with one thing leading to another, Frank was soon discussing the big Percheron draft horses his brother-in-law Lawrence entered in all the pulling competitions in southwestern Utah. He explained that Lawrence worked for the Soil Conservation Service, being one of those fellows who got out and measured stream flow all over the state. For example, he made measurements of the Virgin River and it was really surprising how much muddy water went down that drainage.

When Frank came to a pause, Washley said, "I'm glad you stopped in, because I've been wanting to talk to you. Time was a case like your brother's was hopeless. Lifelong psychosis, nothing to do about it but lock up the poor deluded soul. But these new drugs, they're nothing short of miraculous! Even the chronic cases—it makes it so we can get them out of straightjackets and padded cells, we can treat them like people again."

"Thanks just the same," Frank said. "We've made up our minds to take him home. That's what I'm here for, to get you primed up to let him go."

"Not just yet, please. Prospects for him are rather bright, I'd say. We'll help him get his life rolling forward again."

"He ain't got anywhere to roll forward to," Frank said. "He thinks he's a girl named Alice. He plays with dolls."

"We can bring him out of that. That's exactly what we mean to do."

"We're going to take him," Frank said. "We made up our minds."

Washley looked very discouraged. "Really, believe me, I don't like to pull rank on you, but in this case, well, I can't release him."

"My mother never signed anything. We want him out."

Frank got up and Washley came around and leaned against the edge of his desk. "There's a possibility your brother is dangerous. Keep in mind that he performed a terribly violent deed upon himself. How would I settle it with my conscience if I released him and he attacked you or your mother? Consider your mother. What if he turned his knife against her?"

"He doesn't look violent," Frank said. "He looks peaceful. We'll take a chance on it."

"I'm sorry," Washley said.

Shaking his head bitterly, Frank left the office. Going along Center Street he kicked a tricycle some child had left on the sidewalk, popping the spokes on its big front wheel. He stood at an intersection waiting for the light to turn green, reviewing how Washley had tangled him up in his big words like a carp in a net. The light changed and Frank crossed. There had been no traffic along either street, and he wondered why he had stood there waiting. The world was full of traffic lights, Washley being one of them.

Dora served supper in her big kitchen, which was also her living room, furnished with a sofa, a buffet, and a television set. The table showed slight touches of elegance—starched napkins and a rose in a small crystal vase. Dora set on salad, lentils, chicken fricassee, and cherry pie, saying to Frank, "The lentils are for your mother and the chicken for you. She says you haven't repented of eating meat."

"No, ma'am, not yet," he said.

"Neither have I," Dora said. "But I certainly do respect Margaret's principles."

After supper Frank inspected the family photographs on the buffet while the women washed the dishes. In one frame Nathan and Dora posed with three daughters and a son. Other frames showed the grown-up children with spouses and children of their own. A small, ornate frame held a picture of Dora and Nathan at their wedding, which Frank studied closely. The big surprise was that Nathan was almost good looking. Knowing that disgusted Frank. It was just like him to bungle things by growing old and toothless.

Dora began explaining how she, a Salt Lake girl, had come to marry Nathan Woodbarrow. They had met at the university and after they had married, he had quit college and they had moved to Springville, where he had sold real estate and had done a little speculating. They had a frame house, white with yellow trim, and every summer Dora planted borders of tulips and snapdragons and bluebells. They kept a cow and raised their own vegetables and fruit.

"When we lost that house," Dora said, "it was a bigger trial than you might think. Losing a house is almost like losing a loved one. It really is." She pulled open a drawer and found a snapshot of a small frame house surrounded by elms, which she showed to Frank and Margaret. "I don't blame Nathan. It was 1933 and lots of people lost their homes."

That was when Nathan went back to Escalante and started over. He bought the old Jamison place, the one which Frank's grandfather and grandmother had homesteaded, and tried to make a go of farming. Dora and the children moved to Provo.

"For a few summers the kids and I went to Escalante to be with Nathan. But I got so I couldn't stand it. Flies thick as a carpet on the screen door. Water from a barrel. An outhouse for sanitation. That's my failing. I'm not worthy of my pioneer ancestors. I didn't have the fortitude to live like they did. I left poor Nathan to struggle all by himself. If I had stayed by his side, if I had showed more faith in that place down there, he might have pulled through and kept it."

"Posh!" Margaret said. "Nobody can make a go of farming down there. You have to do something else besides farming like teaching school."

"Well," Dora said, "shall we have a hand or two of Rook?" She pulled a deck from a drawer and went to the table, where she began to shuffle cards.

Later Frank put down his bedroll between two bookracks in the book shop. Every time he roused, he could see a wall clock with a neon sign saying "Sanders Paper Supply." Toward morning he heard footsteps in the kitchen and then in the doorway of the shop. It was Margaret. She groped until she found a chair, which she dragged into the aisle where Frank lay.

"Are you awake?" she said.

"Only way I couldn't be is if I was dead."

"How did your visit go? What did Dr. Washley say? I decided not to ask in front of Dora. It isn't right to burden her with all our secrets."

"It didn't go good. He didn't budge an inch. He says they're going to cure Jeremy with tranquilizers. Leave him here and he'll be fine. Take him home, he'll tear us to pieces. He'll go for us with a knife."

"Go for us with a knife? That's silly."

"Sure it is. We're going to get him out of there. I've been thinking what to do next. I'm going to visit that lawyer in Richfield and see what he says."

"You'll do it, Frank, I know you will." Her voice became peevish. "Psychiatrists are strange people. This Dr. Washley is a little off the beam. You can tell it just by looking at him. It comes from being around too many crazy people, which is exactly the reason we are going to take Jeremy home. How can he help acting insane in a place like that. All those oddities you see in the day room! The stories you hear about the locked wards upstairs!"

"It's a jail; that's exactly what it is."

"But I must say, Frank, if there's anything that has brought me a little comfort in this dark, dismal time, it has been you getting straightened out and living the way a good Latter-day Saint boy ought to."

"I've been warned," Frank said. "I had a vision."

"A vision?"

"Yes, ma'am, a real one."

She was silent for a long time, then said in a hoarse whisper, "Is it too sacred to tell? Ought it be saved for a proper place?"

"It was the night after Jeremy cut himself off. I was in the back of my pickup trying to sleep. I heard the Holy Ghost, like a big bird flying overhead. Then I had a vision. It was a gunsight and a big eye watching me and a gunbarrel following me wherever I walked."

"A gunbarrel!" she gasped. She got off the chair and knelt at the head of his bed. She squeezed his hand in both of hers, whispering, "I feel the truth of your vision, Frank, I feel a confirmation. You have had a witness, no question of it. Keep it close to your heart and don't talk it around. We'll seal our lips, both of us. It's as sacred as God's name."

"God has his sight on me. It scares the liver out of me."

"Oh, no, don't be afraid!"

"Maybe God expects me to hunt for my true punishment," he said. "Like Grandma searching the sandhills."

"My goodness, that would be wonderful—your true punishment!"

"But I don't know if I'm man enough to face up to it," he said. "I've been nothing but devilish and mean all my life. It won't be easy to make up for all that backsliding."

"Be cheerful, Frank!" she said eagerly. "God loves those he chastises. He lets the others go down the wide, wicked path to hell without any worries. He has picked you out, he is calling you for something special." She pressed his hand to her lips. "Oh, my, I've got all shaky. I could sing a hymn or shout hallelujahs!"

After an early breakfast Frank drove to Draper, which was a spread-out little farm town—orchards, plowed fields, here and there a cluster of houses. The white frame house where Frank knocked was half hidden down a lane in an orchard. The woman who answered didn't fit his notion of a polygamist, being young and pretty and dressed up in heels and hose as if she was about to leave for a secretary's job in Murray or Salt Lake. She took Frank around back and showed him the empty garage where he was to stack the wheat, then led him to an old chicken coop, saying as he peered in, "That's the produce you're supposed to take." There were about fifty boxes of apples and a big mound of Hubbard squash.

Hours later, when he had pulled into Richfield, Frank looked up a lawyer named Rossler D. Jarbody, whose office was over a men and women's clothing shop on Main Street. The stairway was dark and smelly and the walls of the tiny receptionist's room were decorated with handmarks as if about once a week Jarbody let a herd of greasy-fisted kids run through. A couple of chair cushions had split, spilling mud-colored stuffing.

Frank knocked on an inner door and a voice told him to come in. Jarbody, leaning back in a swivel chair with his feet on his desk, was tall enough to play center on a basketball team. The colors of his clothes snarled and spit at each other: a royal blue suit, a purple and black polka dot tie, red and green Argyle socks.

"Don't move an inch," he said. "My fee is twenty dollars an hour. Minimum charge is five, which means you sit down in that chair right there, you pay five dollars no matter what else happens."

"Gosh," Frank said.

"Take it or leave it."

Frank looked in his wallet. "Okay," he said.

"Have a chair. Now what's on your mind?"

"I want some help. I want to get my brother out of the insane asylum."

Jarbody hauled his feet off his desk and swung around to take a good look at Frank, who went on to explain it all—Jeremy mutilating himself; the doctors at the Utah Valley hospital committing him to the state hospital without any sayso from the family; Jeremy thinking he was a girl and playing with dolls; the family, which was Frank and Margaret, wanting him home.

"If that isn't bizarre, if that doesn't beat all," Jarbody kept muttering. Then, when Frank had finished: "I'm not your man. First, I don't know anything about the legalities of mental health. That isn't my specialty and I don't hanker to get into it either. Second, I don't particularly favor lunatics. I think they ought to be kept off the street, I think the booby hatch is just exactly the right place for them." He looked at his watch. "That'll be five dollars. Stay one more minute and it goes up to ten."

"Well, what are we going to do?" Frank said. He had got watery eyed. "We've just about had all we can take. It's worse than having him die, and now we're supposed to sit back and forget about him. We're supposed to sell him off like a slave and let that dictator who runs the hospital do whatever he wants with him, which won't do him any good, I can tell you that. He ain't ever going to be what he used to be."

"Holy Moses," Jarbody said. "All right, here is some advice. There's an attorney in Salt Lake who gets into strange cases like this. His name is Algernon Bullard. He's a Gentile, he hates Mormons, at least the regular, run-of-the-mill kind. He doesn't know what the word reverence means. For a nickel he'd blow his nose on the president of the Church or one of the twelve apostles or the state governor or a county commissioner. Sometimes he defends polygamists.

Last I knew, he defended a draft dodger. Got him acquitted on a technicality. I'm going to give you his address and you can use my name as a reference."

"That's what we need, that's just exactly what we need," Frank said.

Driving south from Richfield, Frank was thinking how Jesus had said woe unto the lawyers for they lade men with burdens grievous to be borne. Jarbody's fee had come to fifteen dollars, half the amount Frank was making for a five day haul for Farley. It cheered Frank up to think maybe Jarbody would get it in the neck come Judgment Day.

Frank arrived in Panguitch in the late afternoon and stopped for a chat with Lonnie and Jessica. Lonnie said his horse was okay and invited him to stay the night. Frank was embarrassed to throw his bedroll down on Lonnie's sofa when he could go home and sleep in his own bed, but wanting company he did it anyhow.

The next morning he stopped at Farley's mercantile in Glendale. The store was dim and crowded with tall racks of cereal, canned vegetables, and soap, and for a moment Frank felt lost in the woods. In the back were four bar stools and a little counter and a grill. Bertha sat on one of the stools, embroidering.

"Farley ain't here," she said. "He's over at Alton."

"I'll just keep going then," Frank replied. "I'll make Short Creek this afternoon and get unloaded and reloaded and head off for Pioche tomorrow morning. I should be back to Alton with the hay day after tomorrow."

"How about some breakfast?"

"No, thanks. Just had some in Panguitch."

"Care for mint tea and a cookie?"

"No, ma'am. I have a weakness for strawberry soda pop."

She got a bottle of pop from a cooler and put a couple of cookies on a plate and he climbed onto a stool. She set out a cup of tea and a cookie for herself and sat one stool away from him. Straight ahead was a mirror with a Coca-Cola insignia. Bertha had a flat, pasty face and resentful little lips and she wore a faded calico dress. Frank shouldered above her by a good twelve inches. A lock of his brown hair projected over his forehead like a cantilever. He took big bites, chewed fast, and gulped his pop.

"I've never been to Short Creek before," Frank said. "I've heard about it all my life. It's almost as famous as New York City."

"Not much to see," Bertha said. "A bunch of farms, some houses, a lot of sage brush and sand."

"I understand Onis somebody or the other is the big prophet down there."

"Big prophet according to their lights. Me, I favor Justin Higgins over among the folks in Johnson Canyon. You can tell the difference when a bunch of people have really got the Spirit among them like they do over there."

She served Frank several more cookies. "One of these times when Farley walks into this store, I'm going to be gone, and that's where I'll be gone to—Johnson Canyon."

Frank scratched an ear and took another bite of cookie.

"I don't like that man. He's got an evil spirit."

"Who?"

"Farley. My so-called husband."

"He seems like a pretty nice fellow to me," Frank said.

"He seems like. Seems like and is are different as night and day. I guess you met Gomer, didn't you?"

"Yes, ma'am."

"When he took her out of a whorehouse it wasn't with my consent. If he'd asked me I'd have told him where his revelation came from. It came out of a privy pit; it came out of the heart of Satan. She was a whore then; she's a whore now. He's up there to Alton today. What's he doing? He's bedding her. Once? That ain't enough for that buck. Two, three, four times a day when he's around her."

Frank had turned red. It wasn't fit for a woman to talk this way.

Her voice deflected in odd angles of anger and spite. "Gomer's pregnant. She's three or four months along and Farley, he jumps her every chance he gets. You know what he claims? Him and her keep a tally, they mark it down on a paper every time they couple. The reason is this. She kept a count how many hellish men came to her in the whorehouses where she worked—up at Fallon, down to Caliente, who knows where else? Something like six, seven hundred. So her and Farley are undoing them all, one by one. Before he gets on top of her, they kneel down by the bedside and hold hands and say a prayer. They think God takes off one of those six or seven hundred sins every time they do it! Forgives Gomer, forgives the man who done it to her, him not even knowing he's being forgiven!"

Frank wiped his mouth on a napkin and stood up. "I surely thank you for these nice refreshments."

She stood up too. "A man don't have business having carnal knowledge of his wife unless she asks him. A woman don't have business asking him unless she wants to have a baby. Doing it when she's pregnant, that's nothing but adultery. Nothing but filth."

Frank edged toward the door and she followed. "So tell me, is it of God or of Satan what those two are doing?"

"It doesn't seem right," he said.

"That's true, true as day. It ain't right. It's stable work, it's the law of the cow and the bull, it's plain old lechery."

"I imagine that's just about the truth."

"Now I've forgot your name."

"Frank Windham."

"Yes, Frank Windham," she said. "I hope your sins don't weigh you to the earth. Whatever they are."

In Orderville, a few miles down the road, he stopped and had a chat with Leola, giving her a report on Margaret and Jeremy. Then he drove on through Carmel Junction and Kanab and across the Arizona line to Fredonia. Fredonia was the town where he and Jack and Red had gone to sin with that painted lady named Sally; also where he had kicked the stuffing out of that Forest Service fellow. He hoped God would forget all about that.

He turned off Highway 89 and headed west on a graveled road. He had to slow down to not much more than a crawl because the road, rutted and choppy as corduroy, pounded the tires and made the steering wheel lurch and swing. Mid-afternoon he topped a crest and saw far off the notorious polygamist colony of Short Creek. The rolling land bore junipers, sage brush, and scattered frost-killed fields. Here and there were houses, their metal roofs glinting in the sun, their chimneys smoking. In a barren swale stood a big white building, which might have been a church or a school. Behind everything a giant rim of red rock, stretching away east and west, cut the world in half. Without question, Short Creek was a long way from anywhere.

Frank pulled off onto a narrow side road and stopped at the first house, in front of which stood an old-time hand cranked gas pump.

A silent, unsmiling woman pointed out a house a half mile down the road. He drove on. Having knocked, he leaned on the veranda rail, slapping his gloves against his leg. A heavy woman in a long brown dress came out. Her hair, tied into a pouchy little bun in back, was luminously white. By her face, which was half pretty, she wasn't more than fifty.

"We had word from Farley you were coming. I'm Betty Bollinger. Onis Bollinger is my husband."

An old man pushed by the woman, tugging the ends of his stringy grey beard from a muffler which coiled around his neck. His soiled Army overcoat was latched by three giant safety pins.

"This is my father, Mr. Windham. His name is Osmer Jacobson. He'll show you where to put that produce in the schoolhouse basement. There isn't any light down there. There's no electricity in this town. Be careful for your head because the joists are low. Figure on supper with us. You'll hear the supper bell. Come sharp because a group of us eat in common and you've got to be on time."

The joists of the schoolhouse basement, a good foot lower than Frank's scalp, were draped with dusty ropes of cobweb. Frank didn't care. He unlashed the tarps covering the load and began to carry apple boxes, two at a time, down the stairs. Osmer took a seat on a stump at the nearby woodpile. Pretty soon school let out and dozens of happy, shouting kids milled around the truck. Some of them played on the teeter-totters and in the swings, pumping hot and wild; others chased, mostly boys after girls. Some of the girls wore duplicate dresses. It was something to see five sisters walking hand in hand, their heads going up like stairsteps from little to big, their hair braided into pigtails, their calf-length dresses cut from the same pattern and the same bolt of cloth.

After a while, when most of the kids had scattered for home, Osmer took a prune from his coat pocket, pitted it with a pocketknife, and popped it into his mouth. He gummed it with fast rolling motions of his toothless jaws, just as Nathan would have. A left-over boy, perhaps seven years old, wandered up and sat on a stump by Osmer. Orange freckles littered his nose; an inverted bowl of clipped, straw colored hair bounced above his ears.

"Here, Jimmy, eat this," Osmer said, offering him a pitted prune. "This is Jimmy Bollinger, Onis's boy by his wife that lives in Pioche."

Jimmy chewed the prune two or three times and swallowed. "Hold up there!" Osmer cried. "Get some goody out of it. Let it set on your tongue a little. You eat prunes like you was a runaway horse."

Squinting wistfully, Jimmy said, "I sure would like to sit in that truck a minute."

Frank opened the door and the boy climbed in. He seemed embarrassed for a second, then forgot everything except his daydream. Kneeling so that he could see out, he seized the steering wheel with both hands, twisting this way and that, while from his throat arose a throbbing hum, a muted motor laboring on mysterious, faraway roads.

Around seven Frank showed up for supper, which was more like a church social than a family meal. The dining room was lit by four kerosene lanterns. People had come in from other houses—six men, counting Frank; eight women; close to thirty kids. Frank met Onis Bollinger, a man nearing sixty, grey headed, lean, big nosed. Onis called on another man to say a blessing on the food, which he took a good five minutes to do, blessing the leaders of the nations and praying for a moist winter and thanking God for favorable cattle prices as well as asking him to make the food fit for consumption. Then people lined up at the serving table, chatting and smiling but not laughing much. Frank could see the real boss, at least in this room, was Betty Bollinger, who it turned out was Onis's first wife. She and another woman ladled out beans cooked with a little pork. On the trestled tables where people sat to eat their beans were platters of cornbread and butter, molasses, and milk.

Onis had Frank sit next to him and asked about his family.

"My dad was Miles Windham from Panguitch. My mother was a Jamison. Her dad was Tertullian Jamison from Escalante."

"I know all about them good people," Onis said. "I used to be bishop over in Tropic before I converted to the Principle."

He made a sign to Betty and she poured Frank another glass of milk. "I'm going to tell you about the big raid," he said. "We got raided in July of fifty-three. Governor Pyle, state of Arizona, had to make the voters think he was tough on polygamy. He got on the radio, said we were in a state of insurrection, making treason against the holy laws of Arizona. He said our wives weren't anything but whores, said we were keeping them in slavery. About a hundred officers invaded us. One bunch by the Arizona road, another by the Utah road. They came during an eclipse of the moon so it would all be a big secret. They were going to go door to door like the Gestapo and wake us up out of our sleep and arrest us. But our folks up and down the road let us know. We went over to the schoolyard, every last one of us, men, women, and kids, dressed in our Sunday clothes, and when the officers came tearing into town, making a dust so thick some of them banged up each other's cars and with their sirens screaming and their red lights flashing, we began to sing 'America.' Unconditional surrender."

A murmur went up and down the tables. Somebody said, "It made you wonder if this was America or Russia."

Frank already knew about the big Short Creek polygamy raid of 1953 because word of it had come out on all the radio stations and in all the newspapers and in the national newsmagazines.

"After a while," Onis said, "things began to look better for us. They couldn't find nobody to testify, and people from everywhere wrote letters to the Salt Lake and Phoenix newspapers about how Governor Pyle didn't have a thing over Adolph Hitler and Joseph Stalin. Also, the state got tired of paying board and room for our wives and kids. They let us men out on bail, told us they'd have us back for trial pretty soon. But they never. Some of us just picked up our wives and kids and came right back here to Short Creek."

"That's something," Frank said.

"God's looking out for us."

Slipping away from his place, Jimmy came around and leaned against Onis, who turned half about. "Go finish your supper, feller." Onis turned back to Frank. "This is my boy Jimmy. He don't mind any better than the rest of my kids."

"Him and me have already met," Frank said. "He helped me load those beans."

"What did you learn in school today?" Onis asked his son.

"There's a place called England."

"Well, that's something. Where is it?"

"I don't know."

"Maybe it's somewhere near Salt Lake City or over around Las Vegas. What do you think?"

"Likely it is," the boy nodded. "I guess that's where it is."

"It's across the Atlantic ocean, feller. Now get on back and empty that bowl."

Onis pushed a molasses dish toward Frank. "That boy don't even know where England is. Better off not knowing. The more you know about the world the more you know about sin. Isn't that about right?"

Later Frank threw down his bedroll on the pineboard floor in the big dining room. Kneeling on his bedroll to say his prayer, he asked God to look with mercy on these misguided people. He also asked God to preserve him from sorrow over Marianne. Whenever he thought about her, he felt as if he had lost a piece of himself, as if something was gone, like one of his lungs or half his liver. He said amen and got in bed. Although there was a good deal of treading around upstairs and slamming of the back door as people went out to the four-hole privy, he soon became drowsy and drifted off.

After a while he woke up sharp. It was dead dark, but he knew somebody was in the room. "What do you want?" he said, getting up onto an elbow.

"It's me."

Frank could tell it was Jimmy. "You better get back to bed."

"I got to go to the toilet."

"Don't you have a chamber pot?"

"You aren't supposed to do what I got to do in a chamber pot."

"Gosh," Frank groaned. He got up and put on his pants, coat, and shoes and the two of them groped their way outdoors.

When they came back, Jimmy said, "Can I sleep with you?"

"You better go sleep in your own bed. This floor is hard," Frank said. He was on his hands and knees, groping in the dark for his bed.

Jimmy left but shortly returned, dragging something and asking, "Where are you?"

"Right here. But you still can't sleep with me. Get back to your own bed. Your mother will get worried about you."

"She's in Pioche. Uncle Osmer told you that."

"I forgot. Who looks after you?"

"Aunt Marie."

"Well, Aunt Marie will wonder where you are." Frank sat up and rewadded his coat to make a better pillow. "Go get in bed with your dad."

"He's over to Aunt Cristobel's tonight. I think that's where he is. Maybe he's at Aunt Katherine's."

"How come you don't stay in Pioche with your mother?"

"I'm a comfort to Aunt Marie. She doesn't have any kids. She doesn't say her prayer and ask for some, I guess." He had got close and Frank could hear him spreading his blankets. He gave a sigh and became quiet. After a while he said, "Where does your mother live?"

"Right now she's in Provo. She looks after my brother who got hurt."

"I had a little brother but he died."

"That's too bad. My brother just as well be dead."

Frank could hear the boy raising and dropping an arm. After he had sighed again two or three times, his breathing became deep and regular. Frank doubled one of his own blankets and laid it over him.

Frank was on the road at sunup, having filled the gas tanks at the old fashioned pump by the house next to the graveled road. A couple of hours later he drove the truck into Hurricane and pulled onto a paved highway. He got into Cedar City at eleven and bought a strawberry soda pop to wash down the sandwiches Betty Bollinger had made him. Then he turned west on a wide graveled road headed for Nevada. Mid-afternoon, ten or twelve miles short of Panaca, he had a breakdown. As the truck was laboring up a steep hill, steam suddenly swirled from under the hood and a wet, metallic odor filled the cab. He pulled the truck onto the shoulder and got out. A radiator hose had split and hot, rusty water splashed onto the gravel below.

Frank walked toward Panaca for an hour and a half before a car came along and gave him a ride. Considering that Panaca wasn't much more than a post office and a service station, he was lucky to find a radiator hose that would fit. He had to pay for it with his own money. Then he borrowed a five gallon can, filled it with water, and got out on the road. Long after dark he caught a ride with a man who commuted once or twice a week between a mine the other side of Caliente and his home in Enterprise.

While they were riding along, Frank asked if there was still a whorehouse in Caliente.

"Sure thing, if that's what you're after," the fellow said, his voice showing he didn't have much use for whorechasers.

"I wasn't interested in patronizing the place," Frank said. "I happen to know a lady who worked there. I mean I know her in a decent way. She ain't in that line any more."

"What's she doing now?" The man's heavy work gloves and aluminum safety hat sat on the seat between him and Frank.

"She's a housewife."

"Who in heck would marry an ex-whore?"

"This here polygamist over in Kane County. He says he's making her over. Cleaning her up."

"You must be a regular Mormon," the man said. "Like me."

"That's right. I'm hauling for some fundamentalists. I never had anything to do with them before. A curious bunch, though when you get right up to a table and eat with them, they're people like anybody else."

"Sex fiends is what they are."

"I don't know about that. Some of them hold you don't get on top of your wife unless she's decided she wants a baby. It's her decision, not yours. Thinking that way, a fellow might have some long, lean times even if he had four or five wives."

"Likely story."

"What's your opinion?" Frank said. "Do you think a married couple ought to go after it when they aren't trying to get the lady pregnant? Say she was already pregnant. What about it then?"

They could hear the rumble of tires and the clatter of gravel against fenders. "It happens all the time," the man said. "It seems like a man just can't leave his wife alone."

"It seems like to me God wouldn't favor it," Frank said. "The New Testament says if you look on a woman to lust after her, you have committed adultery with her already in your heart. It says if your right eye offends you, pluck it out. If your right hand bothers you, cut it off."

"You're not supposed to take that serious."

"You find funny things in the Scriptures," Frank went on. "The Old Testament says he that is wounded in the stones or hath his privy member cut off, shall not enter into the congregation of the Lord."

"My golly, that's a joke!"

"I don't know," Frank said. "I've got a brother who went crazy and cut himself off. Nuts and pecker, the whole shebang. Nothing left."

"You're kidding, buddy. Don't fill me up with crap like that."

"It's so. He's nothing but a steer."

The man dropped Frank off at the truck and drove away. The sky was black and a cold desert wind blew. Having no flashlight, Frank worked by feel under the hood. He skinned his knuckles a half dozen times because his pliers kept slipping off the spring clamps that held the burst hose. By the time he had finished he was chilled through. He filled the radiator and started the engine and nursed it into a steady roar.

Just then a vehicle came over the crest of the hill, its lights on high beam. When it got close, it slowed and then came to a stop directly in front of the truck. A man climbed onto the running board and Frank rolled down the window.

"Got a jack we could borrow?"

"What's the trouble?"

Suddenly the man put the muzzle of a pistol into Frank's face. "Cut the motor and set your brakes. Then get out of that cab."

A moment later Frank was lying face down in the road with the man standing over him. "Listen, you son of a bitch, my buddy is going to back our truck up to yours, and then you're going to get up and start loading those sacks off your truck onto our truck real fast. Real fast! Because if you don't load them real fast, I'll kick your teeth in." He shoved the pistol into Frank's neck. "I'll kick them in and make you swallow them."

Frank climbed onto the trailer, blinded by the beam of a flashlight. He lifted a sack, carried it to the end of the trailer, then stopped.

"Get a move on," a new voice said.

"I can't see."

A light fell onto the bed of the waiting truck, and Frank saw he had to step down six inches. "Okay, mister," the new voice said, "you've got your bearings. Now hustle."

They kept shouting for him to move faster and by the time he had finished, he was panting hoarsely.

"Jump down, feller, and get in the cab. Leave the door open and just tuck your arms into the spokes of that steering wheel."

One of them tied his wrists to the steering column. "That hurts," Frank said. "You're cutting off my circulation."

"That tears me to pieces," the man said. He punched Frank in the mouth. "If I had my way, we'd cut your goddamned balls off

and stuff them down your throat. How'd that be for cutting off
your circulation?"

They raised the hood and Frank could hear them ripping out
the wiring. One of them came back to the cab. "Here's your final
instructions. Don't be dumb and get loose too fast. You catch up
with us and we'll blow your head off. My advice is you don't look
up the sheriff. He don't want to hear about it. And pass the word
along when you get to them Bible pounders on that ranch above
Pioche that you polygamists have got a lesson to learn. You ain't
wanted in Lincoln County. Tell them to count on more of the same."

"I don't have no part with those polygamists," Frank said. "I'm
just driving for them."

"Tough luck, buddy. Don't be so stupid next time."

The men got into their truck, and Frank watched their taillights
become smaller and smaller and disappear over the hill. Though
still sweating, he was shivering violently. He had a quick fantasy
about grabbing the gun away from the fellow and pulling his head
and shoulders inside the cab and banging his face as hard as he could
on the steering wheel twenty or thirty times. When the other fellow
came dashing over to see what was going on, Frank could see himself
pushing the pistol out the window and firing so close that it tore
his face off.

Then he became hysterical because all that was nothing but a wild,
vain fancy, and here he was tied up for the night on a lonesome
road without a coat and the temperature bound to go below thirty-
two. He shouted and twisted and jerked until the bristling hemp
had rubbed his wrists raw and he could feel a cool evaporation trickl-
ing down his hands.

He heard a flutter of wings. Inside his belly he was sucked
up into nothing. He couldn't take a vision tied up like this. He
had to be loose and free for running in case it was something he
couldn't bear.

He squinted his eyes tight and waited, but nothing came to him
except a picture of his poor bloody wrists tied to the steering post.
So it was nothing to worry about, just a false alarm. But the picture
wouldn't go away. The steering post grew and grew until it looked
like a gate post, and there Frank stood with his wrists tied, hugging
the post as if he loved it.

A baler ram cranked in his chest. It was a true vision; God had showed him his true punishment. He would have to study how to slice the fat off his belly, the vanity off his back. He would have to sell his horse and saddle, trade off his pickup, get rid of his gun, do away with his fancy boots and jeans and carved leather belt and ten gallon hat, and tell Margaret to take back her cows or let him sell them for her. He would have to give up roping and riding and hunting. That was it exactly, the way his life was supposed to be, sucked out and ciphered down to zero.

One car went by in the night. Frank leaned his forehead against the horn button, but the car didn't stop. Just after dawn another car drove by. A hundred yards past, it stopped and backed up. It was the man from Enterprise on his way back to the mine near Caliente. He pulled open the truck door and took a look.

"Still here, huh? I guess you couldn't get her started."

"I've been hijacked," Frank said. "I've been tied to this steering post all night."

"I'll be danged," the man said, stepping around to view the empty trailer.

At a ranch on the other side of Pioche, Frank had a conference with Tina Bollinger, Onis's wife, who appeared to be in charge of things. A seamed, puffy goiter showed above her collar. Her eyelids drooped a little as if she had lost her endurance and thought only of sleep. "I don't know where we'll make up for those beans from," she said. "But you just well load up the hay and take it over to Farley. We sure can't eat hay."

She put on a coat and climbed into the truck with him, and they followed a winding two-track lane through the junipers, emerging where a stack of baled hay bordered a stubbled field. She lifted her skirt and climbed onto the trailer, ready to position bales as Frank threw them on.

"I know your little boy Jimmy," he said.

"I expect he is doing fine. I haven't seen him in some time."

"Seems to be. It isn't any of my business, but I was wondering how long he'll stay over there in Short Creek."

"He'll stay over there as long as Marie wants him. Which will be till he's grown up, I imagine. Marie don't have any children so I lent her my boy. There's nothing like plural marriage to beat the selfish out of you. If you want these shoes I'm wearing, you can have them. So what do I care if those beans are stolen? We'll just do without beans this winter, won't we?"

The truck was loaded by five. Frank decided to sleep three or four hours and leave in the dark for Utah. Tina let him throw down his bedroll on a cot on her back porch. When he woke, he had no idea how long he had slept. He went into the kitchen, where a fancy cut-glass lamp burned on a bare, grease-spotted table. Tina gave him a bowl of cereal and a glass of milk. The room smelled of burned kerosene. From outside came faint sounds—the lowing of a cow, the barking of a dog. Something went round and round in his head like a runaway clock hand, making him wish he hadn't got out of bed.

He arrived at Farley's ranch mid-afternoon, having been delayed by the overheating engine on the long, switchbacked climb over Cedar Breaks. No one came from the house as he backed the trailer into the stackyard and went to work unloading the hay. When he had finished, he went to the house and knocked. Hearing a crying child, he pushed open the door and saw little Brackley Vinharth belted into his high chair. As Frank unstrapped him and picked him up, he bellowed like a dehorned calf.

The table was set for three and a pot of soup simmered on the stove. Holding Brackley in one arm, he carried the pot to the table and set it on a pad. He sat on a chair and ladled a bowl of soup, which was potatoes, onions, and cream seasoned with black pepper. He took up a spoonful, blew on it, and sipped at it.

Brackley was still wailing. Frank pulled out a handkerchief and wiped the child's nose. He spooned more soup and blew again. "Here," he said, "you try this one. It's real tasty."

Brackley stopped crying, puckered his lips, and took a tiny taste. Frank blew again and the boy opened wide, taking in the entire spoonful. "We're in business," Frank said cheerfully. He began trading off, first giving himself a spoonful, then giving Brackley one.

Somebody made a noise in a back room and shortly Gomer and Farley emerged, half dressed and tousle haired.

"I'm here with the hay," Frank said. "Also, me and this boy are having dinner."

"Knew it was you," Farley said. "Could hear you out there unloading."

Gomer took Brackley and hugged him, crooning, "Auntie Gomer loves you." Turning to Frank, she explained, "Silas came by and took Judy and the other kids to St. George yesterday to see the dentist. They won't be back till tomorrow. Brackley's staying with me."

She put the boy in the high chair, tied on a bib, and gave him a bowl of soup. She ladled soup for Farley and herself and refilled Frank's bowl. Farley finished tying his shoelaces and said, "Had a good haul, I hope. No trials or tribulations or anything."

"Lots of trials and tribulations," Frank said. "I'm sorry to tell you about it. The beans got hijacked. Stolen, every last sack." He stopped eating and told the story.

"Drat," Farley said, as melancholy as a beagle. "A bunch of poor, rocky beans don't mean nothing to people like that. They just want to do us a dirt. Now the whole system has busted down. Without the beans, the hay ain't paid for. Without the hay, the wheat ain't. Without the wheat, the apples and squash ain't. So now what we going to do?"

"Maybe we should fast and pray," Gomer said.

"At least we'll get to do some fasting," Farley grumbled. "Anyhow, Frank, bring in your bedroll and stay the night. In the morning we'll load more wheat on the trailer. Got a deal worked out with a bunch over in Huntington Canyon. They mine coal, and that's what we could use a little of."

"Sorry," Frank said, "I'm quitting."

"Can't quit," Farley said. "Had a vision, saw you doing a work of great mercy, saw you helping out these poor polygamists who don't have nobody else who gives a damn about them."

"One haul is all the mercy I got," Frank said. "I was hoping you'd pay me off and we could drive down to Glendale tonight so I could get my pickup and go home."

"That's another problem," Farley said. "I was hoping you'd hold off till after the next haul for your pay. Could write you a check. It'd bounce. Got no money. Cold out. Think I see some coming in next week."

Gomer brought a cake from the cupboard. "Judy made it," she said, serving each of them a piece. "She used dried apples and raisins. It's good."

"Darned sorry about not paying you off," Farley said. "Sure will do it. First chance I get."

Frank glanced at Farley, who was hunched over his plate, scooping in cake like a starved man. He reminded Frank of a dairy bull—big in the shoulders, smaller in the haunches. Frank glanced at Gomer. Her skin, almost the color of olive oil, matched her bronze hair. When she moved, her breasts swayed beneath her robe, reminding him of Marianne. God moved in mysterious ways. He visited a man and fled, leaving behind signs, riddles, visions, wonders. His meanings came clear strangely, at odd times and places. Frank knew he wouldn't make love to a woman again in his whole life.

6.

Farewell, All
Sinful Pleasures

In December Frank found a steady job driving a delivery truck for Ashael Lamson, who ran a bakery and a wholesale grocery operation in Richfield. A few days before he began work for Ashael, he made another attempt to pry Jeremy from the state hospital, driving to Salt Lake and calling on Algernon Bullard, the feisty Gentile lawyer whom Jarbody had recommended. Bullard sat in his ninth floor office, comfortably tilted in a padded, high backed chair, puffing calmly on a fat cigar and listening intently to every word Frank said.

"Is this Dr. Washley a Mormon?"

"Yes, sir."

"Okay, Mr. Windham, you're on," Bullard said. "We'll go for Brother Washley's throat. Now the more involved I get, the more money it's going to cost you. It's thirty dollars for a letter. It's a couple of hundred if I have to go down to Provo in person. Cheapest thing is for you to use my name and see if you can scare him into letting your brother go. Here's my card."

"Thank you, sir."

"Now, don't get wild with your threats. Just tell him the next step is you'll go to court and Algernon Bullard is the lawyer who's going to help you do it. Remind him your mother never gave her consent. Emphasize that fact. Tell him you intend to make that a big issue in court."

It was snowing lightly while Frank drove from Salt Lake to Provo. Underneath the skiff of new snow the streets had patches of black ice left over from earlier storms. Dora gave him an affectionate greeting and fed him a sandwich. He walked to Penney's and between customers had a good chat with Margaret. Then he walked to the hospital where, after visiting with Jeremy and waiting an additional hour and a half, he finally got in to see Washley.

"I've come for my brother," he said, shaking the director's hand. "I'll just take him along with me today."

Washley's pencil-line mustache seemed to waver slightly, like a bit of yarn floating in a bathtub. "Not possible, not at all possible," he said. "He is still a profoundly psychotic personality. In fact, he is a rather discouraging case. We have tried three kinds of tranquilizers. I can't honestly say that we have broken through the psychosis in even the most rudimentary way."

"So we just as well take him home and see what we can do."

Washley cocked one leg over the other, arched his thin, tapered fingers, gazed at the light fixture, and began to instruct Frank on the technicalities of Jeremy's case. It was uncanny how some aspects of it fit the classical definition of an Oedipal complex. It did appear that between Jeremy and his mother there had been a fundamental transversion of identities, or, if you wished, a kind of exchanging of roles, the son behaving as the mother, the mother as the son, or, as the daughter, since it appeared that Jeremy's view of himself as male had always been tenuous and weak, largely overcrowded by his desire, or his mother's desire, that he be female.

Listening to all that, Frank felt as if Jeremy and his mother and he himself, for that matter, were as dead and finished as so many rotten carp in a slough. Big words were like sticks and stones; somebody who knew how to use them could pound a man hard.

"This here is my lawyer," he said, handing over Bullard's card. "I aim to have Jeremy out. I hope you'll just up and release him the regular way. But if you don't, I'm going to court over it."

As soon as Margaret arrived home in January, Frank became serious about renouncing the vanities of the world. The first vanity that went was gluttony, because anyone who ate Margaret's cooking regularly was eating for mere survival. She had recently decided that sweets were partly to blame for Jeremy's problem, which meant a ban on all of them, even honey, corn syrup, and sorghum. Eggs were also partly to blame for Jeremy's tragedy.

"Considering that eggs come from inside the chicken," she told Frank one early morning as she served him a breakfast of cracked wheat mush and milk, "I'm surprised how people can stomach them. Have you ever noticed that a fresh laid egg is wet? Ugh. Also, have you noticed the unlaid eggs in a slaughtered hen? They are leathery."

So Frank was eating grains and fruits and vegetables, cooked and raw, and also kelp imported from the ocean and alfalfa sprouts that Margaret grew in a south window. When once in a while something tasted good, he felt guilty about it. He kept himself hungry enough to get down Margaret's other meals by giving away his lunch every day to a fellow who worked in Ashael's bakery.

Another vanity Frank got rid of was his gelding, Booger, which he traded to Theodore Amsdew for a low grade milk cow. He also turned his pickup over to Leslie Holway, who ran a Texaco station at the north end of town. Leslie took over the payments and swapped Frank two tons of weedy hay for his equity. Frank suffered every time he saw Leslie driving his shiny blue pickup around town, and he felt as if he had played Judas to Booger by putting him into the hands of an Amsdew. There never had been an Amsdew who knew how to handle livestock. Like all the other Amsdews, Theodore stunk and had a grimy, pasty skin that wouldn't come clean with any amount of scrubbing.

Frank gave his saddle and lariat to Jake Rollins to help pay for winter pasture for his cows and bull. He also gave his thirty-thirty to Red as a gift. He thought for a long time before doing that, lying awake nights remembering all the innocent animals he had slaughtered just because he liked to see them hunch and die. Red had quit running around with Jack Simmons and had gone to Cedar City to the junior college for fall quarter, which made Frank think Red might use the rifle more righteously than he had. He gave his fancy western clothes to Jack—his best cowboy boots, twill pants, pearlbuttoned shirts, and wide brimmed Stetson. That took a lot of thinking too, because for all Frank knew, his fancy clothes would just egg Jack on in his waywardness. Jack cussed, boozed, and ran wild with the girls more than ever, not having sense enough to know that God had a gunsight trained on him and eventually would boil up and pull the trigger.

"Well, bless my old pink asshole," Jack said the night Frank brought the fancy clothes out to the Simmonses' ranch near Henrieville. "What are you giving me all this stuff for? I can't just take it from you like this. I oughta pay for it." He stood in the living room in his jeans, undershirt, and stockings, a girlie magazine in his hand.

"I want you to have them free," Frank said. "I'm through using them and it'd make me feel better knowing somebody I like has got them."

"Holy cack," Jack said, rubbing a shirt collar between his fingers. He put on the shirt and buttoned it, pulled on the boots, placed the Stetson on his head, and clattered back and forth across the wood floor. Peering into a small mirror above the sofa, he said, "Ain't that nice? Frank, you old buzzard, you are one fine buddy, that I gotta say."

"They look danged good on you."

"They do so. Danged good."

Frank took a chair and they talked a little about what they had been doing lately. Every minute or so things got quiet and they sat rubbing their chins or scratching their collarbones till one of them thought of something else to say.

"These here nice clothes you've give me are for goodby, ain't they?" Jack said. "We really ain't close friends no more."

"Sure we're close friends."

"The things I've been hearing must be true. The word around is you've repented and got righteous. And Red, why, hell, Frank, he's a candidate to be bishop. Last time I tried to entice him off for a frolic, he delivered me a sermon. My gosh, a real sermon! Now is the time to trim your lamp with oil, he says; now is the time for working out your salvation in fear and trembling. Son of bitch, if that ain't something!"

"Really, now, I better be going," Frank said, standing and putting out his hand.

"It's just like a funeral, Frank. It's like you guys had died."

On a Sunday evening in late January Frank milked his cow, which he had named Chloe after old Grandma Amsdew, who was long dead but still talked about in Panguitch. The evening was cloudy and the brisk, cold wind smelled of snow. Chloe's ancestors might have included Holsteins, but the line had gone to seed in this cow, which was stunted and bony and had bulging, spooky eyes and the temperament of a blasting cap. Her flappy, deflated udder held a scant two quarts of watery milk, and her teats were like sausage tips filled with gristle—short, thick, and hard to squeeze.

Frank drove her into the milk shed, where he had hung a lantern, locking her head in the stanchion and chaining her legs with hobbles to keep her from catapulting him through the roof. During the afternoon she had lain in wet muck, sheathing her flank with manure, which Frank peeled away with a putty knife. He washed her udder with warm water from a pail and settled down on a one-legged stool. When he gripped her teats, she raised her tail and humped her back, threatening to urinate. He eased off on her teats, whereupon she eased off too because she was too smart to squander her last defense.

"For crying out loud," he said, "go on and pee. Get it over with."

But she wouldn't and after about the tenth time, he stood and smashed the stool to pieces on her backbone. She bellowed and lunged and collapsed in a heap. He unhobbled her legs and levered her up with a four-by-four timber, feeling terrible for half killing a poor dumb brute. He peeled off more manure with his putty knife and washed her udder again. He squatted on his heels and gripped the pail between his knees. He stripped down hard on her teats, and jets of milk rang in the empty pail. Soon the milk foamed and the jets streamed down with a quiet, rhythmical swish. Chloe rolled her eyeballs and trembled, but she didn't dance, hump, or lift her tail. Frank wasn't feeling so bad now, having decided that splintering a milk stool on a cow's back was an important part of animal husbandry. Furthermore, it fit in well with the way God treated human beings. He broke up furniture on their heads, so to speak, but it was for the good purpose of making Christians of them.

Somebody in a rattling truck had pulled up in front of the house. A door slammed and footsteps came down the driveway. The corral gate scraped open and the footsteps sloshed in the muck of the corral. It was Bishop Bidley. "What I have come over for tonight," he said from the doorway, "is I and the stake president have recently put our heads together and come up with the idea it's time to advance you in the Priesthood. You might just as well be an Elder instead of a Priest, and President Ehrlinde says let's get on with it and ordain you next Sunday after Sacrament Meeting."

"Maybe we ought to wait a while," Frank said.

"What for?"

"I'm still working on straightening myself out."

"Who ain't?"

"Why don't you just tell me to go move Casto Bluff with a shovel and a wheelbarrow?"

"You'll grow into it. Getting advanced in the Priesthood isn't that big a thing."

Frank and the bishop walked down the driveway and said goodby at the back door. Frank went in, washed his hands, fitted a clean white cloth over the lip of the pail, and strained the milk into a shallow pan. He rinsed the cloth and the pail and carried the pan to a cupboard.

Margaret had set out bread and cold milk for Sunday supper. Before eating they had family prayer, kneeling with their elbows propped on chair seats. Margaret asked Frank to pray. At the table, she said the blessing on the food. Then she asked, "Who was that out at the corral with you?"

"Bishop Bidley."

"What did he want?"

"He has in mind to ordain me an Elder next Sunday."

"It's about time," she said. "I've fretted they might hold it against you for running wild this past year or two." She cut another slice of bread and crumbled it into her bowl of milk. On the breast of her blue Sunday dress she had pinned a brooch of plated gold. "Well, an Elder!" she exclaimed. "That does give me satisfaction."

While he was helping her wash the dishes, the phone rang. "Oh, my, oh, my," she muttered into the mouthpiece. When she had hung up, she said, "Your uncle Salsifer is very sick. He began to bleed from the bowels about three this afternoon. Helen put him in the car and took him to Richfield. From what she said on the phone they're working on him right now. Transfusions and such things."

After supper Frank went out into the snowstorm that had just begun and got an armload of firewood. He stoked the stove in the living room until the fire danced and rumbled behind its isinglass window. Seated on the sofa, Margaret stitched on the patchwork quilt top which she called her memory quilt because each of the irregular pieces had been cut from cloth belonging to a loved one, living or dead.

"Here," she said, pointing to a bit of blue and yellow plaid, "this was cut from a shirt Salsifer had when he was in high school. Poor, dear Salsifer! I have a feeling he'll surely die."

From time to time she glanced at Frank, who sat at the oak secretary, copying from his grandmother's journals. There were five of the small clothbound notebooks in which Jerusha had scribbled with a smudging pencil. They had lain for many years in the bottom of a small trunk, first in the attic of Jerusha's house in Orderville, then in the basement of Margaret's house in Panguitch.

"I want to you to see Mother's journals," Margaret had said to Frank on the first Sunday after she had come back from Provo. She led him into the basement and unlocked the old trunk. It held other keepsakes too—a moth-eaten blanket; a ruffled temple dress of white satin, now turned yellow; a plated, oddly dented table spoon; a collection of tiny ceramic animals. The five notebooks were tied into a bundle by a strip of blue cloth.

"These are a sacred writing," Margaret said as she untied the strip. "Mother was tuned to the other world. She was so spiritual, she had dreams and visions and promptings. She wrote them down in these little books. They are a private revelation for us, a family Scripture."

The journals weren't easy to read. The pencil lead had blurred; Jerusha's l's and d's were exactly alike; sometimes she had been in a hurry and straightened out curves and bumps, turning an entire word into a wavy horizontal line. But after he had spent four or five evenings browsing, Frank figured out the handwriting. Most of the entries were commonplace, telling about mending Salsifer's pants and Margaret's smocks or making a dozen loaves of wheat bread, half of them for barter, or brooding a clutch of white ducks or catching suckers in an irrigation ditch. But some of the entries had character and authority and he carefully copied them onto lined paper.

So on the snowy Sunday evening in late January he labored over a couple of entries, frowning and biting his eraser and printing each word in block letters since his own cursive writing was no improvement on Jerusha's. Margaret looked up frequently from her stitching, waiting for him to read to her. "Okay," he said at last, "listen to this one."

Aug 12th 1899 today my little doter Lucy Belle is much
on my mind, it being her deathday a day for solemn reflec-
tions. I had a dream it has been two months about, the
night of her birthday she would have been eight years of
age. In my vision I saw her opposite on a river bank,
the flowing water seperated us, I called she did not answer
did not seem to see me. I woke fearful and asked God
for an interpretation but did not think I saw any. I have
been plaged with fear she is alone on the other side a false
interpretation. Today churning butter a true interpretation stole on me. She wants baptism, she cannot go into
the waters being dead God gave me heart to know this
is my duty. I will go to the pools of the creek privitly lest
I cast perls before swine & will lay myself beneath the
water for her.

"That's so beautiful, that's so wonderful," Margaret said. She
wiped her eyes and blew her nose and tried to stitch, still muttering, "So spiritual, so spiritual."

"Do you want to hear this other one?" he asked.

"Oh, yes, I'm so interested in all of them."

"It embarrasses me some. It seems awfully private."

"Good heavens, go on and read it. Nothing Mother wrote could
offend a righteous heart."

October 4th 1899: Tertullian my beloved husband took
leave of me this morning after a visit of four days, he came
late with many apologies, it being hard to come over the
mountain to Orderville when crops in Escalant are in need
of harvesting. I said I wasnt a jealous woman, didnt keep
track of days he spent with Cynthia, not now or ever, I
said it was acceptable to me if she had more of him than
me, I know he is a duteous man. Rested together these
four nights chastely.

"There's a saint for you," Margaret said. "Father neglected
her criminally, yet she never complained. She was so generous,
so forgiving."

"I guess Grandpa had to stay where the crops were, didn't he?"

"Certainly. I never said anything else. But when the courts ordered men to keep their wives in separate houses, it was always the second wife who had to move."

"I thought Grandma liked living in Orderville."

"Well, certainly she did. But Father didn't agree to Orderville all at once. At first he put Mother and her children out on the ranch in a two room shack. That was me and Salsifer and Andrew and Lucy Belle. And that's where Andrew and Lucy Belle died. Rosie and Lewis died before she moved out to the ranch. That house on the ranch was nothing but a two room shack."

"I know," Frank said. "The foundation is still there on Wesley's place." He glanced again at the sheet on which he had transcribed the entries. "Grandma says they rested together these four nights chastely."

"Certainly," Margaret said. "I will say this for Father: he honored a woman's delicacy." She held a piece of cloth against a blank in the quilt top and trimmed it with scissors. "My advice for you regarding intimate things after you are married is to respect your wife's feelings. I believe women are more spiritually attuned, they are more naturally pure than men."

"I'm not getting married. It isn't on the books for me."

Margaret snorted. "Of course you're getting married. Everybody should have an eternal mate. That's part of the Gospel. Besides, God didn't give us any other way to have children."

"It isn't my calling to have kids."

"Oh, I do count on you having some children, Frank. What about Leola's children and Susan's? Where would our family be without them? We'd be a dead end, wouldn't we?"

Frank put down his sheets and pencil. "I feel like I've been told and instructed, I've been set apart. God means for me not to get married."

She lined up two pieces of fabric and began to stitch, her lips pursed skeptically. Frank shifted his chair and leaned forward, earnest and eager. "God blessed me with lust. He made me rich with lust. What for? So I could overcome it, so I could conquer it."

"Gracious, such words!" Her face slowly coloring, she squinted and turned the block in her hands round and round. "You no more than any other man," she said at last. "Lust is any man's nature."

"All I know is there isn't any in between for me. God said to me, I've called you out of the world, so cut off your lust, root it out, turn your back on it, be as a little child, be like Jesus, be perfect."

"I can hardly get hold of all this."

"You don't have to get hold of anything. Just stop talking about when I get married. I'm not getting married."

When she spoke again it was low and solemn. "I have to hand it to you, Frank. I never thought you'd be the one who'd come forward and be spiritual. But there it is, yes, there it is. It's a noble purpose you've got. You have your grandmother in you, no question of it. If you can do it, Frank, if you can make it, you'll be too good for this earth, you'll be an angel, not a man."

Frank felt proud but not for long. In bed asleep he had a dirty dream. He saw Marianne dressed in shorts and halter sitting on the edge of the ranchhouse table. With a brazen smile she unlatched her halter and dropped it at his feet. She seemed so real that when he woke up, pumping his penis like a churn handle, he could hardly believe it was a dream. He got out into the dark, cold room, stripped off his union suit, and sopped the semen off himself. He threw the underwear on the floor and got back in bed naked and shivering. He went to sleep, putting off the reckoning of his depravity until four o'clock, when he got up for his day's work.

He milked his cow, got in wood for the day, and ate breakfast in a hurry because six inches of wet snow had fallen and he had to leave earlier than usual for Richfield. He followed the county snowplow, driving carefully and thinking about masturbating in the middle of the night when his Christian will was dead and gone. The deed slipped and spun in his mind like truck tires in a mucky corral. Sometimes as he drove wide awake down the highway and saw a crevice in a rocky canyon, he remembered the crevice between Marianne's legs. Even among the clean, pure scenes of Nature he couldn't have decent thoughts, God having arranged Nature so that it showed a man back his own dirty mind.

At the Richfield city limits, he stopped briefly to put on a tie, part of the delivery uniform which Ashael had required him to buy, it being Ashael's theory that delivery men were more responsible and energetic when they had to pay for their own uniforms. On the back of his coat—a brown aviator's jacket with an imitation fur collar—black letters spelled out "Lamson Distribution" and "Harvest

Bread Bakery." The same words were painted in red on Ashael's trucks and on a sign in front of his big brick building, which was both a warehouse and a bakery.

Frank backed up his truck to the loading dock where two other trucks were already parked. As he went inside, he could hear Ashael clanging on a big iron triangle to announce the Monday morning rally for his employees. In the warehouse walkway, surrounded by stacks of flour, shortening, canned vegetables, and packaged notions, Frank joined the other employees—two truck drivers, a secretary, a warehouse man, a dough mixer, a baker, a packager, and a pots and pans scrubber. First they sang a verse of "America" and pledged allegiance to a little desk flag that had been placed on a stack of canned peas. The dough mixer, a hefty woman named Aramissa Kranpitz, offered a lengthy opening prayer and the secretary handed Ashael a clipboard with the rally agenda.

He glanced at the clipboard and returned it, then commenced pacing back and forth, swinging his arms and muttering, warming up like an athlete before strenuous exercise. A tall, bony man with a head domed like a fire hydrant, he wore the same uniform his drivers wore. He began to orate. "Our new Fluffy Harvest Bread is selling like hotcakes. I have advertised it in all the newspapers and it's catching on, just like I said it would. We're proud of that bread. Aramissa here took a special trip up to Salt Lake and learned a few things and we got some tricky yeast and a new high-powered mixer, and, ladies and gentlemen, there isn't a bakery in the United States can put out a fluffier, lighter loaf than Lamson's Harvest Bread Bakery. Now, you drivers, push that bread. I want sales up, up, up. Also, please remember, we've got a wholesale special on canned asparagus and green beans. Push those products."

Afterward, while Frank and the other drivers stocked their trucks, Ashael shoveled snow from the dock, pausing a moment to call to Frank, "Be sure to put in some extra of those Fluffy Harvest loaves."

"Sure will," Frank said. Actually he was down on the new bread, which lumped up in his mouth and stuck to his teeth. It was all froth and dead air space, something you could insulate sleeping bags and winter coats with.

"Moreover," Ashael said, pushing a shovelful of snow off the dock, "Mrs. Rasbuttar down in Joseph reports you don't wear your tie when you deliver to her store."

"It must have slipped my mind to put it on," Frank said, tugging his tie up a little tighter.

"Also, I'm disappointed about the number of new deliveries we aren't picking up over on Highway 91. Didn't we set a goal for you? Didn't we say you were going to stop and ask in three new stores each day you drive down that route?"

"Yes, sir."

On Mondays, Wednesdays, and Fridays Frank delivered south on Highway 89 as far as Panguitch, then east on Highway 12 past Bryce Canyon to Escalante, with an extra leg out to Boulder on Mondays. On Tuesdays and Thursdays he followed the state road over the mountain to Highway 91 and went south through Beaver and Cedar City.

"All right," Ashael said, "wear your tie and smack 'em hard. Let's show some corporate pride."

"Yes, sir, I'll keep on my tie and I'll drop in on some new stores tomorrow when I head over that way. And on Thursday too."

"Atta boy!" Ashael said. "The Lamson way, bigger every day."

Frank returned to the bakery to pick up a sheet cake for a retirement party at the courthouse in Junction. Aramissa Kranpitz was having her daily argument with the pots and pans scrubber, a runty man named Billy Walters, who was a Mason. Aramissa lived in Monroe with a demented sister named Rendella, who pushed a wheelbarrow cross-country collecting junk and badmouthing the authorities of church, nation, and county. Aramissa stood six foot three and had calves and biceps like fence posts. She was good at making dough, so fast and efficient, in fact, that Ashael wouldn't rein her in, and she handed out orders and opinions to the other workers like a Marine sergeant.

Frank set his lunch sack above the sudsy sink where Billy was scrubbing a mixing bowl. "There you go. An extra lunch."

"Oh, wow," Billy said, "thanks a whole lot! Your mother sure makes fine sandwiches. I keep telling Jenny we'll have to get her recipe for meat spread."

It wasn't meat spread, it was ground soybean loaf mixed with vegetable oil and sage. It tasted like chicken mash, but that didn't matter to Billy, who was gaining weight eating two lunches every day. Billy's teeth were crooked and overlapped and his throat was patchy with whiskers he had missed when shaving.

"I was just showing Billy this nice little book," Aramissa said to Frank. She held out a thin old volume titled *Masonry Revealed, or The Connivances of a Subtile and Treacherous People.*

"It a damn lie, nothing but a big damn lie," Billy said. He had a high voice which turned into a squeak when he got excited.

Aramissa, wearing a white bakery dress and apron, leaned her chunky posterior against a mixing table. "Now listen to what Mr. Isaac Q. Whartmither says about the Masons. 'There is little doubt that a general influx of Masons into a country condemns that country to internal dissension and moral paralysis.' That sounds about right, don't you think so, Frank? Sevier County can't quite get on its feet due to all the Masons running around."

"There ain't but nine of us," Billy said.

"Maybe that's nine too many. Now," she said, leafing on, "this chapter is called 'Secret Signs and Symbols Unveiled.' Look at this here drawing. Two fellers hugging up like loveydoveys. The signs of fellowship, foot to foot, knee to knee, chest to chest, hand to back, cheek to cheek. I declare if they don't look like a couple of homos!"

"Ha! You Mormons stole your temple ceremony from us Masons. Joseph Smith was a Mason and that's what he did, he stole the temple ceremony."

Aramissa whacked him on the head with the book. "You keep the name of Joseph Smith out of your vile mouth."

"What I want to know," Billy said, "is how come you Mormons wear them funny little green aprons in your temple."

Aramissa said, "You just shut up about things you don't have no business talking about."

"If that ain't silly, them funny little green aprons."

"It ain't for you to make light of sacred things," she said, hot as a blow torch. She grabbed a long handled brush, swirled it in the sink, and scrubbed it through his hair. He shouted, scooped up sudsy water in a two quart measure, and splashed it down her cleavage. She squalled and made a lunge for him. He dashed for the men's rest room and locked himself in. She pounded on the door with the brush, shouting, "You just well come out of there. I'll get you sooner or later."

Before he left Richfield, Frank stopped at the hospital, a single storey frame building, to see how his uncle Salsifer was doing. With Salsifer were Helen and Ammon, who was another of his sons.

Salsifer appeared to be asleep, his head on double pillows, his face sunken, grey, and whiskery. An oxygen tube ran up one nostril; blood and glucose dripped through a tube into his arm.

Helen said, "I'm real glad you came," and then, as she hugged Frank, whispered in his ear, "You won't ever see him alive in this world again." She wore shoes with run-over heels and no stockings; her dress, once blue, had faded to a color close to grey.

Ammon shook Frank's hand and said, "As soon as they get the ambulance gassed up, we're taking off with him for Salt Lake. They're going to cut out his big gut."

"He hasn't stopped bleeding all night," Helen explained, "though they are keeping ahead of it with transfusions."

"You showed up just when I needed you," Ammon said. "I want some help giving him a blessing."

Ammon was a turkey grower and an elementary school teacher in Manti—short, stocky, and bald like his father. Little blue veins branched across his cheeks and he had a ruddy dewlap under his chin. He spilled a drop of consecrated oil on Salsifer's head and said a prayer of anointing. Frank crowded close, joining in laying on hands while Ammon said another prayer sealing the anointing and telling his father God would comfort him and ease his pain. Salsifer's eyes remained shut; his mouth was open, his teeth gone, his breath sour.

"Squeeze his hand," Helen said. "I think he knows when you touch him."

Frank squatted and took his hand whereupon Salsifer coughed and said, "Dad, is that you, Dad?"

"This ain't your dad. It's Frank, Margaret's boy. I'm driving out on a delivery run and I wanted to stop and see how you were doing."

"Frank?" Salsifer had opened his eyes. "Frank, the roper. The one who drags the calves in so the others can brand them."

"That's me."

"The cattleman."

"No more. I've given that up."

"I thought you was Dad," Salsifer said. He lifted his head off the pillow and stared across the room. "Well, there he is now. Dad!" His head fell back and he closed his eyes. "That's him, Frank. I knew he was here."

The hair prickled on the back of Frank's neck. Turning to Helen and Ammon, he said, "Grampa has come for him." Helen clapped a hand over her mouth and Ammon took out his handkerchief.

The old man opened his eyes again. "That Jeremy wasn't much of a hand with cattle. Didn't do much but get in the way. Them range oysters puked him. They sure did."

"It's a terrible affliction, what has happened to Jeremy," Helen said. "He was the beautifulest boy. I can't hardly stand to think about what he did to himself."

"It don't matter," Frank said. "Everybody has misery in this world. That's what this world is for."

That night when Frank got home, Margaret told him Salsifer was still alive. When he got home Tuesday evening, she told him he was dead. The Salt Lake surgeon had taken out two-thirds of his colon and sewed him up, and he had seemed to be recovering. However, early Tuesday morning his heart had stopped and wouldn't revive. The funeral was already planned for ten-thirty on Saturday morning in the Antimony meetinghouse.

While they ate supper, Margaret made a list of everybody she had phoned. She had given word to Leola and Susan, of course, and to numerous Windhams up and down the state, and also to the Jamisons descended from Aunt Cynthia, whom Salsifer's children might not have called because of the old grudge between Cynthia and Jerusha.

"When it comes to a funeral, it's time to put down our animosities," Margaret said. "We will all be united in the Celestial Kingdom. We will assemble as a glorified family in due order and rank. All the offspring of Mother and Aunt Cynthia will line up behind Father, and a holy peace will prevail. There will be no bickering and backbiting, you can count on that."

"I thought all us Windhams would be lined up behind Grampa Windham," Frank said.

"Well, of course, it's the husband's line that counts. You and I will certainly be marshalled into the ranks of the Windhams." Her mouth puckered as if she had had a sip of turpentine.

"Speaking of animosities," Frank said, "there's another one we might ought to settle right about now. I've pondered a good deal those cows you gave me. I want to get out from under them. Either

I sell them and give you the money or I turn them back over to you.
I'm through being a cattleman."

"I wouldn't have those cattle back under any circumstances,"
Margaret said. "Growing animal flesh for the table is ungodly. Sell
them and clean our hands of them."

"I have in mind offering them to Raymond cheap."

"Cheap? Why cheap?"

"So he'll think better of us. Also I'll give up my claim to that forest
range for summer pasture."

Margaret flared up. "I can't think of a single reason why we should
kowtow to Raymond. He has a hot temper and sticky fingers. He's
a penny pincher and a grudge holder."

"Let's give up on it," Frank said. "Let's patch up with him."

"All right, if you are so set on patching up, you take care of it.
I don't want to know anything about it."

Frank didn't know what he would do with his old bull, which
couldn't jump cows. He didn't have the heart to sell him to a dog
food plant. Also he didn't know what to do with the little piece of
land on the upper Paria. Though he had missed a couple of
payments, the former owner refused to foreclose, saying he wanted
his money as agreed. Now that he had a job Frank felt duty bound
to resume payments.

They settled down in the living room with a warm, rumbly fire
in the stove, Frank reading the Bible, Margaret sewing in a few final
pieces on her quilt top. About a half hour later, Lonnie and Jessica
dropped in to offer condolences.

"We were wondering if you might have extra folks coming in
for Salsifer's funeral," Lonnie said. "If you get an overload here,
you can send some over to our house, kids and all. We've got
three empty beds."

Lonnie and Jessica had been married for forty-five years and had
come to look almost like twins. They both had thick grey hair, his
shingled and hers feathered; wide, coarse noses; and glasses whose
thick lenses made their eyes pop with surprise. Being a little deaf,
they often ended up talking at the same time, their voices harmoniz-
ing uncannily, his being a bass, hers a wobbly soprano.

"I've got troubles," Lonnie said. "I've got shingles."

"The poor man," Jessica added. "There isn't any cure for them
but time. It takes four or five months to get over them."

"Want to see them?" he asked, starting to unbutton his shirt.

"Lonnie Windham!" she squeaked. "Not here!"

Lonnie and Frank went into the kitchen. Lonnie took off his shirt, unbuttoned his union suit, and pulled it down, showing his fat, hairy back. A scarlet welt, wide as a man's hand and speckled with tiny, watery blisters, reached around one side from his backbone to his belly button.

"That does look mean," Frank said.

"You want to see the scar on my butt?" Lonnie went on. "When I was about growed up, maybe a little younger than you, I sat down on a double bitted ax that was leaning haft up against a stake in Jordan Biglow's wagon when we were hauling wood." He unbuckled his pants and pulled the union suit off his buttocks, showing a thick purple scar five inches long.

"That's something!" Frank said. "Who sewed you up?"

"Dobb Hendersen's wife. She used a regular sewing needle and cotton thread, like I was a sack of corn meal. She said she enjoyed every minute of it. She said it was a proper revenge for all the abuse men give women."

Lonnie buttoned up and they returned to the living room. Sitting by Margaret on the sofa, Jessica pulled a portion of the quilt top into her lap. She said, "Now look here at this, Lonnie. Margaret calls this her memory quilt."

"See this patch here?" Margaret said. "You'd wonder why I would put faded gingham into a quilt, wouldn't you? Well, it's because it came from one of Mother's old aprons. In fact, the quilt was her idea. She started saving pieces of material that had something to do with her folks. But Mother never got around to making it, so I took over her pieces and just kept on adding to them, and last summer, why, I decided it was time to go ahead and start stitching."

"That beats anything I ever saw in my whole life," Jessica exclaimed. "I do like it, I just really do. A memory quilt!"

"I want to show this quilt to some of Aunt Cynthia's children," Margaret went on. "It's got as many pieces from her line as it does from Mother's line. I certainly want Marilla to see it. That woman won't lay off badmouthing my poor mother. She thinks my mother was worse than the Gadarene demons. I'd just like to show her how Mother never held grudges and neither do I."

That night the sky cleared and the temperature dropped to twenty-five below zero, and when Frank went out before dawn to start his truck his nostrils burned. As daylight came and he drove past fields and pastures, he saw horses and cattle clustered for warmth, their breaths steamy, their shaggy hides white with rime. In the little stores along his route he found people huddled near glowing stoves, awestricken and perhaps a little frightened by the wondrous cold.

"My good heavens," said Mrs. Rasbuttar when he went into her store in Joseph, "close that door quick." Seated by a roaring stove with the *Richfield Reaper* in her lap, she wore thick cotton hose, a wool sweater, and a scarf looped around her neck a half dozen times.

A shopper, a knit cap pulled low over her brow, rotated a tin of corned beef in her clumsy mittened hands. "Isn't this kind of high, Cora?" she asked.

"I could come down a nickel," Mrs. Rasbuttar said.

The shopper wandered around to the bakery stand where Frank was stacking loaves of bread and packages of cookies and cupcakes. She took up a loaf of the new bread. "We got a new thing on the market, ain't we? Lamson's Fluffy Golden Harvest."

"This is better," Frank said, handing her a loaf baked from the old recipe. "It won't gum up your teeth. You get more for your money too. That loaf there has been pumped up like a tire; it's two thirds air."

Mrs. Rasbuttar, who had been listening, said, "I kinda like that Fluffy loaf."

"You can't do a day's work on it," Frank said. "It's just something to tickle your tongue. You just as well spread your butter and jam on a piece of cardboard for all the good it does you."

Past Junction, he took the side road to Antimony, and when he was through stocking the shelves in the mercantile there, he pulled over to Raymond's and Helen's house. A bright sun stood in the morning sky. Everywhere the snow sparkled, glistened, blinded—in the rutted street, in yards and corrals, on the high mountains that rose both east and west. Across the street at Salsifer's house, the shades were drawn and no tracks disturbed the smooth, snowy yard.

Rebecca, who should have been at Piute high school for the day, answered Frank's knock. She said her mother was still in Salt Lake and her father was around back in his workshop making a coffin.

Frank pushed into the workshop without knocking and closed the door. A stove made from a cut off fifty gallon barrel glowed red. Hammers, saws, chisels, and wrenches hung on a wall over a cluttered workbench. In the middle of the floor a half finished coffin rested on two sawhorses.

When Frank said hello, Raymond looked up, grunted, and went on sharpening a handsaw. He wore the same denim shirt and runover boots he had worn during the fall roundup. "I'm sorry about Uncle Salsifer dying," Frank said. "I hope you and your family won't sorrow too much."

"Everybody's got to go."

"Well, that's true. Everybody has to go. Looks like you're moving right along with that coffin."

"Ain't much different than any other box. Just bigger."

Frank took a close look. The top and bottom had been sawed from cement stained plywood. He scratched at a bit of hardened concrete and blew the dust off his fingernail, saying, "It seems like you'd use fresh lumber for a coffin."

"What for? The ladies are going to cover it with satin cloth anyhow. Plywood is expensive stuff." He looked as if he was getting ready to tell Frank to mind his own business.

"Dying in Salt Lake, Uncle Salsifer has got sent to a mortuary, I guess," Frank said.

"That's right."

"Likely they will want to put him in one of their coffins."

Raymond straightened up. "By damn, that's so."

"Selling coffins is a big sideline with those mortuary folks," Frank said. "I've heard that's where they make their money, like car dealers making theirs in automatic transmissions and fancy mirrors."

Raymond said, "Son of bitch!" He flung down the saw and walked to the door. "How the hell can you fight them bloodsuckers from two hundred fifty miles away?"

The two men went out. Although the air was bitter, icicles hanging from the eaves sparkled with sunlight. "I have a proposition," Frank said. "We will sell those cows of Mom's cheap if you want them."

"Holy Moses, do you think I'm daft?"

"No, sir."

"Your ma, she says once she'll sell them cows to me, then she jerks the rug out from under me and makes me look like a fool, and then she sends you over when we got a funeral to pay for and says she's changed her mind."

He was shivering and hugging himself and he said, "Come on in the house. I can't take any more of this cold." When they had seated themselves in the living room, he said, "What do you mean, cheap?"

"One tenth under market."

"Last fall's market?"

"Present market."

A car churned by in the street and Raymond craned his neck to see who it was. "I see you're driving for Ashael Lamson. I was curious what you was going to do after you quit Wesley Earle. It isn't any of my business, but I wondered why you quit him. You two had a fight, I imagine."

"We never had a fight," Frank said. "One reason I quit was I wanted to go home and take care of Mom. Another was I couldn't live very spiritual among that outfit."

"They're Episcopalians or something."

"Lutherans. There wasn't anything wrong with them. Just with me. So I moved."

Rebecca came into the room and sat on the arm of Raymond's chair. Despite a weak chin she was almost pretty. She scratched on Raymond's head and said, "You've got dandruff, Daddy."

"There's sure something fishy about it," he said.

"About your dandruff?"

"Gosh, no" he said, irritated. "I'm talking to Frank. Ten percent under present market. There's got to be a catch."

"No catch," Frank said. "We're just trying to patch up with you. Me and Mom both want to get out from under those cows and we'd like you to have first chance at them if you want them. And I won't be saying anything more about summer range on the forest."

Raymond flamed up for a minute. "That was a dirty damned thing you were trying to do, horn in on range we've been using for forty years. There isn't anything rottener in this whole world than stealing range."

"It was dirty," Frank agreed. "I apologize for letting temptation get the best of me."

Raymond put on his coat and walked out to the truck with Frank. He shook his hand and said, "Okay, I'll take those cows. Tell your mom I feel much obliged."

Frank drove back to Highway 89 and went on making deliveries through Circleville and Panguitch. At Minnerly's mercantile he chatted briefly with Margaret, who had been rehired as a cashier, telling her about the deal he had made with Raymond. She had a bottle of prune juice under the cash register and wondered whether he wanted some of it. He said no and drove on, soon turning east on Highway 12. Except for a few spots which the high, bright sun had bared, the road was snow-packed. In Red Canyon he met Wesley Earle driving a new copper colored GMC pickup. Wesley didn't wave; probably he didn't know it was Frank in the Lamson truck. Frank had run into Clara twice while delivering at the grocery stores in Escalante. The first time she had been delighted; the second time she had been hardly polite.

He stopped at Ruby's Inn at the entrance of Bryce National Park. Ponderosa pines towered over the lodge and snow was deeply banked against its thick log walls. In the kitchen a cook named Peggy Lindburne signed the delivery bill. She was petite and pretty, having frizzly curls, a pug nose, a tiny waist, and a voice as sweet and clear as a little girl's. Each time Frank showed up she wrinkled her nose with a grin and made wisecracks and asked all kinds of friendly questions. She had hired on at Ruby's Inn because she had a three year old son whom she wanted to keep as far away as possible from her ex-husband in Connecticut.

"Have you been having a lot of fun lately over in Panguitch," she said, returning the clipboard.

"Same as always."

"I know you're dating somebody in Panguitch," she giggled. "Who is she? Somebody I know?"

"Well, it's true. I do date somebody regular. Her name is Chloe."

"Chloe? Is she cute?"

"Cute ain't the word for it. She's out of this world. She dresses slick, puts on lipstick and smelly perfume, and has got the prettiest legs you ever saw, though her feet are somewhat lacking. She's sweet and quiet and patient and long suffering and pious and just has an all around wonderful personality."

"Come on now, do you really have a girl named Chloe?"

"Sure. She's kind of bony in the hips and her ears stick out and her nose is wet and she belches a lot. She's got shifty black eyes and if I didn't tie her up when I tried to milk her she'd kick me over the fence."

"That's a cow!" Peggy burst out.

"That's right. Her name is Chloe."

"Oh, Frank, you're a scream."

He zipped up his coat and pulled the furry collar up around his ears. "I'll see you Friday," he said.

She put a foot on the rung of a stool and tied her shoe lace, showing a plump, pretty knee. "They're fixing up a sleigh ride on Saturday night for a Florida party that are coming in on a charter bus. Do you want to drive over and go on it? Afterward there'll be hot cider and doughnuts in front of the fireplace in the foyer."

Frank peered into the seething, sizzling deep fat fryer. He shook the basket a couple of times, then pulled it from the fryer and dumped a fish patty into a warming tray. "I'd sure like to come over to your sleigh ride," he said, "but I really can't."

"Some other time then."

"No, no other time either."

"That's okay. I was quite certain you had somebody."

"I don't. It ain't on the books for me to have somebody."

"That's okay," she said again.

He went out, locked the cargo doors on the truck, and drove on down the dugway toward Tropic, bitter and depressed. He knew he was damned. He had done well, but not well enough. Having been smitten on one cheek, he had failed to offer the other; having surrendered his coat, he had refused to give up his cloak.

His sins still reached as high and stretched as wide as Fifty Mile Mountain; they pressed him down and under like a billion tons of rock and dirt. He didn't have the sweet spirit of sacrifice. He resented those who had his pickup, horse, rifle, and clothes; he begrudged them all, even Jack and Red. He was puked by his mother's food and endlessly irritated by her earnest exhortations. He went two thirds crazy on weekends, wishing he had somewhere to go, somebody to see. He despised Ashael Lamson, no, he hated him, for acting the czar of canned corn and penny candy in southern Utah. Worst of all, day and night his belly was ripe with lust; lechery roamed inside him, rattling every door, trying every window. Even now, as he drove away from Peggy Lindburne, he wanted to turn around and go back. She had just offered herself, had asked him to hold, kiss, and have her. He wanted in the worst way to say yes.

On Saturday morning a big crowd showed up for Salsifer's funeral in the Antimony meetinghouse. All of Jerusha's descendants were there, Salsifer's children and grandchildren and Margaret's too, and a good many of Cynthia's descendants and of course dozens of friends and neighbors from all over Garfield County, including Lonnie and Jarvis Windham and their wives and also Nathan Woodbarrow. To take care of them all, folding chairs had been set up on the podium and in the foyer and aisles.

The coffin sat, lid open, on trestles between the podium and the front pew. For an hour before the service people filed in, shook hands and hugged and cried, and shuffled by the coffin to take a last look at Salsifer Jamison. A tall woman, tottering along on spike heels in front of Frank, said, "Don't he look natural? Just like every day." Sure as daylight, somebody at a funeral always had to say the corpse looked natural. Salsifer didn't look natural unless, of course, natural meant looking shrunk, fallen, and dead.

The coffin was nice—lined inside with cushioned bunting, covered outside with patterned white satin, and fixed with chrome handles and hinges. Along a seam the satin bloused a little. Frank took a close look and, good gosh, he saw that the coffin was homemade. Raymond had finished his cement-stained box, the Antimony Relief Society sisters had covered it, and the Salt Lake undertakers had learned a thing or two about little town initiative.

The program, a purple ditto on white paper, was very satisfactory. The pallbearers were six grandsons. Ammon Jamison was to give the opening prayer. The three Holbert sisters from Koosharem would sing a special number, "I Went to the Garden Alone." Leola would read the life story—Margaret had been asked first, but she said she couldn't keep from crying. Bruce Hinderblom, a son-in-law, would preach the sermon; he was a professor of economics at BYU and was supposed to be high on spirituality. The Antimony ward bishop would deliver closing remarks and Raymond would dedicate the grave.

When Leola took the pulpit, she shook her beefy shoulders and gazed around the hall, her eyes squinted, her head tilted, her nose sharp as a hawk's beak. She seemed ready to say, "All right, you damned quarrelsome Jamisons, if you don't like my speech, you can just kiss my you know what."

But that was all bluff. She started off in a low reedy voice, and nobody could take exception to what she said. She knew where to begin a life story, which was at the Creation. She mentioned the great council in heaven when the spirit children of God voted to reject Lucifer's plan for a guaranteed salvation based on coercion and to accept Christ's plan for an earthly probation based on free will. She proudly pointed out that Salsifer had not been among the third of the hosts of heaven who had sided with Lucifer and had been cast out of heaven, never to receive mortal bodies. Furthermore, it was evident Salsifer had been extraordinarily valiant among the spirits who remained in heaven because his sojourn on earth had been delayed until this, the glorious final dispensation, and because, instead of being sent to earth to dwell among Roman Catholics or Hindus or Arabs or some other kind of benighted people, he had been placed among a high and princely Latter-day Saint family, the Jamisons.

After the funeral, the pallbearers put the coffin into the back of a pickup and everybody followed along in cars and trucks to the cemetery. The grave lay open, its walls smooth, its corners square; beside it gravel heaped high and red. The pallbearers lowered the coffin with ropes into a rough pine box that waited in the bottom. Raymond's son Jeff clambered into the grave and nailed a lid on the box.

The weather had warmed up a little and a new storm was threatening. A stiff wind blew, stirring thick grey clouds overhead and drifting old snow against gravestones and fence pickets. Old people and small children remained in the cars; the people standing around the grave hunched their backs and pulled up their collars. The women wore long coats, but most of the men—those from the little towns and ranches—didn't. An overcoat was a sign of a city man. Nathan Woodbarrow was at the edge of the crowd, wearing a suit coat, his thin body shaking, his face turning blue. Frank went to Margaret's car and fetched the jacket he wore while driving for Ashael.

"Put it on," he said to Nathan.

"Put it on yourself."

"I'm okay," Frank said, draping the jacket over his shivering shoulders.

Raymond began his prayer of dedication by calling on the Lord God Almighty, the creator of all things, the giver of life and all blessings, and he mentioned numerous things God already knew about, such as his having raised up a prophet in these latter days, even Joseph Smith, and in the fastness of the Rocky Mountains having established his earthly kingdom, the Church of Jesus Christ of Latter-day Saints. Then he got around to Salsifer, whom he praised as a mighty pillar of Israel and an edifying example of righteousness unto his descendants, cousins, neighbors, and friends. He took a full ten minutes to dedicate the grave, which showed that even a mealy mouthed man could have a lot of the Gospel stored up inside.

When he said amen, some of the men grabbed shovels and went to work filling the grave. For a minute or two the gravel thumped and rattled on the lid of the pine box; then it struck quietly, like hooves in plowed ground.

"There goes old Salsifer," Nathan said to Frank. "Him and me bumped into each other many a time over the years. I bought cattle from him, sold him hay more than once. He did real well by himself. He built up three, four hundred head of cattle, most of them pureblood Herefords. He had money to retire on. Him and Ora Jean bought a camper and a fishing boat and they spent some nice summers up at Koosharem Reservoir and Fish Lake."

"I remember of him fishing a good deal in his later years."

"That ranch of his is the nicest bottom land on the East Fork of the Sevier."

"It's pretty range, no question of that."

"I wanted a ranch like that," Nathan said. "That's exactly what I wanted. I didn't want to be a hay farmer."

"It's not doing him any good now. Raymond's got it."

"At least he had it. I never had nothing. I wish me and Dora had us a fancy pickup and a camper with a big bed and an icebox and an oven and a potty in it. I wish me and her had us a fishing boat with a motor on it. We'd visit the lakes, that's what we'd do. We'd be having us a vacation in our old age."

The wind had whipped tears into Nathan's eyes and he was rubbing them with a knuckle. His thin grey hair was combed down slick with oil. His cheeks were brown and leathery, and his forehead, where his hat kept off the sun every summer, was muddy white.

"Actually me and Dora have in mind her coming down to stay on the ranch a while this spring before the weather gets hot. Our boy Archie has offered us a nice trailer house with a bathroom and shower. All we gotta do is tow it down and fix it up with a septic tank."

"Good idea," Frank said.

The grave was filled and heaped and people were getting into their cars. Family members had been invited to the schoolhouse for a lunch prepared by the Relief Society sisters. Frank told Nathan to come along, but he said no. He was standing by a gravestone, a marble shaft, scratching at a weathered spot with a fingernail.

"What I can't hardly believe is I'm going to die poor," he said. "I've lived the Gospel all my life; I've responded to the call of the authorities; I've said my prayers and been good to my neighbors. And what do I have to show for it? I don't have no Social Security. If you work for the railroad or the steel company, you get a fat pension. But not if you're a farmer. Not a penny of retirement."

"Everybody dies poor," Frank said. "There isn't any other way to die."

"I lost a house in Springville in 1933. I mortgaged it in 1928. I was going big in Utah Valley real estate. There wasn't anybody who didn't think he was going to get rich. I never told Dora it was mortgaged. So one day I had to go to her like a dog with his tail between his legs and tell her, You don't have a house any more."

They were alone in the cemetery. The wind had already started to grizzle with snow the red clay of Salsifer's grave. Frank couldn't get over Nathan's envy of Salsifer, his lust for worldly vanities. Frank was jolted and scared. The living were in graves as much as the dead. Everyone who breathed was locked in a coffin, was hugged in the dark silence of the gravelly earth. In due time Nathan would be put down into hell. He had done well, but not well enough. Having been smitten on one cheek, he had failed to offer the other; having surrendered his coat, he had refused to give up his cloak.

"It's getting awful cold," Frank said. "Drive me down to the schoolhouse, would you?"

Nathan gave Frank his jacket and they got into Nathan's sedan, which hadn't improved since Frank had last seen it. Nathan sawed violently on the steering wheel and the old Ford lurched down the rutted, icy road.

"That house Dora lives in," Nathan said, "is her house. She bought it. I never put a penny into it. That's how well I've done."

"That don't matter," Frank said. "Dora ain't a woman to begrudge anything to anybody."

"I love her," Nathan said. "I truly love her."

"Sure you do."

"I'm so lonesome it's about to kill me. It was better when you were there, Frank. I still can't get used to not hearing you over there in your bunk breathing. I wake up in the night and listen and there's nothing. Maybe a mouse in the closet, that's all."

They parked in front of the schoolhouse. Frank held out his hand and Nathan shook it but went on talking. "Things have gone downhill at the ranch. I never saw a bunch more out of sorts than those Earles. Wesley don't say a word at meals anymore. Sometimes he just looks up at Marianne and all of sudden she breaks out and bawls and gets up and heads off to her room. Then Clara says to Wesley, Haven't you got any mercy? She smells like vomit half the time."

"Clara smells like vomit?"

"No, Marianne."

"Why would she smell like vomit?"

"I ain't got no opinions on that."

Frank said goodby and watched while Nathan drove his car away, the exhaust roaring, the muffler swinging on baling wire. When Frank got inside, people were lined up at the counter between the kitchen and the big classroom where Relief Society ladies were serving fried chicken and browned rice. Some people were already eating at the long tables, which had been set with silverware and butter, rolls, and jam. Marilla sat at an empty table, waiting for her daughter Emily and her husband and children to come through the serving line.

"Come right here and sit by me," the old woman said as Frank passed by. "Do I know you?"

"Yes, ma'am," he said, taking a chair. "I'm Frank Windham, Margaret's boy. You're my aunt."

"I knew you were somebody. I like the looks of you."

"Thank you."

"I don't see any pretty little wife hanging around."

"No, ma'am. I'm not married."

"What are you waiting for? Are you going on a mission?"

"Likely not."

"Do you believe in the Gospel? Have you got a testimony?"

"Yes, ma'am."

"Well, go preach it then."

"I'm taking care of my mother."

"Oh, that's a good boy. You can't do better than that. Though it's a waste you aren't married. If I was a girl I'd set my cap for you."

"Thank you."

"Thay have put your uncle Salsifer away."

"That's true. He's buried and gone."

With thin fingers Marilla tied and untied a small knot of green yarn. Her hands had shiny, transparent skin and lumpy blue veins. "The stories I could tell you about my mother. You wouldn't believe half of them. But they are true, every word." She leaned close and spoke lower. "She was never done justice to. Father favored Jerusha. He built Jerusha a big rock house in Orderville with a dozen rooms, and she didn't have but two children, whereas my poor mother who had seven children lived cramped up in that tiny brick house in Escalante—four rooms plus the lean-to Father slept in. You had to go outside to get from one part of the house to the other."

Jerusha's house in Orderville, the one Leola now owned, wasn't a mansion. It had six rooms, not a dozen. Its floors sloped. Its wall surfaces were cluttered with pipes and wires because the walls were solid stone and mortar. The windows were off square and their cracks were stuffed with oakum and putty. Probably Marilla had never been inside that house. Probably her feelings wouldn't have been different even if she had. People needed grudges as much as they needed food and shelter.

When Frank had heaped his plate with chicken, rice, and other good things, he wandered around the room looking for a seat. Emily had tied a bib on Marilla, who ate food the way a chain saw cut wood. She saw Frank and waved wildly with a drumstick. He smiled and went on by. The tables were crowded with fifty or sixty eating, chattering, laughing people. Salsifer was already water under the bridge. Fathers and mothers and kids, uncles and aunts, cousins, friends, a family. Together they were folding up their grief, putting it away, pocketing their fear, remembering reasons for being hopeful and happy.

"Right over here, Frank," Leola called. Lawrence had dragged up an extra chair, making a place for him. With them were Ammon and his wife Glenda and a couple who turned out to be Cyrus and Rhetta Jamison from Ogden. Cyrus was Cynthia's grandson and a dentist. It was easy to see he had money because his grey flannel suit was new and unwrinkled and still had a nap to it.

Leola told them that Frank would be ordained an Elder on Sunday afternoon, whereupon they all congratulated him and commented on what a big thing it was to hold the Melchizedek Priesthood, which empowered a man to go to the temple, bless the sick, and lay on hands for the gift of the Holy Ghost. Squeezing his arm, Leola said, "I never lost faith in you. All that time you were living over on that ranch, I told Mom to relax and to quit worrying about you. You were just frisking a bit, kicking up your heels and passing a little air. That's all you were doing."

Frank cleaned up his food in a hurry, every bit of it, and seeing some of the men going back for seconds, he did too. When he had finished that, he went back for thirds. The sisters at the serving counter were tickled; they enjoyed seeing a big fellow eat heartily. People were standing up, finding coats, shaking hands and kissing and hugging. Lawrence and Cyrus were still at their table, threshing out whether Coca-Cola was against the Word of Wisdom. Cyrus claimed it was because it had caffeine in it, just like coffee. Furthermore, if you left a ten-penny nail in a glass of Coca-Cola overnight, it would be corroded to the size of an eight-penny nail.

"The damage Coca-Cola does to the teeth of Americans is frightful," Cyrus said. "I keep a ten-penny nail in my office just to show my patients. That is, it was a ten-penny nail before I let it corrode. No question of it, Coca-Cola is just as evil in the sight of the Lord as coffee is."

Frank hardly listened. He was mad, disgusted, glum. He was thinking about his plate heaped three times over with drumsticks, breasts, thighs, rice, lettuce, crusty rolls, and moist applesauce cake. He had no excuse, no defense. His Christian conscience had protested and he hadn't listened. Seduced by chatter and cheer, he had soaked his tongue and stoked his belly, had surrendered to gluttony, had apostatized to hoggishness.

When he went outside, he found Raymond and Margaret on the school steps being cordial to each other. Raymond was saying how much he appreciated getting the cows at such a good price, and Margaret was saying it wasn't anything, just a little token of appreciation for Salsifer's sake. Raymond asked Frank if he would help move the cows on the next Saturday, and Frank said sure. As he went out of the gate, Helen met him and gave him a hug.

"That is generous of you folks," she said. "Thank God you took steps to make up between us because Raymond never could've. I just love you a whole lot, Frank."

Helen wasn't anything to look at, spindle legged, flat chested, bucktoothed, spittle lipped. Yet Frank hoped that if he ever got old and sick he could have a woman like her to take care of him. She had nearly killed herself nursing Salsifer for two or three years, running back and forth between his house and hers at all hours of the day and night. She was the one who had cried hardest at the funeral, the one who still had red eyes and a sniffly nose.

The wind had died and the clouds seemed ready to break. People were clearing a skiff of snow from their windshields, slamming doors, starting engines. Cloyd was showing his new Plymouth hardtop sedan to Lonnie while Susan and Jessica chatted at the side. A two-tone red and white, the Plymouth sported slanting headlight hoods, chrome strips, and high sweptback tail fins that made it look like a jetfighter. Frank peered inside. It had air conditioning, an automatic transmission, and carpet on the floor.

"It's a 217 V-8 engine," Cloyd was saying. "Good gas milage and pretty snappy too. I don't know how fast it'll go. I quit trying at ninety the other day."

"Right pretty, right pretty," Lonnie said.

Cloyd swept snow off a front fender, bent down, and scrutinized a spot. He pulled out a handkerchief and rubbed the spot, a happy man. Frank got behind the wheel of Margaret's car, a six-year-old Chevy with a dented front fender, a six cylinder engine, and a column mounted manual gearshift. He watched Margaret, still on the steps, now talking to Marilla and Emily.

Margaret said the Jamisons were more righteous than the Windhams, which was likely true. Leola said the Jamisons were a noble and princely family. Sure enough, most of them paid tithing, said prayers, refrained from foul language, attended meetings, and kept the Word of Wisdom. But not a one of them could take a breath without making a compromise with the world. They had to butter their eggs and salt their greens. They brushed their teeth with peppermint paste and freshened their faces with smelly lotion. They had to have lacy dresses and fancy suits. They lusted on freezers, automatic washers, and TV sets. They wanted cars with air conditioners and sweptback fins. They stamped their names in gold on leatherbound Scriptures and bought thick-piled carpets for their churchhouses. They thought all these distractions and vanities were God-ordained, as if goods, gadgets, and devices were the end of Creation, as if free enterprise and the law of supply and demand were the reason for the Lord's crucifixion.

Frank was jolted, he was scared. He remembered Salsifer's leathery dead face and the rattle of gravel on the big pine box. In due time the Jamisons would all be put down into hell. They had done well, but not well enough. Having surrendered their coat, they had refused to give up their cloak.

7.

The Wedding

Early Sunday morning Clara Earle phoned saying she was on Main Street with a flat tire and asking Frank to help her fix it. He found her parked at Milne's cafe.

"There's nothing wrong with my tire," she said. "I didn't know how else to arrange a private talk. Can we go into Milne's for a few minutes?" They took a booth and Clara ordered coffee. She tried to smile, showing her misaligned, tartarred teeth. "I imagine you know why I'm here. She's pregnant, Frank, and everything is ruined, absolutely ruined."

She rummaged in her purse for a handkerchief and dabbed at her eyes. She was dressed for Sunday in a black jacket and a ruffled blouse; her grey hair was cut short and parted on one side. "The sensible thing is for her to go back to Illinois and have the baby and put it up for adoption. My sister, bless her heart, has offered to take her in."

Frank fidgeted with his cap and sniffed at the corral odor that clung to it. Inside he spun like a radiator fan.

"But she won't hear of giving up the baby, Frank. She won't budge, she's hard as a rock. She says, I'm going to raise the little bastard; it won't be any different than raising a goat. Such cynical talk! But, good heavens, I never thought I'd be grandmother to an illegitimate child. It never entered my mind. And the fights she and I are having, Frank, they are truly hellish. The obscenities that girl knows!"

A nickel and some pennies lay on the tabletop, which Clara pushed back and forth with a stubby finger. Frank was wondering

223

what Abraham Lincoln, who was on the pennies, would have done in this situation; he certainly hadn't lain down sick and fearful and let the Southerners run amuck and destroy the Union. It was time for Frank to butt in and tell Clara to save her breath because he couldn't be the daddy.

She went on, sad and confidential. "Sometimes you'd think she has no remorse whatsoever. She tries to stand up to Wesley. They have shouting matches and excel in calling one another names. But of course Wesley always wins. Marianne crumbles and runs to her room. It's awful, Frank. My poor little girl. She is so unhappy."

She took a sip of coffee, rotated the cup, took another sip. "The only way out is for you two to get married. There isn't any other way. If she keeps the baby, she has to be married. You won't have an easy time talking her into it. I have to say, you aren't exactly high on her list of nice people. She says she wouldn't marry you for anything. She says you took advantage of her, Frank. She says you told her deliberate lies."

His evils stood forth like cockroaches on a tablecloth. It was Jack who had told him a woman couldn't get pregnant while having a period. He wondered where Jack had got that idea.

"I could be bitter awfully easy," she said. "That was unmanly of you."

"Yes, ma'am, it truly was."

"You had better not come to the ranch to see her. Wesley wouldn't welcome you. You can catch her in town when school lets out some afternoon. And when you talk to her, Frank, please talk hard. Don't pay any attention to the harsh, mean things she might say. Don't take no for an answer." She reached an anxious hand toward him. "You will treat her good, won't you, Frank?"

Before he went home, Frank called on the bishop, who was milking his Jersey cow. He listened gravely, mumbling and shaking his head, and agreed that Frank's ordination should be postponed. His fur-fronted Yukon cap sat far back on his head. The grey whiskers on his nose were a half inch long, probably because he needed new glasses and couldn't see that his nose wanted trimming.

He swung on his stool and faced Frank. "I sure wouldn't be daddy to somebody else's baby. But you're in a pickle and I don't know what you're going to do."

They crossed the corral, their boots sucking in and out of the mire. "There ain't any use for everybody in town to know about this right now, though sooner or later it'll come out, you can count on that," the bishop said, pausing at the gate. "For the present the reason why we're canceling your ordination is this. We've got two or three young men getting old enough to be made Elders. We've decided to hold up on you a bit so we can have a nice big occasion and ordain two or three at once."

"My mother isn't going to believe that."

"So you just go home and come straight with her right now. And, brother, I gotta say, I'd hate to be in your shoes while you're doing it."

At home Frank dressed for Priesthood Meeting, then, having time to spare, went into the living room where a fire crackled in the stove. At the secretary he prepared to write a letter, pulling out a pad of creamy writing paper and filling his fountain pen from a bottle of ink, all the while sniffling.

"Have you got a cold?" asked Margaret, who had put her head into the room. Fluffy bunny slippers encased her feet and a shower cap circled her head.

"No, ma'am." He got out his handkerchief and dabbed his eyes and blew his nose. "It's time we got Jeremy home. I'm going to write Washley a letter and tell him we want him home now."

"Well, I certainly wish you would," she said. "There isn't a day goes by that I don't mourn over that boy being locked up with all those crazy people." She went on to the bathroom and he began his letter:

> Dear Dr. Washley,
>
> My brother Jeremy is in your hospital who thinks he is Alice. Please get ready to let him go. We have had enough shilly-shallying around. We do not want to fight but will go to court if we have to. My mother never signed for Jeremy to go into your hospital and we will see what the judge says about that. We are not troublemakers and would rather get along. Please write and let us know when we can come get him. A Saturday is best because I work five days a week.
>
> Sincerely yours,
> Frank J. Windham

After he had addressed and sealed an envelope, Margaret looked into the room again. "My land, boy, it's way past time for Priesthood Meeting. Hurry right over."

"I just don't have the courage to go," he said. "The bishop is calling off my ordination."

"Calling it off? What on earth for?"

"The reason he's giving out isn't the real reason, which is what I've got to talk to you about. I've got to get something off my chest."

"Oh, my heavens," she said, entering the room and seating herself.

"It's about Marianne and me. When I was living out on the ranch, her and me got too friendly. You asked me one day if I was a fornicator and I said no. I lied to you. The two of us, that's what we were doing all along."

Her long, hollow cheeks were now the color of the nearby lamp table, a pale varnishy yellow.

"I wrestled that all out with the bishop a long time ago," he said. "Him and me both thought maybe since I'd turned over a new leaf and put it behind me I could forget about it. But something new has come up. I'm in bad trouble. She's going to have a baby, which I didn't know till this morning. Clara didn't have no flat tire. She just wanted to get me alone so she could give me the news. So there isn't going to be any ordination today."

The blood returned to Margaret's face in a rush. "A fornicator? A street-running, slop-loving fornicator! What did I ever teach you to make you become a fornicator? What kind of wonderful person am I to have a son like you?"

"It wasn't anything you taught me. I thought it up myself."

"And a liar," she said.

"Yes, ma'am, a liar."

"I won't have it," she said, rising and standing arms akimbo in the center of the room. "I have a broom and I know how to clean my house. I don't have to put up with a fornicator and a liar. Why should I associate with that sort of person?"

She stamped angrily into the kitchen and drew a glass of water. Frank followed, leaning in the doorway while she drank. "Just day before yesterday," she said, clattering down the glass, "I was exalting myself. I said to myself, there isn't anybody like my boy Frank. Not since my own saint of a mother I never saw anybody try harder than my boy Frank to live the commandments. I was making myself big over that. If that isn't the way of pride!"

"Yes, ma'am," Frank said, "I'm nothing at all."

"You are an empty vessel and a sounding brass. All that big talk of yours about never getting married, about being called of God to resist your lust."

"I didn't know she was pregnant when I said all that."

"Shame on you, Frank, for letting your lust choose you a wife." She began to wail. "Now you have to get married to a Gentile girl. God help me. My shame is laid open for everybody to see. Everybody in the county will know."

Monday morning as he began driving his delivery route, Frank resolved to find Marianne when Escalante high school let out at four. He knew that determined human beings could force themselves to marvelous deeds. Wounded soldiers could deliver themselves to field hospitals to have legs amputated without anesthetic. Condemned prisoners could walk unforced from their cells to the gallows.

In Circleville he carried a tray of bread, cupcakes, and turnovers into Grundler's grocery store. Ormus Williams was telling Sam Grundler about the wonderful experiences his boy Donnie was having on his mission. Ormus pulled a tattered picture postcard from his bib pocket. "Isn't that a cute little town? It's on the Rhine River and the German folks who live there grow grapes and make wine for a living. Donnie and a bunch of other missionaries went to a wine festival there. Of course they didn't imbibe." Ormus showed the postcard to Frank. There were houses with tiled roofs, a church with a steeple, hillsides covered with vineyards, a steamer on a broad, silver river.

"He labors in Heidelberg, which has got a famous university," Ormus went on. "They got a wine keg there big as this store. I swear to goodness it is. I wish I had brought that postcard to show you."

Later, pushing on down the road, Frank had a long think about Donnie Williams, an ugly half-pint kid whom Frank had bowled over like a cornstalk during a football game. Now he was preaching the Gospel in Heidelberg and taking sightseeing trips to villages on the Rhine. Wasn't that a vanity? Wasn't a wine barrel big as a grocery store a vanity?

Those thoughts brought Frank around to the vanity of all vanities, which was him getting married to Marianne Earle. Every morning she'd want to cook a big breakfast of ham, eggs, and hash browns, and he'd have to eat it. She'd fill his mind with silly chatter about goat roping and horse training. She'd decorate the walls with posters of starry-eyed girls and false Lutheran slogans. Every evening he'd have to watch her get undressed.

He got into Escalante at mid-afternoon and, after delivering at Hinton's on one side of Main Street, he made a U-turn and delivered at Lowry's on the other side. As usual he hadn't had lunch and his stomach felt like a cement mixer. Since the fine points of Christian abstinence seemed futile for a man who hadn't mastered the gross principles, he bought a quart of milk and ate stale turnovers—two cherry, two apple, one lemon, one chocolate. Then he drove to the high school and parked at the curb. Down the line of waiting vehicles he could see Wesley's stocktruck.

At four the doors burst open and students streamed out, the boys wearing Levi's, denim jackets, and Stetsons, the girls wearing wool skirts, loafers, and long coats. Some of them got into parked cars and pickups and others headed home afoot. The kids from the ranches and from Boulder climbed into a little yellow bus waiting at the corner.

Marianne came out carrying an armload of books. When she reached the stocktruck, she put the books on a fender and dug into her purse for the keys. Frank got out and walked toward her. She looked up and stared, then picked up her books and climbed into the truck, locking the door. As she started the engine he put his foot behind a front wheel.

She rolled down her window a crack. "Move your foot or I'll run over it."

"Go ahead," he called, "run over it."

She shut off the engine and got out, saying, "What do you want?"

"I came to see you. I wanted to know how you are."

"I'm fine."

She was astonishing and unfamiliar. Her hair was untidy and tangled. Her face was pale as peeled juniper; the features he had liked the least, the cleft chin, the long bumpy nose, were stronger, starker, more deeply whittled.

He said, very fast before he lost his nerve, "I know about the trouble you're in."

Her eyes got wide and her mouth tried to make words and a red flush came up her neck and jaws.

"I wore rubbers," he said. "Every time but the first and the last."

"You wore rubbers! What do I care if you wore rubbers? Did you look me up to tell me that?"

She turned to go, but he caught her arm and said, "I didn't think it could happen when a woman was in a period."

"Who told you I'm pregnant?" she said. "It couldn't be anybody but my mother."

She tried to pull her arm from his grip but he didn't let go. She twisted his fingers, then sank her nails into his knuckles. He gripped tighter. Her nails dug deeper. All at once she quit, slumped, began to cry.

"My God, Frank, how could you think I'd do it with anybody else? But that doesn't make any difference. I wouldn't marry you for anything in the world. I don't care if Mom cries her eyes out; I don't care if Dad shouts till he blows off the roof."

He released her arm and looked at his bleeding knuckles. "I'd try to be good to you," he said.

"You can't."

"I'd try."

"I never could love you," she said. "Not again. No matter what, I couldn't."

"Maybe we shouldn't be thinking about whether we love each other. Maybe we should be thinking about what that baby needs."

"You make me want to vomit, Frank. Please go home and leave me alone."

He scratched his neck and looked around.

"Really, just go away and don't come back."

"All right," he said.

She climbed into the truck and started the engine. He stood while she backed from the curb. She looked at him once and he could see the silver on her cheeks.

He watched her truck disappear at the intersection. A thin line of clouds divided the sky overhead; the elms around the churchhouse across the street stood grey, leafless, and lacy. For a moment, like a hooked trout or a roped calf just released, Frank couldn't grasp that he was free. Then it hit him and he wanted to shout. Though he had been ready to take Marianne, she wouldn't accept him. God had hardened her heart. He had paroled Frank, put him on probation, given him another chance.

He drove on to Boulder, arriving a little before dark and making his weekly delivery there. Then it was a long hundred mile trip back to Panguitch. The pavement was a dark river between banks of snow. The headlights flashed against road signs, against trees, against cliffs and dugway walls. Inside the cab, the steering wheel vibrated, the instrument panel glowed, soft air rushed from the heater.

His good mood had already left him. A little movie played in his mind and he couldn't close his eyes to it. He could see a couple of woman having a gossip in a grocery store—perhaps Hinton's in Escalante. One of them wore a purple muffler that dangled to her knees, the other a pert little black lambskin hat. Frank was there too, stocking bakery shelves across the aisle.

The lady in the black lambskin hat said, "You see that fellow right there at the bakery stand? He's a Windham boy from Panguitch."

"I know some of the family," the lady in the purple muffler said.

"He's quite given to church going at present, I understand. Lives a very sober life. Takes care of his mother. He's put up as a Mormon who does everything he's supposed to. I mean, *everything*."

"Well, isn't that just fine. You don't find many like that."

"Except for one thing. He has gone and got Marianne Earle pregnant. You won't see her at school much longer. A girl with a watermelon under her smock can't go to high school in this town. She'll just sit around her father's ranch and twiddle her thumbs. And here's the fellow who got her that way, walking around free and easy."

"Well, if that doesn't burn me up!"

"He doesn't care if that baby is born without a name. He doesn't care if his own little bastard grows up on a ranch not ninety miles from where he lives. Gracious, no. He has to look out for his mother."

In Escalante Frank turned onto the road to the Earle ranch. At the ranch he parked, walked through the picket gate, and knocked on the door. Wesley opened and peered out, his hand holding a newspaper, his shirt half unbuttoned, his hair tousled.

"I've come to have a talk with Marianne," Frank said.

Wesley turned on the porchlight and saw who it was. "You bounder," he said. "You cad. You prevaricator. You seducer. I've just got one word for you. My lawyer, Mr. Tenny Rostom from Cedar City, will be calling on you to work out child support payments. We intend to have you foot the bill for Marianne's confinement too. Now you can leave. You aren't welcome on this ranch."

"Who is it?" Clara said, coming up behind.

"It's me. Frank."

"Oh, lord," Clara said.

"I want to talk to Marianne again."

"Not on your life," Wesley said.

"Oh, yes," Clara insisted, "oh, dear, yes."

Wesley slammed the door. Frank stood still and voices came through the door, Wesley shouting, Clara murmuring. Then the door opened and Clara said, "Come in, Frank." She took him into the living room, saying, "Sit down. Marianne will be here in a minute."

He was alone in the room. A gold-faced German clock ticked on the piano. From the radio came a calm, quiet voice advertising suits at Auerbachs in Salt Lake. A Belgian rug with a thick wooly nap lay in the middle of the room. Over the fireplace hung the head of a trophy desert ram; under it was a twelve gauge shotgun.

Marianne stood in the doorway, her bare feet peeking from beneath her pink flannel night gown. She said, "I didn't want you to come here."

"I've got to say one more thing. It isn't decent for that little kid not to have a name."

"It can have my name," she said. "It's been okay for me."

"I can't just walk off on that little kid."

"You aren't going to get to," she said. "Dad's planning on having a little talk with you about child support."

"He's already mentioned it," Frank said. "You bet, I sure will make payments."

"All right, now go home." She leaned against the door jamb. "Please, Frank, leave me alone."

"You hate me," he said. "You wouldn't want to marry me."

"That's right. I hate you a lot. You don't want to marry me either. You never did want to."

"That's true. I never did."

"Well, then, that about takes care of things, doesn't it?"

"What if we got married for about a year?" he said. "We could live together like a brother and sister. We'd treat each other like Christians, like God wants us to do. Then when the baby has been here for a while and things are all settled down and people aren't paying much attention, we'll just get us a divorce. I'll keep paying support money and maybe once in a while you'd let me come see the little critter so it'd know it had a daddy somewhere in the world."

Marianne crossed the room and sat on the sofa, curling her feet under herself and adjusting her nightgown. She shook her head. "That is about the dumbest idea I ever heard in my life."

"It isn't so dumb. It's a pretty good idea."

"What's so good about it?"

"Because for a while we really will be married. So our kid really will have a name."

"It'd just be hell living together for a year, now wouldn't it?"

"It wouldn't have to be. Not if we treated each other like real Christians."

"I never heard of married people living like a brother and sister. That isn't what people get married for."

"That's what we'd get married for. We'd live righteous. We wouldn't be carnal with one another."

"You're crazier than your brother Jeremy."

Frank swore under his breath, kicked a chair leg, and went to the door. "All right," he said, "tell your dad to send that lawyer along. I'll work things out with him."

"You don't have no call kicking that chair!"

"I know it. I ain't got any self control. I'm sorry."

On the steps outside he stood a moment zipping his jacket. The barnyard floodlights cast odd patterns of brightness and shadow upon the snow; the bunkhouse window glimmered; the immense sky pulsed with faint, dusty light. The door opened behind him. "Come back in here a minute," Marianne called.

"Maybe we don't have any choice," she said when he had returned. "Like you say, it isn't decent for a kid not to have a daddy's name. But, by God, Frank, if we do it, we'll sleep in different bedrooms."

"That's right, that's exactly what we'll do."

"And I won't cook for you. You'll get your own meals."

"Yes, ma'am. I'll cook for myself. I'll be glad to cook for you too."

"I wouldn't eat anything you had cooked. Just take care of yourself."

She went down the hall. Frank heard her open a door and say, "We're going to get married," and he heard Clara say, "Thank God."

Clara came from the hall, smiling brightly. She hugged Frank and kissed him four or five times. She returned to the doorway where Marianne and Wesley had looked on and led Marianne to Frank, putting their hands together, then holding them tightly with her own. "I'm so happy. You are so beautiful, both of you. Don't ever let go of each other."

Wesley wiped his feet on a throw rug as if they were muddy and came forward to shake Frank's hand. "Glad to have you in the family," he muttered. Then he hugged Marianne, who was sniffling.

They all sat down and had a big talk about where to have the wedding. Clara favored the Lutheran church in Richfield with a long white dress and a veil for Marianne and a nice dark suit for Frank. Frank shook his head and said Margaret would for sure want Bishop Bidley to perform the ceremony at the North Ward chapel in Panguitch. Marianne said she wouldn't be caught dead in a long white dress and she didn't see why she had to be married by a Mormon bishop.

"That whittles it down to the justice of the peace in Escalante," Wesley said. "That's old Mr. Obenheimer. He shaves about every other week."

"Not in his filthy old house!" Clara wailed. "Oh, I just couldn't stand that."

They decided to think on it for a while. Clara wanted to get Frank some supper, but he said had better get on home to give Margaret the news. On his way to the door he paused by the sofa where Marianne sat with a leg propped up, inspecting her toes. Frank scratched his arm pit and looked around.

"Marianne," Clara said, "he wants to say goodbye."

She tilted her head and gave him a cheek. He bent down and pecked it.

"God bless you both," Clara said.

Wesley followed Frank out and stood with him beside the delivery truck, saying, "Now that we are out of the presence of the ladies, I mean to tell you a few things. Clara said if I didn't endorse this wedding idea, I could move out of our bedroom. Ponder that a moment. I have been told I can move out of my own bedroom. That is the second time in an otherwise long and peaceful marriage that I have been threatened with the loss of connubial bliss. Do you realize that the human male toils and sweats and engages in the combat of the market place simply to purchase his bedroom tickets? We are slaves to sex, Frank. We are held in ignominious bondage by nuptial privileges."

"That's the truth, I expect," Frank said.

"But that is neither here nor there. Clara is not present now to defend you. Frank, you are a goddamned rascal."

"Yes, sir, I know I am."

"I trusted you. I exalted you. I put power into your hands, as Potiphar did for Joseph in Egypt of old. I opened financial doors before you. Having done all that, I explicitly enjoined you from my daughter. I warned you thirty times over. And what did you do? You went straightway and seduced her. You sat at my table and ate my food and accepted my wages, and all the while you were prostituting my daughter. Furthermore, I don't care for your religion, Frank. You Mormons are archaic and obscene. You are far worse than the Lutherans, and God knows how I detest them. You are a throwback to animism and ancestor worship."

"Yes, sir," Frank said, "I believe you are just about right."

"I wanted her to go to college."

"I know you did."

"She's the bright one, Frank. I don't expect anything of Jeanette, who is just as goodhearted and thoughtless as her mother. But Marianne, she could have gone back east to college, she could have gone into biochemistry, which is what I should have done. My gad, Frank, do you know what exciting things are happening in biochemistry? Have you ever heard of DNA? Deoxyribonucleic acid?"

"No, sir, I never heard of it."

"There has been a staggering breakthrough. Nobel prizes are being given because of it. Scientists have figured out the chemical pattern for genes, Frank. And she could have got into research on something like that. She's good at chemistry. She's good at mathematics. She's good at biology."

"I know she is," Frank said. "She's also good at barrel racing and goat roping."

"Trash, trash, trash! Oh, the sorrow of it, seeing her waste that bright, sensitive mind!"

"Yes, sir, I understand."

"However," Wesley went on, "now that you know how disillusioned I am with you, I want to go forward on a more positive vein." It turned out there was something Frank could do to redeem himself. Wesley hadn't had any luck finding a permanent replacement for Frank, three men in succession having hired on and quit.

"So it just came to me," he said, "while Clara was in there threatening to put me out of my own bedroom, maybe you and Marianne could live right here on the ranch and you could go back to work for me." By April he wanted a new aluminum pipe sprinkling system in operation on the new sandhill farm, and he wanted similar systems on the other farms before summer was over. Besides that, he had plans for a new feedlot and four giant sheds for hay storage.

"You have a crafty side to you, Frank," he asserted, "but there's no question, you are an exceptional worker. Things do get done when you're around."

Frank had in mind he and Marianne would live in Panguitch for their year of marriage so that he could keep an eye on Margaret. What he really wanted was for them to live in Margaret's house, but Marianne wasn't likely to go along with that arrangement.

"Now what we'll do," Wesley went on, "is get you two kids a nice used trailerhouse, something considerably bigger than that thing Nathan's son Archie towed down for him and Dora. Then later on when your family gets bigger, we'll build you a fancy house out on one of the farms."

Frank could see what that would add up to. If Wesley planted Marianne and him on the ranch, they would be in a position to inherit it. A big hay ranch! My gosh, the old natural man in Frank got up and did some walking around.

"So how about it?" Wesley said. "Is it a deal?"

It couldn't be a deal. It would mean Frank would have to leave Margaret, and nobody but an ungodly skunk would trade his mother for a hay farm and a wife he didn't love. It would also mean he'd have to put up with Wesley until Wesley got old and died, which would be more hell on earth than anybody deserved. Then it occurred to Frank that he could leave Marianne easier, when the time came, if she was already settled on her father's ranch. He didn't have to think a second more. He took Wesley's hand and said, "It's a deal."

"That's a good fellow. My gad, Frank, I believe I am cheering up. Well, well, the follies of youth! We mustn't be too dismal about them." He chuckled and gave Frank a dig in the ribs with his elbow. "Welcome to the married man's club. Remember what I told you. You'll work your butt off to buy your bedroom tickets, and every once in a while, just to keep you in your place, your wife won't make good on them."

On Saturday Frank helped Raymond move the cows he had bought from Margaret. Raymond offered to take the old bull and sell him for dog food. Frank said no, and with Lonnie's pickup and trailer he hauled the bull home to Panguitch and put him in the corral with the bony little cow. The bull, which spent most of the time lying in the shed, didn't bother to get up when Frank came in to milk. He didn't seem to mind when Frank set the milk pail on his paunch or leaned against his back.

On Sunday the Earles had Frank and Margaret over to the ranch for dinner, and together they settled the details of the wedding. It would be at Ruby's Inn on Saturday in two weeks. Mr. Obenheimer would perform the ceremony, duly shaved and dressed up, of course. A small number of friends and relatives would be invited and a little buffet luncheon would be served. Then Frank and Marianne would take off for a short honeymoon in Las Vegas. Clara was putting up the money because she said it broke her heart to think of them not having a honeymoon. They would drive down in Wesley's new pickup, which had a carpeted floor and a radio, and when their honeymoon was over, they would tow back a trailerhouse. Wesley had been on the phone and had located three used trailers under fifteen hundred dollars, from which they could pick the one they liked best.

When dinner was over Frank and Marianne had a minute alone in the living room. Frank slumped in a deep, soft chair, rumpling his grey doublebreasted suit and showing off his new knit socks. His neck and temples were freshly shingled and the usual shock of brown hair stuck out over his forehead. Marianne sat on a straightbacked chair, one leg cocked over the other, a high heeled shoe dangling from her toe and a garter showing above one knee. She wore makeup and her short auburn hair had resumed its former curl and shine.

Frank said, "I don't know if we ought to be going on a honeymoon. It doesn't sound proper."

"It wasn't my idea," Marianne said. "It was Mom who thought it up."

"Why didn't you tell her no?"

"You go tell her no right now."

"If she was my mother I would. I wouldn't hold off a second."

"Yeah, I'm really impressed how much you put your foot down around your mother. How come you never took any roast at dinner just now? You looked at your mother and handed on the platter."

"You don't have any call bringing that up. A vegetable diet is good for you. You don't see cows eating meat, do you? They get along fine."

"Good grief!" she said. "Now I know for sure I'm not cooking for you. You can get your own crummy vegetables."

Frank rolled his eyes and grated his molars. Then he got control of himself and said, "I don't want to quarrel. I want to treat you like a sister. I want to be good to you."

Marianne put both feet on the floor and pulled her hem down a bit. "Well, I didn't think it was a good idea to go on a honeymoon either. But Mom cried and said it looked like we didn't love each other."

"It's okay. We'll do it. But we've got to take different rooms in the hotel."

Marianne flared up again. "You're damned right we'll take different rooms. I wouldn't let you touch me for ten thousand dollars."

The next morning at the warehouse in Richfield, Frank gave Ashael two weeks' notice. Ashael said if he had known Frank was going to quit so soon he wouldn't have hired him. They were sitting in Ashael's little office, and Ashael was leaning back in his slatted chair with his feet propped on his yellow oak desk.

"I've had reports on you, Frank, and they aren't favorable. Turns out you wear your tie loose most of the time. You know very well a neat, tidy uniform is one of the conditions of your employment by Lamson Enterprises."

"I try to remember to tighten it up before I make a delivery," Frank said. "Once in a while I forget. It seems like I can't wear a tie tied up tight all day long. It makes me feel like every day is Sunday."

"And I hear you've been talking against my new Fluffy Harvest bread."

Frank squinted his eyes and rubbed a nostril with a knuckle.

"I predict a lowly future for you, Frank," Ashael said, bouncing a wire yeast beater against his thigh. "You'll never climb in the business world. You lack enthusiasm."

"Yes, sir, that's right, sir. I just don't think I was cut out to deliver bread and pies and canned vegetables. There's something about all them that don't give me any pleasure."

That night when he got home Frank found the walls ready to fall down. A letter had come from Dr. Washley at the state hospital, driving Margaret into a frenzy. Although canning season was six months away, she had carried empty jars from the basement and now stood at the sink, scrubbing furiously. "There it is," she said, stabbing with her brush toward the letter, which she had laid out on the table.

> Dear Mrs. Windham:
>
> In response to Mr. Frank Windham's recent letter, I am willing that your son, Jeremy, return to your home on a trial basis. I will count on you to continue his chemotherapy. I strongly attribute his currently docile character to the medication we are providing. Also I will expect a quarterly visit here at the hospital. If this is acceptable, you may arrange to come for him at your earliest convenience.
>
> Yours truly,
> Anthon F. Washley, M. D.

"Hot dog," Frank said, "he's coming home at last!"

"Him coming home, you getting married," Margaret said faintly. "It's too much, far too much."

"It's a sign that God heard our prayers. He's sending Jeremy home to be with you while I'm gone."

"Oh, this is terrible, terrible. I counted on you being here. What on earth will I ever do?"

"There won't be nothing to it. You'll feed him wholesome food and take care of him. He'll be a thousand times better off here at home."

"What will the neighbors think when I say, This is my boy Alice? What if he wants to haul his dolls all over town and show them to people? What if he won't mind when I tell him to do things?"

"I'll be around a good deal. Every weekend I'll drive over for Sunday. If something special comes up, you can phone and I'll come over any time. And Leola too. She'll help out. Orderville isn't so far away."

"God take care of us," Margaret said. She picked up Washley's letter with wet fingers and, finding herself unable to focus on it, dropped it. "Well, he can't come till after this wedding, that's all there is to it. I can't do two things at once."

Frank put an arm around her. "I won't be away from home for long. Just one year and I'll be back to stay with you and Jeremy. I mean it. Marianne and me aren't getting married for keeps."

"Don't talk nonsense," she said angrily. "She's got you and she'll keep you. You won't ever be home again."

"She hates me. I make her vomit. I don't blame her, seeing what a low down, deceitful coyote I was. So we've made up our minds we're busting up in about a year. We're getting married just to give the kid a proper name."

"That's wicked," she said. "You don't mean that."

"We've talked it over and we're not going to do what married people usually do. We're going to sleep in different rooms. This honeymoon is a big fake. Reason we're having it is Clara wants us to. But we aren't doing what people do on honeymoons. And when the baby gets here and people know who its daddy is, we're splitting up. That's the plan."

"That's abominable!"

"No, it isn't. I'll send her money and I'll go visit the little thing so it knows me."

"What makes you think you can get by without sleeping with her. That's a pipe dream!"

"We're going to practice chastity like Grandma and Grandpa Jamison. If they could, why can't we?"

"Yes," she said, her nose wrinkling with disgust, "just like Grandma and Grandpa Jamison!"

"We're going to," he insisted. "She's agreed on it. We're going to live like a brother and sister. My mind is made up. Getting married is just another test, another way to practice self control."

She looked as if she wanted to spit.

"I have it in me," he said. "I ain't going to touch her. I promise you."

"Your promises," she said, "aren't worth a turnip peel."

While Margaret fixed supper Frank phoned Leola and she and Lawrence drove up from Orderville, arriving within an hour. Leola thought Jeremy ought to come home immediately. "You just go right on up there and get him next Saturday before that Dr. Washley changes his mind. Frank will be here in the evenings next week, and I'll come up every morning to help him get settled in. And after Frank's wedding, if you need to, you can bring him down to Orderville and stay at our house for a while."

"Oh, gracious," Margaret said, "what will Mr. and Mrs. Earle think? I'll bet they don't have any derangements amongst their relatives."

"People will just have to get used to him," Leola said. "The sooner they start, the better off everybody will be."

On Saturday morning Frank and Margaret drove to Provo. They spent an hour in Washley's office getting instructions, advice, and several prescriptions. Washley was very pleasant with them and said perhaps Jeremy really would be as well off at home. Jeremy sat waiting for them in the day room, at his feet a suitcase holding his clothes and a carpet bag holding his dolls. He was leafing through a new Sears catalog. His crew cut was freshly barbered and he wore new Levi's and a plaid shirt.

Margaret hugged him and said, "Now leave the catalog where you found it and we'll go right along."

An aid said, "It's his. Mrs. Woodbarrow brought it over."

As they were driving west on Center Street, Margaret said, "I wouldn't mind looking at that catalog myself."

"It isn't a catalog," Jeremy declared. "Thou shalt live from every word which proceedeth from the mouth of God."

"It most certainly is a catalog."

"Not if he says it isn't," Frank said. "Looks like it's Scripture."

"God give me strength," Margaret murmured.

"He will, he surely will," Jeremy said.

They went to Dora's for lunch before leaving for Panguitch. Dora was behind the counter waiting on a woman. A new assistant, a college girl, was at a rack helping another woman. Dora bustled out with great cheer.

"There you are! My, don't you look fine, Margaret? Frank, you handsome young man, let me give you a kiss. And here's my little Alice. Bless your heart, dear." Jeremy bent down to her and she gave him a long hug. "In your absence, Margaret, I've been visiting him twice a week."

"Oh, thank you, thank you. What a support you are, Dora."

When the customers had left, she introduced the college girl, Jenny Wheeler, who was working Saturdays in the store. "We're getting ready for my big vacation in May. Jenny will help take over while I'm down in Garfield County with Nathan. I'm just so excited. He writes me every week about the progress he is making on the trailer. You've seen it lately, haven't you, Frank?"

"Yes, ma'am, he's fixing it up real fine," Frank lied. The shabby trailer hadn't been touched since Archie had delivered it in early January.

Dora left Jenny in charge of the store and took the others into the kitchen, where she put Frank to setting the table and Margaret to dicing apples and grating carrots. "I have been keeping up with the news about you, Frank," she said . "A week from today you are getting married. I'm sure Marianne Earle is a wonderful person. I wish you both great happiness."

"Happiness!" Margaret said in a weak, croaking voice. "It's terrible what has come to pass."

Hugging her, Dora said, "Don't you cry, dear. Everything will turn out for the best."

When everything was ready, Dora called Jenny in and they all sat down. Dora said, "Alice, would you like to say the blessing on the food?"

"Yes, ma'am," Jeremy replied. He closed his eyes, placed his clenched fists against his forehead, and leaned low over his plate. "Heavenly Father, we pray for the California condors, that they may develop a more practical way of launching into the air. We also pray for the parakeets of Dutch Guiana, which are illegally sold in pet shops."

"Also bless this food," Frank said.

"Yes, Heavenly Father," Jeremy went on, "bless this food that it may strengthen and nourish our bodies. And keep in mind the state buffalo herd on the Henry Mountains that it may enlarge and prosper."

"Also thanks for this food," Frank said.

"Yes, oh Lord, we thank thee for this food. We thank thee for abundant winter snow wherewith our summer shall be wetted."

"In the name of Jesus Christ, amen," Frank said.

"Amen," Jeremy said and looked up.

"Goodness gracious," Margaret exclaimed. "Is that how they bless the food in the hospital?"

"It was a lovely blessing," Dora said.

Jeremy shook out his napkin, which was of fine cotton with a satiny fleur-de-lis in the center. He spread the napkin over his plate and scrutinized the pattern. "Poison ivy," he muttered.

"What's that?" Frank asked.

"Poison ivy," Jeremy said, pulling away from the napkin. "See there, a three leaved plant, shiny with toxic oil. Poison ivy induces severe dermatitis. They have invented a vaccine for it but it isn't effective. The foremost rule for poison ivy is avoidance. Stay away from it."

"Oh, no, dear," Dora protested, "that's not poison ivy; that's a lily blossom, a fleur-de-lis. The royal house of France took it for their coat of arms." She looked at her napkin with admiration. "Isn't it pretty?"

Jeremy held up his napkin. "Yes, it is pretty."

Margaret said, "Put your napkin on your lap and have some of this good casserole, Jeremy."

"My name is Alice," he said.

Margaret put down her fork and stared. "We are going to get one thing settled right now, young man. I have had enough of this Alice business. It's Jeremy from now on. Do you understand that?"

"Alice."

"Jeremy," she said, giving his arm a hard pinch.

He bellowed, "Oh, I'm hurt, I'm hurt." He dragged his chair to a corner and seated himself with his back to the table. He shook and sobbed and snuffled and wiped his nose on a sleeve.

"Well, if that isn't strange," Margaret said. "You just come right back over here and eat your food."

"You've got to call him Alice," Frank said.

She pushed back her chair and stood, tears streaming down her cheeks. She walked halfway to him and paused. "Aren't you my Jeremy?" she said. "My little Jeremy?"

"I'm your little Alice."

"Oh, sweetie," she said, "I don't care if you're Alice. Come back, Alice. Come back to the table."

He got up and turned and Margaret opened her arms and took him in, patting his back and saying, "My poor little Alice, my poor dear little Alice."

When they got home to Panguitch late that night, Jeremy circled through the house, ground floor and basement, four or five times, picking things up and setting them down. His bedroom was ready, a light orange counterpane turned down, artificial flowers arranged on the table, blue pajamas hung over the back of the chair. The next morning he and Frank put on their heavy coats and went out to milk the cow. Frank waited at the corral gate while he explored the snow covered lot, kicking out a buried bucket and giving a log a lick with the ax.

"What do you think of this here bull of mine?" Frank said. "He's got a lame leg and doesn't do much but rest. However, one of these times when that little cow comes in heat he'll manage to get on top of her."

In the milk shed Frank threw hay into the manger and shut the gate on the cow's neck. "This cow is named Chloe. Now I want you to sit on that stool and try your hand at milking her. When I'm gone you'll have to do it all the time."

Although Jeremy grunted, grimaced, and squeezed, milk emerged from the teats in weak, dribbly streams. Finally he quit, saying, "My hands are tuckered."

"Good enough," Frank said. "You keep trying night and morning till you get your fingers built up. She isn't an easy milker."

After breakfast Frank and Jeremy went to Priesthood Meeting. About forty men and boys were assembled in the chapel for opening exercises. A stake high councilman took some time warning the brethren of the North Ward against being dissentious and uncooperative with the brethren of the South Ward. Then Bishop Bidley took the pulpit and after giving ward announcements called attention to Jeremy. "We want to welcome home Brother Jeremy

Windham. This good brother has had a bad shaking and has been off in the state hospital and now he's back in Panguitch and we want everyone of us to do our little bit to smooth things out for him."

Frank stood up in his pew and said, "Bishop, can I say a word or two?"

"You bet. Give us what's on your mind."

"I just want to alert everybody that my brother doesn't like to be called Jeremy anymore. He likes to be called Alice. I'd take it as a personal favor if you would all remember to call him Alice."

Three or four pews ahead a couple of deacons snorted.

Frank leaned forward and shook his fist. "Anybody who picks on my brother will answer to me. I don't care who you are, big or little, if I catch anybody picking on him, I'll thrash you."

The bishop said, "Sit down, Frank, and don't get yourself lathered up." He squinted and looked around the hall. "There's nothing in Scripture that says a man can't be called by the name he wants to be called by. Come Judgment Day we're going to see Sister Alice standing on the right hand of the Savior. The Lord has put him among us for a special reason and we better not let the Lord down. Brethren, keep an eye on your kids and if you see them making fun of Sister Alice, larrup the daylights out of them."

On Saturday morning enough people to fill a gymnasium showed up at Ruby's Inn for the wedding—Leola and her family; Susan and hers; Lonnie and Jessica; Jack and Red; Nathan; Mr. Obenheimer, the justice of the peace, and his wife; and fifteen or twenty Lutherans whose names Frank couldn't keep straight. Pine logs blazed in the giant cobblerock fireplace, their smoke scenting the air. Silver ribbons looped along heavy ceiling beams and spiraled down thick supporting posts. On a table sat a fancy three tier wedding cake flanked by two bowls of pink punch distinguished by signs reading *with* and *without*. At another table Peggy Lindburne, the cute pug nosed cook who had signed Frank's delivery bills, was setting out platters of tiny sandwiches. She waved and gave Frank a big smile.

"My gosh," Frank moaned to Margaret, "who invited so many people?"

"We did. That is, Clara and me." Margaret wore a high collared dress checkered in light lavender and brown.

"Holy Moses, this is worse than a Mexican bull fight. Everybody has come to see me killed."

"Don't blame me," Margaret said. "It was Clara who insisted on a crowd. I couldn't very well not invite anybody at all from our side, could I, seeing how many she meant to invite? I must say Clara certainly doesn't seem to have in mind this is just a temporary marriage. Not at all."

"I don't care what she doesn't have in mind," Frank growled. "One year, that's all I'm putting into it."

Wesley, sipping from a little glass, had been standing with Jack and Red near the punch bowls. He had on his fanciest outfit—lizard skin boots, twill pants, corduroy coat, and silver ten-gallon Stetson, which he had pulled low on his brow. Just now Clara was giving him a scolding for getting an early start on the refreshments. "That's for after, not before. Now please go over there and help the Stapleys swing that piano around where we want it."

Frank sidled up to Jack and Red and said, "Who invited you?" Red wore a regular Sunday suit, Jack a pearlbuttoned shirt and the boots Frank had given him.

"Mrs. Earle requested our company," Jack said. "She knew what wonderful, long-suffering, generous friends we've been to you all these years. She thought we'd want to give you a last goodby."

"This is awful."

"Cheer up. One of these punch bowls has got anti-freeze in it."

"For crying out loud don't you guys get drunk."

"What do you mean you guys?" Red said. "Don't count me in with this reprobate. I'm going on a mission next month."

"The end of a good man," Jack said, shaking his head dismally. "And this here little ceremony today, that's the end of another good man. Frank, you poor hoot owl." Then he pretended to brighten up, nodding toward Marianne, who stood by the fireplace with Nathan and Jeremy. "Of course there's something to be said for having a little regular loving every night, ain't there?" He socked Frank on the arm. "You old studhorse, how come you never told us you were getting into her britches?"

Frank wandered to the fireplace, where Marianne still stood with Nathan and Jeremy, none of them saying a word. Marianne was the prettiest he had ever seen her—lipstick, eyebrow pencil, heels, and a shiny new blue dress with a white sash.

He said, "Do you think we ought to shake hands?"

"What for?" she replied, smelling of vomit.

"Maybe I ought to kiss you on the cheek."

She put out her cheek and he kissed it.

"This here is my sister Alice," he said, gesturing toward Jeremy.

"We introduced ourselves," Marianne said curtly.

Nathan said, "It'll be good to have you back on the ranch, Frank. I sure do wish you and Marianne lots of happiness. I brought you a juniper gnarl for your wedding gift. You know, one of them nice round knots you can use for a paper weight. I sanded it and waxed it and polished it up till it's all shiny."

"I always wanted one of them," Frank said. "Thanks a whole lot."

Clara had called Marianne across the room. Watching her teeter over the cobblerock floor, Nathan said, "I never would've figured on this coming to pass."

"Me either."

"Them Earles aren't bad people, Frank, considering they are Lutherans."

"No, sir, I believe they are pretty decent."

"She's a good girl, Frank."

"Yes, she is. I'm not blaming anybody but me for my troubles."

"You don't have to see them as troubles, I guess."

"Well, that's how I see it. Troubles are all I got."

Nathan rubbed his brown, oily chin.

"Speaking of troubles," Frank said, "you got a few of your own coming up. We saw Dora last Saturday. She's getting everything arranged to take a little vacation in May."

"That's what she says in her letters."

"Thing is, she's not just blowing hot air this time. She really is coming. She's getting some helpers trained up who will run the bookstore while she's down here."

Nathan stopped rubbing his chin.

"You better get that trailerhouse fixed up."

"I had in mind doing it."

"Well, you really better do it. Either that or skip the country."

Clara called Frank to help Marianne bring in the flowers. "Let's get the baskets set up and get everybody's bouquets and corsages. They're in the trunk of my car. And then we'll be ready to start."

The parking lot outside the lodge was icy and snow was banked up six feet high around its edges. North of the lodge a snowy plain rolled away toward distant blue mountains; south rose a forest of tall ponderosa pines. Marianne went ahead of Frank, and when he came around Clara's car, he found her bent over, spitting and drooling.

"Let me take your handkerchief," she said. He handed it to her and she wiped her mouth. "I'm going to vomit right in the middle of the ceremony. I know I will."

"It's a circus in there. Everybody is here for a party. They think we're doing this because we want to."

"It's that damned honeymoon I'm dreading," she brooded. "I can't spend four days in Las Vegas alone with you. I'll vomit every minute."

"We'll make the best of it," he said. "We can take in some shows and I wouldn't mind seeing Boulder Dam and maybe we can find some good books to read."

"I don't know how I can live in a trailerhouse with you, I honestly don't. I just don't want to be around you, Frank, that's all there is to it."

When they had got inside with the flower boxes, Clara put the baskets beside the fireplace where she wanted the bride and groom and justice of the peace to stand, and she got corsages and boutonnieres pinned to Margaret and herself and Frank and Wesley. Then she gave a big bouquet of yellow and white flowers to Marianne and said everything was ready.

Mrs. Stapley struck a loud chord on the piano, a massive old upright decorated by fancy carvings. Peering through thick lenses, Mrs. Stapley galloped into a heroic medley sounding more or less like parade music. Mr. Stapley stood at her side, one hand behind his back, the other ready to turn pages. Mr. Obenheimer planted himself before the fire, holding a Bible and an old envelope on which he had scribbled some words. A spot of shaving cream showed on his ear lobe and the knot of his tie struck off at an odd angle. Mrs. Obenheimer, in a calico dress, grinned happily, exposing dentures with pumpkin colored gums.

Frank and Marianne stood side by side in front of Mr. Obenheimer and the ceremony began. Marianne kept her lips pursed tight and every few seconds her heels teetered on the cobblerock floor. Frank's brown cowlick stuck out over his forehead. His big red neck swelled over a tight collar and his giant hands dangled from the sleeves of his grey doublebreasted coat. He couldn't concentrate on the advice the justice of the peace was giving them about loving one another, couldn't follow the business about taking each other for better or worse till death did them part. He kept his teary eyes down, noting that Marianne's big ankles weren't out of proportion with her calves, which were bigger, also noting that the yellow and white bouquet matched up pretty with her blue dress and white sash. The first thing he knew, they had both said "I do" and there was a long silence and he knew it was time for action. He leaned over and gave her a little kiss on the lips.

Mrs. Stapley crashed into a hymn of love and praise and Jack hooted out, "Kiss her hard, you badger, kiss her hard."

Marianne stood with her eyes closed and a tear or two on her cheeks and her lips still puckered, so Frank gave her a big wet kiss. Then people crowded around shaking hands and hugging and kissing. Mrs. Stapley pounded into a popular song, and Jack grabbed Marianne, whirling her into a dance. She stumbled and swayed and started to laugh.

Peggy Lindburne, in a white waitress uniform, said to Frank, "Do I get to congratulate the groom?" After kissing him, she said, "She's a real pretty girl. I hope you have lots of joy."

Jack swung Marianne around to Frank, shouting, "Get out of the chicken coop and dance with your bride."

People pulled back and made a little square, but Frank hesitated. Marianne put her arms around him and he couldn't do anything but dance.

"That danged Jack," he growled. "I hope his teeth rot out."

"Be decent," she said. "People want us to dance." She pulled herself up close and put her cheek against his. "Who's that waitress?"

"She just works here. She signed off the ticket when I delivered."

"That was a pretty cozy kiss she gave you."

"She ain't anybody," he said.

Soon others began to dance—Lonnie and Jessica, Lawrence and Leola, Wesley and Clara, swirling and swaying near the edges of the room where the cobblerock gave way to puncheon floor. A call went up to have Frank and Marianne cut their cake, and people began loading plates with sandwiches and cake and filling up glasses at the punch bowls. They milled around for a bit and finally separated into little clusters of Mormons and Lutherans, smiling and nodding in a quiet, cautious way. Clara dug into one bunch after another, saying, "You've just got to come over here and tell Frank's sister about what the PTA is doing in Monroe," or "I want you to tell Mr. and Mrs. Jahonie where you caught those trout last summer." It wasn't long until things were noisy again and people were chattering and laughing like they were all best friends.

Wesley and Jack struck up a friendship at the punch bowl marked *with*, discussing flour mills and uranium prospecting. After a while Wesley saw Nathan by himself at the fireplace. He filled two glasses and started slowly across the room, gazing upon his wobbly hands and muttering "Damnation" as punch splashed from the glasses.

"Nathan," he shouted, "oh, Nathan, I say! Old friend, comrade, amigo! It pains me to see you standing apart from all society. Here, we'll drink together."

Nathan held up outturned palms. "I can't drink punch from that bowl, thanks just the same. It's against the Word of Wisdom."

"My God, the word of wisdom! Man, it is mete that we be merry. That is the word of wisdom."

"I can't do it."

Wesley stared back toward the bowl he had just left, then peered at the glasses in his hand. "You won't drink with me?" he said in a surprised tone. "That's ungrateful."

"No, sir," Nathan said, "I'm not ungrateful."

Wesley relaxed the fingers of one hand and a glass dropped, shattering on the cobblerock floor. Instantly the room became silent.

"Ungrateful," Wesley said loudly, "clearly ungrateful! Nobody gives a damn about J. Wesley Earle. His dissertation was granted distinction. His committee chairman advised him to specialize in biochemistry and apply for a position at Berkeley or Yale. My God, who is he now? A piddling hay rancher, trapped in the godforsaken wastes of southern Utah." He relaxed the fingers of the other hand and the second glass shattered on the floor.

"Daddy!" Marianne shouted. "You're drunk!"

He turned, glaring, and said, "Ungrateful."

She squatted and began to pick up shards of glass. Wesley pulled her up and hugged her. "You're nothing but a child," he cried. "Hardly out of the cradle! Cut off from your prospects! Cut off, cut off!"

"Oh, Daddy," she wept, "I'm just so sorry."

Jack shouted, "If this ain't a hell of a way to run a wedding! Come on, lady, get that piano going. Let's have some more of this good food. Let me dance with the bride again. I never got but a minute last time."

The piano started and Wesley gave up his daughter to Jack and turned to Nathan. "Forgive me," he said, putting an arm around the old man.

About noon Frank and Marianne left Ruby's Inn in Wesley's pickup, headed for Las Vegas. A quarter mile down the road Frank stopped and took off the tin cans Jack and Red had tied to the rear bumper. He circled the pickup, taking another look at the big letters printed in white shoe polish on the door panels and hood: *just married, true love, whoopee.*

"Those weasels make me sick," Frank grumped as he climbed in. "When we stop at Leola's we'll wash those words off." The plan was for them to stop a minute in Orderville to change from their wedding clothes.

Marianne was getting a head start on changing. She had pulled up her skirt and was unlatching her garters and peeling off her hose. Frank couldn't help watching, and her big white legs and her lacy slip looked awfully nice. If he and she were going to get along like a brother and sister, she would have to keep her dainties covered up.

"It was really nice of folks to give us all those gifts," he said.

Margaret had given them pots and pans. Lonnie had slipped Frank a ten dollar bill to help out on the trip. Leola had presented them with a beautiful quilt in a pattern of embroidered sea shells. Wesley and Clara had handed them a little note written on fancy stationery telling them that Clara's Chrysler was theirs, which meant of course that Clara would be getting a new car. Jack and Red had given them a double-bitted ax and, sure enough, Nathan's gift had turned out to be a heavy juniper gnarl.

"At least we'll have a car," he said.

She didn't reply.

"Can you believe those two skunks giving us an ax!" he exclaimed.

She was staring out the window.

"I wish Nathan would keep his gnarls to himself," he went on. "What in heck are we going to do with that thing?"

She shook her head slightly.

He could tell her spirits had dropped down among the angleworms. She sat braced against the seat as if she was in a dentist's chair, her arms crossed and her bare feet stuck under the heater vent. He wondered how they were going to make it through a year of marriage if they couldn't come up with something to talk about on their honeymoon. He quit trying to talk and listened to the rumble of the speeding pickup. When they came to Zion's National Park, he asked her if she wanted to get out and take a look at the Great White Throne.

"Why?"

"Seems like folks on their honeymoon ought to take a look at it. That's what it's for."

"Go ahead," she said.

He hiked up a switchback trail for three or four hundred yards. There was no snow in the canyon, the sun was shining, the air was almost balmy. The bottom was filled with leafless trees, box elder, maple, and ash, and here and there a stream glinted yellow brown. Rising slopes were rust-grey with brush, blue-black with firs. High overhead loomed giant cliffs, crests, monoliths, pinnacles, cut from solid rock in tints of grey, red, and cream. For a minute he felt as he had in the old days before God had struck Jeremy—loose and free like a mustang or hawk.

They arrived in Las Vegas at dusk and Frank pulled in at the Fremont Hotel in the city center. Inside he asked for two rooms, one for himself, one for his sister. After unpacking they went down to supper in the hotel coffee shop where, steak dinners being cheap, Frank ordered a top sirloin. Although he was ashamed of himself for letting down on Margaret's healthy vegetarian principles, his misery was the kind that needed red meat. Marianne ordered a toasted cheese sandwich and left about a third of it. When he asked if she wanted to take in a show, she said, no, she was all pooped out. He bought himself a magazine in the hotel candy shop, and by nine-thirty they were locked up in their separate rooms.

He read for a while, had a shower, and put on the new pajamas Margaret had bought him. Before getting into bed, he stood at the window and looked out. Across the street, above the portico of the Golden Nugget casino, a giant marquee blazed. A neon prospector, hefting a pick, bent and straightened, bent and straightened amid hundreds of racing, blinking bulbs. A crowd flowed on the sidewalks, men and women in all kinds of clothes, suits and sport shirts, high heels and flats. Frank picked out a couple, a short pudgy man, a tall thin woman. He puffed on a cigar and talked in a serious, important way, his hands gesturing. She laughed with excitement and her teeth glimmered. Frank knew it was all vanity. He just wished he didn't feel so envious.

Around midnight a loud knock woke him up. Groggy and uncertain, he shuffled to the door and opened a crack. There was Marianne in fuzzy slippers and flowery bathrobe, her curls tangled and messy.

"I can't sleep," she said, starting to sniffle. "The drapes won't keep out that awful blinking light. I'm so lonesome I just can't stand it."

"Gosh," he said, "come in. There's no sense you being lonesome."

She took a chair and sobbed. "I'm sorry I woke you up. It's terrible of me to do that, but I just hate this place. Let's go home tomorrow, Frank."

He sat on the edge of the bed and ran a hand through his tousled hair. "Tomorrow's Sunday. We likely can't pick up one of those trailers till Monday."

The room vibrated with light from the winking, pulsing marquee across the street. He was wishing he could turn it off. It wasn't decent to sit there plain as day in his pajamas with his hair mussed up.

Then a good idea hit him. "I'll tell you what. I'll get the blankets out of your room and make me a bed on the floor and you can sleep in this bed."

"Oh, I couldn't do that."

"I don't mind," he said. "I used to sleep on floors all the time when I was driving truck for your dad."

She was still sniffling so he dug in his suitcase and handed her a handkerchief. He stood nearby, thinking this might be a good time to talk over how they were going to live like a brother and sister, and then his hand reached out, as if it belonged to somebody else, and began to rub her shoulder. She reached up and started patting his hand, and there they were, rubbing and patting, rubbing and patting. Finally he bent over and gave her a little kiss and she put her arms around his neck, keeping him down until the little kiss got to be a big, long, wet one. He knew he needed a rescue. Right that minute he needed a policeman or a Mormon bishop or, heck, a clergyman of any kind or a high school principal or a newspaper editor, just anybody with some authority and a little bit of intelligence to come pounding on the door and save him.

He pulled her up and they hugged and kissed, she crying a little, saying, "I loved you so much, I did love you so much."

The first thing he knew, he had unbuttoned her bathrobe and tugged up her nightie and his hands were going everywhere. Like a man back from a long thirst on the desert, he couldn't stop drinking. He was astounded how good she felt, every inch of her, her tangled hair, her wet cheeks, her arms, her sagging breasts. She let the bathrobe slip off and pulled the nightie over her head and stepped out of the slippers. They migrated toward the bed, hugging, kissing, and fondling, and before long they lay down and made love.

At dawn he looked through the drapes. The marquee of the Golden Nugget still blinked and flashed and raced. The street was empty except for a delivery van and one late reveler, a man in a flowery short-sleeved shirt who tottered on the curb, looking as if he didn't know what to do next. Heading for the bathroom, Frank glanced at Marianne, who lay on her side, an arm exposed, her tousled head sunk in the fluffy pillow, her breathing deep and regular.

He sat on the toilet, planting his elbows on his knees and his chin in his hands. He felt wretched. He was wondering how God was feeling this morning up on the royal star of Kolob. Would he already know that his servant, Frank J. Windham, had once again had sex with a woman, or would he leave details like that to his staff? Frank wondered how he could let God know that this awful reversal in his repentance was only temporary. It wasn't likely God would give much account to promises a man might make in a hotel room in Las Vegas. All of which made him further ponder why God put up with the notorious state of Nevada with its gambling and drunkenness and whoredom. In particular, why had God allowed this modern Sodom and Gomorrah to exist side by side, to share a common border, with Utah, his new Zion, the home of his true saints? Sometimes it seemed that God subjected his servants to excessive trials and tribulations, of which a honeymoon in Las Vegas was a good example.

After he had shaved, combed his hair, and brushed his teeth, he found Marianne sitting up in bed with her bathrobe on. "Could we go eat breakfast pretty soon?" she asked. "I think if I get something in my tummy I won't vomit this morning."

She went into the other bedroom and shortly emerged in jeans and blouse, dragging a comb through her snarls and fluffing and patting around her head. In the coffee shop, she ordered ham, eggs, toast, hash brown potatoes, orange juice, and milk and then began to talk about the wedding in a cheerful voice. She laughed about Mrs. Stapley, who played a piano like she was killing flies.

"Bless Nathan's heart," she said. "He cleaned my boots. They were in the hallway, muddy from the last ride I took last fall. He polished them and brought them up from the bunkhouse Friday night. I cried a little and said, I won't ever go riding again, and he said, Sure, you will."

Frank ate his pancakes and eggs without much comment. It was funny how a carnal deed could cheer a person up. He hoped Marianne wasn't forgetting this marriage wasn't supposed to last more than a year. However, for the time being, he'd rather have poked out one of his eyes than say something that would make her blue again.

After breakfast Marianne wanted to see the sights in the city center. Frank had a notion he ought to go to church, but he decided a little Sabbath breaking didn't add up to much compared to the other sins he had been committing. As they wandered around, Marianne hung on his arm and marveled over the bright sunshine, balmy air, palm trees, and green grass and all the out of state cars. They went by a massage parlor, a penny arcade, a dirty movie house, and a bookstore with a big yellow and red sign saying "Stephano's Adult Books."

They paused before a tiny white wedding chapel furnished with a couple of pews and three or four pots of plastic Easter lilies. "We could have got married in there and saved all the fuss," Marianne said.

They found a slot machine in a drugstore where Marianne went to buy sunglasses. She put a quarter in the slot and pulled the handle, sending pears, bananas, and bells whirling round and round.

"I'll have to see your I.D., miss," a clerk said. "Minors can't play the slots."

"I'm not a miss," she said.

"That doesn't matter. Law says minors can't game."

"That's the stupidest law I ever heard of!"

"Don't start a ruckus, lady, or I'll call a security man."

She fumed as they went along the sidewalk. "Well, aren't they self-righteous? Minors can't do this and minors can't do that. Everything that goes on in this town, and I can't even play a two-bit slot machine!"

When they got back to the Fremont, she went to her own room to take a nap, which suited Frank just fine. Though he lay on his bed and tried to sleep, his mind kept tracking back to the adult bookstore they had passed. A store like that would probably have a book telling whether a woman could get pregnant while she was having a period. He locked his door quietly and tiptoed down the corridor. Outside he took off as fast as he could walk.

Up front Stephano's Adult Bookstore had tobacco and candy and a lot of regular magazines and out of town newspapers. The back was more interesting. There were a lot of magazines on whose covers tough looking ladies showed their breasts and crotches. There were also a half dozen racks of paperback novels with titles like *Deeper and Deeper, Motel Weekend,* and *Unholy Romance.* In a display case marked "Fantasy Aids" were some strange devices made of plastic, rubber, and fake hair. Seeing he had come to the wrong place, Frank headed for the door. A man with a cigar leaned over the counter. He was squat, swarthy, and bald and had a big Jerusalem nose and black chest hair curling out of his collar.

"Whatcha need?" he said.

Frank decided this had to be Stephano and he certainly wouldn't be shocked by Frank's little problem. "I was trying to find a book that would say if a woman can get pregnant when she's having a period."

The man straightened up and squinted his eyes until the cigar smoke had cleared off a bit. "She sure as hell can," he said. "Don't try it without rubbers, mister. You can get them in them machines you see in the rest rooms. Just put a quarter in the slot and turn the handle."

"It ain't for now," Frank said. "I was just wondering."

"You just got married, I bet."

"Yes, sir. Yesterday."

"Happens we got some books in your line. Come here and have a look."

The man waddled along an aisle Frank hadn't gone down. "Right there," he said, pointing to a little section of hardback books. "Marriage manuals. Anything the newlywed wants to know. Store policy is, You handle, you buy. If you're serious, I don't care if you thumb through a few before you make up your mind."

Frank got into one titled *Sex and Affection in Marriage*, written by Basil V. Phoxhalter, M.D. He stared a while at the chapter on sexual physiology, which gave sketches on male and female plumbing, letting him see just exactly how women were rigged up. Then he stopped in the chapter called "Varieties of Intercourse," which also had a lot of sketches. He regretted looking into this book because of all the dirty notions it put into his head. A man and a woman could make love standing, kneeling, or lying on their sides. They could do it belly to belly or front to back. And if they got tired of all that, they could even do it on a stool.

He studied the sketches and read the instructions three or four times, just so later on he could remember how rotten and perverted marriage manuals could get. Then of course, since he had spent a good half hour browsing in the book, he had to buy it and it cost twelve bucks. Once he got down the street, he pitched it into a city garbage can. About the time he got back to the Fremont, he remembered he never had found where Dr. Basil V. Phoxhalter said a woman could get pregnant during her period.

In the afternoon Frank and Marianne drove the pickup out on the Strip, where everyone said the future of Las Vegas lay. There were a few giant casinos and a great deal of open, barren desert. One marquee, a quarter of an acre in size, proclaimed none other than Elvis Presley, the fantastic, sensational king of rock 'n roll.

"Gosh," Frank said, "can you beat that? I didn't know he was real. Maybe we ought to go buy tickets and watch him work."

"He's not much," she said. "The way he humps around a stage you'd think he was a billy goat making babies."

"That's true. However, we might never get another chance to see him. It's like they had brought Hitler or Stalin over for public inspection. You'd go see him just to find out what he really looks like, wouldn't you?"

"Let's not waste our money," she said.

They ended up going to a little dinner show across the street from their hotel. The entertainer was a country singer named Jason Hugo from Fresno, who did an impersonation of Hank Williams. He wore a creamy western suit and brown alligator boots and had a guitar inlaid with mother of pearl that under the bright spotlights shimmered white, green, and purple. He was backed by two fiddlers and an accordion player, also in fancy western suits.

For eight dollars apiece Frank and Marianne were having a crab and salmon dinner. Jason Hugo didn't seem to mind that waiters were running in and out, taking orders, setting down platters and glasses, and asking whether the potatoes au gratin were okay or whether somebody wanted a refill of coffee or a little more dessert. He sat on a stool in a bright spot strumming his guitar and talking in a faraway voice about the history of country-western music. From time to time, as he talked about Hank Williams's lonely existence, the little orchestra came to life and Hugo strummed like a locomotive picking up speed and pitched himself into singing "Lovesick Blues" or "Your Cheatin' Heart" or some other song Hank had made famous.

When she had finished eating, Marianne edged her chair closer to Frank's, pressing her leg against his and leaning an elbow on his shoulder. She was all caught up by the show, shaking her curls, gasping a little, letting a tear or two trickle down her cheeks. "Isn't it sad," she whispered, "how he died in his limousine, just riding and riding and nobody knowing he needed help?"

Frank nodded. He was feeling awfully good about her just now. It was an all right woman who liked Hank Williams, even in an impersonation, better than Elvis Presley.

When they were standing by her door in the Fremont, she tilted her head and closed her eyes and there was nothing he could do but give her a kiss. One thing led to another and pretty soon Frank unlocked his door and they went inside and went on hugging, kissing, and fondling, stopping once in a while to kick off their shoes or slip off her dress or unbuckle his pants.

"Did you ever hear about making love on a stool?" he asked.

"Never did."

"Do you think we should try it?"

"There doesn't seem to be a stool here."

"There's that chair. How about it?"

"All right," she giggled.

Later they lay on the bed for a long time, relaxed, uncovered, arm to arm and thigh to thigh. The light from the Golden Nugget waxed and waned in the room. He was thinking how odd it was to lie by a naked woman without wanting to do anything except let his finger circle around on her breasts and belly.

"It doesn't make any sense, us having two hotel rooms," she said.

"I guess that's right."

"We are married," she said.

"Yeah, we are."

"I never did think much of your idea about us living like a brother and a sister."

"Pretty dumb idea. I don't have one inch of self control."

"I guess you couldn't ever love me," she said.

He didn't reply.

"Would you want to try?"

"Maybe I shouldn't try. I think God is against it."

He felt something crawling upward inside his gullet, like ants or garden beetles. For the first time since he had met her, he wanted to love her. He got up on an elbow and looked at her belly, which was nearly flat now but before long would be a big half moon. He leaned his ear against it and listened hard.

"What are you doing?"

"I can hear the baby."

"That's my digestion."

He knew it was his baby inside. He lay down again, wishing it was somebody else's.

They were quiet for a long time. Then she said, "I've been thinking all day about us making love, whether it was right or wrong, me knowing you don't love me. I didn't know what I was going to do when we got to my door out there in the hall. Then I thought, Good gravy, we're going to be married for a whole year; we can't live like monks and nuns for a whole year."

She got up on her elbow and looked down into his shadowy eyes. "If we can treat each other kind and decent, then it sure isn't any sin if we do what other married people do." She swung out and sat on the edge of the bed, her shoulders slumped, her breasts rolled onto her belly. "I guess I need to know how it's going to be. Yes or no."

"Okay," he said, "we'll treat each other kind and decent and we'll do what other married people do."

"I'm not going to think about anything for a year," she murmured. "I'm not going to try to figure out how bad it's going to hurt when you go away again."

Early the next morning Frank had another good session on the toilet, feeling remorseful over his weak, spineless, wishy-washy, mealy-mouthed promise to Marianne. However, he couldn't keep up his remorse. He got in front of the mirror and lathered up, canting his jaw and scraping off the bristles with his razor. Then he went into the bedroom and asked whether she minded making love after breakfast. She didn't mind.

Mid-morning they drove to a trailer dealership on Eastern Boulevard and looked over the three used trailerhouses Wesley had located on the phone. When Marianne had picked the one she wanted, Frank told the dealer they'd be after it about noon on Wednesday. Following that, they went shopping for swimming suits so they could use the pool on the hotel patio. Marianne's was a red one piece suit with a flouncy little skirt that would keep people from guessing she was pregnant. Back in their room before lunch, she put on her suit and got in front of the mirror, craning her neck this way and that to get a better angle on herself.

"It's okay, isn't it?"

"Right nice," Frank said. He really did like a woman with a little heft to her legs. "How would it be if we get on that bed for a little while before we go out swimming?"

"Gosh," she said.

"We don't have to. I can wait."

"I don't mind," she said, stripping off her suit.

Out at the pool there were tiled walks, potted palms, planter boxes full of little white flowers, and trellises twined with ivy. The sky was bright and blue, the air was balmy. A few people were swimming and diving; a lot more were dangling their legs over the edge of the pool or burning themselves on towels or reclining in deck chairs with books, cigarettes, and icy drinks. Frank and Marianne swam for a while and she got playful and tried to dunk him. Then they sunned on bathtowels. Frank watched two bronzed young men dive off the board who probably had come from southern California. In the summertime his back was browner than theirs, but not his legs. It took leisure, it took money, to get a pair of tanned legs. For a minute, watching them dive, he got to feeling as he had felt up the trail in Zion's Park a couple of days before—loose and free like a mustang or hawk.

As they padded barefooted toward their room, he made up his mind not to pay attention while she stripped. There was no more sense in making love three or four times a day than there was in eating two breakfasts every morning. Also, he had heard of men coming back from their honeymoons hollow-cheeked, slump-shouldered, and weak from too much sex. However, when they were in their room, he couldn't help watching her like a hungry kid.

Having glanced at him a half dozen times, she finally said, "If you want to, it's okay with me." So they made love again.

In the late afternoon they drove out past Henderson and Boulder City to the Hoover Dam. Frank had read a lot about the dam and was keyed up to see just how it had been built. It was a massive curved concrete wall planted between the rocky cliffs of a deep canyon. On the upstream side a lake, its blue water lapping a few yards below the top, reached away to a distant bend in the canyon. On the downstream side the dam was a giant vertical swale—vast, rolling acres of dry, drab concrete. At its base hydroelectric turbines hummed. Bright power lines swooped upward toward metal towers jutting from downstream cliffs. Water roiled from the turbines, green and foamy and sparkling.

"I wish I had been here when they were building this thing," Frank said as they gazed off the downstream side. "Gee whiz, wouldn't it be fun to drive a truck or run a bulldozer on a project like this!"

He pointed out the sections in which the concrete had been poured and the grooves which had been blasted into the solid rock of the cliffs to anchor the dam. Fifteen or twenty workmen had slipped and fallen into the concrete as it had been poured. They were still there, he told her; once the pouring had started, it couldn't be stopped.

Tourists from a sightseeing bus clustered around the elevator building, listening to a guide. When with a wave of his arm the guide disappeared through the doors, they followed by two's and three's. A little man broke off and headed along the roadway, stopping beside Marianne to peer over the railing into the gorge. He wore a rakish blue golf cap, a tails-out sports shirt, yellow and brown plaid Bermuda shorts, and blue sneakers.

"Ye gods," he said with great satisfaction, "this is what I've been waiting to see. Look at all that cement. There must be a cubic mile of it. Doesn't that give you ideas though? How about paving this whole godforsaken, barren, useless desert? And I'm not just talking about Nevada. I mean the whole West, every inch of it. There isn't an inch of pretty anywhere between San Bernardino and Omaha, not one damned inch! I used to say, Give the West back to the Indians. But this dam gives me ideas. Pave it, every bit of it. Bury it under concrete."

Frank stared at the little man. "That's a wormy idea if I ever heard of one," he said. "There's lots of pretty places in the West."

"You call that pretty?" the man said, sweeping his arm toward the cliffs and rocky terraces and spotty patches of yellow grass and prickly pear.

"You ought to see it at sun-up."

The little guy leaned over the railing and spit. "The West hasn't got enough people in it to be worth the trouble. Say I want to take the train from Los Angeles to St. Louis. Good God, it takes two days to make it because I've got to cross the West. It's a nuisance. Pave it, turn it into parking lots, make a race track out of it."

"I hope you're joking, mister," Frank said, "because if you aren't I'm going to knock you goggle-eyed."

"Come on, let's go," Marianne said, tugging on Frank's arm. "He's crazy."

"I know he is and that's why I'm going to teach him a lesson."

With a sudden jerk the man flung his golf cap to the sidewalk. He put up his fists and began to weave and bob. "Threaten me, huh? I'm not helpless, fellow. I know something of self defense. Go ahead, I'm ready for you." The little man was shadowboxing in a wild frenzy. "I'm not afraid of you, lumberhead," he panted, slowly dancing away from Frank. "I execrate the West. I urinate on it. I wipe my ass on it."

"What a grasshopper like him says doesn't make any difference," Marianne pleaded.

"There are some things people have got to learn a little respect for," Frank said.

The doors to the elevator building had opened and people were spilling out onto the sidewalk and roadway. "Lordy, let's go," Marianne whispered hoarsely and Frank let her pull him along.

"Ha!" shouted the little man, dancing forward now. "You're all talk. You're all air. You don't have the guts to stand up to a real fighter."

In the pickup, as they drove toward Las Vegas, Marianne laughed and laughed. "That's something, that little piss-ant getting your goat. You're as bad as my dad."

He glared at her and shook his head mournfully. It seemed whatever he did was either sinful or stupid.

Though it was supper time she said she wanted to go up to their room and freshen up. When she got out of the bathroom, he was slumped in the armchair, beat down and blue. She got onto his lap and leaned her cheek against his.

"If you want," she said, "we can make love again after dinner."

"How about let's make love now? Then we'll do it after dinner too."

"You look kind of run down."

"I'm perking up."

"All right," she said. "I sure don't mind."

8.

Yoked to
Unbelievers

The Old Testament said that Jacob worked seven years for his father-in-law to earn Leah, another seven to earn Rachel, and seven more just to give good measure. Frank had in mind working only one year for his father-in-law, which was all the time God had given him to clean up the mess he had made by getting Marianne pregnant. He planned to rip into Wesley's projects like a millsaw and finish every one of them—to compensate Wesley not for taking Marianne away but for giving her back.

Wesley made Frank his foreman. "The whole operation is your baby," he said. "You hire and fire. You say what and when, who and where. Consult me when you think you really need to, but don't bother me with trifles."

Wesley was going all out on being a gentleman rancher. He spent more time than ever on the telephone investing in cattle futures, was still on the Water Board of the state of Utah, and was president of the Intermountain Hereford Breeders Association. Planning to run for county commissioner in the next election, he had accepted a position on a fund raising committee for a new hospital in Panguitch and another on a committee for the beautification of Escalante.

Frank didn't relish being foreman. A foreman couldn't pitch in and get a job done with muscle and sweat. He had to lie, pet, cajole, butter, and flatter; and even all that wouldn't work in the case of Nathan, as Frank told Wesley one afternoon in the middle of April.

"If Nathan won't work for you," Wesley said with great heat, "fire him. It's your baby. You hire and fire. You say what and where, who and when."

Clara followed Frank to the kitchen door after his little chat with Wesley, saying piteously, "Don't you fire that poor old man."

"No, ma'am, I sure won't," Frank said. "Not on your life."

Her eyes were full of affection. "You are so kind and clever and energetic, Frank. You'll figure out a way to manage Nathan, I know you will."

The next afternoon, a Thursday, Frank refueled and serviced the diesels on all the pumps. He drove an old white Dodge pickup Wesley had bought for knock-around use, in the back of which he carried a big grease gun and a fifty gallon barrel of fuel oil. Though it was sunny, a fierce wind blew and the sky was red with dust. The willows around the catch ponds had leaved out and the alfalfa fields were already a rich, deep green.

When he went out to the sandhill farm he took Nathan along. After servicing the diesel, they stood awhile contemplating the new sprinkling system. Like big, shiny stems of joint grass the aluminum pipes stretched across the field in segments, which had to be unjointed after sprinkling, carried to a new part of the field, and rejointed.

Frank dug in his coat pocket and pulled out a couple of candy bars. "I swiped some candy from Clara. Here, have one."

"That's kind," Nathan said, looking pleased. "Thanks a whole lot."

"About this time of day, a fellow needs a shot of sugar," Frank said, ripping off a wrapper and throwing it down. A man could duck his head and flail directly into a brush patch, or he could circle around it. Circling around was what Frank had in mind with Nathan. He meant to be subtle as a serpent.

At thirty yard intervals along the pipes, sprinklers rotated slowly, pulsing out great arcs of water with a clacking, splashing music, ka-swish, ka-swish, ka-swish. At a certain point in their rotation the wind-sprayed arcs caught the sun in shimmering rainbows.

"Ain't that pretty?" Frank said.

Nathan was busy gumming his candy bar, having put his false teeth into his bib pocket.

"Watch those sprinklers go, everyone of them whirling around ninety miles an hour. They sound like an orchestra. They could put you to sleep."

"I can sleep fine without them," Nathan said.

"We'll save a lot of water using sprinklers. That means we'll save a lot of diesel fuel."

"What we save in fuel, we'll lose in hay," Nathan said. "You can't soak a field with sprinkling like you can with flood irrigation."

"I guess you can," Frank said. "Farmers back east don't flood irrigate. What's rain if it isn't sprinkling?"

Nathan looked disgusted. Rain wasn't the same kind of thing at all.

"By the end of the summer," Frank went on, "Wesley plans to have sprinklers on every field he has. That means we've got to get a couple of high school boys to change the pipes."

"Don't pussyfoot around. If Wesley wants me to supervise the sprinkling, let him say so."

"That's just exactly what he wants."

"Let Wesley tell me himself," Nathan insisted. "I'm working for him. I ain't working for you."

"He won't," Frank said. "I already asked him to talk to you."

"Well, ain't that something!" Nathan exploded. "My experience and insight and wisdom ain't good enough for him. You marry his daughter and he makes you foreman. That's the thanks I get, is it? I've killed myself off for him; I've held on in my old age, working like a man thirty years younger, to help him make a go of it on these hay farms."

"He's grateful to you, I know he is," Frank said in a hurry. "He's got his mind on a lot of other things."

"Don't try to smooth things over," Nathan said. "I see I've fizzled out on this ranch. There's nothing for me but going up to Provo and living off the welfare of my wife and kids. I'm through. It's the end. I just hope you know it's you who has run me off this place."

Mid-afternoon at the ranch Marianne asked Frank to hook a plow to a Ford tractor so that she could till the garden. She watched from the fender of the stocktruck, her legs dangling, her red smock awry, her unbuttoned Levi's tightened over her belly with a shoestring.

"That bolt doesn't go there," she said.

"It sure does," he said.

Pretty soon he saw it didn't and found another bolt.

"I told you so," she said.

"Why don't you hook this plow up yourself?"

"I'm a queen bee. All the other bees take care of me."

He started the engine, which was tetchy and had to be nursed along. When it roared vigorously he opened the garden gate and Marianne steered the tractor in. She backed up to a ditch, lowered the plow, and went forward, turning a bright, moist furrow. By then Jerry, LaMar, and Harvey had arrived from town. They were working late afternoons and Saturdays, and when summer came they would work full time. Frank gave them the task of laminating two by twelve planks into beams for the new hay sheds.

"When you get them nailed together," he told them, "hunt me up and we'll lift them onto the posts. I'll be around the toolshed."

As he walked by the ranchhouse he saw a strange sight—the billy goat standing spread legged on the roof of Clara's elegant new Lincoln. The goat, his jaws busily masticating an old sock, gazed about with calm yellow eyes. The ranchhouse door slammed and Clara shouted, "Get off that car, you son of Beelzebub." She tore a loose picket from the fence and sent it sailing through the air. It missed the goat and also, luckily, the car. The goat lifted his tail and emitted a shower of pellets.

"Help me!" Clara cried, wringing her hands.

Frank took up the picket and advanced toward the goat, which jumped off the opposite side of the car and raced bleating around the fence corner. By now Wesley had come from the house. Clara turned to him and said, "How does he get out? This is the third time this week. I checked the fence. There aren't any holes in it."

Wesley examined the car roof, saying, "Your Lincoln is soiled, sweetheart." Taking the picket, he led Frank and Clara after the goat, which circled the house, crossed the driveway, and jumped onto a wagon, where he urinated

"That malicious sidewinder," Wesley said. "He knows very well human beings loathe urine and feces. That was calculated and cunning. It's further evidence that animals hate people."

"That's nonsense," Clara said. "He's just a poor dumb brute."

Five minutes later the goat was still free, having led Frank, Wesley, and Clara around the bunkhouse, between the two trailerhouses, behind the catch pond, and back to the corrals. Marianne shut off the tractor and left the garden. Coming from the tackshed with a halter, she said, "I'll saddle up Chowder and rope him."

"No, you won't," Clara said. "You're not getting on any horse in your condition. Frank can rope him."

"He doesn't know how," Marianne said. "Goats aren't like calves. They're smart and tricky."

"Go ahead and rope him, Frank," Wesley said. "And when you get a loop on him, put in a good lick for the human race. Jerk him down hard."

"Oh, no," Clara cried, "nothing rough, please, Frank. The poor animal doesn't know any better."

Frank went into the corral and cornered Chowder. He led him out, saddled up, and tied on a lasso. "Okay, boy," he said, "let's show that stinking critter a thing or two."

For a minute the goat dashed among the trucks and tractors so that Frank couldn't get a clear throw. Finally he broke across the driveway, and Chowder dug into the dirt and went after him. Frank threw his loop and pulled Chowder in. The goat dodged and the loop came down empty.

"You can't rope for nothing," Marianne said, laughing loud.

Frank kept his eyes on his hands, which were coiling the lasso. "Okay, boy," he said to Chowder, "this time is it."

The horse and goat ambled around a semi trailer three times. Suddenly, the goat bolted and Chowder was on his tail. Frank listened with his knees, which gripped the gelding's heaving ribs, and Chowder told him which way the goat would dodge. The goat saw the loop coming and tried to turn. It missed his head but as Frank jerked the line, it tightened up on a front leg. The goat catapulted into the air and thudded onto his back. He struggled to his feet, bleating pitifully. A sharp, white bone stuck through his hide and blood drenched his leg.

"Oh, the poor thing," Clara cried out.

"You rough bugger," Marianne said.

Frank was off the horse and walking along the tightened rope. The goat struggled, his bloody leg held askew by the rope. Frank grabbed him and threw him down. "Nothing to do but kill him with a broke leg," he said. He handed his pocketknife to Wesley. "Here, open this for me." In a moment he took back the opened knife and with a sudden slash laid wide the animal's throat. Blood spurted into the air, drenching Frank's arm. The goat gargled hoarsely, kicked, and died.

"Forgive us, Lord, oh, forgive us," Clara moaned.

"Damn good thing," Wesley said. "That boy could climb fences. That's how he was getting out."

"J. Wesley Earle," Clara said, low and grim, "it delights your hard heart to see that dumb brute laid low in the dust. Doesn't it just delight your hard heart?"

"Now, sweetheart," Wesley said, "don't you get upset. I was just talking, that's all. To be truthful, I'm appalled by this unfortunate accident."

"You have never stopped badmouthing my goats all these months. From the minute I first begged you to let me have a little livestock project of my own, you have ridiculed and carped and criticized."

"Now, lovey, don't you carry on like this," Wesley pleaded. "I'm just as torn up as you are over that poor dead billy. We sure will get you a new one. And we'll fix that fence so nothing can climb over it."

Wesley put his arm around Clara, who was sobbing with her face in her hands. "Come on, honeybunch, let's go to the house. Let Wesley fix you some hot tea. That'll make you feel better. Time for a little tea."

As Wesley led Clara to the house, Frank got on Chowder and dragged the carcass across the driveway. He dismounted and heaved it into the back of the white pickup. Later he would throw it out in the junipers.

It was after dark when Frank went into the trailerhouse, where Marianne was at the stove cooking spaghetti and meat sauce. Having taken off her Levi's, she now wore the red smock, white panties, and cowboy boots. The house was full of smoke because the spaghetti water had boiled over onto a burner and the hamburger fat was popping and fuming. The table held dirty dishes from lunch, which Frank stacked and carried to the counter, where a huge mound of soiled dishes was carefully hidden beneath a flannel Indian blanket. He lifted a corner of the blanket and found a place for the lunch ware.

"It's about time to wash some dishes," he said.

"I'll get to them in a day or two."

He went to the cupboard and couldn't find plates for supper. Returning to the stack of dirty dishes, he picked out a couple of plates and glasses and carried them to the sink. The sink was full of debris from salad making, carrot peelings, lettuce leaves, and apple cores, which he dug out and shook into the wastebasket.

"Shall I just rinse these dishes?"

"No, sir," Marianne said, "bust out the dish pan and make some suds."

When he had washed and dried the plates and glasses, he set the table. By then she had put on the spaghetti and salad, and they sat down. He looked at her and she shook her head, saying vociferously, "No, I don't want to kneel down and have family prayer."

"It seems like we ought to."

"Lutherans don't kneel down and say family prayer twice a day. At least not my kind of Lutherans."

"Would you say a blessing on the food?"

"Sure." She ducked her head and recited, "Come, Lord Jesus, be our guest, and let these gifts to us be blest, Amen."

It sounded like paganism to Frank, but he felt lucky to get that much out of her. Although God had given him stewardship over this household for one year and would expect him to conduct it according to a righteous pattern, Marianne wasn't cooperative. Like people said, you could lead a mare to water but you couldn't make her drink.

While they were eating, a knock sounded at the door and Clara came in. She pulled a chair to the table and sat down, glancing repeatedly toward the heap of dishes under the flannel blanket.

"I've come to apologize for getting so emotional over that goat," she said. "I know you didn't mean to break its leg, Frank. Also, considering how badly it was injured, cutting its throat was the proper and humane thing to do, though I admit I don't want to watch something like that ever again. What a terrible sight, blood spurting out like a fountain!"

"Frank likes to kill things," Marianne said.

"I don't either," he protested.

"Another thing," Clara went on, "I want you to know I have the highest regard for Wesley. Please don't interpret my little outburst as a sign of disrespect. Your father is a wonderful man, Marianne. He is the best of providers. He indulges me in a thousand whims. He goes out of his way every day to make me comfortable and happy."

"Sure he does," Marianne said.

"He does," Clara reemphasized. "I don't take it as a wrong that he exerts leadership in our home. It's proper for the husband to be the head of the household."

"Head of the household!" Marianne said bitterly. "I thought when people got married they got to make a few decisions on their own. Lord! When I got married I didn't get rid of any bosses. I just picked up one more."

"I don't boss you," Frank said.

"You sure do," she said. "You run this house like a dictator. You're a fascist. You're worse than Hitler and Franco."

"Marianne!" Clara cried.

"Good gosh," Marianne said, "I'm joking. Can't you tell when I'm joking?"

When it was bedtime Frank went into the tiny bathroom and sat on the toilet with his chin in his hands, having a good think. Shortly Marianne crowded in and stood at the basin. Now she wore an unbuttoned shirt and panties and high heeled shoes. High heels at bedtime were just one of her oddities, which Frank wouldn't have tried to count. She had enough to fill a barn.

She began to floss her teeth, using a strand which had been dangling from a corner of the mirror. She tried to get ten or twelve flossings from a single piece. Then she lathered her toothbrush with hand soap and brushed her teeth. She said she didn't mind the taste and it was a lot cheaper than toothpaste. She had glued some inspirational signs on the mirror, one of which said, "Do what Jesus would have you do today" and another, "Smile and the world smiles with you." Her Bible was balanced on the waste can, open to the Epistle to the Ephesians. She spent a good deal of time reading on the toilet.

The basin was directly in front of the toilet, which meant that when she bent over to spit out lather, her buttocks brushed Frank's nose. He straightened up and poked her with a finger. She turned around, her heavy, pointed breasts swinging before his eyes. He couldn't help himself. He lifted a finger, pressed a nipple, burred his tongue like a doorbell, and said, "Anybody home?" Looking down with great contempt, she backed slowly into the hall. She hefted her breasts in her hands, rotated her body like a machine gun turret, and fired: "Rat-a-tat-tat, rat-a-tat-tat, rat-a-tat-tat." Then her voice zoomed like an airplane pulling out of a dive and she disappeared down the hall. Frank knew he had been shot down.

Frank went into the little bedroom, put on his pajamas, knelt by the side of the bed, and said his prayer. He prayed for President McKay and the twelve apostles, for President Eisenhower and the leaders of the nations, and for Margaret and Jeremy. He prayed that Jeremy would stop getting into pouts when people in Panguitch refused to call him Alice. He prayed extra hard that he wouldn't make love to Marianne this evening. He had told God he would try to limit his carnal activities to one night a week as a sign he wasn't forgetting that sooner or later he would get out of this mess and return to righteous living. He had decided on Friday night.

When he got up from his prayer, he saw she had been watching from the doorway. "You must have had a shopping list a mile long," she said. "You must have been asking God for a whole department store. You look like a Mohammedan, kneeling down like that."

"Kneeling is the best way to pray."

"I pray in my heart," she said. "God doesn't care if I stand, kneel, or sit. He doesn't care if I'm climbing a tree or cleaning out a corral just as long as I pray in my heart."

"When you kneel down to pray," Frank said, "it's like putting high octane gas in your car. Your valves quit pinging and you can get up the hills faster."

Marianne pulled down the covers and crawled on her hands and knees to the far side of the bed, which was against a wall. "I don't know how come I have to sleep on the wall side," she said. "It's not you who's having a baby. I'm getting tired of hauling my big belly over you every time I need to go to the bathroom in the middle of the night."

Frank wasn't going to quarrel with her; however, he wasn't going to give in either. If a man and a woman were going somewhere together in a car, it was the man who should do the driving. By the same principle a man got the favorable side of the bed.

He turned out the light and got in bed and pulled up the covers. They both sighed and shifted and wiggled, trying to find a comfortable place on the mattress. After a while she said, "Do you think most married people kiss each other goodnight when they get in bed?"

"Gosh, I don't know," he said. He knew what she wanted, though, so he got up on an elbow and leaned over and gave her a kiss.

"I also really like it when you kiss me goodby in the morning."

"All right, I'll try not to forget."

"Tomorrow is Friday," she said.

"It sure is."

"Are we going to the movie?"

"You bet. And before that we'll go over to the cafe and have hamburgers and French fries for supper. Or whatever you want."

"I like a night out," she said. "And then we're going to come home and make love."

"That's right."

"You know something? I wouldn't care if we did it tonight too."

Though he got a hot feeling in his belly, he said, "Let's hold off till tomorrow night."

"I don't know why you're so worried about having a little sex. That's what you're supposed to have when you're married."

"Sure," he said, "that's what you're supposed to have if you want to live like a carnal, sensual, devilish animal."

She snuggled against his shoulder, slipping a hand under his pajama top and stroking his breast.

"I could make you do it," she said.

"I know you could."

"I really could."

"I know you really could."

"Why shouldn't I then?"

"I don't know," he said. "I was just trying to hold off till Friday. I'd just feel better if I could make it through to Friday."

"You poor skunk," she said, pulling her hand away.

On Friday afternoon, returning from the sawmill with a load of lumber, Frank stopped at Hinton's store and picked up a sack of flour for Clara. Before leaving, he took a look at a fishing outfit, a long, springy rod and a closed faced spinning reel which operated with a thumb release and could hold a hundred yards of monofilament line.

"Gosh darn," he said to Sally Hinton, who was clerking, "I'd sure like to get a couple of those outfits for me and Marianne. We'd go out on opening day and slaughter the trout population."

He wasn't serious, of course. For one thing, fishing was a vanity. For another thing, the reel cost eleven fifty and the rod six forty. He had the money but he was trying to bank every spare penny to leave with Marianne when he took off.

At the ranch he showed Harvey, Jerry, and LaMar how to construct rafters from the lumber and left them sawing, pounding, and singing. As he went by the garden he saw Marianne irrigating with rubber boots and a shovel. She had harrowed and furrowed that morning and had spent the afternoon planting onions, lettuce, radishes, and peas. He was feeling guilty for not buying her a fishing rod, which would have tickled her pink. He considered washing the dishes that were stacked half way to the ceiling. That would be a nice surprise for her, and the dishes might not otherwise get done for another five or ten days. For a minute he bowed up at the idea and tried to forget it. He liked washing dishes about as much as cleaning hog pens.

However, doing a big batch of dishes was exactly what his rebellious spirit needed. He went into the trailerhouse and threw the blanket off the heap. Plates, cups, glasses, mixing bowls, casserole dishes, all were stacked so high, one inside another, that they teetered when he touched them. He had to hand it to Marianne for being a clever stacker; it stood to reason that stacking would come natural to a girl who lived on a hay ranch. Still, it looked like she could have washed the dishes in the same time it took her to figure out where to put the next bunch.

Lacking proper equipment for a big job, he went over to the ranchhouse and asked Clara to lend him a couple of wash tubs, saying, "I need something to soak dirty dishes in. I'm fixing up a little surprise for Marianne."

Clara was exasperated. "I'm embarrassed to own her for my daughter. That horrible, unsightly, unhygienic pile of dishes! I ask myself why she troubles to throw a blanket over them. I wonder what homekeeping magazine suggested that. I wouldn't wash those dishes for her, Frank, not for a million dollars. She is a trashy girl."

Back at his house, Frank filled the tubs with plates, bowls, and cutlery and poured in hot, sudsy water with a bucket. When they had soaked, he began to wash and dry. Before long every dish towel he had was sopping wet. He went back to the ranchhouse and borrowed a half dozen towels from Clara.

"I just wouldn't do it if I were you," she said. "I'd eat off the bare table before I'd do that girl's work for her."

"She has a pretty tough row to hoe," he replied. "Being pregnant doesn't sit too good with her."

Marianne, coming from the garden as he crossed the driveway, called, "What have you got there?"

"I borrowed some towels. I'm cleaning up a little mess at our place."

She carried a battered straw hat in one hand and let a shovel drag from the other. The hat had pressed a rim into her tangled curls; her nose had burned cherry red; muddy sweat had tracked down her temples.

"You're doing the dishes!" she cried when they had got inside.

She dried while Frank finished washing, after which they showered and got ready for their evening out. While he sat on the edge of the bed pulling on his socks, she hugged him and nuzzled his neck, saying, "You're so good to me." Her robe was open and her breasts drooped on her round cantelope belly.

For about thirty seconds he tried to talk himself into waiting until after the movie to make love to her. Then he said, "Do you want to pull off those panties and garter belt?"

"You bet," she said.

When they were through, they lay with their arms around each other. "My big old tummy," she apologized, "it sure gets in the way."

"We can manage." He kissed her and let his hand drift up and down her back. Sometimes he felt as if he was falling in love with her. Right now with his lust slunk off to sleep like a run-out hound, his arms still had an itch for holding her. Her big bumpy nose, her high cheeks, her cleft chin, they were just fine; they didn't seem ugly anymore.

They dressed, she in her smock and skirt and heels, he in his Sunday pants and a white shirt, and they got into the Chrysler Wesley and Clara had given them and drove to town. She sat so close to him that they took up only half the seat. At the Rim Rock cafe he ordered two hamburgers and French fries, she a hot beef sandwich; they agreed to forego dessert so they'd have room for popcorn and soda pop at the movie. They took seats in the middle of the theater, and when they had finished their popcorn and drinks, they held hands.

The movie, *Cattleland Fighters*, featured a ranch girl named Bessie whose brother had been captured by a cattle baron. A kind, gentle drifter named Rory came along. Though he was against violence, he was a master with a Winchester and was drawn into Bessie's fracas with the baron. He was too late to save her brother, whom Bessie found hanging from a limb, but in a big shootout he killed off the baron and the bad eggs among his men. At the end Rory and Bessie rode across the spread which was now securely hers; though they were quiet and sober, having been chastened by frontier violence, they were in love and their future was bright.

When the theater lights came on, Marianne squeezed Frank's hand and said, "Wasn't it good?"

"It sure was," he said.

While they drove back to the ranch, she sat close again and they mused in silence. Frank's mind was full of distant mountains, mysterious valleys, and strange heroic music. At last he said, "I'd give anything to live in the olden days. Why did I have to be born now?"

"Me too," she agreed. "There's nothing anymore like those days."

They were still quiet while they got ready for bed. She left her heels and hose and skirt in a pile on the bedroom floor and put on a gauzy little night gown. While Frank stripped off his shirt and pants, he went over his latest contract with God. He hadn't promised in so many words to make love once and once only on his day off from righteousness. Given that fact and considering how stalwartly he had been abstaining on the other days of the week, he couldn't see that going at it twice on Friday should make much difference.

So he got on the bed with her and they tugged her night gown up around her armpits and made love. Then they lay for a long time on top of the blankets. Marianne had put pillows behind her back and sat propped up a little, an arm around his shoulders and a breast against his cheek. She ran her fingers through his hair and traced them along the ridges of his ear.

"I sure do love you," she whispered.

He was feeling the same way but he couldn't let her know.

When Frank climbed out of bed before dawn and put on his work clothes, Marianne got up on an elbow, looking groggy, and mumbled, "I'll have you some scrambled eggs in two minutes."

"Go back to sleep," he said.

He put on a jacket and went out into the fresh, cold air. The barn and sheds loomed in the dark. A gray rim of morning stretched over the eastern horizon. Chowder nickered, a goat bleated, a robin chirruped. From Hogan Wash came the faint throb of the diesel, which had been pumping water all night.

He went into the toolshed and closed the door, groping until he found the wall switch and turned on the light, a dangling bulb. The odor of motor oil filled the shed; scattered on the concrete floor were wrenches and parts of an engine—a cam shaft, gleaming pistons, a head with gaping cylinders. He stretched on tiptoe and felt along a narrow shelf nailed to a joist. He pulled down a tiny notebook, a stubby pencil, and a leather strap.

He dragged a stool from the workbench and sat under the light. Opening the notebook, he added two marks to a long row; wetting the pencil tip in his mouth, he carefully totaled the row. Forty-six marks. Forty-six times he had had sex with Marianne since their wedding day. It frightened him to see how the marks were accumulating because he didn't know how to undo them. They were lining up like pickets in the fences of hell.

It was time to add up the good deeds he had performed during the past week, time to see what credits he might have accrued. He had said his secret prayer both night and morning. He had read from the Scriptures every evening except Friday. He had been kind to Marianne, hadn't said sharp words to her. He hadn't exalted himself because he was foreman and hadn't got mad at Nathan. He had forgiven Wesley for his pompous words and unnecessary meddling. He and Marianne had gone to Panguitch on Saturday afternoon to be with Margaret and Jeremy. On Sunday he had attended Priesthood Meeting, Sunday School, and Sacrament Meeting. He had stopped by the bishop's house and had given him a tithing check, a tenth of his gross pay.

Now it was time to tally his shortcomings. He was chagrinned, embarrassed, ashamed how he had wallowed in sex, not once, but twice, how he had reveled in Marianne's flesh. Furthermore, he had eaten for his belly, relishing every bite of ham, steak, and sausage, savoring hotcakes and honeyed muffins. He had said son of a bitch four times, piss once, damn twice, also shit twice. He was loose minded and gamesome about his driving; more than once he had caught himself doing seventy miles an hour in the old pickup. He had lusted on his work. One afternoon he had got all tied up and absorbed with working on the new sheds, later coming awake and realizing he hadn't thought about God and spiritual things for three or four hours. Finally, he had killed the goat, provoked by its yellow unrepentant eyes; hot and vengeful, he had delighted to see its blood spurt.

His book wouldn't balance. His checks were written against insufficient funds; no one but Lucifer would cash them. He had a standing order with a broker in one-way tickets to hell. He had a trunkful of them, good any day, any hour, any season.

Frank pulled the leather strap through his fist four or five times. Cut from an old harness, dark with oil and dirt, it was a foot and a half long, an inch and a half wide, a quarter inch thick. Every Saturday morning he gave himself ten slashes. They were nothing at all, a token, a sign of what he would do if he was free to please God. He went to the door and peered out. Pale light lay over the ranch. Windows were grey in the houses. A calf bawled, a dove cooed. He closed the door and took off his shirt, preparing for Sunday.

Late that afternoon Frank and Marianne drove to Panguitch in their Chrysler. The wind bent tall-stemmed grass along the roadside and chased silvery clouds through the high bright sky. In Red Canyon Marianne said, "Tomorrow while you're going to the Mormon meetings, I'm going to drive up to Richfield and go to the Lutheran service."

"Well, why not? That sounds like a good idea."

"Lutherans worship God, too, you know."

"Course they do."

"Your mother doesn't know they do. The way she looks at me I can tell she thinks I'm a zoo animal. She's trying to make up her mind whether a Lutheran is a clam or a lobster or maybe some kind of a plant."

"No, she isn't. She's respectful of Lutherans."

"I'd just soon run my arm through a wringer as stay at your mother's house tonight."

"You could have stayed at the ranch."

"I know I could have. But I didn't. If you go visit your folks, I go visit your folks."

Having pulled the rearview mirror aside so she could see her hair, she drew a comb from her purse and touched up her curls. "You know, I'd go with you to the Mormon service tomorrow if you'd go with me to the Lutheran service next Sunday."

He looked straight down the road, ignoring the dry, sandy wash on one hand and the wall of fanciful red erosions on the other.

"You wouldn't do that, would you?" she said.

"I guess I wouldn't."

"Hell no, you wouldn't. Mormons are sellers, not buyers. They don't import religion. They just export it."

"You don't know nothing about Mormonism."

"You don't know nothing about Lutheranism."

"Never said I did."

"When we got married," she said, "I had in mind we'd go to your church one Sunday and to mine the next. I thought we'd show respect for each other that way."

"I don't want to miss my own meetings unless there's a real good reason," he said.

"A Lutheran church isn't a pool hall, you know."

"Course it isn't."

He felt bad. A bullheaded person like Marianne never would listen to facts. Looked at one way, a pool hall was better than a Lutheran church; at least the people who went there on the Sabbath knew they were being ungodly.

Margaret and Jeremy were working in the garden when Frank and Marianne pulled into the driveway. Jeremy wore a red leather hunting cap, stained with sweat, and a chambray shirt buttoned at the collar. Margaret's hair was wispy and windblown and she had on slacks which bunched at the belt because they were three or four sizes too large. Margaret hugged Frank, then went for Marianne, who dutifully put out a cheek for a kiss. Margaret held on for a moment, gazing down at her belly. "A little bigger, I do believe," she said. "I can hardly wait till time is up."

Marianne drove to the drugstore on Main Street to find a magazine. Frank went to work repairing a chicken coop because Margaret had changed her mind about eggs and wanted to get another flock of hens. Margaret and Jeremy returned to the garden where they were planting radishes along a furrow which Jeremy had carefully groomed with a handrake. Five days a week Jeremy worked for a local farmer, Rulon Smythe, who paid Margaret forty cents an hour for his services. Jeremy planted corn, spread fertilizer, cleaned ditches, and fixed fences; he also helped haul and saw juniper for sale as firewood in Cedar City and St. George. Jeremy and Rulon got along fine. Rulon called him Alice and wasn't bothered by him talking to himself.

Later Frank took a milk pail to the corral, where the grizzled old bull and the scrawny, spook-eyed cow stood waiting for their evening hay. When Frank got close the cow took off at a run. When he had her cornered, he lambasted her with a pole till she wobbled. The bull took it all in without moving an inch.

Marianne, who had been watching over the fence with Margaret, said, "Well, at least he ain't partial. He's just as likely to kill a cow as a goat."

Margaret frowned, maybe because she didn't like to hear a woman say ain't.

"He killed us a goat the other day," Marianne explained. "He roughnecked it to death. Roped it by a leg and broke the bone out of the hide. Then he put his knee on its neck and cut its throat. He doesn't need a gun. All he needs is a pocketknife."

"When a critter won't mind, I kind of forget who I am," Frank said. "Chloe isn't hurt any. It'll give her good manners for a while so Alice can milk her easy."

While he milked, Marianne sat in the open door of the Chrysler, which was parked by the back steps of the house. She turned on the radio to a Richfield station which was broadcasting a parody by Homer and Jethro called "How Much Is That Hound-dog in the Window?"

Margaret leaned over the corral fence and said to Frank, "Isn't it about time to get rid of that bull. He eats twice what the cow does."

"Maybe so."

"You left him here to breed our cow. I just well tell you, he hasn't got what it takes. He can't get off the ground. He's too stiff and halt."

"I'll do something with him by and by," Frank said. He didn't know what it would be; he still couldn't stand the idea of making dog food out of the old fellow.

"Your wife is a crusty girl," Margaret said, glancing toward the Chrysler. "She's offish and cold. No matter what I do, she won't let me get close."

"It looked like she was hugging you a while ago."

"That doesn't mean anything," she said. "That's just good manners. She doesn't like me."

"She just doesn't know you very well. Give her time."

"The first weekend you two came over after your honeymoon I suggested she might come to church with us. The way she acted, you'd have thought I was forcing vinegar down her throat."

He swung angrily around on the milkstool. "What did you do that for?"

"So she could see the Gospel up close, that's what for."

"You aren't going to get anywhere inviting her to church," he said. "She's a dyed-in-the-wool Lutheran."

For supper Margaret served egg and spinach custard, which Marianne poked at two or three times with a fork before giving up and making her meal on brown bread with butter and milk. Frank thought the custard was one of the nastiest things he had tasted in months, but he ate it heartily and held out his plate for another serving, saying, "This sure does grow on you." He didn't want Margaret to know how he had been enticed away from a healthy diet while living with Marianne.

After the dishes were washed everybody went into the living room. Frank intended to read in Margaret's Book of Mormon. Marianne had a new *McCall's*. Jeremy pulled down the writing leaf of the secretary and set out a checkerboard. Margaret began stuffing envelopes with an announcement about the Panguitch chapter of the Daughters of the Utah Pioneers.

Jeremy played checkers with himself, making a move every five minutes or so and then spending the time in between on other things. "That's so he'll forget why he made the last move," Frank told Marianne. "That way he doesn't cheat."

"That isn't so dumb," she said.

From a brown paper sack Jeremy pulled a nude rubber doll, declaring, "This one wets." He went back into the sack and found a piece of flannel, which he tied over the doll's crotch. Having kissed the doll and replaced it in the sack, he glanced at the board and shoved a checker with his finger. He leaned back and looked at the ceiling. "The bane of banes is dry breasts. Dry breasts run in this family."

"They most certainly do not," Margaret protested. "Certainly not on the Jamison side. I never knew a Jamison woman whose milk didn't come in proper when her baby was born."

"My poor dead Millicent," Jeremy said. "Dead and gone. Before she departed she had her patriarchal blessing. It gave her promises." He shoved another checker on the board. "The truth swims around like turtles in a tank and nobody sees it. Nobody bumps into it. Just us Mormons. This is how you make a Piute firebundle. You shred juniper bark into fine bits. You wrap them in coarse strips of bark. You touch the bundle to a dying campfire and it smolders all night, giving you a kindle in the morning. The bane of banes is fire. Oh, the tragedy of standing near a stove. Boiling water, scalding steam. You can see right through her, but she is not an evil spirit. No one has ever been threatened by her."

"Ah, ha," he cried suddenly, jumping one checker with another. "I had him all along and he didn't know it." He removed the vanquished checker and shoved another forward.

Marianne wasn't getting anywhere with her magazine. Her mouth was open a little and her eyes were wide.

Jeremy got out of his chair and squatted by her. "Can I touch you?" he asked, looking at her belly.

She looked down at the little mound beneath her breasts, covered by a brown pleated smock. "If you want," she said.

He put out a hand and softly stroked her belly. Returning to his chair, he said, "She's dead."

Marianne flushed, sat up straight, said quickly, "It's not dead. It moves inside me all the time. It kicks me."

"Don't pay any attention to him," Frank said. "He doesn't mean anything real."

"My Millicent is dead," Jeremy said. "The big hippopotamus did away with her at the hospital. She's gone, gone, gone."

"You mustn't dwell on Millicent all the time," Margaret said. "Show Marianne some of your other babies."

He put a hand in the paper sack and pulled out the rubber doll that could wet. "This one is named Jenantha."

"She's real cute," Marianne said.

"She's named after her great grandmother."

"There aren't any Jenanthas in our lines," Margaret insisted.

"Alice has got lines we don't know about," Frank said.

Jeremy swept the checkers from the board and said to Marianne, "Play me a game."

She looked at Frank who shrugged his shoulders. She got up and pulled a stool close to the secretary as Jeremy placed the black and red checkers at opposite ends of the board. "I'll take red," he said. "Red is Lamanite color. Black is the color of the descendants of Ham."

"He'll beat you," Frank said. "He's a regular coyote at checkers."

"That's okay," she said. Jeremy had already pushed a checker forward.

"Now that's just sweet to behold," Margaret said, glancing up as she tucked a last announcement into an envelope. She began to address envelopes, looking up every minute or so at Jeremy and Marianne. After a while she said, "Alice's face looks somewhat like my mother's. Don't you think so, Frank?"

"I don't know. I never saw your mother."

"I can't get over how Marianne's father is farming our old homestead," she said. "Did you know that, Marianne?"

"Yes, ma'am, I know that. I've seen the foundation of the old house."

"My mother was so remarkable. When the court told Father he had to keep his wives in separate houses, Mother went bravely out to the homestead. She had already lost two babies, and on the ranch she lost two more. They are all buried in the Escalante cemetery. Not side by side, however."

"It's your move," Jeremy said. Marianne had been watching Margaret; now she looked at the board and pushed a checker

"Gotcha," Jeremy said, jumping her piece

"My poor sorrowing mother sought the Lord in the sandhills," Margaret went on. "She knew there were reasons for God taking those babies."

"Marianne doesn't want to hear about all that," Frank said, closing the Book of Mormon.

"The truth is, my mother saw the Savior at Reston Spring. It's a lost place in the sandhills. I've never been there."

"I've ridden there with Frank," Marianne said. "It's nothing but a seep."

"It's your move," Jeremy interrupted. She pushed a checker and he jumped it.

"The reason her babies died," Margaret said, "that reason was her vanity, her passion for the world. She never told me in so many words, but that's what I think."

Frank had gone to the doorway. "That isn't something Marianne wants to hear. For crying out loud, let's go to bed."

"I do want to hear it," Marianne said.

Light from a lamp lit Margaret's round nose, her long jaw, and her hollow cheek, over which tears had begun to slide. "It was a spiritual education to know my mother. But we don't always learn what our teachers teach us, do we? If I had learned my lesson, I wouldn't have lost my little Elizabeth."

"My gosh," Frank muttered from the doorway, "let's go to bed."

"Elizabeth was so sick," Margaret went on. "It was after the twenty-fourth of July, very hot. She ate some clabber, maybe it was spoiled. She got summer complaint, vomited, had diarrhea. She suffered for three days, couldn't keep anything down, dehydrated, got weaker and weaker. It wrung my heart to hear her scream. She looked at me in such a way! She was wondering why I couldn't give her ease. I couldn't stand to see her suffer. I said to Miles, Dedicate her to the Lord. But he wouldn't. He got huffy, went off into the other room. I went out back into the garden. I stood under an apple tree and I told the Lord to take her. I said, If you will ease her suffering, I promise not to murmur, I will accept it. When I went back into the house, she had gone to sleep. She lived a little longer but she didn't suffer any more."

They were all crying, Frank hardest of all. Marianne said, "I'm sorry she died, I'm really sorry."

"It was my lesson," Margaret said. "You have to learn it one way or another."

At ten thirty Frank and Marianne went downstairs to bed. The room smelled of paint because the week before Marianne had painted the woodwork with white enamel. The walls were the dirty, chalky green they had always been. The bed creaked and swayed when they sat on it to undress.

When they were in bed Marianne asked, "What was your grandmother's name?"

"Jerusha."

"And she lost four babies?"

"That's right. She lost four."

"I didn't ever know you had a little sister named Elizabeth."

"I wasn't born till after she died. She was only three."

"You're such a sad family. Do you know that?"

"I guess there's nothing to do about it."

"Poor Jeremy," she said. "I'd rather look at a corpse. He gives me the shivers. I wish he hadn't touched my belly."

"It won't hurt anything."

"Why did God let all these terrible things happen to your family?"

"He let them happen because we don't deserve no better."

"I've got to have a hanky," she said, sniffling hard.

He got out of bed and felt in his pants pocket for a handkerchief. She blew her nose and put the handkerchief under her pillow.

"I sure wish you'd hold me," she said. She lay on her side, tucking up her knees, and he curled around, hugging her from behind. She said, "It feels so good when you hold me."

Later Frank woke up, still hugging her. He knew he was lost. He couldn't keep his hand from roaming along her thigh and hip, along her ribs, over her shoulder, around her soft breasts. He couldn't keep his fingers from unbuttoning her nightgown. She mumbled and stirred and the bed creaked.

"Will you let me?" he whispered.

"Now?" she murmured.

"I've just got to do it."

"Gee whiz, I'm sleepy."

"Please."

"They'll hear upstairs," she said. "This bed rattles worse than an empty truck."

"I don't care."

"Get it over with as fast as you can," she said, arching her back and slipping off her panties. The bed rocked, groaned, squeaked, and thumped. He finished, rolled off, and lay quiet, staring into the dark.

"Do you feel bad?" she said.

"Yes."

She snuggled against him, tracing her fingers over his chest, letting them come up his neck, twining them in his hair. "I think Jesus loves you," she said.

He put his hand over hers, saying, "Jesus lets sinners fall in love with each other."

"What do you mean?"

"I'm in love with you."

"Oh, God," she said, going rigid and pulling away.

"I wish I wasn't. It wouldn't have happened if I'd treated you like a sister like I promised I would."

"I can't take any more lies. They'll kill me."

"I'm not lying," he said. "I've got where I can't stand to think about splitting up."

She pressed against him, legs, belly, face. "We don't have to split up, Frank! Honest, we don't have to!"

He was silent and she said, "Do you really love me?"

"I don't know," he said. "Sometimes it seems like I really do."

A long time later, she said in a soft, sleepy voice, "I pray for you every day, Frank."

"Thank you. I pray for you too."

"But also I say, Sweet Jesus, please don't be like Frank thinks you are." She shifted and the bed creaked and after a while they both went to sleep.

The next morning Frank was out early milking the cow. When he returned to the bedroom he found Marianne stepping into a lacy maternity slip. While he changed into his Sunday pants, he asked, "Are you still going to church in Richfield?"

"Sure thing," she said. She inspected the collar of his coat, which hung over the back of a chair. "We ought to get you a new suit. That thing looks like you bought it in a thrift store."

"It's good enough," he said. "Do you want some breakfast? It's about ready."

"That depends. Is it something decent?"

"Of course it's something decent. It's cracked wheat mush. Mom'll give you sugar if you holler for it."

"Which you don't dare do." She put on a navy blue skirt and a light blue smock.

"You look real nice," he said as they went up the stairs.

He ate in a hurry and got up from the table, saying, "Me and Alice are heading off for Priesthood Meeting."

She said, "Okay. Don't save me any dinner. Half a dozen people will ask me to eat with them after the service."

"Drive careful," he warned, giving her a little kiss.

At the North Ward meetinghouse Frank and Jeremy went down to the basement where the Elders quorum met, Frank having recently been ordained an Elder and Jeremy tagging along because the fellows in the Priests quorum made fun of him. Zachary Forsyte, the Elders president, was tossing hymn books to the quorum members. "Brethren," he said, "the opening song is 'Redeemer of Israel.' Sister Alice, give us a pitch."

Jeremy hummed and Zachary waved his arm with authority and said, "Okydoky, let's do her." The men began to sing and for half a minute they did well. Then a loud singer wandered off key and in another half minute the quorum sounded like chickens at feeding time. "Pretty bad," Zachary said when they were through. "It's lucky the Lord judges by intentions, not by performance."

Zachary, a wiry little man with a big sunburned nose, drove a school bus for the Garfield County school district and worked part time as a professional hunting guide. There was a story around about how he had hanged a mountain lion in the Henry Mountains. He claimed his dogs treed a young female that had a trap dangling from a hind paw. He could have easily shot her and collected a bounty, but he said he was conservation minded and wanted to build up the lion population. He lassoed her around the neck, threw the shank of the rope over a big limb, and tied it so that she was stretched out and could do nothing but perch. Then he crawled out on the limb she was perched on, meaning to get the trap off. The limb broke and he fell, cracking a rib when he hit the ground. The lion fell too but the rope caught her up short and broke her neck, and there she dangled like a criminal, stone dead.

Zachary called on Frank to say the opening prayer. After that, he lined up volunteers for running a hamburger concession at the Memorial Day horse show at the Panguitch arena. "Now another matter," he went on. "The bishop said I should castigate this outfit for slacking off on ward teaching. Anybody here got his home visits already done for April? Raise your hands, brethren." Everybody was looking at the floor or paring fingernails or digging in pockets for something. "All right, consider yourselves castigated. Let's get on top of that ward teaching."

After Priesthood Meeting, Frank and Jeremy went upstairs to the chapel for the opening exercises of Sunday School. While the congregation sang the first hymn Frank peered around, wondering where Margaret was. As the sacrament hymn began, he saw her coming down the aisle. Close behind her was Marianne, who as she pushed into the pew smiled ahead at Frank.

When she had got her skirt adjusted, Marianne whispered, "Your mother wanted me to come." Down the pew Margaret was sharing Jeremy's hymnal. Her eyes were red, as if she had been crying, yet her face was shining and her song was loud and vibrant.

"It smells like floor wax in here," Marianne whispered.

"Sure enough," Frank said. "Now you better be quiet. They're going to bless the Sacrament."

Two young men from the Priests quorum were breaking bread into bits. "Are they ministers?"

"Heck, no. Just fellers."

"Is that your minister up there?" She nodded toward a man sitting on the podium.

"We don't have any minister. Just a bishop. And that ain't him. That guy is the Sunday School superintendent."

"Where's your bishop?"

"I don't know. Maybe down the hall in his office."

"Does he wear a robe."

"Gosh, no."

"Doesn't anybody wear a robe?"

"Heck, no. Nobody at all."

"That isn't much fun," she said. "That's like washing your feet with your socks on."

One of the young men knelt and blessed the broken bread and the boys from the Deacons quorum passed it among the congregation. "I guess I'm not supposed to take any of that," she said.

"That's right. Just let it go by."

"What would it do, poison me?"

"Can't you be quiet?" he said, looking at her hard and mean.

When Sunday School adjourned at noon, they chatted and shook hands with people in the foyer and then paired up to stroll home, Marianne and Jeremy in front, Frank and Margaret behind. It was a beautiful spring day; the sun was shining, the air was calm, trees were budding, tulips and daffodils were in bloom.

"So," Marianne said to Jeremy, "according to Mormons, it wasn't on the cross where Jesus atoned for the sins of the world."

"It was on the cross," Jeremy said. "Certainly on the cross."

Since this was the Sunday before Easter, the lesson in Sunday School had been about the Crucifixion.

"From what the teacher said, I gathered Mormons think it was in the Garden of Gethsemane where he made the Atonement."

"Yes, it was in the garden," Jeremy agreed. "Just like she said."

"Well, make up your mind. Was it in the garden or on the cross?"

"I'll read up on it. I'll research it. Then I'll let you know."

Marianne said, "To tell you the truth, I wasn't sure Mormons believed in the Atonement at all."

"Yes, we believe in it. We don't believe in anything more than we believe in the Atonement."

"I don't think Frank does."

"Yes, Frank believes it. He has a great testimony of the Atonement."

"You can't tell it by the way he acts," she said. "He doesn't act very atoned."

Frank put his hands in his pockets and kicked a rock off the street, then pulled them out and kicked another rock. When Margaret took his arm and slowed him down, he gestured impatiently, not trusting Jeremy to say what ought to be said. Jeremy read bird books and church books and sometimes he could talk ten minutes straight without saying anything crazy. Other times he mixed things together like a tossed salad—birds, religion, fire, boiling water, invisible girls, and his poor dead Millicent.

When Marianne and Jeremy were well ahead, Margaret said, low and insistently, "You mustn't be fooled by that girl's brassy way of speaking. We have misled ourselves regarding her true character. Inside her crusty shell is a tender spirit, Frank. She is of the honest in heart."

"I ain't sure she isn't crust all the way through."

"Please don't say ain't. Now I admit I have more or less endorsed your notion of leaving her in due time. I have judged her to be an unfit match for the noble blood that runs in your veins."

"Noble blood hasn't got anything to do with me splitting up with her."

Marianne and Jeremy had reached the house and stood now on the porch, scrutinizing a planter filled with pansies. Noon sun fell on the greening lawn. In the street Margaret pulled Frank to a stop.

"The Holy Ghost has descended on her."

"On who?"

"On Marianne."

"On her?" He laughed, then choked.

She shook his arm angrily. "She came back, Frank. It was about a half hour after she left for Richfield. I was in the bathroom fixing my hair. The door was open and she came down the hall and looked in. She said, 'Would you like me to come to Sunday School with you?' " Margaret bit her lip and closed her eyes. A meadow lark trilled in somebody's back yard. "I burst into tears, Frank, I wept, I sobbed. I couldn't get control of myself."

She straightened his tie without realizing she was doing it. "I could see it worried her, me carrying on like that. I said, Oh, you sweet child, God has answered my prayers; my cup is full, it runneth over."

"Her coming to Sunday School once doesn't mean anything," he protested. "You heard her pulling Jeremy's leg just now, putting me down, saying I don't believe in the Atonement."

"She's just covering up," Margaret said. "She is ripe for conversion; she's ready to be a Mormon. If you've ever had an inclination to respect the advice of your mother, Frank, I hope it will be now. I surely do instruct you to give up your idea of leaving that girl."

"You don't know anything about her. She thinks Mormons are a joke."

"Maybe she isn't entirely to your taste; maybe you think you can do better for yourself. But you have married her, Frank, and you have begat your own flesh and blood with her. Oh, I have suffered over your baby; I've wept nights thinking about it! What a tragedy, what a terrible sin to deliver that innocent spirit into the hands of the Lutheran church. And now the Lord is paving the way to bring Marianne into the true church. And not just her, but Wesley and Clara and that cute little Jeanette too."

"I feel as bad as you do about that baby."

"I hope you'll heed me, Frank." She looked at the ground. "I don't think getting along without a wife is one of your gifts."

"Sure it is."

"You don't have to apologize to me for taking advantage of your privileges," she said. "It is better to marry than to burn, the Apostle Paul says. Marriage is marriage and people will do what they will do."

He could feel blood come up his neck and into his ears. He could hear the squeak and groan of the old rusty bed.

"I'm not blaming you," she said. "I feel terrible for putting you and Marianne into that dark little room with that ramshackle bed. We'll paint those walls and next time we're in Provo we'll go to Woolworth's and find a nice picture to hang up. And we'll certainly get a better bed."

9.

Dross and Refuse

On Tuesday afternoon Frank and Nathan replaced a burned-out universal joint on the pump at the sandhill field. A cold, gritty wind blew and fleecy clouds raced like squadrons of fighter planes over the rim of Fifty Mile Mountain.

"I imagine you have been somewhat disgruntled with me," Nathan said while he helped Frank push and pry. "You have been worrying about when I would up and quit."

"No, sir, I haven't," Frank replied. "I've been disgruntled with too many other things to worry about you."

"I have decided not to up and quit. I have given you cause for grief and I apologize. If you want me to superintend this sprinkler system, I'm ready to do it."

"You bet, that's what I wish you'd do."

"I have been resisting progress. I have been worse than those rascals in the railroad unions. I've made up my mind to stop fighting these new fangled devices."

"That's the right way. They're coming, no matter what."

As they put away the wrenches and screwdrivers, Nathan said, "I expect I'd better tell you me and Marianne had a long talk yesterday. I told her a lot of things about the Church. Also I gave her a book."

"She has gone plumb loco," Frank said, stopping short. "She don't believe it. She don't now and she won't later neither."

"She sure seems interested in Mormonism."

"Seems is right. Her being interested is phony as a three dollar bill."

They got into the pickup and slammed the doors. "From what she said," Nathan went on, "I expect she'll be around asking me more questions."

Frank spit out the window. "Well, answer them. I ain't her boss."

When he got home Marianne told him they were having supper with the folks at the ranchhouse. There was a special guest, a woman named Gomer Chittenden, who had turned up at Hinton's store in Escalante that afternoon asking for Frank. "Mrs. Hinton phoned out to the ranch, so Mom and I drove in to see what this lady wanted. We brought her back with us. Her husband is in jail, and she expects you to do something about it."

"It's no skin off my nose if Farley Chittenden is in jail. That's probably just exactly where he belongs. He still owes me thirty dollars for driving truck for him." Frank had stripped off his shirt and was washing his face and dousing his hair in the kitchen sink.

"I hope you can do something for her. She's pregnant as all outdoors. Looks like she might have her baby any minute. Me and Mom have more or less adopted her because she's needy and doesn't have anybody else to turn to. Dad is madder than hell, but Mom has fought him off."

"I side with your dad," Frank said. "You ought to pay more attention to what he thinks."

Clara was in the kitchen baking enchiladas and mixing raspberry punch. Wesley, Nathan, and Gomer were in the living room pretending to listen while Jeanette played recital numbers on the piano. Gomer looked like a lost child—tense, hopeless, ready to burst out crying if somebody gave her half a chance. Her bronze hair hung in oily strands, and her big belly had warped her blue knit dress until its hem wouldn't cover her bare knees.

As Frank put out a hand for a shake, she struggled from her chair and words came rushing out. "Please, Mr. Windham, Farley sent word I was to talk to you. He said you'd know what to do. He said to get you down to see him without fail. It was Bertha who turned him in. I kept telling him to spend more time with her. She swore out a complaint against him for bigamy. They arrested him in Carmel Junction. It was two weeks ago tomorrow."

She dropped his hand and sat again, burying her face in her hands and sobbing. Her hem was half way up her thighs. Clara and Marianne had come to the doorway to watch.

"Where is he?" Frank said.

"Kanab jail."

Nathan said, "When it's one of his wives that has made the complaint, they've got him. That's all they need. Someone who will really testify."

"How much is the bail?" Wesley asked.

When she said, "Twenty-five hundred dollars," he whistled.

"What have you been doing these two weeks?" Clara said.

"I went down to Short Creek and asked Onis Bollinger to help out. He said, Nothing doing, Farley has got what he had coming. Last week Silas Vinharth came by and took Judy and the kids away. He said he didn't dare leave them around. I was at the ranch all alone five days. Finally a man came with word from Farley. Farley's word was I should find Mr. Windham."

"What does he think I can do?"

"I don't know," she said in a weedy voice. "Not anything, likely. Nobody can do anything."

"Don't ask her what you can do," Marianne burst out hotly. "Go see him and find out."

"I can't raise twenty-five hundred dollars."

"Well, go see if there's something else you can do."

"Suppertime," Clara called out. "Everybody to the dining room, please. The enchiladas are getting cold."

Clara put Gomer between herself and Jeanette, opposite Frank and Marianne. Wesley sat at the head of the table, Nathan at the foot. Jeanette said grace and Clara got the enchiladas and salad going around the table. For a while the only sounds were the clatter of knives and forks and the click of Nathan's false teeth. Clara looked around the table. "I think a little speech is in order. Gomer, we want you to know the Earle ranch is honored by your presence. We would consider ourselves privileged to have you stay right here in our guest room for as long as you need."

"I couldn't do that, ma'am."

Clara went on in great indignation. "Can you imagine being an expectant mother, on the threshold of giving the world a new life, yet not having any loving hands to care for you, not having any place for shelter?"

"That is damned rotten," Marianne agreed.

Clara continued. "The Earle family will not be found lacking in this sorrowful situation. We are taking Gomer to Richfield to the doctor tomorrow. And we will see that the baby is born in the hospital where Gomer can be properly cared for."

Clara stared hard at Wesley, who coughed and rolled his eyes and said, "That is correct, absolutely correct. Earle Ranch Enterprises will underwrite this project in all necessary ways."

"I didn't have in mind anything fancy," Gomer said. "I was just going to have Judy Vinharth till she left."

"No midwives," Clara said decidedly. "When you told us you haven't been to a doctor a single time during your pregnancy, I was appalled. Gracious, this is the twentieth century."

On Friday morning Frank and Nathan fixed up Nathan's trailerhouse for Gomer. They patched window screens, installed new cabinet doors, and cemented plastic topping to the counters, which Frank trimmed with a router. Then they swept and vacuumed the floors and washed the cupboards, refrigerator, and stove. About noon Wesley came in, dressed up for town. After lunch he was heading for the livestock auction in Salina to bid for feeder calves.

He ran his thumb along the edge of a countertop and scrutinized a hinge on one of the new doors. "Real fancy work," he said. "You fellows ought to take up cabinet making and get out of unremunerative trades like agriculture."

"It ain't bad," Frank agreed. "I kind of get a kick out of it."

"I'm much obliged to you," Wesley said, turning to Nathan, "for making this trailer available to Gomer. I can't say I relish having a polygamous woman in the house day and night."

"Happy to be of service," Nathan said.

"Also I'm tickled about you taking over the sprinkling."

"Yes, sir. Progress is progress. This is one of the most advanced, up-to-date, scientific hay ranches in Utah, and I'm proud to do my little bit."

Frank could see Wesley and Nathan were eating off each other's plate for a change. Neither one seemed worried about Dora showing up expecting to live in the renovated trailer. Wesley had said if she did they would clean up the bunkhouse for Gomer.

Wesley sat in the dining nook and said, "Now, Frank, a word with you about Mr. Chittenden. I notice that Marianne dings at you every day about visiting him in jail. You are of course a free citizen and at liberty to visit whoever you want. Furthermore, it would be to my advantage to have him out of jail supporting this woman he has made pregnant. But repugnance wells up within me toward polygamy. I find I have no tolerance for it, no moral forbearance, no fellow feeling whatsoever, though I am willing to support Gomer for a time in hopes of rehabilitating her. Therefore, Frank, banish from your mind all thought of tapping the Earle accounts for Mr. Chittenden's bail. Tell Marianne her father draws the line at that point. Not one damned penny for his bail. Is that clear?"

"Yes, sir, that's clear as day," Frank said. "I never had any notion of putting up his bail anyhow. I haven't even made up my mind to go visit him."

A few minutes later they went to the ranchhouse for sandwiches and vegetable soup. Gomer wore one of Marianne's maternity outfits, a yellow skirt and smock which matched her bronze hair and olive skin. Clara and Jeanette, who were going to town with Wesley, wore new Sunday dresses. It being Good Friday, they planned to attend evening church services in Richfield. Jeanette's hair, the color of willow bark, was a circle of bouncy curls and she had on faint lipstick and a little eye shadow. She was excited because Easter Sunday would be her first communion.

Clara was vexed with Marianne. "I do wish you were coming to the service tonight. Afterward they're giving a little reception for Jeanette and the others having first communion on Sunday. We might borrow you from Frank just this one evening."

"Nothing doing," Marianne said. "Friday's our night out. I wouldn't miss it for anything."

Halting a spoonful of soup mid-air, Frank said, "Maybe I'll go myself. I've been getting curious about Lutheranism."

Clara gave a little cry of surprise. "Why, Frank, that'd just be wonderful!"

"Can he come with us, Daddy?" Jeanette squealed. "Can he have the afternoon off?"

Wesley spluttered. "Frank being foreman, he doesn't have to consult with me about his time off. But I think he is being ironical with us, sweetheart."

"No, sir, I'm not being ironical. Lutheranism is a wonderful old religion, which us Mormons don't know half enough about. It would be real interesting to know about all the revelations and visitations Mr. Luther must have had."

Marianne said, "If that ain't the biggest crock I ever heard of in my whole life!"

Jeanette, cutting her sandwich like a steak, said, "Maybe you'd come to my first communion on Sunday, Frank."

"You bet, that's just exactly what I'll do. I won't come tonight but I'll come Sunday. I've been feeling for a long time me and Marianne ought to trade off going to each other's church a little so we can show respect for one another."

"You big phony," Marianne said. "I'm the one who said we ought to show respect for one another. You said you weren't interested. That was last Saturday."

"I've changed my mind. I've been thinking hard about Lutheranism all week. I've decided I've got to help you be a good Lutheran. A person can slack off on their religion if they aren't careful. I don't want you to do that."

Clara was becoming a little teary-eyed. "Isn't that just splendid! Isn't it just an answer to prayer? You two have so much in common as Christians that it's a crying shame you have to quarrel about religion. My, yes, Frank, we will be just so happy to have you come along."

Wesley said, "This has certainly turned into a love feast. A great outpouring of ecumenical spirit, you might say." He looked at Nathan. "How about you, Brother Woodbarrow? Do you feel any special promptings on this occasion?"

"It ain't any of my business," the old man muttered.

All afternoon Frank worked on a feeding trough for the new calves Wesley would bring back. He kept hoping he'd be man enough to hold off on making love to Marianne until after the movie. It turned out he wasn't.

The movie was called *Swordsman of the High Seas*. A handsome English ship captain, held for ransom by pirates, found himself in chains next to a beautiful woman. They fell in love and through luck and the assistance of a penitent pirate managed to escape when the vessel put in at an island. They roused the local population, seedy immigrants from various European countries, leading them in a successful attack upon the pirate ship. After much swordfighting and many deaths they gained the loyalty of the surviving pirates and sailed for England, where they would be married.

After the movie Frank wasn't in a mood to go home. He headed the Chrysler toward Boulder, listening to the clatter of gravel on the fenders and feeling the rush of cool air through a window. When the road entered the canyon of the Escalante, the car swayed and swung and circled, its headlights gleaming on yellow cliffs, scattering across acres of slickrock, boring out into the darkness of the gorge.

"That was a good movie," Marianne said, snuggling close.

"Yeah, it was."

"I was glad they killed that pirate chief. He was a son of bitch."

"Me too."

"Are you really going to go to Richfield to the service Sunday?"

"You bet," he said. "I wouldn't miss it for anything."

As he slowed down for a fat Hereford standing in the road, she said, "Are you going to go see that poor Mr. Chittenden in jail tomorrow?"

"I believe I won't."

"You said you would."

"I changed my mind."

"You know something," she said, "you've been a mean rotter all week."

"Me! You're the one that's been cranky."

The cow backed off the pavement and Frank picked up speed. The car had just crossed a bridge and was starting up a long, winding dugway. A round white moon stood high in the eastern sky.

"Don't you want me to be a Mormon?" she asked.

"It isn't a question of if I want you to be a Mormon. It's a question of if you should be one. You're trifling with the commandments. God isn't laughing about it."

"I'm not trifling," she said. "I really would try to believe it. I'd do everything I could to believe it."

As the car rounded hairpin curves she put her arm around his shoulders and held on tight. Inside him was a bed of oak coals, sifting, settling, glowing red, blue, and white. He was burning up, thinking about them staying together, about her being around to kiss goodby every morning, to say hello to every evening, to go to the movies with every Friday night, not for one short year but for all his life.

Ahead was a pulloff overlooking the Calf Creek gorge. He drove onto it, shut off the engine, and turned out the lights. Moonlight glowed strangely on knolls and ridges and plains, between which washed large pools of darkness.

They kissed and he said, "If we stayed married we'd have to change our ways."

"What would we have to do?"

"We wouldn't have sex except to make babies. We wouldn't eat fancy food—just plain stuff to keep us going. We wouldn't keep a fancy car like this one. It's a vanity. We wouldn't ride and hunt and fish for fun. We wouldn't laugh loud."

"Other Mormons don't live that way."

"I know they don't," he said. "But I have to."

"Isn't there any other way?"

"Not if you're with me."

"That's really tough," she said, sounding run out and tired.

She turned on the radio, twisting the knob until she tuned in a station from Albuquerque. "It's a nice moonlit night here in the Land of Enchantment," an announcer was saying. A couple of fiddles began sawing, a bass began plunking, and a country voice came on with, "The saddest words I ever heard were words at parting, the sweetest days were the days that used to be."

"Lord, that's pretty," Marianne said. "It just about makes me want to cry."

She snuggled up to Frank again, her head in the hollow of his throat, her curls tickling his chin. After they had sat for a long time listening to cowboy songs, she unlatched his shirt buttons and her hand went light and easy over his breasts and belly. He kissed her hard and undid her smock and she took off her bra. Her shoulder, her breast, half her round basketball belly glowed in the moonlight drifting through the windshield. Pretty soon she unzipped his pants and he slipped his hand under her skirt.

"This is stupid," he said. "There's no way we can do it in a car with your big belly."

"Let's go home then," she said. They buttoned up and he started the engine and backed from the overlook.

"The reason we can't stay married," he said, "is I don't have any backbone. Being close to you I couldn't leave you alone."

"Couldn't we ever make love? Not even on Friday nights?"

"Just to make babies. That's all."

"There's no sense me worrying about being a Mormon then," she said. "It'd be hell, always wanting to hold each other and never being able to do it."

"Yes, that'd be hell."

On Saturday morning when Marianne asked Frank to visit Farley Chittenden in jail, he said he would. Phoning from the ranch-house after breakfast, he told Margaret that he and Marianne would be very late that night getting into Panguitch; also that they would be going to the Lutheran church on Sunday for Jeanette's first communion.

For a minute Frank could hear only the hum of the long distance connection. Then Margaret said, "I had in mind Marianne would certainly want to go to our meetings tomorrow."

"She isn't going to be a Mormon," he said. "Me and her have talked it over a good deal this week. I'm going to help her be a good Lutheran. We're going to take turns, going to her church one Sunday, going to mine the next."

"Frank, I do not recommend that you attend a Lutheran service for any reason. That's a first step toward trouble, just like smoking. First one cigarette, then two, and pretty soon you're an addict."

"Don't you worry," he said. "The Lutherans won't get their hooks into me."

After lunch he and Marianne left for Kanab in their Chrysler. The sky was broken, at times grey and somber, at other times patched with blue and brightness. They sat both in the driver's half of the seat, her arm around his shoulders, his hand on her thigh. When they went by the turnoff to Alton, he said, "Out there is the ranch where Gomer stayed. You can't believe how Farley got her. He took her out of a whorehouse."

"A whorehouse!"

"That's true. She was a whore in Caliente and also up in Fallon. Maybe other places too. The prophet Hosea appeared to Farley and instructed him to go into the whorehouse and bring her out and give her the name of Gomer."

"That's crazy. I don't believe you."

"Take it or leave it, that's the way it happened," he said.

"I wish you hadn't told me about it. I was feeling real sorry for her. Now I don't know if I feel sorry or not."

They hunted around Kanab until they located the sheriff at the rodeo grounds where he was helping the Lion's Club set up a couple of privies. The sheriff was six foot four, had a bushy walrus mustache, wore cowboy boots, and belted his Levi's low beneath a bulging belly.

He sauntered over to the Chrysler with Frank and took a good look at Marianne. "Is that one of Farley's wives?"

"No, sir, that's my wife."

"How many you got?"

"I ain't a polygamist."

"Looks like she's in a family way."

"Somewhat," Frank said.

They followed the sheriff's car back to the courthouse, which was a big rectangular building of purple sandstone. He led them in the front door and down a hall past an office where residents could pay their water bill and on through a trial room having a judge's bench and jury box. They entered an office furnished with two battered wood desks, half a dozen chairs, a picture of George Washington, and a sawed-off shotgun chained to a rack.

"Me and the judge share these quarters," the sheriff said, putting on a pair of spectacles and shuffling up to scrutinize Frank. "If you ain't a polygamist, how come you're down here?"

"I was asked to come."

"Who asked you?"

"A lady."

"One of his wives. How many has he got?"

"I don't know," Frank said. "I don't take census on polygamists."

The sheriff scratched his belly and pulled a bundle of keys from his pocket. "Can you raise the twenty-five hundred?"

"No, sir, I can't."

"How much can you raise?"

"Zero. I'm not studying how to bail him out. That's his business."

"I believe the judge is getting in a mood to dicker," the sheriff said. "To tell you the truth, that first wife of Farley's who filed charges, Bertha, she won't be worth anything as a witness in a trial. She's gone off and took up with another polygamist outfit over in

Johnson Canyon. So we aren't likely to empanel a jury over this little matter. If somebody was to make the judge a reasonable offer on some forfeit bail, I think he would take it."

The sheriff locked Frank and Marianne in Farley's tiny cell and said he would be back in a half hour. Farley was beside himself with joy, jumping off his cot, wringing his hands, and throwing his arms around Frank. His hair rimmed his bald spot like aspens around a meadow and his mustache grew down to the points of his chin like Genghis Khan's. A green tee shirt stretched over his burly shoulders; a pair of jeans sagged on his frail hips.

"Oh, Frank, Lord love you, boy, I knew you were coming! Lying right here on this bunk I saw you in vision yesterday morning. I saw you and a pregnant lady." He smiled broadly and took both of Marianne's hands. "Frank's little lady. Heard he had got married. Ma'am, I'm Farley Chittenden. Honored to make your acquaintance. I love anybody Frank Windham loves."

He put a long muscly arm around each of them, squeezing hard. "Ain't it strange? In vision I saw this pregnant lady alongside Frank. Figured it was Gomer. Didn't think there might be other pregnant ladies in the world. Thought Frank would show up with Gomer. How is my little sweetheart? Tell me she's okay before my old heart busts."

"She's okay," Frank said. "The Earles have taken her in. Marianne here took her to the doctor in Richfield the other day. You can quit worrying about her. She's in good hands."

"Bless your daddy and mamma, bless them, bless them. Heavenly Father won't let this go unnoticed."

He shoved books and papers aside on his littered cot. "Me and Frank'll sit on this bed, and, Marianne, you take that chair. Got things to show you. Big things brewing in this little cell. The burning bush has been here. Saw it one night, right there in that corner. I despaired, Frank, I cried out, O God, where art thou and where is the pavilion that covereth thy hiding place? That son of a bitch Onis Bollinger has throwed me to the lions. Me, that was one of his ordained apostles. But God spoke to me. Said, my son, as well might man stretch forth his puny arm to stop the Missouri River in its decreed course, or to turn it up stream, as to hinder the Almighty from pouring down revelation upon his servant, Farley Chittenden."

He gripped Frank's knee. "I'm called to set his church right, Frank. God has revealed to me he has withdrawn his spirit from all the earth. Said even Onis's bunch has fallen into apostasy. Saw the burning bush right there in that corner last week when the lights were out. A voice called and I harkened."

His eyes were glinty and he spit when he talked because he was in such a hurry. He rummaged among his papers and pulled out a map. "The world right here in my hands. Already decided where I'll send my first missionaries. The church of Jesus Christ restored and set right at long last by the hands of Farley Chittenden. Look here! That's for you, Frank. Argentina! The Spirit instructed me you was to go to Argentina and preach the Gospel. Going to ordain you an apostle. Might make you a member of the first presidency too."

"I'm not interested in being an apostle," Frank said. "Maybe you ought to just put a lid on that burning bush stuff for a while. Maybe you ought to concentrate on getting out of jail first."

"Yes, sir, I'm counting on you for bail."

"You still owe me thirty bucks for driving your truck."

"Shame on me, shame," Farley said. "I ain't forgot. Got to have your help, Frank. Don't know anybody with money. Lord told me it was Mr. Earle who would put up the money. Said, I have opened the windows of heaven upon Mr. Earle."

"No, sir, that won't work," Frank said. "Wesley thinks polygamists are worse than Confucians."

Farley stared at the floor and bit a thumb nail. "Haw," he said, "I've got a plan. Made a plot. You're in it. Drive over to Johnson Canyon. Find Justin Higgins. Big prophet over there. False prophet. Find Bertha through Justin Higgins. Tell her Farley has suffered agonies over his sins against her. Tell her God rebuked Farley because of his wrongdoings against Bertha. My first wife! Got married in San Bernardino. I was thirty-six, she was forty. Tell her Farley remembers the little darling he married down in San Bernardino. Tell her to drop them charges. That's the whole idea. Drop them charges."

"She isn't going to drop the charges. That's pie in the sky."

"You could head over there right now," Farley urged. "It ain't that far to Johnson Canyon. I can draw you a map. Tell her I've got a plan. Going to gather my wives. Going to spend equal time with them. Not going to favor one over the other. Except my first wife, which is proper. Got an aching heart for the little gal I married down in San Bernardino. Tell her that."

"She won't pay any mind to me."

"You're my Aaron. Speak for Moses, man."

"We'll do it," Marianne said with finality.

Frank and Marianne took the graveled road east from Kanab. Fifteen miles out they turned north into Johnson Canyon. Ten miles farther they turned into a side canyon rimmed by high cliffs of rich red rock. Beyond the cliffs rose immense ridges layered with alternating terraces of blue timber and white rimrock. The road narrowed to a rutted track. It dipped into sandy washes, snaked over powdery sagebrush flats, tunneled through juniper groves. Frank drove cautiously, turning tight, easing into dips, keeping a soft foot on the accelerator. The trick was to keep the low slung Chrysler on the high edge of the ruts.

"It's this country that drives people crazy," Marianne said, swaying with the lurch of the car. "It's so pretty; it's wild and clean and godly. But sometimes it makes me feel so lonesome I can't stand it. It isn't just the polygamists who go crazy down here. Everybody has more or less gone crazy."

"Now that ain't true."

"Yes, it is," she said. "All the Mormons I know have gone crazy. There's a good deal of Farley in all of them. Including you."

"I'm not crazy."

"Not a whole lot maybe, but somewhat crazy, yes, you really are."

He rubbed his chin, looking hurt. A half mile farther he said, "Talk about crazy. It wasn't me who wanted to drive out here and scout the sagebrush for Bertha. I can't figure out why you're so interested in these polygamists."

"I'm interested because they're down and out. Everybody else is down on them, has turned their back on them. Aren't those the kind Jesus wants us to help?"

"That's so," he said, giving her a sidewise glance.

Some miles farther the canyon widened, and they drove into a swale silvery with grass. Across it, maybe a mile away, were cars, a windmill, a corral, a fire, some people.

"Good gosh, what are those folks up to?" Frank said.

They drove closer. It was nearly dusk and the wind had died. There were no houses or barns, only the rolling, silvery swale and the wide purpling sky. The windmill was a circle of spoked vanes on a tower. The fire burned high and smokeless. The thirty or forty people crowding around it wore suits and ties and ankle length dresses.

Two men walked toward the approaching car. One of them held up a hand and Frank stopped. The man leaned into the window and said, "This is a private gathering. All this land around here is private property."

"I want to talk to Justin Higgins."

"We are having a service. Back your car down the road a piece so you aren't disturbing, and we'll come along and see what's on your mind."

When Frank had backed the car for fifty yards, he and Marianne got out and waited. "We're looking for Justin Higgins," Frank said as the men approached.

"I'm him," said the man who had told them to back up. He was tall and willowy and had a burned, wrinkled neck, a pointed chin, and deepset eyes.

"What we want is a word with Bertha Chittenden," Frank said. "We were told you could tell us where to find her."

"What do you want of her?"

"A word with her."

"What kind of word?"

"About her husband. We've got a message."

"Nobody by the name of Bertha Chittenden is here."

"We were told she is."

"This is a private gathering. We'll thank you kindly to go back down the road."

"We have in mind seeing Bertha Chittenden," Frank said.

Higgins's voice took an edge. "We have in mind you leaving. Bertha Chittenden isn't here. Never has been. Goodby. Take care you don't high center driving out."

Higgins and his friend went back up the road to the group around the fire. As Frank opened the car door and slipped into the seat, Marianne started up the road, muttering, "He's a liar."

Frank jumped out and caught up with her in a hurry. "Do you think you're going to arm wrassle them or something?"

"I'm going to find that lady."

"Don't you go over there. That isn't a bunch to mess with."

She pushed off his hand and walked on, her hair bouncing, her hips swaying. Her pink smock caught light from the sky. In the west the evening star shimmered above a rim of charcoal clouds. The bonfire burned bright, and vague, musical words rose from the people around it. Frank watched, his foot resting on the bumper of the Chrysler. The group opened when Marianne arrived and Higgins stood in front of her. She looked around, said something, waved her hand. Higgins said something. Marianne spoke and gestured again. A woman stepped forward and stood by Higgins. Marianne turned half around and pointed down the road. She left the fire and the woman followed.

As they approached Frank, Marianne said, "This is my husband."

The woman scrutinized his face, put out her hand, and said, "We done met." She was Bertha, no mistake about it. In the near dark Frank could make out her flat, pasty face, her thin, grudging lips. She wore a long dark dress under an open coat.

"So give me the word from Farley and get on your way."

"He wants you back," Frank said.

Bertha snorted. "I'll bet he does. I'll bet he hates jail worse than anything else in his whole life. I think that's just fine, him eating crow, sending word he wants me back."

"He knows he did you wrong," Frank went on. "He says God rebuked him and warned him he had to treat you better. He's suffering over it; he's remorseful about it. He wants to gather his wives and treat them equal like a husband ought to. He says he'll turn over a new leaf, he really will."

Bertha turned to Marianne, saying with disgust, "Is that what you dragged me over here for, to listen to that? You don't know anything about Farley. He's all mouth, all promises. The only thing I feel happy about these days is knowing that mink is in jail. Tell him to put his money where his mouth is; tell him to get rid of his whore."

"We've got Gomer up on our ranch," Marianne said. "She doesn't seem like a whore."

"She still goes by Gomer, does she? Farley and his revelations! God phones him up daily for advice. Do you know what God told him to do? Bed her every day. Twice, three times a day when he was around the ranch, which was most of the time. Him and her knelt by the bed, held hands, said a little prayer, then played the animal. How come? Every time they did it, according to Mr. Prophet, they erased one of her early sins, they got forgiveness for the whoring she did. Does that sound godly? Does that sound like a true revelation?"

"My gosh," Marianne said.

"However, that doesn't make any difference. I'm not going back to him no matter what."

It was full dark now. The sky moved with stars, the bonfire danced and flickered. A fox yipped, a sheep bleated. With a slow, haunting music the people at the fire began a hymn, voices wavering, going off key, coming back, drifting away into the strange night.

"They've started the service," Bertha said, glancing toward the fire. "You better get going. This isn't a favorable place for you folks to be. They follow the true Aaronic law out here. They're getting ready for Easter. There's four horses and a lamb in that corral. Come midnight Justin and three others will load them and head for Pine Point. When the road peters out they'll ride the horses. One of them will carry the lamb on his saddle. There's an altar up on Pine Point where, come sun-up, they'll sacrifice the lamb. They'll shed its blood to signify the Crucifixion. Every Easter, that's their practice out here. It's the true Aaronic law."

"Criminy!" said Marianne.

The singing had stopped and a man's voice floated on the air. "A thing has happened," Bertha whispered. "I'm not saying it was wrong, but I feel like I'm still in a churn. I came over here to marry Ross Drummer. Him and me exchanged letters all last year. It was Ross who told me how to put Farley in jail, told me where to go to file a complaint. Ross wrote I was to come over here and be his wife. I wrote I would do it. Last letter I had was in February. I got Farley in jail, boarded up the store in Glendale, and came over here."

Frank and Marianne gathered close, straining to catch her hoarse words. "I found out Ross was dead. Had been since the first of March. He atoned himself. It turned out he sometimes went to bed with men. Every time he went to Salt Lake, he did it. He had lived in hell's fire for many years. He had a black witness, knew he was damned, asked to be cleansed by his own blood. They took him out, I'm not saying who; they dug a grave, prayed together, then somebody held him by the hair, cut his throat, pointed the spurt of blood into the grave. He wanted to be cleansed by his own blood. It's the only way if you've had a black witness."

"My God!" Marianne said.

"So I don't know what I'm going to do," Bertha said.

"Go back to Farley," Frank said.

"It's too late for that."

"He's still in love with you. He talked about when you got married down in San Bernardino a long time ago. He can't get you off his mind."

"Please don't say no more."

"You and him must have been awful close once upon a time," Frank said. "That's what he wants to go back to."

Her throat clicked oddly.

"I can't keep shut up any longer," Marianne broke in. "I told Frank to come over here and find you because I felt sorry for Farley. But I've got over feeling sorry for him. It's too damned easy for a man to tell a woman he's in love with her. That way he can buy twenty-five hundred dollars worth of bail for ten cents worth of words."

"That's the truth."

"And I'd get out of this place if I were you."

"Thank you, sister," Bertha said. "I don't know you but I've got a feeling about you."

"Bust off with all these damned polygamists!"

"I don't know what I'll do. I'm waiting for God to say. I've got a testimony of plural marriage. True things aren't ever easy. Now you folks get on. Thank you for your kindness in coming."

When Frank and Marianne arrived in Panguitch at two in the morning, Margaret was frantic with worry. They calmed her down, and Frank also called Wesley and Clara because Margaret had phoned and got them excited too. At dawn Frank got up and milked. He sat on a one-legged stool, his head against the cow, which fed next to the bull at the outside stanchion.

Margaret came into the corral, bundled up in a coat. She turned an old bucket upside down and sat near Frank, asking, "Are you making motions to sell that bull?"

"I've got to get to that," he said. "Somehow or other I don't want to see him go."

"Are you still set on going to that Lutheran service?"

"Yes, ma'am. But it don't mean nothing at all. I'm just doing it for Jeanette." He squirted milk at the neighbor's cat, which had come into the corral. The cat lapped at the wavering stream and afterward licked its wet fur.

Margaret said, "I surely thought Marianne would want to come to our church today."

"She has changed her mind."

"I don't know about that, Frank. I have begun to wonder if you changed it for her. It would be a terrible thing for you to stand between that girl and the truth."

"Yes, ma'am, but I didn't do that. All I did was call her bluff. She got to thinking it'd be easier for us to stay together if she was a Mormon. But we're not staying together."

"Oh, dear me, Frank, that's a wicked idea. Please stop thinking it. Get down on your knees and ask the Lord to help you get it out of your mind."

He flared up. "Do you want me to be a backslider all my life? If I stay with her, it won't turn out she is a good Mormon and our kids will grow up righteous. What will happen is I'll fall away."

"Not if you pray, not if you do your duties properly."

He stuck a finger into the milkpail and picked a hayleaf off the foam. "If I stay with her, I'm headed down to hell and no turning back. So I'll likely be coming home to stay pretty soon. I had a stupid idea I should see her through till the baby's born and then a little more beside. I'm about to give up on that."

"It will break my heart for your baby to grow up a Lutheran," she said.

At nine-thirty Wesley and Clara picked up Frank and Marianne and drove on toward Richfield. Beside Jeanette they had Gomer, who had suffered labor pains in the night and couldn't be left alone on the ranch.

Clara, sitting between Wesley and Gomer, exclaimed with a sweeping arm, "What a glorious Easter morning!" The sun was bright, the air quiet. Cottonwoods greened along the Sevier, which made its way north in placid loops and rippling runs. Cattle and sheep grazed peacefully in roadside meadows.

"Imagine how the two disciples at Emmaus felt," she said. "A stranger fell in with them and they told him about the great tragedy of the Crucifixion, not knowing Jesus had risen. While they ate supper with the stranger, their eyes were opened and they saw the resurrected Lord. Isn't that marvelous?"

"Yes, that's marvelous," Jeanette said, looking angelic in a new lacy white dress.

Wesley said, "It wouldn't be inappropriate on this Easter morning, would it, to ask Frank and Marianne about Mr. Chittenden?"

"Oh, yes, please," Gomer said in a rush, "how is poor Farley doing? Is he frail and wasted?"

"Not by a long shot," Frank said.

"Is he getting out? Did he tell you what to do?"

"No, ma'am, he isn't getting out and what he told us to do didn't work. He sent us to find Bertha in Johnson Canyon to see if she wouldn't drop her complaint."

"Won't she?" Gomer cried.

"Not a chance," Frank said. "Especially with Marianne working on her. I thought for a second she was softening up. Then Marianne piled in and told her to stay away from skunks like Farley."

Marianne pinched him hard and said, "Thanks a whole lot for making me popular." She leaned forward and placed a hand on Gomer's shoulder. "The truth is I'm totally against polygamy. I don't think it's good for anybody, especially you, Gomer. If I was you I'd find me another husband."

"Now if that isn't positively rude! You have made her cry," Clara said, digging in her purse for a Kleenex. "Polygamy is part of Gomer's religious convictions and we are duty bound to respect it."

Wesley said, "I can't say I had ever met a polygamist before Gomer came to stay with us. Do you mind telling me, Gomer, who performed the marriage ceremony for you and Mr. Chittenden?"

"Onis Bollinger," she said in a teary voice.

"And what county commissioned him to perform marriages?"

"No county. Just God."

"Just God! Think of that!" Wesley said. "I imagine Mr. Bollinger has a church which you belong to."

"Yes, sir."

"However," Frank interrupted, "Farley is down on Onis and is setting up his own church now."

"I suppose Gomer will belong to this new church," Wesley said.

"He never mentioned any new church to me," she said, "but if he makes one, I'll sure be a member of it."

"That's an admirable confidence in your husband's spiritual leadership," Wesley remarked.

Frank said, "Farley asked me to be an apostle in his new church, but I turned him down."

"An apostle?" Clara said. "I find that a little presumptuous of Mr. Chittenden."

"You can't fault him," Wesley said. "He's another Martin Luther down here in tumbleweed country. He's just engaging in a little reformation, Utah style, that's all."

"The reason I'm down on polygamists," said Marianne, "is some damned ungodly things are going on out there in the boondocks. I won't mention everyday, run-of-the-mill things like visions and revelations. Over there in Johnson Canyon they've turned into priests of Baal. They were having a service last night out under the sky, singing and preaching and praying around a fire, getting ready to haul a lamb up on a mountain and sacrifice it on an altar. But that isn't anything. Last month they sacrificed a man. They cut his throat and bled him out, then buried him."

"A man!" Clara said.

"That's what Bertha said. I don't know if I believe her."

"I believe her," Frank said.

Marianne gestured angrily. "Then why didn't you do something about it? Why didn't we stop in Kanab and tell the sheriff on our way through last night?"

"Maybe that fellow had it coming," he said. "He was a sodomist. Story was he asked to have his blood shed so God would forgive him."

"My God!" she exclaimed, clapping her forehead and sinking back.

"That story doesn't sound credible," Wesley said. "It's got to be rumor; it can't be anything but folklore."

"I wouldn't be a Mormon for a hundred million dollars," Marianne muttered.

Frank grunted. "Them folks out there in Johnson Canyon aren't Mormons. They're Fundamentalists. They've been excommunicated."

"There isn't a speck of difference," Marianne said. "You and Farley, you and that Justin Higgins, you're all one and the same."

The Lutheran church was a white frame hall with a gabled roof and a thin tapered spar serving as a steeple. Along the inside walls hung banners decorated with crosses, doves, and angels. Above the altar in the forward wall, arched windows let in light through glass of amber and cherry. Short pews, occupied by sixty or seventy people of all ages, ran down the hall in double rows. An electric organ sounded and from a wing marched a little procession—four children, one of them Jeanette; a young man carrying a lighted taper; and a minister wearing a white gauzy tunic over a black velvet robe.

"My gosh," Frank whispered to Marianne as the taper bearer lit candles on either side of the altar, "how come they need those candles? Isn't this place wired?"

"They're symbolic," she said. "They stand for the light of the Gospel."

The minister, a lean, grey-haired man, said a few words and the congregation arose. The minister read, with pauses allowing the congregation to repeat in unison, "Almighty God, our Maker and Redeemer, we poor sinners confess unto thee, that we are by nature sinful and unclean, and that we have sinned against thee by thought, word, and deed."

"What are we doing?" Frank whispered.

"We're confessing our sins together," Marianne said.

Frank looked around. No question about it, Lutherans were odd.

There were other readings by the minister and recitations by the congregation. Then came a hymn, which didn't sound different from a Mormon hymn. Holding a side of the hymnal, Frank tried to pick out Marianne's voice from the others. Hearing her high, sweet, quivery notes, he felt lustful and glanced sideways at the mounds under her pretty flowered smock. Knowing it wasn't right to lust on a woman in a church, even if it was Lutheran, he tried to concentrate on the words of the hymn: "And from my smitten heart, with tears, two wonders I confess, the wonder of his glorious love and my own worthlessness."

"Amen to that," he whispered as the congregation sat down.

"To what?" she whispered back.

"To my own worthlessness."

She looked peevish. "You overdo it. You've got to have quitting sense when it comes to guilt and confession."

The minister preached a sermon on the Resurrection in a voice so soft and gentle that Frank had to strain to catch his words. Then came the rite of confirmation, as the program termed it. The minister called forward Jeanette and two other girls and a boy and told how they had completed a year of catechism and were ready now to become full fledged members of the congregation. While the minister asked questions and the young people answered in unison, Frank stuffed his hands in his coat pockets and stared at his shoes, which he noticed were in need of polish. He perked up when the minister said, "Do you renounce the devil and all his works and all his ways?" and the young people said, "We renounce them."

"It ain't much of a test to ask somebody that question," he whispered to Marianne. "I could have answered it for them."

"It's not supposed to be a test. It's a ceremony."

While the four new members knelt at the hardwood rail before the altar, the minister gave each a little wafer from a basket, then gave each a sip of wine from a silver goblet, whose lip he wiped with a napkin between sips. Next it was the congregation's turn. Clara and Marianne stood and when the usher gave them permission they went forward and knelt at the rail.

Wesley moved close to Frank, whispering in his ear, "Pure superstition! The idea of the Crucifixion is a relic of barbarism, a throwback to a primitive mentality, and by gad, Frank, Christianity has institutionalized it, has brought it down against the tide of civilization during two long millennia. Here we are in the twentieth century, a time of enlightenment and science, and these people are still celebrating the bloody death of a god."

"Yes, sir, likely so," Frank said.

Having received the communion, Clara and Marianne came down the outside aisle, pushed into the pew, and sat down. Marianne took Frank's hand and squeezed it hard, looking at him with wet, emotional eyes. "Why can't you believe his blood was enough?" she whispered. "Why do you have to shed yours too?"

He didn't know what she meant.

After the service people gathered to chatter and gossip on the front lawn, the ladies as bright as flowers in their new Easter dresses of pink, blue, yellow, and gold. At the foot of the flag pole, on which

the American flag gently flapped, Mr. and Mrs. Richens were per-
suading the Earles to come to dinner.

"Your bunch too big?" Mrs. Richens said to Clara. "Pshaw!
Not at all, not at all. We're just so happy to finally meet your
son-in-law, and as for Mrs. Chittenden, why, we'll just be tickled
pink to have her along too. Now do come! Dinner in forty-five
minutes sharp."

Still a little embarrassed, Clara said, "We are quite a party but
we'll come, Ida, and thank you for your kindness."

Wesley sidled up to Clara, waving toward the street where
Marianne helped Gomer into the car. "We've got a problem. It looks
like Gomer has gone into labor."

A committee meeting took place around the car, determining who
would remain with Gomer at the Richfield hospital. Wesley said
nobody needed to stay, doctors and nurses being hindered in their
professional services by loitering visitors. They could check in on
Gomer's progress by telephone from time to time and drive from
the ranch the next day to see the new baby. Clara called that a
heartless breach of duty. A woman in travail needed moral support
even if those giving it were sitting in a waiting room. It was clear
that she should stay because she had insisted the family take on
Gomer as a project. Then Marianne settled the issue by saying she
intended to stay no matter who else did or didn't. Of course Frank
said he would stay with her.

After Gomer had been admitted, Frank and Marianne had lunch
in the hospital kitchen. Afterward, while he read magazines in the
waiting room, she sat with Gomer. From time to time he looked
into the room where Gomer lay, her hand in Marianne's. Silent and
tense, she was slow in dilating and it looked as if the baby would
be a long time coming.

Frank took a walk to the opposite end of Richfield. Along the
way he found a man breaking the Sabbath by repairing a lawn mower
engine. Squatting on the driveway where the fellow had spread
parts, Frank said, "I never saw the guts of one of them one cylinder
outfits before."

"Simple as hell," said the man, whose mouth went all the way
to his ears when he smiled. Frank knew he was a Jack Mormon
because he smelled of tobacco.

Frank examined the tiny, gleaming cylinder, which had flanges at either end for bolting it into the housing. "Me and the wife are up at the hospital waiting out a delivery," he explained. "It's a friend who hasn't got anybody else to look after her. She's a polygamist lady whose husband is in jail. I've been waiting to hear her holler but she hasn't."

"Wait'll it gets to the end. She'll holler then."

"God fixed it up so having a baby would hurt," Frank said. "He said to Eve, in sorrow thou shalt bring forth children."

"Don't believe everything you read in the Bible."

"It fits," Frank said. "God doesn't mind feeding people misery." He put a finger into the cylinder. "The reason it hurts is a big baby has to come out a tiny hole. I just don't see how it can loosen up enough for a baby to come out."

"It'd surprise you how the damn thing stretches. The doctor can put a hand up inside if he has to. A baby's head is big as this." The man put his clenched fists together. "I watched one of ours come. It slipped up on us. The missis was on the toilet when her water broke. We headed for the hospital but we never made it to the front door of our own house. She had it in the hall. A neighbor lady took care of things till the doctor got there. I saw the whole thing."

"Did she holler?"

"She always hollers. She pants and puffs and screams and says I'm the one that caused it, and says she's never going to let me on top of her again, not once. But of course when the baby gets here, she falls in love with it and forgets all about that."

"My gosh," Frank said, "women have it tough."

"True, true. They aren't a favored race."

When Frank put his head into Gomer's room in the evening, things hadn't changed. Gomer gripped Marianne's fist with both hands; every time contractions came she squeezed as if she was juicing an orange. Frank said Marianne should get a bite of supper before the hospital kitchen closed for the night.

"I'm not hungry," said Marianne, who looked almost as bad as Gomer. "I'm damn mad at Dr. Reuther. That fake! During all these months I've been seeing him, I've had him pegged for a compassionate healer. I thought he was a second Albert Schweitzer. But he hasn't looked at Gomer since two-thirty this afternoon. He's home sitting on his fat butt waiting for the nurse to phone him with word she's finally got dilated."

"I imagine if the doctor and nurses aren't worried, you don't need to be either."

"But she's in pain," Marianne snapped. "Don't you understand that?"

"She's okay," Frank said. "There's no sense giving her the idea she's worse off than she is." He leaned over Gomer's bed. "How are you doing? Can you make it okay?"

Gomer's eyes circled before they lit on Frank. She nodded her head and said, "I'm making it." She grimaced and grabbed Marianne's fist. A minute later, relaxing, she looked again at Frank and said, "Would you give me a blessing? I was sick with the flu and Farley and Silas blessed me. It did me so much good."

"I can't administer to anybody."

"Why can't you?" Marianne said. "That's what Mormons specialize in, isn't it? They hold the Priesthood so they can heal people, don't they?"

"I never healed anybody. I wouldn't know how."

"I would surely take it as a favor if you would bless me," Gomer said. "Things would go better if you would."

"My gosh," Frank said in a panic.

"Bless her," Marianne commanded.

"I'll have to get some help. It takes two."

"Okay, go get somebody."

The nurse at the desk gave Frank the name of a Richfield bishop. Frank dialed and no one answered. The nurse was new in town and didn't know any other Mormons. As Frank got into his car street lights were coming on. Driving down Main Street he saw a tall, shadowy figure locking a door; it was Rossler Jarbody, the lawyer who had his office over a store. Frank made a quick U-turn and pulled in behind Jarbody's car.

"Howdy," he said, getting out.

"Who are you?" Jarbody said, about to slam his door.

"Frank Windham. Client of yours once upon a time. You gave me the name of a Salt Lake lawyer who helped bust my brother out of the insane asylum. I paid you fifteen bucks."

"Got a problem? Going to jail?"

"I was wondering if you were a Mormon."

"Are you trying to get yourself sued for invasion of privacy?"

"There's a poor polygamist lady having a baby over in the hospital who wants to be administered to. I'm trying to run down somebody to give me a hand."

Jarbody laughed like a hen clucking. "That'd be the farce of the century, Rossler D. Jarbody laying on hands for the healing of the sick. I'm as wayward as the Afghan railroad."

"You're a Mormon."

"Don't get your hopes up."

"You owe me a consideration," Frank said. "Fifteen bucks was a lot of money to pay for nothing but another lawyer's name."

"You don't want me. A man in my spiritual state would do more harm than good."

"She isn't real hard up. I don't think she's in any danger. It's just to make her feel better while she's in labor. Also to make my wife feel better, who is sitting with her."

"This is sheer lunacy. I won't do it."

"It won't take but five minutes."

"My gadfrey," Jarbody said, "you're serious." He locked his door and climbed into Frank's car, muttering, "This isn't rational; it just isn't rational."

"Where do we get some consecrated oil?" Frank said as they pulled from the curb.

Jarbody hummed a minute, then said, "Swing down First East. I'll check the houses as we go by. You'll have to do the asking. I can't afford to be seen doing this kind of thing. It'd ruin my reputation."

In a minute he said, "Here. Go in and ask Jerald Zimmer if he doesn't have some oil. Don't mention my name."

Frank knocked and the door was opened by a tweedy little man wearing a long striped tie and a white collar so big it would have fit around a power pole. "Sure, sure, sure, I always got olive oil," he said. "You bet, you bet, glad to have you use it. It's out in the truck."

He led Frank to his driveway, jerked open a battered old Ford, groped in the glove compartment, and pulled out a Coca-Cola bottle stoppered with a cork. "There, that's about half full of consecrated oil. If you get back late and the lights are out, just stick it in the glove compartment. I keep it there in case I need it out at the farm. Never know when an emergency will come up. Healed a horse one day. He was down with compaction. Me and Ralph Tershelshire gave him a blessing, using some of that oil. He healed up quick. Passed a pile, as you might say. Right as any horse today."

In the hospital corridor Frank and Jarbody met the doctor, who took a hard look at Jarbody, then another hard look at the Coke bottle in Frank's hand. "This here is consecrated oil," Frank explained. "We're Elders. Mrs. Chittenden asked us to administer to her."

Uhmhuhing and ahmhahing as if he had no objections, the doctor twisted his head and watched Jarbody proceed down the corridor. Nobody could miss Jarbody. He was six foot six and wore a grey suit, a pink shirt, and a fluorescent ruby tie.

"Absolutely embarrassing," the lawyer whispered. "Reuther will spread the word about me. I'll swear, Mr. Windham, this is bizarre. I can't believe I'm doing it."

"What did the doctor say?" Frank asked when they entered Gomer's room.

"She's coming along," Marianne replied. "But it'll still be a while."

"Gomer," he said, "this here is Rossler Jarbody. He's going to help me administer to you."

"Oh, thank you."

"Now one of us has to anoint with oil and the other to seal the blessing," Frank said.

"I'll take the anointing," Jarbody said. "Just tell me what to say."

After he had spilled a drop of oil on Gomer's forehead and said a little prayer, he and Frank together lay hands on her head and Frank said a longer prayer. As he got into it, Frank cheered up and decided he'd risk a few promises.

"And we say unto you, whereforeasmuch as ye are faithful, thou shalt be healed and delivered of a fine baby boy which thou shalt call Jezreel. And it shall come to pass soon. Very shortly. Very, very shortly. Therefore have patience. Amen." The part about patience was for Marianne.

"A boy? Named Jezreel?" Jarbody said. "You must be as crazy as your brother."

"That's the way it felt," Frank said. "I might be wrong, of course."

"Oh, no," Gomer said, "you won't be wrong. God told Farley a long time ago we were to name him Jezreel. The next one will be a girl and we'll name her Loruhamah."

"That is correct," Frank said. "Book of Hosea. Look it up for yourself."

"Holy mackerel," Jarbody said, "this is a nest of the occult."

"I do feel better," Gomer said. She turned her eyes to Marianne, who still sat nearby. "Go get yourself some supper now. I just do feel better."

Later when Frank and Marianne let Jarbody out by his car on Main Street, the lawyer said, "An exceptional experience! On the whole I don't object to making people feel better. However, Mr. Windham, I won't be all torn up if I don't run into you again. Glad to have met you, Mrs. Windham. I hope you both have a nice evening."

"Much obliged for your help," Frank said. Then he and Marianne went up the street to a drive-in where they had hamburgers and milk shakes.

A couple of hours later the doctor came back to the hospital and the nurses wheeled Gomer into the delivery room. Marianne dragged a chair down the corridor and sat outside the double doors, Frank following with another chair. It wasn't a cheerful place to sit, Gomer's cries and shrieks tumbling through the closed doors like water through a screen. She shouted for Farley and her mother and somebody named Miss Angela and goddamned the doctor and the nurses for being so rough and goddamned Bertha for not letting poor Farley out of jail. She said she couldn't take any more and prayed for death and asked why God had forgotten her.

Marianne sat upright and rigid, gripping the arms of her chair. Her curls had unraveled into tousled strands and her cheeks were the color of milk gravy.

"For heck's sake," Frank said, "let's go sit somewhere else. We can't do any good here."

"No, I'm not leaving."

"She doesn't know you're out here. Us sitting here doesn't mean a pickle to her."

"No, I couldn't leave her."

In a minute she asked, "Will you pray with me?"

"Sure I will."

"Let's ask the Lord to let us carry some of her burden, to direct some of her pain to us so she doesn't hurt so bad. Will you do that?"

She took his hands and began to pray silently. Closing his eyes, he tried to concentrate on accepting some of Gomer's pain. In his mind he could see a ditch full of clear water. He thought of himself opening a headgate, letting part of the stream flow into a lateral ditch. He wondered where he would feel the pain. Maybe in the belly. No, more likely in the crotch. Gosh, maybe in the back. But he didn't feel a thing.

In a minute Marianne released his hands and said, "There, our prayer is answered. I think she is easing up a little."

No question, there was a lull. But a minute later Gomer was whooping and shouting again. Frank looked to see what Marianne thought about that. Her eyes were closed and with each shout she flinched. It looked as if God was giving her plenty of pain; however, he hadn't eased Gomer's.

Abruptly Gomer's cries stopped and the wail of a newborn child began. Marianne struggled from her chair, slipped on her high heels, and pushed into the delivery room. Though Frank expected the doctor to order her out, she didn't appear. He slumped in his chair and cocked a foot over a knee, noticing that it was after midnight. He was awfully glad the baby had arrived. From the sound of things or rather from the silence of things, he judged Gomer was feeling much better.

The doors swung open and out came a nurse and Marianne, who held the baby in a flannel cloth. "It's a little boy," she said, leaning over to give Frank a look. The baby had a wrinkled, muddy face and an abundance of damp black hair. Marianne and the nurse went down the corridor toward the nursery. Frank followed, dragging the chairs he and Marianne had sat in. He settled down in the waiting room and went through some magazines for the fourth or fifth time. The doctor came by, putting on his suit jacket. "Pretty good delivery," he said, smiling at Frank. "Mother and son are doing just fine."

When Marianne joined him in the waiting room, Frank said, "Let's go. It's way after bedtime."

"Not for a minute. Let's make sure Gomer is okay."

Soon a nurse wheeled Gomer by, heading for her room. She was dozy and only murmured when they said goodnight. They walked to the parking lot, Marianne leaning on his arm. As he helped her into the Chrysler, he handed her the corked Coke bottle. "We gotta take this back to Mr. Zimmer's place. He said to leave it in the glove compartment of his truck."

He drove along First East and pulled up at Zimmer's curb where overhanging mulberry boughs shaded the glow of a street lamp. As he reached for the bottle of oil, she held it to her breast, saying, "Would you bless our baby before you take back the oil?"

"You want a blessing? Now?"

"Yes, now," she said, handing him the bottle.

"I'd rather not do that. Tomorrow we can get Uncle Lonnie and the bishop to give you a real blessing."

"No, I want you to do it here. Please bless our baby." She turned on the dome light and pulled up her smock, exposing her round, white belly.

"Have you gone loco?"

"Put some oil on my tummy," she said, "and then lay on your hands and give our baby a blessing."

"No, by gum, I ain't going to do that. Get your smock down before somebody comes up the sidewalk and thinks we're getting ready to make love."

"Please."

"Oh, lord, Marianne, don't make me do this."

"Please."

"What'll I say?"

"Bless it to be healthy and strong. Bless its mother so she will have courage. So she can go through with the delivery."

He uncorked the Coke bottle, dribbled oil on her belly, and laid on his hands.

"Right here," Marianne said, moving his hands a little. "That's where the baby is."

He said the little prayer of anointing, then stopped. "I don't know anything more to say."

"Say whether it will be a boy or a girl."

"I don't know what it will be."

"Bless its mother, Frank," she cried, clasping him around the neck. "I'm so scared. I can't go through what Gomer went through. I just can't. Promise our baby you won't leave. Promise it you'll be its daddy. I can't stand to have you leave, Frank. I can't raise our baby alone. I just can't."

His neck ached from the clamp of her arms, his mouth was full of her hair. His hand groped purposelessly over her breasts, tangling in her bunched up smock.

"I promise I'll live like you want, Frank," she wept. "I'll be a Mormon. I'll swallow my foolish pride and make myself believe in it. We'll live the way you said we would have to. We'll have separate bedrooms. We won't have sex much. I'll learn how to cook plain. We'll get rid of our Chrysler. I'll sell Chowder. I'll get rid of my fancy clothes. We won't play cards and go to the movies. We won't laugh loud."

"You poor damned thing," he said.

10.

The
Cowboy Jesus

A couple of weeks later Bertha Chittenden withdrew her complaint against Farley and returned to her store in Glendale, whereupon the circuit court judge released Farley from jail. Marianne and Clara whined at Wesley until he agreed that Frank could hire Farley on the ranch as a mechanic, carpenter, and all-around handy man. Everybody pitched in for an afternoon to clean and paint the bunkhouse for Farley and Gomer, Nathan having moved into his trailer because Dora was expected almost any day. The bunkhouse was a poor place for a family—a hot plate for cooking, a cold water tap, bunks pushed together to make a double bed, and an outdoor privy. Nonetheless, Farley and Gomer said it was just dandy.

One evening Farley borrowed the Chrysler, drove to Glendale, and begged Bertha's forgiveness. A couple of days later he announced that she was moving to Escalante. Through a realtor he had swapped the store in Glendale for the drive-in hamburger stand in Escalante, which Bertha would operate. Farley let it be known that he planned to alternate between nights on the ranch with Gomer and nights in town with Bertha. Also, as soon as he could buy a car, he planned to drive every other weekend to Pioche to visit his wife Hanah.

Early one morning Wesley spoke to Frank about all that. "Seriously, Frank, do you think I am putting myself into legal jeopardy by harboring this nest of polygamists?"

"No, sir, I don't think there's any danger."

323

"I find it downright obscene to be told of Farley's sleeping arrangements. Yesterday he was very emphatic about telling everybody, my wife and yours included, that if they couldn't find him in Gomer's bed on a certain night then they were to look in Bertha's and there he'd be."

"He just wants everybody to know he isn't playing favorites. That's what got him in trouble before."

"That stallion! He's as horny as a wagon full of antlers. Oh, my sweet departed mother! What would she think of my tolerating this ruttish behavior? Tolerating? Encouraging, Frank, encouraging! I am giving those lewd people implicit support and encouragement by accepting them without protest."

"They ain't lewd according to the way they figure," Frank said. "It wouldn't do no good to protest anyhow. You can't knock anything into the head of a polygamist by protest. You have to use something hard."

"I can see what's happening," Wesley said indignantly. "Earle's Old Folks Home and Goat Farm is now broadening its horizons. It's diversifying; it's getting into other lines of enterprise. We're opening a resort for polygamists, a refuge for lechers on the lam. We'll call it Earle's Bower of Bigamy or Earle's Haven for Harems."

"That's danged funny," Frank chuckled. "But you better not let your wife hear you say that."

Another change at the ranch was that Marianne had become completely serious about Mormonism. She received missionary lessons every Saturday night at Margaret's house and attended Sunday School and Sacrament Meeting with Frank, Margaret, and Jeremy. At home she threw out her Lutheran books and hung a print of Joseph Smith on the wall. She agreed with Frank's idea about making every evening at home into a little Sunday School by reading the Scriptures and having pious discussions. In particular she was trying to become the special kind of Christian that Frank said God loved. She cooperated with him in living chastely, making up his bed on the dinette every night and keeping herself clothed in his presence. She cooked food that was nourishing without being tasty or enticing, which wasn't difficult because she had never been much of a cook. She renounced frivolous clothes. She carried her dresses with lace and ribbons and her jeans, boots, and Stetson to the ranchhouse, asking Clara to keep them for Jeanette or give them to charity.

She scheduled her baptism for the Saturday following Memorial Day and her confirmation for the day following that, which would be Fast Sunday. Frank disapproved, saying she shouldn't be baptized till she had overcome her doubts. She said baptism would help her overcome them, which satisfied Margaret, Bishop Bidley, and the stake missionaries who were giving her lessons. She insisted that Frank be the person to baptize her.

On the evening before Memorial Day everyone on the ranch went into Escalante to inspect Bertha's drive-in, which was ready for a grand opening. They found Farley perched on a ladder out front, making adjustments to a new neon sign, a large oval with blue stars and red lettering which read *Canadian Blizzard Hamburgers Hot Dogs Shakes.*

"Where'd you come up with that name?" asked Harvey.

Hair flaring, teeth glistening, Farley explained. "A name that sounds cold, that's what you need in this country. Hot summers is what we've got. People sweating like hogs, panting like lizards, dry and thirsty, grateful for a little shade, selling their souls for a cool breeze, wondering if the heat will ever quit. Can't help but patronize a place that sounds cool."

He had asked those on the ranch having strong backs to help install a new grill. He lifted the back door from its hinges and Frank, Harvey, LaMar, and Jerry tugged, heaved, and tilted, maneuvering the old grill out and the new one in. When the grill was in position Farley crawled under with his wrenches and went to work hooking it up. The customers who showed up at the service window stared in surprise at the big crowd inside. Bertha took their orders, telling those who wanted hamburgers to come back later. She also invited her company to give orders. Mixing shakes and drawing Cokes, she clenched her tiny lips and kept a frowning eye on Gomer, who leaned against a sink holding Jezreel in her arms.

"Oh boy!" Jeanette cried when Bertha handed her a cherry malt. Dipping up a spoonful, she licked with a long, wavy tongue.

"Don't fix anything for Frank and me," Marianne called. "We're off poisonous stuff like that."

Clara said, "Goodness gracious, is that what the missionaries are teaching you?"

Farley lay under the grill, his legs protruding, his breath huffing, his wrenches clattering. Homemade oaths rose through the grill vent. "You guzzleruck! Sheezoram and Keezeram, bless me! Oh, batpizzle!"

When he groped for a larger wrench, Jeanette placed a wet dishcloth in his hand. "Oh, howl!" he exclaimed, having examined the cloth. "Oh, cry and weep!"

Jeanette snickered, then put the wrench into his outstretched hand. "Are you really a prophet?" she asked.

"What's that? Who wants to know?"

"Me. Jeanette."

His protruding feet twitched. "Your daddy and mamma wouldn't want me to answer that. When you're growed up maybe. A time and place for all things. No discussions about prophets now."

"Say what you want," Wesley said. "I don't sit on any board of censors."

"Are you really a prophet?" Jeanette repeated.

"Well, then, yes, ma'am, I am."

"How do you know you're a prophet?"

His voice came from the vent hollow and muffled. "I've had visitations and whisperings. I've seen the burning bush. Heard God's voice. Communed with the resurrected. Wrestled with angels."

"How come you're a polygamist?" Jeanette asked.

He came crawling out, puffing and heaving. He sat a moment, his back propped against the grill. "I'll tell you no matter who scoffs. Grew up a polygamist's son in Bountiful. Rebelled against my father, said I'd be a regular Mormon, said I'd show him. Wasn't no kind of Mormon for many a year. Was in the War of the Pacific. A sinful Marine. Tasted of the world, suffered in consequence. Fought on Iwo Jima, fought on Okinawa. Saw many friends slaughtered. Came round the bend in a trail, sunset one day. Little Jap, his rifle up. My rifle down. Pam, he fired! Saw the bullet. Saw its trajectory in the low sunlight, an arc, real pretty. Knew my time was up. But it wasn't. The hand of the Almighty came down. Hand of deity, big as a wash tub. Transparent like glass, palm and fingers. Kerthud! Bullet hit the hand, fell to the ground. I was saved. Thanked God, repented. Vowed I'd be a polygamist. Have been too."

"What happened to the little Jap?" Wesley asked.

"I shot him. Could I have one of them milk shakes?"

Soon afterward, the party broke up and everybody except Bertha went out into the warm evening where a flight of gnats droned around the glowing neon sign. Farley and Gomer climbed into the old white pickup and left for the ranch. Wesley and Nathan sat in the Lincoln, waiting for Clara to finish a conversation with Marianne. Harvey tinkered under the hood of his battered Plymouth, while on the radio inside Jerry and LaMar tuned in a vociferous country song, "He's too old, he done got too old, he's too old to cut the mustard any more."

Frank helped Harvey secure a distributor wire with friction tape. As they finished he said, "On your day off tomorrow I imagine you fellers will take in a bunch of cemeteries, decorating graves and what not."

Harvey snorted. "Haw! We're going up New Canyon and catch some trout. The Fish and Game planted the creek yesterday for the opener on Saturday. We thought we'd get a head start and catch ours before all them California dudes beat us to them." He banged his head on the hood as he stood up. His hair, bristling in odd weedy lengths, gave the appearance of a lawn cut by a maladjusted mower. His belly was long and cylindrical, like a section of highway culvert dressed in clothes.

He looked at Frank. "Are you and Marianne going out opening day?"

"We've got a baptism to tend to."

"Kee-rect!" he exclaimed, pounding himself on the temple. "I keep forgetting about that. Gotta say a word to your wife." He ambled toward the Lincoln where Marianne and Clara stood on opposite sides of an open door.

He put out a hand to Marianne, saying, "In case I don't see you tomorrow or Saturday, congratulations on getting baptized."

"Thank you, Harvey."

"I want you to know I think you're an awful nice person."

"That's sweet. Thank you very much."

"Being in the church, you can't help but be happy. Well, gotta ramble. See you later." He strolled to his car, clambered in, and drove away with Jerry and LaMar.

"The church!" Clara choked. "For the Mormons there's only one church. Nobody else gets into heaven. Just them alone. To tell the truth, that's the hardest part for me to swallow."

"Nobody is making you swallow it," Marianne said. They faced one another, their hands gripping the doortop between them, their eyes angry and anxious.

"I don't know why you have to be baptized again. We had you baptized a long time ago. If you can't see what you are doing says about me and your father, you are simply blind. It says we are heathens. It says all these years we haven't been Christians."

"Now, Clara," Wesley admonished, "be temperate, be temperate."

"Both of you have gone off the deep end," Clara said. "You've just got lost in the woods. Never doing anything for fun. Never eating desserts and bacon and eggs."

"We eat eggs," Marianne protested.

"You've turned into fanatics. You're becoming like those folks there," she said, gesturing toward Bertha, who worked behind the plate glass of the drive-in.

"We're not turning into polygamists," Marianne said. "We're just trying to be the best Mormons there are anywhere."

Nathan said, "Humph!"

"Frank's mom doesn't eat meat of any kind," Jeanette declared.

"You just shut up," Marianne burst out. "Nobody invited you into this conversation."

"Don't you talk that way to my daughter," Clara shouted.

Marianne turned on her heel and strutted stiffly to the Chrysler. She slammed the door and sat looking straight ahead.

At dawn Frank began to cut hay. A holiday was no different from any other day for him. Except for refueling and eating a brief lunch, which Marianne brought to the field, he stayed on the swather until evening. When he came in Marianne was chopping a salad and tending a pot of beans. After washing his face and combing his hair, he took a seat at the dinette and listened to her troubles. During the morning, beside preparing his lunch, she had milked goats, washed dishes, and hoed the garden, all the while brooding on her mother's rudeness and hostility. During the afternoon, while Gomer helped at the drive-in, she had tended Jezreel, who had fussed and cried and filled his diaper a half dozen times.

She set the pot of beans on the table, pausing to say, "I wish you'd button up." He murmured and buttoned his shirt over his brown, glistening belly. Returning with the salad, she gave him another close look. "Why don't you wear a tee shirt under your shirt? Your nipples show through, don't you know it? How am I supposed to live righteously if you flaunt your body before me all the time?"

"It's too hot to wear a tee shirt."

"Borrow one of my bras."

"Oh, for crying out loud."

They knelt in front of the dinette and Frank said a prayer. Then they sat at the table and Marianne said grace in a Mormon way.

"There's no salt in these beans," Frank said after his first mouthful.

"I know it. I left it out on purpose."

"Maybe you don't have to make them taste this bad," he said, staring at his bowl as if he intended to shove it away.

"I'm eating mine," she said. "You had better eat yours. You need to keep up your strength."

He reached for the salt shaker.

"If you put salt in them beans I'm going to be mad," she said. "If we go part of the way on being righteous, we go all of the way."

He withdrew his hand from the shaker, put a spoonful of beans into his mouth, and went to work chewing.

After supper he took a shower and put on his pajamas and while she took a shower he made his bed on the dinette. She put on a bathrobe over her nightgown, and for a few minutes they sat on straightbacked chairs and read passages of Scripture to each other.

Frank got out a little contraption he had made from two buckskin gloves, which were sewed together at the fingertips and joined at the wrists by a leather band with a buckle. As they sat on the edge of his bed, Marianne pulled the gloves onto his hands, circling his wrists with the band and buckling it tight. The contraption was to keep him from masturbating in his sleep.

"Now," he said, "if I holler in the middle of the night and tell you to get this thing off me, don't you dare do it unless you're sure I'm awake. No matter what I say, don't unbuckle that strap until I'm plumb woke up."

She said sorrowfully, "This is about the hardest thing for me to take—tying you up. That's what a wife is for, Frank, so a poor fool man won't want to jack off."

"Now just be quiet," he said with sudden heat. "We're doing fine, ain't we? We haven't been carnal in over a month and I haven't loped my mule ever since I worked up this device."

"Is it okay if we lie down together for a little while now?"

He nodded and rolled onto the bed. She snuggled close and, leaning on an elbow, kissed him, saying, "I sure do love you."

"I love you too."

She murmured, as she pressed her face into his neck, "This is the best part of the whole day."

They dozed and when they awoke she said, "I, a poor sinner, confess before God that I am guilty of many sins."

"Please don't tell me about your sins," Frank said. "I've got too many of my own to worry about."

Nonetheless she said, "I want to purify myself. I have loved evil today. I spoke crossly to Jezreel. I spoke crossly to the baby in my tummy. I am filthy minded, having lusted on a man in *Life* magazine. The sweet milk of the Gospel is sour in my mouth. I can't get a testimony of the Book of Mormon, owing to the hardness of my heart. I forgot to say my secret prayer at noon today. I am worse than goat drizzle and pig manure."

"Hold it, hold it!" Frank cried. "Practicing humility is something you ought to do in private."

"Furthermore," she went on, "this afternoon, taking a little nap with Jezreel, I daydreamed about the cowboy Jesus, which is a false daydream. The real Jesus will come with fire. I saw the heaven opened and beheld a white horse. He that sat upon him was called Faithful and True and in righteousness he doth judge and make war. His eyes were as a flame of fire and he was clothed with a vesture dipped in blood and his name is called the Word of God."

She raised onto an elbow and kissed Frank a final time, muttering, "Goodnight." She slid off the bed and helped him get under the covers. Turning out the light, she went to her room.

For a while Frank lay worrying about the next day. At four he would leave for Salt Lake in a flatbed semi. Arriving there midday he would take on a load of sprinkling equipment and return to Provo, where he would pick up Dora, who had decided she wanted to arrive in Garfield County in time for Marianne's baptism. He and Dora would drive on immediately, hopefully making the ranch around midnight.

When he finally slept it was fitfully. He suffered from a recurring nightmare, anxiously remembering during brief waking moments a posthole big as a silo and a post so large that he couldn't devise a way to slide it into the hole. He hoped to locate a crane or a forklift by telephone but his tied hands prevented him from dialing. With his hands locked up he felt whipped and done for; he felt as if he was dying.

In the early morning he woke up shouting loudly for Marianne. The light came on and she stood in the doorway. He sat up in bed, his frightened eyes circling the room. He shook his tied hands and said, "Take these damned gloves off. Right now! Get them off!"

She stood stock-still.

"Take them off!" he shouted, rolling off the bed.

"You're having a bad dream," she said. "You aren't woke up."

He stumbled across the room, thrusting out his arms. "It don't make no difference what I'm having. Unbuckle this strap."

"Are you awake?"

"Hell yes I'm awake. Can't you tell when somebody's awake?"

She unfastened the buckle. He stripped off the gloves and slammed them on the floor. Massaging his wrists, he tossed his head in the direction of the bed. "Take off your nightgown. I want to have you."

She remained motionless.

"Take it off!"

"Frank, you aren't awake."

He clamped her in his arms and kissed her hard.

"I'm not going to, Frank. There'd be hell to pay tomorrow if I did."

He gripped her shoulders and shook her till her head snapped. "Oh, lord, let go," she cried. He shook her again. She stumbled to the edge of the bed and stripped off her nightgown and panties, murmuring, "When we're through, there'll be hell to pay."

"You better do it from behind because my belly's so big," she said, rolling onto her side and tucking up her legs. He snuggled into the curve of her butt, kissing her shoulders and neck, letting his hand run wild on her breasts and belly and thighs. When he had satisfied himself, they lay without moving for a long time, she with her knees tucked up, he holding her from behind. Finally he rolled over and sat on the edge of the bed. Rubbing his nose, he stared blankly at a spot on the floor.

"Don't feel bad, Frank. All I ask is you don't feel bad."

"I've ruined everything now. Everything was going just right. Nobody could have done better than you and me were doing it."

"You haven't ruined it. We'll just start over, that's all."

He stood, swayed, looked around. A vegetable grater lay on the sink counter. He walked toward it, pondered, took it up with his left hand. Suddenly he extended his right hand and forced the grater across his fingers and knuckles like a rasp, back and forth, one, two, three, four, five times and more. Skin curled into tiny shreds; flesh lumped and clogged; blood welled, flowed, dripped.

Marianne screamed, rolled off the bed, ran across the room, tore the bloody grater from his hand, and flung it to the floor. "My God, Frank!" she moaned. "My God, my God, my God!"

He stood stupidly in the center of the floor, his arm dangling, blood dripping. She pulled on her robe, found a roll of gauze, and wrapped his hand, his arm tucked under hers. He could feel her breast and her big belly and for the moment he was very calm, very comforted.

"You can't go to Salt Lake," she said. "We've got to take you to a doctor."

"It'll heal up by itself."

"You have to go to a doctor."

"I'll see one when I drive through Richfield."

"No, somebody's got to take you."

He flared. "I said I'll see a doctor when I drive through Richfield."

She tried not to cry. She shook her head, turned away, then broke. Between gasps she said, "Shall I get you some breakfast?"

"If you would." As he went to the refrigerator he added, "Have you got something good? I can't take no more of that damned health food."

"Not much that's good," she said. "I can fry eggs in butter. I can make some sweet toast with cinnamon and sugar."

"That'll be fine."

He dressed, put away his bedding, and restored the dinette. Marianne wept while she cooked and, having served him, wept while she made a lunch.

"Come sit down with me," he said. "I want to say something."

She brought a box of Kleenexes from the bathroom and joined him at the table.

"I hate God."

"Oh, Frank!"

"I hate God and Jesus. I hate the Holy Ghost, too. If I knew how, I'd kill them all. I'd blow them to hell."

"Oh, Frank!"

Wielding his bandaged hand delicately, he shoved egg yolk onto a morsel of toast and put it into his mouth, following with a gulp of milk. He said quietly, "I'm finished."

Her teary eyes were wide and stunned.

"I don't have no will left, Marianne. I can't fight no more. I'm a son of perdition."

He rose and headed for the bathroom. When he emerged she was carrying dishes to the sink. He found his gloves and hat, picked up his lunch, and went to the door.

"Frank," she called frantically, "kiss me goodby."

He kissed her and bent his face into her tangled curls.

"What are you going to do to yourself?" she whispered.

He didn't answer.

"Will I see you again?"

"You'll see me again."

"I'll wait up for you tonight."

"Don't do that. It could be two, maybe even three o'clock before I make it back."

He opened the door and went down the steps into the dark. She stopped him with a call and he stood twisted in the half light falling from the door.

"No matter what you say, Frank, Jesus is kind. I can't believe in no other Jesus."

Frank had agreed to give Farley a ride as far as Junction, where he would take possession of a used car. He parked at Bertha's house on the north side of Escalante, where Farley had spent the night, and walked into the yard, forcing back a barking, whining mongrel. Farley answered his knock, wearing pants and a union suit. He yawned wide as a gully and his hair appeared knocked down and trampled.

In the kitchen Bertha was spooning fried eggs and potatoes onto Farley's plate. She cracked a tiny smile in Frank's direction and offered him a cup of Postum, which he accepted. She wore a faded chenille robe and a net over her mousy hair. While he ate, Farley preached upon the subtleties of buying a used car. Frank hardly listened. He laid his bandaged hand in his lap and drummed the fingers of the other hand on the table. Pretty soon Farley rose and went to the bathroom.

"Have you got trouble?" Bertha said, slipping into a chair next to Frank.

He puckered his lips and shook his head. "No, ma'am, no trouble."

"How did you hurt your hand?"

"Ripped it on a gate a little bit ago. It was dark and I wasn't paying attention. It'll heal up okay."

"You're weighted down with something or other," she said, sipping her Postum. "I can smell it on you."

"No, ma'am."

Sounds came from the bathroom. "Farley plans shortly to drive to Pioche to visit his other wife," Bertha said. "It might be Hanah won't welcome his attentions. Carnal is carnal no matter how many times you pray about it. I'm a widow who ain't a widow. If Ross Drummer was alive, I'd be Mrs. Drummer. But the Lord preserved me. Ross Drummer gave himself to men. What kind of a husband would he have made, tell me that?"

"They cut his throat," Frank said.

"Yes, he asked for it himself. He had a black witness, a testimony of damnation, sealed and sure. He asked to be cleansed by his own blood. It's the only way if you've had a black witness."

"Who said blood would wash clean?"

"Who said? God said!"

"Where did he say it?"

"I'll show you where," she declared. She disappeared into the hall, reappearing quickly with an old leather bound book. "This is the *Journal of Discourses* for 1856. Sermons by Brigham Young, George A. Smith, Heber C. Kimball, a bunch of other early apostles and prophets." She wet a thumb and leafed through the pages, peering closely at the dense, brown print. She pushed the book in front of Frank. There was a sermon by Jedediah M. Grant, delivered on September 21, 1856 in the Bowery in Great Salt Lake City. It was titled "Rebuking Iniquity."

> I say, that there are men and women that I would advise to go to the President immediately, and ask him to appoint a committee to attend to their case; and then let a place be selected, and let that committee shed their blood. We have those amongst us that are full of all manner of abominations, those who need to have their blood shed, for water will not do, their sins are of too deep a dye.

As he pushed the book aside, Bertha whispered, "Have you got feelings of hell?"

"I was a backslider," he said. "I drank, I swore, I fornicated. Then God took off my brother's privates and touched his wits. That's Jeremy. He thinks he's a little girl named Alice. God warned me through him, also through words and visitations. I've heard the Holy Ghost; I know his voice. When you're alone at night and you hear a car rushing far away on a highway, that's what the Holy Ghost sounds like."

"You didn't rip that hand on no gate. I knew you were damned the first day I ever saw you," she said, her eyes soft and piteous, her lips no longer mean and pinched.

The toilet flushed in the bathroom and water rattled in pipes beneath the kitchen floor. Farley emerged, buckling his belt and buttoning his shirt. "Let's roll. Let's make road music. Can't wait to see that Studebaker. Bet she'll fix up easy. Had a testimony about it. It's the right car for me at this moment. No car better than a Studebaker. Old Farley will have wheels of his own again. Won't go begging no more."

As the truck topped the summit between Escalante and Henrieville, Farley said, "Big doings for you tomorrow afternoon. Going to baptize your little wife into the Mormon church."

"Yes, sir, that's the plan."

"Got a little matter on my mind. Still got a call for you, Frank. God exhorts me nightly, says, Get that Frank into my true and single church. Want you to go on a mission to Argentina. Want to make you an apostle. Might make you a counselor in the first presidency if you prove up."

"Much obliged. Nobody ever before offered to make me an apostle. However, I ain't interested."

"I figured you wouldn't be," Farley said sadly.

As they rumbled through Tropic and started up the dugway toward the national park, he said, "My Bertha, she's quite a gal."

"That's true," Frank said. "She has some strong opinions."

"Fell in love with a feller by mail. Ross Drummer! Who'd have ever figured on it? Wasn't my charms brought her back to me. It was him getting himself sacrificed. Ain't that something? Cut his throat! Damn good thing. Good riddance of bad rubbish."

Farley slouched in the truck seat, chewing on whiskers from his long mustache, sometimes clipping one off with his incisors and spitting it out. "Evil little plot them two had hatched up. Going to salt me away in jail. Going to get my store and my ranch. Might have done it, too, she being the only wife I've got in the eyes of the law."

Three deer stood at the roadside, their eyes glaring blue in the headlights. The truck tires rumbled; the transmission whined.

"Well, Ross never put no eggs in Bertha's pail," Farley went on. "Never had a chance. Him and her might have got along fine, him liking men, her liking nobody at all. Reason her and me never had no baby was she'd let me have her just once; then she'd wait to see if she'd have a period before she'd let me do it again. Didn't want us doing it if she was pregnant. Which she never was. The Psalm says, Go at it, make love free and furious, for out of thy lust new souls shall come."

"I never read that in the Bible."

"Whatever a prophet says is Scripture. I'm a prophet."

"I guess there's some logic to that."

It was daylight when the truck rolled through Panguitch. Frank waved at a uniformed man who was unlocking a Conoco station.

Farley sat up straight and watched as the truck passed a car. "Never told you I yearned for my Gomer when she was a whore, did I?"

"Never did."

"Hanging around Caliente, I seen her. Lusted on her. Big ass, tight pants, painted eyebrows, lipstick red as sin. Saw her in the post office, saw her in the cafe, saw her in a car at the service station. Knew she was a whore. Farley Chittenden, God's servant, lusting on a whore!"

"I'm not surprised," Frank said. "She's pretty."

The sun was mounting a blue, cloudless sky. Cool air rushed into the open window. Farley continued. "God said thou shalt not make love to a whore. Said it hundreds of times. Book of Proverbs. For a whore is a deep ditch and a strange woman is a narrow pit. Went to God in prayer. Said, Got to have her, Lord, got to have that pretty whore. My cries went up day after day, night after night. Give me a word, Lord. Tell me how a righteous man can have a whore."

"There ain't no way," Frank blurted scornfully.

"There is!" Farley shouted. "By gum, there is. Book of Hosea. Go, take unto thee a wife of whoredoms and children of whoredoms, for the land hath committed great whoredom, departing from the Lord. Hosea came to me in Pioche. Old time prophet. Said, Get thee into yonder whorehouse in Caliente. Take the one I show you and name her Gomer. It was her! The one I lusted on. Made her into a wife."

In Junction Frank stopped in front of the courthouse and let out Farley, who stood in the open door a moment, smiling winsomely, his teeth gleaming in the three quarter circle of his mustache. Over his shoulder he had flung an old suit coat. "I'll find out where that feller lives and get hold of my Studebaker and be back at the ranch before you know it. Anyway, I said, Give me a word, Lord. Tell me how a righteous man can have a whore."

"Glad you told me. Goodby."

"Adios," Farley said, shutting the door and turning away.

The road north was clogged with traffic, especially in the little cities between Provo and Salt Lake, where there were numerous stop lights. It looked as if all the fishermen in the north part of the state were driving south for opening day, and all those in the south were driving north. Frank fantasized about going fishing with Marianne. He could see them on a pretty bend of the creek high up in New Canyon, fishing with springy fiberglass rods and fancy closed face spinning reels. All of a sudden Marianne squealed, her rod arced, and out in the creek a silvery trout danced on its tail.

He arrived in Salt Lake a little before one o'clock. On a Denver and Rio Grande dock he found half the sprinkling equipment he wanted. The other half, he discovered, was in a Southern Pacific warehouse in Ogden. He loaded and headed north toward Ogden. By the time he had located the warehouse and had loaded, it was after four o'clock. He drove south to Provo, pulling in across the street from Dora's place near seven thirty.

"There you are, Frank," Dora called from the porch, where her suitcases and boxes sat ready to go. Dora herself didn't look ready; she wore a housedress and her pincurls were bound with a kerchief. As he came up the steps, she stared at his bandaged hand. "My word, what did you do to yourself?"

"I kind of got careless with a baler crank yesterday evening," he said. "It's not as bad as it looks." While loading at the Ogden warehouse, he had struck his hand, producing a fresh seep of bright blood on the bandage.

She hugged him and said, "I'm sorry to tell you I'm in a terrible stew. I've never been in such a quandary in all my life! I simply can't make up my mind whether to go or to stay." She took him inside and had him say hello to Jenny, the college girl who would care for the bookshop while she was at the ranch. "Now," she said to both of them, "I am completely paralyzed and I need your most serious and wise counsel. Please instruct me whether I should go or stay."

"Well, for gosh sakes, go," Frank said. "Nathan's counting on you."

"Is he really counting on me? Oh, dear! Yes, I suppose he is."

"Also my mother figures on you being at the baptism tomorrow evening. Me and Marianne too. We would be awful disappointed if you didn't show up."

She turned to Jenny, who had calm brown eyes. "What do you think? Do you really think I should go? You'll be disappointed if I don't, won't you? You are looking forward to running this little shop on your own, now aren't you?"

"Yes, ma'am. I think I can take care of it just fine."

Dora led Frank into the storage room, asking him to unpack a recent shipment, explaining, "It's awfully hard for Jenny or me to manhandle these boxes." Then she glanced at his hand. "Well, aren't I thoughtless? You can't heave boxes with your poor hurt hand."

"Yes, ma'am, I can."

As he pulled a box off a stack and pried it open, she went on with her frantic talk. "May I confide in you, Frank? I am just astonished with myself. I feel very bitter; my negative feelings have risen up and got the better of me. Why should it be me who has to go to him? A six hour trip is all it is, Frank. Do you realize that? Six hours from Escalante to Provo. He hasn't come up in seven years. So why should I go to him?"

"That's pretty shabby, all right."

"What's more, to be truthful, I simply loathe that country. I can't think of anything but outdoor toilets and screen doors plastered with flies."

"It ain't that way nowadays. That trailer has got indoor plumbing and the county sprays for flies."

He carried the box out to the counter and emptied it. When he returned she grasped his sleeve and forced him to look into her pale blue eyes. Her voice was decisive. "I just won't do it, Frank. I won't go. You get in your truck and drive on. I won't detain you a minute further."

She released him and he pried open another box, saying, "Well, then you better phone Nathan and tell him. I don't want to be the one to break the news to him."

"Oh, my! Oh, heaven help me! I can't do that, Frank." Tears rolled down her cheeks. "Why should I expect him to come visit me when I haven't been to visit him? It has been seventeen years since I was last down there, Frank. Isn't that shameful? So what's to be done now? Perhaps we could wait till morning. Yes, wait till morning! Could we do that, Frank? Maybe I'll be more clear headed then. You could sleep in my spare room."

"Maybe that's just exactly what we ought to do. I'm pretty bushed anyhow. I didn't get hardly any sleep last night."

"I will just pray about it, Frank, and see if Heavenly Father will give me some direction."

So he called the ranch, dialing the phone and propping a foot on the stool behind the counter. Clara answered the phone. "No, Marianne isn't here. She's over at your place. Shall I go get her?"

"No, just tell her and Nathan that me and Dora won't be coming in tonight. It's getting late and I'm awful beat out, so I'm going to lay over here at Dora's and get on the road in the morning. Me and her will stop in Panguitch and wait for Marianne and Nathan to drive over for the baptism. Remind Marianne to bring along my Sunday suit."

"I'll tell her," Clara promised. "And she and Nathan won't have to drive over alone, Frank. I do want to apologize for my horrid behavior the other evening at the drive-in. I was in sheer and utter hell all day yesterday. Marianne, bless her heart, has forgiven me and I hope you will too. I certainly am coming to her baptism. I am determined to be supportive, that's all there is to it."

At bedtime Frank waited until things had become quiet in Dora's room before he went to the bathroom. He hated having dainty, refined people go into a place he had just stunk up. His tiny room was crammed with womanish signs—a ruffled bedspread, a deep pile rug, walls in pastel blue, miniature lamps with lacy yellow shades, a host of lotions and colognes on the vanity.

He slept even more fitfully than the night before, over and over drifting off and jerking awake. His hand smarted, his back ached, a leg muscle twitched spasmodically. Eerie, unnerving pictures occurred to him, alternating like pages of a magazine. He saw a man astride a tractor hood, spurring with his feet and clutching in his hand the bloody neck of a chicken. The man shouted, "It's the damnedest thing, ain't it, how a chicken won't die?" He saw bales falling from a baler. They writhed among the furrows and became howling babies. He saw Bertha in her drive-in, making a milk shake. When she handed him the cup, it wasn't milk shake, it was blood.

Late in the night he threw off the blankets and sat up, sweating profusely. He pulled on his pants and wandered into the hall, through the kitchen, into the bookshop. He sat on a chair. The neon wall clock, glowing blue, showed two-thirty. Bookracks loomed like black, irregular cliffs. His eyes had a vision, his hands had a feeling: the bloody spray from Jeremy's butchered crotch, the grisly stub of his penis. He was strangely comforted. If no help was at hand, a man could die from cut off privates. He had only to be determined, only to keep the blood from clotting.

He went back to bed and went soundly to sleep. At dawn Dora knocked on his door and put in her head, saying in a sober, chastened voice, "I'm ready to go, Frank. When I think of him and me being married in the temple, bound to one another for eternity, it seems like I mustn't evade my duty. How can I face him there if I turn my back on him here?"

As they drove, seagulls crossed the brightening sky; farmers plowed fields and sprayed blooming orchards; horses frisked in dewy pastures. "A remarkable landscape," Dora said, gazing out the window. Near Mona they passed a dairy ranch where big Holsteins stood patiently at a milkhouse door. "I admit there is a certain healthiness to ranch life," she said. "I can scarcely wait to meet Clara and Wesley, those wonderful people who have figured so large in Nathan's letters."

"Yes, ma'am, you'll like them. Even Wesley isn't so bad once you get to know him."

"And this strange Farley Chittenden and his wives Gomer and Bertha. I will hardly know how to behave when I meet them. I hope I won't do anything rude."

"Not likely. They are people like anybody else."

Leaving Nephi they drove across a plain where a morning wind swept miles of green wheat into slow, dignified waves. "I feel humbled over meeting your Marianne," Dora said. "I know she will be such a splendid person."

"Yes, ma'am, she's very fine."

After they had turned at a junction in the middle of Levan, Dora said, "I never could get accustomed to barns and corrals in people's backyards. Don't all these little towns seem run down, though?"

"Yes, ma'am, though it's useful having your cows and chickens close at hand."

"Last week I attended the university symphony, Frank, which featured works by Haydn and Brahms. So lovely, so lovely. Now a woman living in Levan actually could drive to Provo in an evening and attend the symphony. But she wouldn't, would she?"

"Not likely."

The truck slowed down for Fayette, a village of perhaps fifteen houses. "Oh, my, if that isn't depressing," she said. "Look, just look at that house over there. Not a single curtain in any window. It's terrible how these little places kill their women. Not physically, but spiritually. They kill the feminine. It's art and music and literature that make womanhood, don't you think?"

"Likely that's most of what it is."

"My word, I have read an intriguing book recently—*The Perfumes of France*. You would suppose in France, of all places, perfume making would be a sacred art, wouldn't you? Not so. Many, many firms have given in to mass production and have turned to synthetic scents. Fortunately a few of the grand old perfumers have stuck to their guns. The House of Chantiers, for example. They buy rose blossoms from local nurseries and laboriously extract rose oil from the petals."

"I never thought of roses as being oily," Frank said.

From her purse Dora pulled a tiny cut glass bottle with a French label. "This is House of Chantiers. I want to give it to Marianne as a baptismal gift. Frank, I want you to make sure she has plenty of cultural opportunities. Don't you dare work that woman to death. Don't you dare cut her off from the civilizing graces."

"No, ma'am, I hope I won't do anything like that. She used to wear perfume before me and her made up our minds to live simple. Also, she likes horse smell. Goat smell, too, I believe. I judge she'd rather rope and ride than go to a symphony. I think she'd like fishing. So maybe you shouldn't give her that expensive perfume. She'd appreciate something like a sack of apples. Also she likes figs a lot."

"Oh, my," Dora said, "I'm afraid you don't know your own wife."

A few minutes later the truck topped a hill and rolled into Gunnison. Frank pulled into a service station and filled the tank. He walked across the street to a pay phone hanging outside a grocery store, from which he called the ranch.

Marianne answered. "Is that you, honey? Are you okay?"

"Sure I'm okay," he said.

"How's your hand?"

"Fine. Fit as a fiddle," he lied.

"Did you stop and see the doctor in Richfield yesterday? Did he fix it up okay?"

"Sure he did. He said it isn't hardly serious at all. Just a little skin gone."

"I'm glad, Frank. I sure have missed you."

"I've missed you too. Now what I'm calling about is Dora and Nathan. Dora's quite a lady. She's heavy on culture and civilization. She goes to symphony orchestras and reads lots of books. She buys perfume made out of real rose petals. Would you like some perfume like that? She's talking about giving you some for a baptism gift."

"What am I going to do with perfume?"

"I told her you weren't much for that kind of thing. Anyhow, what I called for is to tell you to make sure Nathan dresses up extra nice. Make sure he has a bath and don't let him put on the white shirt he wore to church last Sunday. Make him put on a clean one. Also, get your dad to lend him a little aftershave lotion so he smells nice."

"Hold up a second! Nathan isn't here. He wasn't here all night."

"All night! My gadfrey!"

"I saw him take off in his car about three-thirty yesterday afternoon. Now we're all worried about him. Maybe he rolled his car over somewhere and got pinned under it."

"He ain't pinned under no damned car," Frank growled. "That old lizard has run off on Dora, that's what he's done."

"Run off? He wouldn't do that!"

"That is just exactly what he'd do. If that don't beat all!" He stamped a foot and began to laugh. "Geez, I wish you'd told me this last night. Or phoned me early this morning while I was still at Dora's. It would have saved everybody a whole lot of trouble."

"Good gosh. So what are we going to do now?"

Having backed up to a corner of the building, Frank scratched himself like a cow. He was thinking hard. "The gall of that old crawfish, running off on her after I've got her this far down the road! Tell you what. Get on the phone and find out where he is and go get him. When we've gone to this much trouble fixing up his trailer and everything, we ain't going to let him get away with this."

"Do you mean go get him now?"

"Well, of course, I mean now. He won't be any further down the road than Escalante. Find him and get him bathed and dressed and bring him along."

"But what if we can't find him?"

"Find him, that's all; just go to work and locate him. And tell him to keep his trap shut about trying to run away. We can't let Dora down, not now. I'll see you this afternoon at Mom's house. Don't forget to bring my suit."

"Don't hang up, honey," she said in a hurry. "I sure have missed you."

"I missed you too."

"Are you really okay?"

Her soft, distant voice made him want to cry. It made him remember how much he loved the world. The highway and truck, the river glinting in the sun, the clouds climbing into the blue sky, the sage brush plains, the high timbered mountains, the pastures full of horses and cattle, the furrowed fields, the little towns, the people eating, talking, loving, all these numbed him with sweet grief. He was a ram in the thicket. He was waiting for word of a funeral, for word the Jamisons and Windhams were to gather. He was waiting for a call to fill a coffin.

"Are you still there?" Marianne said.

"Yes, I'm still here."

"Six-thirty tonight then," she said.

"Yes, six-thirty."

"After that I'll be a Mormon."

"Correct."

"Something will change, Frank. Something good will happen to us."

"I don't know. Maybe not."

"Yes," she insisted, "something will change. It has to."

"I hope so," he said.

Frank parked the truck in Panguitch a little after twelve. Before the engine had died Margaret came from the house. When she learned Dora would remain for the day, she hugged her and cried, "Wonderful, wonderful!" She paused, staring at Frank's bandaged hand, so he had to tell her about hurting it on the baler.

"The bandage has got dirty; that's why it looks bad. I'll get Marianne to put me on a fresh one before we go to the baptism."

Margaret promised lunch shortly, first wanting Frank to discipline Jeremy, who was creating havoc in the backyard with Lawrence's Percherons and scraper. Lawrence had left his large draft horses in Margaret's corral after competing in the Panguitch horse show on Memorial Day. With unexpected skill, Jeremy had harnessed them, hitched them to the scraper, and begun an excavation.

"He hasn't been a bad boy, Dora," Margaret explained as they walked down the driveway. "He works weekdays with Rulon Smythe and he does the chores around our place. He washes his hands very obediently, and also shaves, though he doesn't hardly have whiskers anymore, and he takes his turn at leading in family prayer. He goes to his meetings and he has a sweet testimony of the Gospel. But just now with Lawrence's horses he has got out of hand. No matter how I threaten, he won't obey."

They stood looking down on a long excavation in the vacant plot beyond the garden. It dipped deep in the center, two swaths wide, one swath being more deeply cut than the other. At one end was a large pile of excavated earth and rock. At that moment Jeremy was guiding the horses and scraper around from the pile, lining up for another cut. The Percherons had tossing, intelligent heads, thick arched necks, shiny bay hides, and white stocking feet. For the moment they pulled effortlessly, their harnesses creaking, the scraper clattering and clanking behind. Jeremy walked beside them with long, taut reins, wearing bib overalls and a shirt with sleeves rolled up.

"Alice," Margaret shouted, "you stop this instant. Frank is here now and we won't put up with this nonsense any longer."

Jeremy scarcely glanced at Margaret. Shouting "Giddap," he spanked the reins against the horses' rumps and pulled a lever on the scraper. As the big animals plodded into the excavation, the scraper revolved and its cutting edge bit into the gravel. With straining legs the horses leaned into their collars and gravel tumbled into the body of the scraper.

"Frank," Margaret pleaded, "make him stop."

Almost immediately a large rock forced the scraper out of the gravel. "Drat!" Jeremy muttered, pulling the horses to a halt. He dropped the reins and walked from the cut. Seizing a crowbar, he returned, thrust in the bar at the side of the rock, and tried to lever it out.

"Isn't this quaint?" Dora said cheerfully. "This is how they used to make cuts and fills before the day of the bulldozer."

"It's a circus and I just won't have it," Margaret insisted. "Frank, will you please order him to stop this pillaging of our backlot? If you have to, take the reins yourself and put the horses in the corral. I told Lawrence on the phone last night this would happen. He just pooh-poohed me. Nothing to worry about, Mother Windham, he said; let him dig a little if he wants; we can fill it in easy. Fill it in easy! Look at that hole."

Frank jumped down to the first cut and down again to the second, where Jeremy labored with the bar. "What in heck are you doing here?" he asked.

"I'm making a pit."

"I see that. What are you making a pit for?"

"I'm going to sit in it."

"My gosh, sit in it! Now listen to me, Alice. Mom is plumb mad over you making this hole and you better quit right now. Dora Woodbarrow is here for the afternoon and it ain't polite not to do something nice for her. Let's put the horses up and after lunch we'll take her for a ride around town. We'll show her some of the sights."

Jeremy thrust in his bar again, then bent to inspect the result, saying, "If I could just get a chain around the end of this rock we'd be in business."

"Like it or not, you have to quit," Frank said.

"I'm not quitting."

"I'm going to make you."

Jeremy looked up dubiously.

"I can do it. I can wrassle you down and haul you out of here just like nothing."

Jeremy began to cry. "How come everybody picks on me all the time? I don't get to do anything I want to do. What do I have to live for? I wish the Lord would take me. I just wanted a pit." He sat down in the dirt, then stretched out and rolled onto his face, howling, "I just wanted a pit." His howls strangled in the fresh-cut ground, ceased as he coughed and spit, and rose again unstinted.

Frank rolled him onto his side and shook him, saying with desperate haste, "For the love of Mike, shut up." Casting a pleading glance toward Margaret, he called, "What will it hurt for us to have this hole back here for a while?"

"Don't you back down, Frank," Margaret shouted.

"I don't have no heart to drag him away. Let's let him go on with his pit. In a week or two I'll borrow Uncle Lonnie's loader and we'll push the dirt back in."

"Isn't it sad how the poor boy cries?" Dora said. "As Frank says, his little pit can't be of harm to anybody. The clean new earth looks rather refreshing, doesn't it?"

"Well, then, Frank, just handle it however you wish," Margaret groaned. "Dora, I'm so ashamed. We're nothing but a sideshow, nothing but a public spectacle."

"All right, Alice," Frank said, shaking his brother's shoulder, "get up and get back to work. And for heaven's sake, shut up that howling."

"I'll try, I'll try," Jeremy blubbered, sitting up and for a moment hugging his doubled knees.

After lunch, Frank took a couple of sandwiches out to Jeremy, who had been digging around the boulder with a pick and shovel. Legs dangling, they sat on the edge of the higher cut while Jeremy ate. The big horses stood patiently switching their tails in the lower cut.

"How are you boys doing?" somebody said. Leaning over the street fence was Jack Stassley, the county sheriff. On the street behind him was his patrol car, motor idling.

"We're doing fine," Frank said. "How about yourself?"

"I've got a touch of hay fever. Something's in the air, dammit all. Though that's neither here nor there. I've been watching your brother off and on all morning. Quite a hole he's making here."

"Yes, sir, quite a hole. He's pretty good with those horses. He's learned a few things working with Rulon Smythe. Also he's a lot stronger than he used to be."

Frank walked from the pit and leaned against the fence, which was of unpainted pickets. Jack adjusted the strings of his turquoise bolo tie and rolled a toothpick with his tongue. "Now what your brother is doing here, ain't that eccentric? It makes your eyes bug out with amazement, doesn't it?"

"It isn't so amazing. It sure isn't hurting nobody. It's on our property."

"And he makes a big scene if somebody won't call him Alice. I saw a bunch over at the service station bait him for fifteen minutes one day."

"Those sons of bitches! Who were they?"

"That isn't the point. The point is he's more or less a public nuisance."

"No, he ain't," Frank said. "He don't cause any more trouble than anybody else. It's just a different kind of trouble."

"I think you ought to send him back up to the asylum. That's what it's for—to take care of people which don't fit in with regular, sensible citizens."

Frank wiped a hand across his forehead. He wished he had his hat, the day having become hot. A white pullet scratched in the pile of excavated earth. The spotted cow and the grizzled old bull stood at the corral fence, peering down on the Percherons.

"I got me two lawyers," he said. "One of them is Rossler D. Jarbody in Richfield. The other is Algernon Bullard in Salt Lake. He's the one who helped me get Jeremy out of the booby hatch. He also defends polygamists. He isn't afraid of anybody. So, Jack, get it out of your head to take my brother back to Provo. If you try, I'll turn those fellers loose on you. I'll put every damned penny I can beg or borrow into it."

"Cool down, cool down! I was just giving you an idea to chew on."

"I've chewed it all I want. It's a stupid idea."

"It don't mean anything to me one way or the other. Whatever you want is fine. Just cool down."

"I ain't heated up."

"Way you talked, I thought you were."

A car went by, its tires crunching on the graveled street. The man driving it waved and Frank and Jack waved back. A woodpecker tapped in one of the locust trees bordering the street. A big curly haired mongrel came trotting along. He paused at the back tire of the patrol car, sniffed, lifted a leg, and marked off his territory.

"I wish this here city would pass an ordinance on dogs," the sheriff said. He stepped away from the fence, then paused to stare one more time at Jeremy, who had resumed his work, bending and straightening in a steady rhythm of picking. "If that just don't look like hell!" he said.

Frank helped Jeremy slip a chain under the tip of the big rock. Then they hitched the horses to the chain and tumbled the rock out, whereupon Jeremy rehitched the horses to the scraper and began to excavate again. Seeing small grassy weeds in the garden, Frank found a hoe and did some weeding. He hacked and chopped and sifted, breaking up the crusty soil, uprooting weeds, banking dirt around the roots of the vegetables. The peas were a foot high and in blossom. The corn was only inches high and the onions and carrots were nothing more than a green whiskery line along two furrows. He forced himself to grip the hoe handle as tightly with his right hand as with his left, and soon bright blood appeared on the crusty, blackened bandage.

About four o'clock Frank's sisters and their families arrived, all wearing their Sunday best. Soon everybody came out to watch Jeremy, who reined in his horses and called hello.

"You could turn it into a silo," Susan said to Margaret.

"I don't want a silo. I'm out of the agricultural business," she replied hotly.

"Maybe he thinks he's making a baptismal font," Susan added. "Maybe this is his way of showing how glad he is for the wonderful thing that is happening in our family today."

"You could bury a gas tank in it if you wanted to turn this backlot into a service station," Cloyd said.

"You could make a swimming pool out of it," Lawrence said. "That's what folks down in Las Vegas are doing—putting swimming pools in their backyards."

"And then you could water your livestock in it, couldn't you?" Leola said sarcastically.

"All I want is for my neighbors not to know how far off the deep end that boy has got," Margaret said miserably.

"Hey, Alice," Lawrence shouted, "let me take her through a couple of times and I'll show you a thing or two." He grasped the reins, lined up the horses, and, as they leaned into their collars, began giving instructions to Jeremy, who followed behind.

"He's gone," Leola said. "There's nothing Lawrence would rather do than show somebody something with those horses."

For supper Margaret served vegetable soup from a simmering pot. Afterward, Dora, Susan, and Leola helped her prepare refreshments for the reception which would follow the baptism. As a concession to her friends and neighbors she had bought a punch mix and had ordered sheet cakes and brownies, which they cut into squares and stacked under waxed paper. Shortly Lawrence and Jeremy came into the house, Lawrence saying Jeremy was satisfied with the depth of the pit.

Jeremy came from his bedroom carrying his rolled-up rug. He had wet and combed his hair and over his bib overalls had put on a Sunday coat. He nudged Frank, saying in a low, ingratiating voice, "Please come sit with me a little."

"I'd better go milk," Frank said, looking at the clock. The service would start in an hour and fifteen minutes.

"You can't milk with that bad hand," Lawrence said.

"There ain't a whole herd of cows out there. I can milk that runty critter with my left hand just fine."

Jeremy renewed his request. "Sit with me just for a little while. We'll bring along a couple of those chairs."

They carried out the chairs and Jeremy unrolled the rug in the lowest cut of the pit and carefully placed the chairs side by side. He sat in one and patted the other. Frank stared dubiously for a moment, then seated himself. They gazed eastward toward the weathered picket fence and the lacy locust trees. The low afternoon sun struck them on the back, casting humped shadows along the cut.

"I've got to say, Alice, this isn't something I relish much," Frank said. "What are we doing it for?"

"We are waiting in the deep pit for the ladder of Lazarus."

"The ladder of Lazarus?"

"Yes, on which we'll climb out by and by. Be patient, please."

"What's going on down there?" said Marianne, who had come up quietly. She teetered on high heels, her hair shiny brown in the slanting sunlight, her dress dotted with tiny pink roses.

"Well, hooray," Frank said, "you made it at last."

"Are you going to offer me a chair?"

"No, ma'am. This is a bring-your-own situation."

"I guess you won't bother explaining all this."

"Alice dug us a pit to sit in," Frank said. "We're waiting for the ladder of Lazarus."

He rose and climbed onto the higher cut. He stepped to the wall, looking up at Marianne, who squatted and put a hand on his shoulder. He said, "I guess you brought the old lizard with you."

She shook her head. "We've been tracking him all day. The folks in Escalante said he was in Hatch. The folks in Hatch said he was in Toquerville. Turns out Toquervillle is where he is. We know for sure because we phoned over there and got hold of a woman who says he's there visiting her husband."

"My gosh."

"I have just met Dora. I don't see how her and Nathan could've ever got married to each other. She's so sweet and pretty."

"So what'd you tell her?"

"So against the better judgment of my parents I told her a big lie. I told her Nathan went to St. George in one of Dad's trucks to get a baler and on the way home the truck busted down in Toquerville. I told her somebody was going over there right after the baptism to get him. So what do you think of that?"

"You bet, that was the right thing to do. That is, if he really is in Toquerville."

"Well, if he isn't, then I say let's wash our hands of the whole affair. One lie just leads to a dozen more."

"I agree," Frank said. "That old badger! He ought to be horsewhipped for running out on a lady like Dora."

"You bet!" Marianne exclaimed. "A lot of men ought to be horsewhipped for the way they treat women."

"That's true."

"May I see your hand?" she said in a softer voice.

He held up the bandaged hand and she said, "You never saw no doctor!" She untied the knot hastily and unwound the blood encrusted gauze, muttering, "Holy Moses." The gauze strip fluttered to the ground and Frank's hand lay exposed in hers, a revolting stew of gleaming knuckle bone, dried tendons, glazed yellow flesh exuding beads of bright blood. She stood and stepped back, looking down angrily. "We're not going to do anything till you've been to the doctor with that hand. I'm not getting baptized or nothing else till you've been."

He shrugged and jumped off into the deeper cut, saying to Jeremy, "I'm going to milk that cow. You better go in and get ready for the service. Unless it's just been called off." He glanced up at Marianne. "Also, Alice, you better not risk leaving Mom's chairs out overnight. She's on the verge of killing you as it is."

As he came out of the pit, Marianne stepped in his way. "Oh, God, Frank," she said, weeping.

They hugged each other and he said, "There's wrapping in the house. I want you to put a fresh bandage on it for the baptism."

They went in and she wrapped the hand, then followed him out to the corral gate, where they hugged again. She leaned her cheek against his chest so that he looked down on her bright hair, her brows, her bumpy nose. "You are headed that way, aren't you?" she said.

"What way?"

"To make yourself like Jeremy. I can see it plain as day. It's the only way you can live."

Heat ran from his heels through his legs into his backbone. For a moment he couldn't think or see or hear. Her tears made tiny points of cool evaporation on his shirt. "Sweet Jesus," she prayed, "help us before it's too late."

She kissed him and went toward the house. She stood on the back porch a moment, her pregnant belly in profile. He went into the corral and settled on a stool at the flank of the spotted cow. He held the pail between his knees, seized a short, stubborn teat with his left hand, and squeezed. Milk shot into the pail with a tinny zing. He heard a belch and smelled the odor of cattle breath. He looked into the eyes of the old bull, which stood not six feet away, calmly chewing his cud.

At twenty after six the group left for the churchhouse, some in cars, some afoot. Frank and Marianne rode with Wesley, Clara, and Jeanette. Clara's eyes were red, showing that she had cried considerably during the day; the three or four handkerchiefs in her hand showed that she planned to cry considerably more during the service.

Lonnie and Jessica shook hands with Frank and Marianne as they came up the church steps; Lonnie would confirm Marianne in Fast Meeting on Sunday. Raymond and Helen were there too, which touched Frank. Helen hugged Marianne as if she'd known her all her life. Bishop Bidley was also on the porch, asking Margaret whether he should send the Relief Society sisters out for additional refreshments, since both the North Ward and the South Ward had turned out in unexpected numbers to see Frank's Lutheran wife made into a Mormon.

Downstairs in the restrooms Frank and Marianne changed into baptismal clothes, a gown of heavy white cotton for her, pants and shirt of the same material for him, white stockings for both. When they had taken seats at the front of the chapel, the bishop started the service. The congregation sang a hymn about Joseph Smith's first vision, and Raymond offered a lengthy invocation. Then the bishop delivered admonitions and sentiments, expressing in particular his admiration for Frank, who he said had the internal fortitude to admit and make amendments for past errors. The bishop recognized the presence of Marianne's father and mother and of her fine little sister, who were always welcome to attend meetings in the North Ward. He said Marianne was one of the sweetest and most sincere persons he had ever had the privilege of interviewing; her conversion was a tremendous boost to his own testimony, being a great manifestation of God's mind and will.

Finally the bishop said the baptism would proceed. Unfortunately the fontroom, which was in the basement, would hold no more than fourteen or fifteen people. Therefore he asked all except close relatives and special friends to wait in the chapel; afterward all would repair to the Relief Society room for refreshments and visiting.

Clear water shimmered in the font, which was surfaced with light blue tile. Clinging to a rail Frank and Marianne descended into the water, Marianne pushing down her floating hem. Cloyd and Lawrence, official witnesses, stood at the corners of the font. Crowding close behind were Susan, Leola, Jeremy, Margaret, Dora, the bishop, and one of his counselors. At the back the Earles stood between Lonnie and Jessica on one side and Helen and Raymond on the other. Slow tears trickled down Clara's cheeks. Helen slipped an arm around her shoulders.

The bishop nodded at Frank, who gripped Marianne's wrist with his left hand and raised his bandaged right hand to the square. He said, "Marianne Earle Windham, having been commissioned of Jesus Christ, I baptize you in the name of the Father and of the Son and of the Holy Ghost, Amen." He put his right hand between her shoulders and laid her back. She came up sputtering in a rush of water. She swept the water from her face and clambered up the steps, Frank following. Their drenched clothes clung to their breasts, bellies, and thighs. Everyone crowded back, making them a path. They went down the hall to the restrooms, leaving a trail of water on the floor.

In the men's room Frank draped his white pants and shirt over the toilet stall and dried himself with a bathtowel. He heard bumps through the wall. Apparently Marianne was knocking around in the ladies' room like a cow in a stocktruck. He glanced at himself in the mirror over the washbasin. His wet brown hair lay flat on his head. His muscled shoulders were tight and tough. His chest and belly were dark from the spring sun, his legs pearly white. His penis and testicles dangled from a patch of brown fur.

He unwrapped the wet gauze from his hand and clumsily replaced it with a dry strip. He put on his briefs, pants, and shirt, combed his hair, and tied his shoes. He tied a knot in his tie and pulled it tight around his collar. He heard Marianne leave the ladies' room and go upstairs. He started to follow, then turned back, needing to urinate. He unzipped his fly and stepped to the urinal.

Having flushed the urinal, he listened to the streaming water. For an instant he thought it sounded like a flying bird; then he thought it resembled a rushing car, heard at night from a great distance. He pushed the lever again, watching the water tumble and splash. The urinal faded from his sight and he saw a stand of scrubby junipers.

Prickly pear and bunch grass grew in the sandy soil; blue-green junipers crowded close. He heard the soft plod of a horse's feet. Beneath the juniper boughs he saw a horse's legs. The animal emerged, a shiny roan mounted by a rider. The cowboy had a beard and he wore boots, ancient chaps, a denim shirt, a creased, sweat-stained Stetson. Touching spurs lightly to his mount, he reined toward Frank. Coming close, he halted and lifted a hand. It was Jesus, his face as kind as an August dawn.

"You're lost," he said.

Ashamed, Frank cast his eyes downward. "I expect I am."

"You are feeling awful bad."

"It's not much of anything."

"It isn't any bother. Hearing your griefs is my business. Go ahead and tell me."

The rider pushed back his Stetson and cocked a leg over the saddlehorn. The roan blinked sleepy eyes and swished his tail.

"My grandmother lost four babies and went crazy in the sandhills," Frank said.

"I'm sorry about that."

"My little sister Elizabeth died and my mother can't get over it."

"I know," Jesus said. "Your family is a sad one."

"My dad died when I was ten."

"That's tough," Jesus agreed.

"Also, my brother cut himself off. He took a hunting knife and laid waste to his privates. Now he thinks he's a little girl named Alice. This afternoon he dug himself a pit and sat in it. He said he was waiting for the ladder of Lazarus. He's pure as an angel. He can't sin, no matter what."

"The poor crazy devil."

"The thing I feel worst about is I can't live righteously," Frank said. "I've got a wife I can't leave alone. I make love to her all the time. I'm cunning and devilish about thinking up new ways to do it too. I hate healthy, decent food. I love ham and broiled steaks and pie and ice cream. I wish I had my shiny blue pickup back and my gelding Booger and my boots and jeans and pearlbuttoned shirts. I wish I had my deer rifle back so I could go deer hunting. I wish I could take my wife trout fishing."

Jesus had pulled a sack of Bull Durham from his shirt pocket and was rolling a cigarette.

"I thought smoking was against the Word of Wisdom," Frank said.

"It is."

"How come you're smoking?"

"I suppose it's a little habit I've got into. I hope you won't take it up."

"No, sir, that isn't one of my inclinations."

"Good. Now go on with your story."

"I hate to say this. The worst thing is, I hate God."

The rider raised his eyebrows but he didn't speak.

"I love the world," Frank said. "I love my wife and my little kid that hasn't been born yet and I love a big truck under me and I love sunrise out over the Escalante breaks and I love the sound of the diesels running the pumps in the middle of the night. That's what I love. I hate God."

"Well, I'm sorry to hear that. Myself, I love God."

"I know you do."

"Go on now."

"There isn't much more to say, except I scraped all the skin off the back of my hand. It's in my mind to do the same as Jeremy did. Except when I cut myself off, there won't be anybody around to stop the bleeding."

"Why can't you believe my blood was enough?" Jesus said. "Why do you have to shed yours too?"

"I don't know."

"There's a lot of crazy in your family."

"Yes, sir, I know it."

"Furthermore, that Marianne is one hell of a good woman. Why don't you just settle down and enjoy her like a husband would who has some good sense?"

"Do you think I ought to?"

"Yeah, you ought to."

Jesus crushed his cigarette on the sole of his boot. He pulled his leg down off the saddlehorn and said, "I've got to ride. It was good to chat with you."

"Yes, sir, thank you, sir."

Jesus pulled on buckskin gloves and took up the reins. "If you want to eat that damned vegetable diet of your mother's all your life, don't blame me for it. Myself, I go for food that tastes good."

"Yes, sir, I'll remember that."

"Do something to make your poor mother-in-law feel better. Your wife getting baptized a Mormon has been tough on her."

"Yes, sir, I will, sir."

"You go see a doctor with that hand."

"You bet."

Jesus pulled his horse around and struck him lightly in the ribs with his spurs. Looking back, he said, "And work on that crap about hating God. See if you can get over it."

"Yes, sir, I sure will."

Pushing the urinal lever, Frank watched as water again streamed over the gleaming porcelain. Above its sound rose another sound, soft and distant, yet distinct and unmistakable, like the soughing of the wind in a faraway forest. He retched, turned to the toilet, and vomited. As he wiped spatters from the toilet rim, he began to cry and couldn't stop. He blew his nose four or five times, went to the basin and splashed cold water into his eyes, tried to think decisive thoughts. Still his tears flowed fast.

He heard footsteps in the hall, then silence, then more footsteps. Putting his head into the hall, he saw Clara, who dabbed at her cheeks with a handkerchief. Her eyelids were puffy, her nose red, her make-up streaked.

"Oh, there you are and you've caught me!" she exclaimed. "I was determined to hide away until I could stop this shameful weeping." Pausing, she stared at Frank. "Why, look at you cry! You poor thing. You act as if your heart was broken."

"Yes, ma'am."

"Well, I've heard that the Mormons weep on numerous occasions, but I certainly wouldn't have expected it just now. What on earth are you crying about?"

"I just can't get hold of myself."

"I would think this is the happiest day of your life."

"I believe maybe it is."

Clara put the handkerchief to her nose and blew forcefully. "I am resolved to stop crying and I hope you are too. Crying makes you look bad and it will give you a headache."

"Yes, ma'am, I think I can stop now. I hope you won't feel too bad about Marianne being a Mormon."

"I am trying valiantly not to."

"It won't hurt her any to be a Mormon. She'll still be a good Christian."

"Of course she will."

"I sure do love and respect you," he said. "I'm real glad to have you for my mother-in-law."

"Oh, Frank, you sweet boy," she said, coming toward him. He stepped from the door and hugged her tightly.

"Now you just wait a moment while I freshen up, and we'll go courageously upstairs together."

"Yes, ma'am, let's do that."

Upstairs a crowd filled the Relief Society room. Plates and cups in hand, men and women chattered about grandchildren, cattle prices, the Memorial Day horse races, and recent testimony meetings of note. They milled slowly in a large circle, at the center of which were Marianne and Margaret. Her hair still damp, her cheeks radiant, Marianne took the hand of each person whom Margaret introduced to her. Those waiting their turn stood with curious, reverent faces, as if she was fresh from heaven and a blessing to touch and to talk to.

Leola had taken Dora under her wing, and her oldest daughter had made friends with Jeanette. Frank led Clara to Wesley and stood with them, introducing them to everyone who came up to congratulate him. Wesley found himself very pleased with the whole affair.

"Yes, ma'am," he said to old Sister Worthenscrop, "I am Marianne's father."

"And are you taking the missionary lessons too?" Sister Worthenscrop had frizzy grey hair and a smooth spoon-shaped chest.

"No, ma'am," Wesley replied. "My wife and I consider ourselves sufficiently papered Christians already. Our home is a feeding lot or a breeding farm, if you will, for fine Christian children, which we produce for a variety of churches."

"Land sakes, do you really?"

"Well, I'm joking, of course, but in a sense, as you might say, yes, we do, ma'am. Have you had any of this white cake with vanilla frosting? I recommend it particularly."

"No, I had a chocolate brownie."

"Now, Mrs. Worthenscrop, I want you to remember my name, J. Wesley Earle, which stands for John Wesley Earle. My parents were Methodists and named me after the great founder of that persuasion. A year from this fall I am running for commissioner of Garfield County. I would appreciate your vote, ma'am."

"Well, you can certainly count on that," she said.

"Remember that name. J. Wesley Earle, running for a two year seat on the Garfield County commission."

After the reception, as the two couples stood in the shadows of the churchhouse, Frank and Marianne asked Clara and Wesley to take Dora to the ranch while they went after Nathan. "Don't let the cat out of the bag," Frank warned. "If she's going to find out he ran off on her, let it be from him, not from one of us."

"I'm sure we don't need instructions in matters of tact," Wesley said.

"He just means it would be easy for us to give it all away without realizing," Clara explained.

"What a grotesque business, us trying to keep this marriage patched up! Have you considered he might not thank us for our intervention? Maybe she won't either."

"Likely they'll settle down to each other all right," Frank said. "When horses haven't been in the harness for a long time they thrash around some but pretty soon they calm down and pull together."

"A curious analogy."

"Maybe not," Clara said.

Borrowing Margaret's car, Frank and Marianne drove the graveled road leading over Cedar Breaks to Cedar City and Highway 91. She snuggled close, her arm around his shoulders. For a while neither said a word. Then, as tall, shadowy pines began to appear in the headlights, she said, "I'm so worried about your hand, Frank."

"I'm going to the doctor in the morning."

"We're going," she corrected.

"Sure, both of us."

At Panguitch Lake they went by campgrounds crammed with the tents and trailers of fishermen. "I have in mind you and me buying some nice rods and reels I saw in Hinton's and we'll go trout fishing. There's lots of good fishing up in New Canyon. That is, if you'd like to."

"Golly, Frank, I would."

As they looped down the switchbacks from Cedar Breaks, he said, "I'm going to buy back Booger. That Theodore Amsdew has damn near ruined him. He don't know anything about horses."

"What are you going to do with him?"

"Ride him. Rope off him."

"That don't make sense if we're going to sell off Chowder like we planned."

"We ain't going to sell him."

"That sure suits me just fine, I can tell you."

As they pulled onto Highway 91 in the middle of Cedar City, she said, "You ain't told me something."

"I know I ain't. Something good has happened to us."

"What was it?"

"I don't know if I can talk about it. I don't mean to be rude; I just won't keep hold of myself if I try."

"Well, don't then," she said. "I can wait."

"I've been thinking when the summer is over and I've pretty well got your dad's projects finished, we could move over to Tropic or Cannonville and rent us a house. I have in mind we'd borrow some money and buy us a big truck and a couple of trailers. I'd go in for hauling sheep in the spring and fall and maybe lumber and hay in the summer. We'd work on getting us a little cattle herd. We could keep an eye on my folks and yours too. When we got on our feet we could build us a house on our little piece up the Paria."

For a while they listened to the thump of the road and the splatter of insects on the windshield.

"Is that all right?" he finally asked.

"You know it's all right," she said. "I could cry but I'm not going to."

"Yeah, let's not cry if we can help it. It's time to be happy."

Arriving in Toquerville around midnight, they found the small clapboard bungalow the lady had described to Marianne on the phone. Shortly after they knocked, a light came on and a man in a bathrobe let them in. Moments later Nathan was before them, his shirt half buttoned, his feet bare, his teeth out, his hair tangled, his chin silvery with stubble.

"You old elk!" Frank exclaimed. "How come you missed Marianne's baptism? Her feelings are plenty hurt."

"Pity sakes, I forgot it was tonight. Forgive me, forgive me," he said, turning to Marianne.

"My feelings aren't hurt. We just want you to come home. Dora is over at the ranch waiting for you."

Nathan wrung his hands and groaned. "She don't want to see me."

"We told her a lie," Frank said. "We didn't let her know you had run off on her. We told her you drove a truck over to St. George and had a breakdown on the way back."

"Merciful heavens, is that really true?"

"It's really true," Marianne said. "She doesn't know."

"Dadgost you, you haven't done me no favor. I thought it was all settled. I had myself steeled up to it, her and me being finished. We wouldn't write no more; we wouldn't make no more phone calls."

"Well, it isn't finished," Frank said. "So let's get a move on. Go take a bath and put on some underwear that's clean and doesn't have holes where they don't belong. Comb your hair nice. Borrow some aftershave too. When you walk into that trailerhouse, you want to be your best."

"What'll I say to her?"

"Don't say anything. Give her a kiss and let her do the talking. She doesn't ever lack for something to say."

While Nathan bathed, Frank and Marianne waited in the living room, he with his head back, trying to doze, she leafing through *Grit* and the *Improvement Era*. When Nathan emerged from the bathroom, he wore a white shirt and a tie; his grey hair was neatly parted, his chin and jaws were shaved clean, his brown, seamed cheeks glistened. He shook his friend's hand, saying he didn't blame him for the fact that Frank and Marianne had discovered his hiding place.

They drove up Highway 91 and over the mountains to Panguitch, where Frank spoke briefly to his mother, thanking her for the use of her car. Then they crowded into the truck, which had remained parked at Margaret's house, and drove on toward the ranch. Fatigue settled on all of them, Nathan and Marianne dozing and Frank fighting to stay awake, cranking the wheel, slapping his jaw, yodeling a little. Close to four o'clock they arrived at the ranch. Marianne went in while Frank walked on with Nathan to the steps of his trailer, where a porchlight burned.

"I don't have anything to say to her," Nathan pleaded.

"Remember all those nice things you used to write to her in your letters—how she was your sweetie and how you were just going wild because you couldn't hold her tight and give her a kiss."

Nathan snorted indignantly. "You don't know nothing about what I wrote in my letters."

"Sure I do. I used to read them when you went out to the privy."

"You skunk. Ain't nothing sacred to you?"

"It was in my backsliding days before I had a conscience."

"That don't matter. Taking everything together, you have been the worst burden God ever loaded onto me."

The door opened and Dora stood there in her bathrobe, looking sleepy and tousled. "Sweetheart," she said. She held the door wide and Nathan went in.

Going into his trailer, Frank turned off the porchlight. A ring of dim light radiated from the open door of the bathroom. He went down the hall. Marianne sat on the edge of the bed buttoning her nightgown. He sat by her and pulled off his shoes.

"I smell something."

"It's that perfume Dora gave me," she said. "I put some between my boobies."

He took off his tie and unbuttoned his shirt. He started to rise, then sat back and tossed them on the floor. "I'll hang them up in the morning. I've never been so tired in my whole life. I haven't had any sleep in three days."

She squeezed lotion onto her hands and began to rub. "Do you want to tell me what was the good thing that happened to us?"

"If I can," he said. "I had a vision."

"A vision?"

"I don't believe I can say any more about it right now. Jesus is kind, just like you always said."

"Oh, lord, Frank."

He had unzipped his pants but he couldn't take them off because she was hugging him tightly. "We don't need to cry," he said.

"It doesn't matter. I'm all right, I'm just all right."

"Can I smell that perfume up close?"

"Sure. You bet," she said, unbuttoning her gown.